Please feel free to send me an email. Just know that my publisher filters these emails. Good news is always welcome.

Prolifick Instinct - prolifick_i

Sign up for my blog for update
prolifick-instinct.awesomeauth

About the Publisher

BLVNP Incorporated, A Nevada Corporation, 340 S. Lemon #6200, Walnut CA 91789, info@blvnp.com / legal@blvnp.com

Praise for His Mistress' Baby

It honestly veers away from being a cliché to being its own little drama. It may be about the usual guy meets girl and guy gets girl pregnant, but what is unique is the 'how' they got there. I love this and would 10/10 read it until the day I kick the bucket.
-Alexus Burton-Wood, *Goodreads*

I chance to have read this as one of my first "wattpad" books. And I fell in love with the story and the motions the characters went through...Wonderful story
-Julynn Pelius, *Goodreads*

AMAZING BOOK!!!
I had so much fun reading this, even though some might think this book is cliche I think it has so many twists and turns! It's a fantastic book and definitely worth reading!
-Preeti Jadav, *Goodreads*

This book was spectacular in every aspect. I loved the way the author allowed each character to have their own personal downfall.
-Jannie Wallace

His Mistress' Baby

By: Prolifick Instinct

BLVNP

ISBN: 978-1-68030-895-2

TABLE OF CONTENTS

This book is dedicated to God, my family, every child in this world, and to all Wattpad readers who supported His Mistress' Baby.

FREE DOWNLOAD

Get these freebies and MORE when you sign up for the author's mailing list!

prolifick-instinct.awesomeauthors.org

CHAPTER 1

"Mom, stop fidgeting. They'll love it. You've put more than enough effort for today. Besides, you're a great cook. Everything is delicious. Trust me, *I know*." Ally gave her mother a knowing smile after a light smack of her lips.

With that twinkle in her soft brown eyes, her mother knew what she meant. Her daughter had tasted most if not all of the dishes.

"Okay." Her mother conceded with a sigh.

Ally understood why her mother was this way. She wanted to impress whoever could be impressed tonight. She knew it would be a great boost for her mom's business, and she was here to support her. Ally was a less than average cook, but she was here to assist tonight. That was the only thing she could do for a woman who took the death of her husband so hard. Her mother's once lost passion for cooking was slowly filling that sense of emptiness she had been carrying around.

Mac Storm had been a wonderful father and a loving husband, but he was not an exemption from cancer's vicious, indiscriminating hands. It had been really hard for both ladies seeing him gradually leave them day by day.

But tonight was all about her mom, and she knew her father would have been proud.

Ally looked around the exquisitely decorated room that was gradually starting to fill with people who dressed and looked every inch of what the night was promised to be: a display of wealth and power.

She had never been one who craved to be among these kinds of social circles, but she might as well feed her eyes with some ridiculously cliche amusements… like that beautiful redhead lady making her advances all too obvious to the young and attractive men. She was obviously irritated by what she had attracted so far, wrinkling her nose at the man in front of her who appeared to be in his early or mid-sixties. It seemed like the young lady cared for the physical appearance that came with the money.

"A woman couldn't be more obvious, I tell ya."

She briefly glanced at the owner of the voice—a friend and an employee of her mom, Katie. She was just an acquaintance, actually. She only made small talk with Katie whenever she was available to help her mom out. They did not have each other's number, nor did they chat over drinks or dinner.

Ally smiled in return.

"And it obviously isn't working," Katie added.

Ally turned to see the redhead turning her pretty neck around, probably in search of someone, totally lacking interest in the man before her.

Katie moved closer to her, almost making their bodies touch. She knew it was no use taking a step back. When Katie was in gossip mode, she loved body contact as if her words would have more meaning that way.

"If my guess is right, she may be searching for the one man they're all waiting for. She hasn't even attracted a single hottie here, and I hear he's hunkier than Hulk himself."

That got her attention, and she faced the young lady, chuckling. "Where do you get your gossips from?"

"They're not gossips," she replied with a straight face, and Ally would have believed her if she did not know about her personality before.

"For real. I have seen him before, not just face to face. He's the real thing, I tell ya. Well, she may have some luck, I guess. I hear he's into redheads. We all have our fetish."

I don't, she thought, and she was not about to ask the woman beside her what hers was. Some things you just want people to keep to themselves. Things like that you do not want Katie to start blabbing about.

"Well, I guess it's your lucky day then," Ally said.

"It's every girl in this room's lucky day," Katie replied with a large grin.

"Katie!" Ally's mom called. She laughed, seeing as Katie did not appreciate the distraction. Her sour face said it all.

"Keep laughing like that, and maybe you'll attract one hunky man yourself."

Before she could come up with a reply, Katie moved on.

She frowned at Katie's comment but was quick to dismiss it. There was no way she could attract anyone dressed in this uniform. She was not dressed for attraction or seduction—far from it. She looked down at her short, blue uniform and raised her hand, adjusting the cap that covered her unruly mass of hair. Of course, she had makeup on, but it was so light, the dim lights probably hid any trace of it.

She turned her eyes back to the crowd, mindlessly fleeting through the room again.

***

It took less than fifteen minutes for the room to start buzzing more than it had been all night, and when she looked at where a few men were gathered, she unconsciously craned her head to see what was going on. When she eventually stopped trying, the pathway cleared and she was able to get a good look. It was not the best angle to view from, but she got the picture of a very attractive man.

He had one hand in the pocket of his pants, and the lady beside him with an elegant figure appeared to be a matching partner for him. He was talking and nodding at the older man in front of him before his head shifted direction.

For a moment, Ally thought he rested his gaze in her direction, but she could not be so sure. If she could not see his face clearly, she doubted he was actually looking at her.

And then he nodded.

It was ever so slightly. She could have been mistaken. She subconsciously had to look behind her to see who he might be nodding to.

Get your head out of your silly imaginations, Ally. You're not exactly looking for a man or a relationship, and the last thing you would expect is for a man like that to take notice of you, she had to reprimand herself.

She smiled knowing how Laurie, her cousin, would reply to that. When she looked back at the scene, everyone had dispersed and she could not locate the man anymore. She got back to the purpose she was here in the first place.

***

Hours had flown by since the event started, and for Ally, the night was turning out to be a total bore. She was not exactly a proud social bee, but this was truly a downer even by her own standards.

"Did you see him?" She heard that same relentless voice from hours ago.

See him, who? she wanted to ask, but she knew too well who Katie was referring to.

His entrance with the ginger-haired woman had made the room come to a standstill. She had seen him alright. Maybe not close enough to see what all the fuss was about, but she had a glimpse, enough to leave an appreciative taste to her senses. His figure and far-off appearance were a sight truly worthy of the three-sixty degree head turns he got.

"Hmm…" Ally murmured with a reluctant nod.

"I guess you have, yes? Every woman in this room saw him. Your mom was looking, too… though she did not look as impressed as we did."

We? Had she been so impressed by someone she had not taken a good look at?

"That would have been a little—" She did not want to imagine her mom drooling over such a man.

Katie swung her hand from side to side as she squeezed her face, waving away what she was trying to say. "You know what I mean."

No, she did not. She did not want to.

Ally turned back to the guests who were preparing for the start of another bidding. *That should be entertaining*, she mockingly thought.

"I told you he had a thing for redheads."

Katie really should give it a break. She knew for sure Katie was not a redhead and neither was she. Redhead or not, the two of them had no chance with the man.

She caught sight of her mother walking out of the room and had the urge to do the same, especially when she could guess her mom's reason for that well enough. She wished her mom would stop smoking cigarettes to relieve her stress. With her eyes still fixed on her mother, she did not see the figure approaching them until she got a jab to the side.

"What was that for?" she hissed at Katie, but the other woman's awkward nod towards the front made Ally look up.

A woman dressed in a figure-hugging olive green dress was towering above her, holding a glass of champagne in her hand.

Oh.

"Good evening, ma'am. Anything you'd like?" Ally asked. She looked at the woman expectantly, waiting for her reply. She looked closely and was almost certain that the woman in front of her looked like the same person she had seen with *him* earlier.

"Would you ladies be kind to offer me the best meal here? I'm starving. I haven't had anything to eat."

She was quick to rise to the request, eager to show off her mother's cooking, when she heard Katie speak.

"I noticed," Katie said, chuckling as if she found something funny.

Both women turned to Katie, enough to shut her up. The atmosphere turned rather awkward.

The lady got a bite out of her recommendation, and she seemed to like it, impressed even. She could feel the woman's eyes assessing her, though. Then again, it could just be her imagination.

After asking for one of the waitresses to get a plate to her table, she walked away. Ally shrugged off her intuition and went in search of her mother, suddenly needing a break from the busy night.

***

She found her mom quicker than she imagined. She had taken the best spot to indulge in her habit—a habit Ally had voiced her disapproval on too many times.

"Mom…"

Her mother turned to her, taking another drag off her cigarette before turning away from her.

"I needed a break," she simply said like it was a good enough excuse.

This habit of hers had started when her father's condition became worse. She had pleaded with her to quit, but her mother had only replied that she had started smoking before Ally was born—an alibi that was quick to her lips for years now. She was at that point where she had given up on asking, just hoping in her heart that her mom would honestly quit by her own free will.

She watched as her mom stepped on what was left of the cigarette and rested a hand on her shoulder. "Worry less about me, darling," she said before walking away.

If only I could, Ally thought as she embraced herself with both her arms, warming her body from the chilly night.

***

Julia had taken a good look at the young woman, assessing her. She had clearly seen the doubt in that woman's eyes, the girl she now knew was called Ally. She had probably guessed she approached the table for something other than sating her hunger.

She had to give it to Ally, she must be a little smart to have noticed that. But she could not help but wonder if that spark of insight alone would be enough to resist the man sitting beside her. She took a look at him, and Xander was not even trying to hide his complete disinterest in what was going on around him.

Julia couldn't help but admit the girl was beautiful upon a closer look, but that was not what she was worried about. She knew very well about Xander's persistence and charm, deadly qualities that a lot of women fell for. Since that exotic beauty came into Xander's line of view, he had been distracted, turning his head to a particular direction for most of the night.

It had really caught her attention when Xander stared in Ally's direction a few minutes after they came in. That was enough reason for her to stand and go take a closer look at the girl that could possibly be Xander's next woman. After all, he was a free man at the moment.

Glancing at the food she had demanded to their table, she wondered if she was ever going to get what she wanted. She has been hoping for years now, but patiently waiting and supporting him did not seem like it was enough.

"I know what you're doing."

She felt his breath fan the side of her face as he leaned towards her to speak. Tilting her head, she offered a mocking smile. "Good. That's what you pay me for."

"She's not business."

She was not stupid. Xander's eyes had been speaking for him all night—and they demand pleasure.

She watched his movement and noticed he was about to stand. "Where are you going? The bid's still on."

"It's nothing of interest to me. You know this was my father's doing. Besides, I already gave a reasonable sum for an art piece."

He must have made the bid while she had gone to see the girl.

That girl…

That was who he was headed for right now. She could bet on her monthly salary.

***

He needed to get out of there. He had fulfilled the duty he initially planned to avoid. He attended the function in place of his father. It was more like a punishment from his old man, and he had been right. It was boring as hell, almost routine… until he saw her.

All night, Xander told himself that it was not the right time to approach her. Now that the guests and workers all seemed relaxed, he might as well take his chance.

He had spotted her walking out of the room, a good opportunity to make his approach. Leaving the rest to Julia, he stood from his seat and walked out of the room. After a minute or so of searching, he found her. He took a minute watching her, careful not to give himself out. She rested her body on an open-air rail, enjoying the night sky as she innocently stuck out her butt. A promise of a delectable backside to have tonight. What would he give to hug close that body he had so unashamedly checked out earlier?

He became more interested and found it funny when he looked straight at her and she turned to look behind her. She did not notice him all night, preoccupied with attending to the guests. It was a situation he was about to correct.

"Beautiful," he exclaimed, referring to the view before him.

Startled, she adjusted herself and turned to look at him.

Her beautiful body was complimented with a more beautiful face. Without the cap she had on for most of the night, he could not help but stare.

He has had women with stunning beauty grace his arm, seek his company, and warm his bed, but something about this one was drawing him in. There was nothing new in her features, but when she turned to him with her mouth slightly agape, he knew this woman was the kind he had never encountered before. He was damn sure of that, but still, there was only one way to find out.

"What a total bore," he said.

"Excuse me?" she said, looking confused at his comment.

"You find the event boring, don't you? I would assume that's why you're out here."

She eyed him carefully, watching him as if trying to know if she was supposed to stay or make an excuse and leave.

"What's your excuse? I wasn't the one invited."

He gave a slow grin, seeing something flicker in those beautiful eyes of hers. Whatever it was, he was not certain of at the moment, but he knew he would be unlocking more emotions in her soon.

"True. I did my part already. It's a waste of time being there. Nothing of relevance, really."

Seeing a slight frown appear on her face, he wondered what she was thinking. Women hardly frowned in his presence especially when he was trying to know them personally. She seemed to be deliberating about something in her head.

"Is this not for a good cause?" she finally said out loud.

"Isn't that what they say? But it's the least of the reason everyone is gathered in that room right now."

"Why don't you leave then?"

"I'm right here with you, aren't I?" he sarcastically asked.

Xander knew what she meant, of course. He was not supposed to be here, but he was grateful for the switch. He must have been watching her for too long because when he obviously added nothing, she made a move to leave.

"I was just taking a break." She hesitated before speaking again, "Well, excuse me, and have a good night."

She was about to leave, but he grabbed her arm gently, stopping her in her tracks and making her turn around to face him.

He saw an expression he had never seen on a woman's face before. It almost looked funny to him that he was tempted to laugh. Her mouth was ajar, probably trying to get words out but failing. He saw confusion mixed with surprise flash on her face.

Then it was gone as quickly as it came.

It really was new to him; a woman who wore all of her expressions on her face without masking them. There was no way he could let her leave now.

"What's your name?"

He never had this much conversation with a woman he wanted. In high school, sure. He was not the man who benefited from his father's fortunes and status then but a normal young boy who worked hard to support both him and his grandfather. Nowadays, women knew when he wanted them, and there was no use dragging the inevitable especially when they wanted him too. But this beautiful one here honestly looked like she did not know either of that yet.

"What are you doing?"

"Your name, beautiful?"

She gave in, still looking unsure. "Ally."

His gaze fell to where the word came out from: her perfect, tempting lips. *Soon*, he promised himself, *I would have a taste.*

"Have dinner with me tomorrow night, Ally."

"I-I don't even know your name."

He was taken aback for a moment, and a frown appeared on his face before it slowly dissolved. She seemed sincere about not knowing his name, and it only made him smile.

She was unaware of who he was. She could not have faked that oblivious look on her face. If she were, she must be a good actress, but she could not be good enough to fool him for hours on end.

So she was a little different from what he was used to… no big deal. He was a businessman by trade, and he adapted well to situations that took him by surprise.

"Alexander Cross, but you can call me Xander."

"Xander," she whispered.

"What do you say, Ally?" He noticed her hesitation and immediately countered. The slight shiver of her shoulders and the discomfort in her eyes made him conclude something; she was attracted to him and was confused by it. He could almost laugh at this situation.

This was absurd, but he loved it.

Her mind might be in doubt, but her body was reacting receptively to the man before her, willing her to reply in a way she probably had never thought about. That much was clear to him.

"You know what I want to do right now, Ally?"

He moved closer, leaving a bit of space between them so as not to overwhelm her. He probably should not be this forward and scare her away, but he felt he should be applauded for keeping his hands to himself this long.

"I want to bury my fingers in those beautiful waves of yours and stare deep into your eyes I can't look away from as I claim that sweet lips of yours," he said, staring down at every part he just mentioned until his eyes rested on the last. "It's what I've wanted to do all night," he continued in a soft whisper clear enough for her to hear. His insides were anything but calm, though.

It was no lie.

He had been aching to do all that and more since he spotted her in the crowd, but she looked like the kind who was not to be rushed. If he got to have her, the least he wanted was to rush the passion they could create together. And that was why her next words froze him.

"Then why don't you?"

CHAPTER 2

Was she sure about this? No, of course not.

But she had never felt these strong emotions towards a man before. Was she stupid enough to ignore her mother's words and the gossips she had read about him? Maybe so.

Was she totally certain calling him to agree to dinner was the right choice? Honestly, she did not know.

"Ahhh!"Ally groaned out loud, hugging her knees before falling back on her bed and rolling her body on it. Why was it so hard to decide?

It had been three days since that night, and she could still vividly remember the embarrassment she felt. She had practically insinuated he jump her! His sudden burst of laughter after a minute of silence made her want to bury herself on that very spot. Xander had obviously realised she was all mouth and that those words had come from nowhere.

There's a hidden passion within you, sweetheart, and we'll unravel it together, his reply replayed in her head once more.

She had been speechless and felt hot all over at his words. He brought out a whole new feeling from within her, for sure.

Something brought a chill to her whole being just as quickly, and it certainly had not been from the cold air; it was from the truth behind his words. As much she had tried to deny it three nights ago, she was sure of it now.

She was attracted to the man, and she had not stopped thinking about her encounter with him.

"Xander…" She tested the name on her lips again.

She was twenty-one, for goodness' sake! Surely, she was allowed to make this decision for herself. Her mistakes would be hers to learn from. Denying she wanted this was helping no one—certainly not her. She would take that leap of faith and follow what her heart was saying.

She was all alone in the apartment she shared with her roommate, Trish, who was currently out on a date with her long-time boyfriend. She wondered if she had a boyfriend what she would be doing on a night like this with a man. She had never felt the need to assess her love life or her roommate's, but now, it was starting to bother her… all because he appeared.

She leapt from her bed, picked up the phone she had been cuddling for hours, and dialled the number on the card she had been staring at for a while. She coughed dramatically as the phone rang, waiting for someone to pick up at the other end—hoping *he* did.

"Hello."

It was him.

Who did you expect it was going to be, Ally? she sarcastically thought. Hearing that voice that had kept her up for days just made her certain she wanted to do this.

"Hello. Um... this is Alicia. Ally?" she hurriedly said, not really sure why she's nervous. Who was she kidding? She was afraid he might not remember who she was.

"Excuse me." She heard him say under his breath. He was with someone; she guessed that was the case when she heard shuffling in the background. He had to be moving away from where he was.

"Even if you hadn't given me your name, I would still know it was you, sweetheart. Your voice did it for me."

"You told me to call if I... changed my mind about dinner."

"And have you?"

"I'm calling, aren't I?"

He chuckled. "Oh, sweetheart, we'll be good together."

What did he mean by that? Good together for a relationship, to be treated differently from other women, or just good enough to set the sheets on fire?

Slow down, Ally. Aren't you thinking too far ahead? She had to remind herself.

She was not naïve. She knew Xander did not just want dinner. He wanted more, but that was hers to give. Right now, she had to face the fact that she was at risk of giving too much without putting up a fight.

"Tomorrow night, then. Seven-thirty. I'll pick you up. Sweet dreams, sweetheart. They'll certainly be for me."

She quickly stopped him before he could hang up. "You don't even know where my apartment is."

"I do. I'll pick you up."

That shut her up. How did he know?

"Listen, sweetheart, I'm in a business meeting. We'll have every talk we can tomorrow, but I have to go now."

"Okay."

***

Xander made sure she cut the call before he did because, somehow, he sensed her disappointment at how short their conversation had been. He was not sure why, but it made him happy. He was giving her time to think and decide on what he *wanted*, and that surprised him.

He wanted her, that much was clear, and he was sure she knew it by now. He had made that known to her. But his decision of waiting for her to make the call when he should have just made her decide on the spot still bothered him. In the long years he had been dealing with women, he had never put the reins in their hands… except when determining if they both wanted the same thing. If any of them wanted out, he would never force the decision.

Not that it had ever been the case.

On top of that, he picked up Ally's call while in a business meeting. With the women in his past, he would have ignored the call and ring back later or have someone else do it. If any of them had been bold enough to ask why he ignored their call, he would have answered he was busy. Easy and simple. If that was not good enough for them, they could leave.

He had never *ever* forced a woman's attention.

He walked back to the meeting put on hold for him and asked them to continue.

Xander was aware of the woman's eyes on him a couple of seats away, but he was not going to give her funny ideas by looking her way. He knew that was what she wanted.

Hell, he knew what she wanted; she wanted him. But he just hated women having a hold of him. Julia knew too much about his personal life; perhaps more than any other girl. She was aware of that, and that sometimes gave her way too much confidence. He had decided not to fuel Julia's notions by involving himself with her again.

He knew the fiery passion burning in him for Ally might be dangerous for him, but he was going to tame it—tame whatever comes with it and have himself call the shots.

All of it.

***

"That was her at the meeting, right?" Julia asked Xander when they were alone, hours after the end of another successful meeting.

He did not bother to give her an answer as he took off his jacket and rolled the sleeves of his shirt to get more comfortable.

"She looks fragile than the rest of them. Do you know what you're getting yourself into?"

Julia made her questions seem casual, but he knew that curiosity was eating at her. He refused to acknowledge what she was trying to say to him.

"Does she know what she's getting herself into?"

That was it. He's had enough. He stood up from where he was seated.

"You don't interfere with my personal business. You just do what I pay you to do," he said, hard and unwavering.

"It's exactly what I'm doing."

He cocked his head to the side at her reply. She looked upset even when she was trying hard not to make it obvious.

"It was not easy getting a woman like Barb away from you with all the ugliness she caused."

He remembered that all too well. The psychotic witch could not take no for an answer and had caused a lot of media attention. He had not handled that situation very well and till now did not understand how Barb eventually stayed away. Had Julia done something to stop the harassment? He never once asked, and she never told him.

He was never letting that happen again, and Julia must know that. He just saw his assistant's questioning as an excuse to know everything that went on with him. He would have replaced Julia himself if she was not such a great professional and a friend.

"Are you even listening?"

"I'll handle my women. Barb was a mistake that would never happen again—or be spoken of." He took his jacket, walking out.

"Where are you going?"

He faced her. "Whatever's going on with you, Julia, purge it out. You're acting like a jealous ex-wife. I need you as my assistant. Nothing else."

"What happened to being a friend?"

He did not bother to give a reply.

Xander got to his suite and dialled a number. It would relieve him of the bad mood he was in, he thought.

"Lissa, I'm at the hotel. Can you come over?"

He got rid of his clothes, needing a shower before his guest arrived.

***

"You look sexy. You sure you really want this?"

A week had gone by, and she could not believe she was still as nervous about going on a date with him as the day she had summoned the courage to call him. This was going to be their second date, but to Ally, she was counting it as the first. They had barely spent twenty minutes together—most of it on the ride to their date—when he got a call from a woman Xander had explained to be his assistant. Turned out he had urgent business ro attend to. He had apologised profusely, and she had seen the regret in his eyes for cutting their time short.

"Am I crazy?" Ally nervously asked, glancing at the mirror to adjust her appearance for the nth time.

"Crazy in love, then."

"I'm not in love with him. I just..." Ally sighed, turning her back to the mirror to face her cousin who was seated on the bed watching her. "I can't explain it. Do you understand?"

"No, I don't." Her cousin Laurie shook her head.

Both girls burst into laughter. They could only laugh at the ridiculousness of it all.

Laurie loved the male kind. If you ask why, she will give you only two reasons they were good to her: the really good sex and the gifts they showered her with—specifically in that order. Laurie was a gorgeous woman, but they looked nothing alike. Laurie was two years older than her, but still, they were best friends. While she was blessed with a mass of wavy, golden brown hair and brown eyes that complemented her golden skin, Laurie was a brunette with blue eyes and had a lighter complexion than hers.

"But with what I'm seeing, you're headed towards that direction. Your mom was right to panic."

Her mom had threatened to call Laurie to talk some sense into her since she was failing at it as a mother, and she did, which was why Laurie was here now. Wrong move. Just because Laurie did not take men seriously, did not mean she was here to discourage her.

That night at the party, she had denied that she was in any way interested in Xander. Her mom must have seen something not to believe her.

"How long have you been seeing this guy?"

"One week." If she could put it that way. They had only seen once in that week, but he had called often.

Xander had roses delivered to her, and the next time he had called, she asked how he knew where she lived and the kind of flowers she loved. It made her a bit uncomfortable to think he could know anything he wanted about her, but he had made it clear that finding out her address was an easy thing and he had only taken a chance on the flowers, hoping she did like them.

Seeing him again on the day of their first date and talking to him over the phone made her realise the indescribable feelings mounting within her for a man she barely knew. He was, indeed, the first man to make her discover different and new emotions.

"And you're sure he's not seeing you just for your body? It's obvious you've got a hot bod." Laurie's voice snapped her out of it.

She smiled. "Well, that's part of it, but... it's supposed to be, right?"

"If you're looking for confirmation from me, you've got it wrong, cousin. You're not me, and I'm not you. What we both want out of men and relationships is *way* different."

Laurie was right. She was not sure she was going to be okay with just sex. She could start getting greedy and want more. It was starting to feel like she wanted more, but did he? Was she getting in too deep?

"But have you two had sex?"

"No. It's been just one week! Besides, I've only seen him once in that one week, so it's impossible we have sex over the phone, right?"

Laurie gave her a teasing look. "Nothing's impossible. If you really wanted to, you could have. I'm sure a man like him will know something about that. You're blushing! You, bad girl. What have you two been doing then?"

One thing was sure. She has never been this crazy for a man.

"Ally!" They heard Trish call from the sitting room.

"What?" she shouted back.

"Your man's here!" came the reply.

She stared in surprise at Laurie.

"It's your fault I got distracted," she said as she hurriedly put herself together.

"Well, I'll finally get to meet him in person. Let's see if his pictures don't lie."

"Don't try anything funny," Ally said in a warning tone.

"Would I?" Laurie asked, faking innocence. "Finish up while I keep him company."

She was done in less than five minutes and stepped out to see Laurie engaged in discussion with Xander though it did not look like much of a conversation because he appeared uninterested. Trish just stared at the both of them.

"I'm ready," Ally spoke up to get Laurie away from him.

Xander did not look like he appreciated whatever Laurie was saying. He happily went to her, holding her in his arms before placing a kiss near her temple. "You look beautiful," he whispered, fanning his breath on her ears.

She welcomed the compliment with a smile. As Xander led her out, she made sure she shot Laurie a stern look. Her cousin just winked in return, giving her thumbs up as she mouthed, *hot.*

"Is she your friend?" Xander asked as soon as they were outside.

"Laurie? She's my cousin. Did she say something to upset you?"

"Do I look upset?" he asked gently as he faced her. "The last time I had someone quiz me because of my date was in high school."

"Is that a bad thing?"

"Depends."

His reaction concerned her. She wanted to know, but before she could ask, her phone started to ring.

It was her mom.

"Excuse me." She moved a few feet away while he went to wait beside his car.

"Mom—"

"Why are you whispering? Is he there?"

This was exactly why she made sure she's out of Xander's earshot before answering. She still didn't understand what her mother had against him. Talking about him was almost taboo to her.

Her mother started telling her off. Getting involved with Xander was stupid, she said. She had to hold back the urge to switch off her phone.

"Your father would be disappointed. Would you dishonour all his hopes for you to be with a man like that?"

Her mom went too far. Bringing her father into her disapproval of Xander was just too much, and she did what she should have done minutes ago. She tried controlling the tears from spilling as she went to join Xander.

"Sorry about that."

He noticed her change of mood. Getting in the car beside her, he saw a stray tear fall. She was not quick enough to hide it from him.

"What's wrong?"

"N-nothing."

"Tell me," he demanded, and she told him the details of the phone call.

"Then we go back to my place."

She looked up at him. "But dinner—"

"We eat in."

She wanted to be excited that he was taking her to his place. It was supposed to make her feel special, but how was she to know if she was the first? Perhaps, she was just one of the many.

Through most of the ride, he held her hand with his less busy one, making her somewhat forget her earlier conversation with her mom. He talked to her and managed to make her smile.

How could this be wrong? she thought.

His place exceeded her expectations by a mile. It was beautiful and expensively furnished. Plus, it had no touch of a woman, from what she saw. It would have been foolish to smile about that. She did, anyway. Secretly, of course.

Xander took off his jacket in full view of Ally, telling her to be comfortable while he tries to make them something. She subtly watched his every move. This was not part of the plan, but she might as well go with it. She did not have much experience with relationships, but she wanted to believe that being invited to his place meant more than sitting in a restaurant.

At least that was what it felt like.

"You look stiff. Are you uncomfortable?"

She had just been thinking.Uncomfortable had not been part of it. She shook her head no in reply to his question.

"Good. I'll make us something," he said as he strode towards his kitchen.

As soon as his words settled, a smile lit up her face, and she followed him, taking the chance to look around. "You can cook?"

He did not answer. Instead, she watched his back as he rolled up the sleeves of his shirt and took a while to look around. When he started to open a ridiculous number of drawers and cabinets, she became suspicious.

"Um... You do know where you keep your things, don't you?"

He still gave no answer.

"Do you need some help?"

She looked at all the ingredients he brought out and could not figure out what was on his mind. What did he intend to cook, anyway? She tried again.

"What are you going to cook?"

"Pasta."

Ally looked around. She did not see any pasta in sight.

"You like pasta, right?"

When she looked up to answer him, she almost laughed. Almost. But it would have been rude, so she sucked it in.

"I love pasta. Thank you."

"I haven't even started."

"I'm sure I'll love it."

She was happy. But was it fair to feel that way when he looked frightened at what he was about to do? He should see the loook on his own face. She did not have to guess twice that he did not have a clue about what he was doing. How familiar was he with his own kitchen?

"If you want to take a look around, you're free to do so. This will only take a few minutes."

A few minutes? If you say so, Xander.

"Sure."

Sooner or later, he would have no choice but to call for her help, but the truth was she was not such a good cook either. Even though her mom was the best at it, she just never picked it up. She was not as bad as not being able to whip a fine plate of delicious pasta, though.

She didn't wander too far. Instead, she had settled with watching the sky in the open space right outside the living room. It was good she brought a jacket along. She took in the view of the lonely street ahead and the night sky.

Dad, would you really have hated the idea of me being with him? Are you disappointed? I really like him, Dad.

A loud crash interrupted her thoughts, and her feet hurriedly took her towards the kitchen. What she saw made her burst out in laughter. There was no keeping that one in. He looked at her, and he did not look too happy.

She took off her jacket and walked towards him, trying to help out with what she could. The kitchen looked a mess with ingredients spattered at almost every spot—just like one side of his face and a good chunk of his hair.

"You can't cook, can you?"

"How do you know?"

She laughed again. "I think this spells it out, don't you?"

"It was not supposed to go like this," he said.

She turned off the blender and stared at the orange liquid dancing in it. She bent to take a closer look. "What is this?"

"You don't need to know."

From her position, she glanced up at him. He looked angry.

"I'm sure I can quickly cook something. I'm not the best at it but—"

"I did not bring you here to cook—and certainly not in that dress and heels."

She looked down at what he meant. "It's fine really. I'll just clear this up and—"

Xander stopped her hand. "Don't."

"Really, I don't mind. It's just food for two. I can manage it. Or are you scared? I'm pretty sure I'm better at it than you." She smiled.

Instead of replying, he stared at her, and that made her extremely conscious of everything, especially him. Without letting go of the hand he held, he caressed her face lightly with his other hand, brushing her hair.

"You're beautiful."

He was staring straight into her eyes now, and she gulped. Too close.

And he was flooding her mind. And now, she was staring at his lips. And now, she really wanted to kiss him.

She really wanted to know what it felt like to have him kissing her. She really did.

"If you keep staring like that, I'll have no restraint to kiss you."

"Why don't you?"

He laughed.

She realised what she said. Embarrassment flushed through her body.

"You're different, Alicia, and I like that. Even though you said that unconsciously, I don't think I can back up from a second challenge from you."

Second challenge?

And just like that, his lips came down on hers. It was then she remembered their first meeting and what she had said to him.

It was hot. Kissing him was hot, and she was starting to feel hot all over. She wanted more, and it was like he heard her inner cry. Without releasing her mouth, he cleared the counter with the swipe of his hand and placed her on it.

The hot taste of his lips and tongue was nothing like she had ever tasted. He made sure he made every inch of her mouth relish the pleasure. She had never been kissed like this before, and she was not sure if she was on the right track, but she certainly was not holding back, and she made sure he felt that in her response.

She could not help the moan that escaped her mouth when he released her mouth and felt the pressure and tugging of his lips on her neck. This was crazy. This was too much. His hand found her thigh, but he treaded carefully as if waiting for her permission.

She tried to manage the words to tell him it was okay when he suddenly froze. As did she.

A light growl was heard, and Xander took a few seconds before he released her totally.

"We should order in."

She could only nod in agreement. A small smile appeared on his face, and he placed a soft kiss on her eyelid as she shut her eyes in anticipation, hoping he would kiss her again.

As he helped her down, she wanted to curse at her stomach for grumbling in hunger at that beautiful moment. She would have been happy if all she got fed for the night were his kisses. He certainly was a guy she could keep on kissing forever.

His attempt at cooking dinner was a total disaster, but it was the most fun she had ever had with any man. He didn't even know where the pots were in his own kitchen! He was the most horrible cook she knew, messing up not only the kitchen but both their clothes.

It had not been just his fault. She happily consented to her clothes getting ruined in that way.

Xander led her to his room and told her to get changed into his clothes while he ordered some food for them.

"Pick anything."

She looked around in his closet. There was not much option, and so, she did take her time. She appeared minutes later in one of his shirts and a pair of boxers she had assumed was new. Everything in his closet looked new.

Ally came in and saw him trying to clean up the mess.

She stood still as she watched Xander approach he, eventually noticing her. She was not so naive not to recognise the look on his face.

Lust.

It probably had to do with seeing her in his clothing, but who knew? He probably had been suppressing a lot of things for a while now. She would not dare admit that she's supressing a whole lot of it too. Their act earlier certainly admitted a lot of things, though.

He walked towards her slowly before gathering her whole body and pressing it into his in a firm embrace as the same emotion flickered in his eyes. "You smell good."

"I smell of you… and ingredients," she muttered, referring to his clothes she had on and the traces of the mess probably still stuck on her skin. A chuckle managed to escape her lips at the thought.

"And that's why you smell good. It's really doing things to me... and I want to show them to you," he said softly, nibbling on her earlobe.

That disconcerted her, and she tried to say something, anything to keep the mood going. "A-are the boxers new?"

Of course, she has to say something as stupid as that in this situation. She mentally blamed him for her loss of words. It was his fault she was not thinking straight.

Xander laughed and released her, only enough to look at her face.

He looked doubtful for a moment, and Ally was worried he might think she did not want him as much as he wanted her. Deep in thought, she did not even realise she was frowning until she heard his chuckle.

He raised the shirt a bit to confirm. "They are new." The doorbell rang. "Must be our dinner."

He released her to get it, and she used that moment to catch her breath and compose herself. She knew they were going to be intimate at one point, but she had not thought tonight would be it. For days, he had been showing her snippets of what was to come, leaving her to her wild imaginations, and she had revelled in it. But honestly, she was nervous of actually going all the way. It was not because she did not want to or that she was not ready. It was a matter of what he really wanted.

There were two things she thought might really excite him—a virgin and an experienced partner. She had only ever been with one guy intimately, she did not even get halfway with the second guy, and the third had been a lousy experience.

"Why are you still standing there? Food's here."

She joined him to sit on the carpeted living room floor where he was taking out their food. While he went to get a bottle of wine and glasses, she got out the rest. The packaging and the meal itself looked like it came from an expensive restaurant. She checked the name on the bag and saw it was the same restaurant he had taken her to on their first date.

When he appeared with the wine, he was out of his clothes and had changed into black shorts and a grey tee. He looked different—much more laid back. She loved the look on him. But like her, the aftermath of their kitchen entanglement was still slightly obvious in his hair.

After they were done with dinner, having minor talks while sipping their wine, he said out of nowhere, "You should wear me all the time."

Amused, she asked, "What?"

"You look sexy and beautiful. Too beautiful."

She shyly took her eyes away and sipped more wine. She was not certain if she was trying to hide behind the glass of wine or gain gumption from it. She just hoped she would not choke on her drink.

"Come here," he demanded with his signature husky voice, and she found herself willingly obeying.

It must have been the latter.

Gumption.

She put down her glass and saw him do the same as she moved on all fours towards him.

***

Xander had tried to keep strong all night. Resisting to take action on his naughty thoughts of the woman currently in the room with him was not easy, but he was doing a pretty darn good job even after that kiss they shared… until now.

Ally was unaware of how she looked right now, he was sure of that.

Desire was radiating all over her, and he suddenly felt like the prey, watching her make her way towards him. He carried her onto his lap, positioning her legs on each side of him. The evidence of his arousal was very prominent, poking her through the fabric as she straddled him, and it made her gasp almost inaudibly.

He chuckled. "That's what you do to me every time I look at you."

"Every time?" she asked, dazed.

"Every time," he replied before capturing her lips with his. He intended to take it slow, but that was not an option now… not with that irresistible taste of her and her hot hands starting to trace his body.

Ally moaned frantically as she got more into the kiss, not denying him access to her mouth or refusing the touch of his fingers. At this point, he was sure she did not know how far she was letting go of her desire. Things were getting heated, and it seemed like she wanted to touch him everywhere just as he was doing to her. She wanted him. She wanted more.

With her lips presently arresting his with no intention of letting go, he got her message. She started grinding her hips against his arousal, unintentionally scraping her fingers on his taut torso. He was not sure how her fingers had found their way under his tee, and he did not care.

He allowed her to go on for a minute before stopping her. He placed his hands firmly on her hips to stop being devoured by her, trying to catch his breath.

This girl was driving him insane.

"What's wrong?"

Xander looked at the sight before him. The woman looked like sex served to a deprived, starving man. Her eyes were innocent, her lips were swollen, her skin was flushed, and her hair was tousled. She was sexier than he had ever seen her. She was robbing him of his sanity, and he knew he could not lose control though a minute or two ago, he would have.

He brushed his thumb and forefinger on her plump lips. "If you continue with that, I would either take you right here on this floor or embarrass myself in front of you."

She must have understood his words and blushed the shade of a tomato.

Amazing. She can't be a virgin, can she? the thought popped in his mind. She couldn't be.

"You've been with a man before, right?"

She looked confused. Of course, any woman would think he was stupid for asking that kind of question in that moment.

"Am I... doing something wrong? Am I going too fast?"

He stared at her, surprised she would even ask that. Was she kidding? She was close to making him get the dire release he needed without being inside her, and she thought she was doing something wrong? She did not even have to do anything.

"I have been with a man before. So no, I'm not a virgin," came her answer, and she started to withdraw.

He should have been relieved. He would never think of taking a lover that was yet to discover the ultimate pleasure a man could give. He was a man who did not do commitments, and he did not want to be responsible for one. However, her answer didn't bring him anything; no comfort or indifference. When she tried getting off his lap, Xander stopped her.

"I just wanted to know so I can be gentle with you."

That was a lie. If she had been one, he would have stopped in a heartbeat—and not just their night but seeing her altogether.

Would he, though? Would that honestly have been his decision? He was having the slightest doubts, and he was glad he was not going to have to find out.

She relaxed her body and kissed him lightly on the lips. "Xander, I want you," she said. Her hips grinded slowly on him as she moved forward to do so. His object of desire below once again stirred at the attention given to its owner.

"But I should warn you that I'm rather inexperienced," Ally added.

He nipped the skin below her neck and replied, "I'll teach you all you need to know."

"Now would be a good time then." She moaned, adding more friction to what she was doing and taking all she could of his body with her hands.

"Oh, hell." He groaned. "Hold on to me tight, sweetheart."

He grabbed her hips, fixing her legs firmly around him as he stood up and carried her to his room—a comfortable place to explore a week's long pent-up desire.

CHAPTER 3

"You lied to me," he said to her with gritted teeth. Xander moved away, almost as if he discovered something poisonous beside him, and sat on the bed. He had just devoured this woman with every passion in his bone only to find out, in a not so gentle way, that she was still untouched.

At least she had been now.

He had wanted to stop. Goodness knew he did, and he tried, but she had not helped. Instead, she encouraged him with every bewitching part of her: her legs and the place he had been buried in deep inside of her. And so, he had angrily taken her and himself to that destination they both craved.

He could not comprehend why she had to lie about it. He could not even look at her right now though the sound of her voice and pleas almost made him want to believe her words. He felt cheated and fooled. However, he was grateful for the fact that he had not let loose enough to forget using protection, and that was the only thing keeping him sane right now.

"You have to believe me, I know. I am sure I was not a virgin."

"Well, you certainly aren't anymore. Were you hoping I wouldn't notice?"

"I swear. I'm telling the truth. If nothing else, it would have been great if you had been my first. It's all I had been thinking before this. I wish I had not let Peter Ross touch me."

"Well, you got your wish. Congratulations, I became your first." He lifted himself from the bed, not shy about displaying his complete nakedness. He was still refusing to face her.

"Why are you like this? I'm starting to get the feeling that there's more than you're letting on. What is it really? What is this about?"

He refused to answer.

"Oh, I get it."

No. She couldn't have had the slightest idea what was running through his mind right now. He finally faced her, but he still could not bear to look at her without that distasteful look on his face. "What did you get?" he asked.

She laughed in disbelief before getting up from the bed and wrapping the sheets around her. After what had happened a few minutes ago, she currently did not look too comfortable putting herself on display.

"What are you doing?"

"Getting out of here."

He watched her drag herself around the room, letting the heavy sheets trail behind her as she picked up her clothes, walked into the bathroom, and locked the door behind her.

He could not help but curse as she disappeared behind the door. This was all going wrong. Then again, should he not be happy that it came to this now and not when things started to get messy, perhaps? He should have been grateful that he would not have to be involved in a situation he tried to avoid his whole life.

Why the hell was he thinking about this?

***

Ally tried to fight back the tears as she dropped the sheets and got into her dress. It did not matter right now if they were stained. She could not think. She did not want to think about anything. She could not even think of the words *'they told you so.'*

One week—one bloody week, and she was going to be referred to as one of his women. *Great job, Ally. Wouldn't your mother be so proud of you?*

She unlocked the door and saw him standing in the middle of the room with his shorts firmly on his hips. His upper body was exposed, and that almost made her change her mind. His hair was dishevelled either from their earlier engagement or from the constant brushing of his hands which he was doing right now.

"Where do you think you're going?" Xander's eyes were hard, and she could not read anything from them.

"I told you, I'm leaving." She dropped the sheets on the bed. This man probably knew more about her body now than she did herself, and it only took less than an hour. "I'll need a lift, of course. If you can't do that, you can at least get me a cab."

She was not so angry to leave his house unreasonably. The road was unfamiliar to her, and she did not want to have to call Laurie to help her out. She felt miserable about how it all turned out already, and Ally knew her cousin would only add more fuel to the fire if she found out. The most she could do right in front of him was to leave here without looking like what she was feeling inside.

"You're not going any—"

"Says who?" She cut him off. "Just a few minutes ago you were thinking of how clingy I might be, that I might be trying to hold on to your almighty self just because you made me a woman, right? Don't even bother denying it. I've come across men like you before."

Not really. She had only come to that conclusion based on one experience she had with this one douche of a guy.

She continued when he parted his lips to speak. "News for you… I might have wished it, but for six years, I have never thought myself a virgin."

"You sound so sure. How could you not have known?"

"I was young and immature, and did not know what I was doing, and he obviously did not too." She muttered the last part to herself, but he must have heard.

"How old were you?"

Embarrassed, she looked away and muttered, "Fifteen. Both of us."

He said nothing.

"I want to leave now."

"And you've never been with another man since then?" he asked, ignoring her words.

"Not intimately. At least it never went that far." She did not know why she was giving him answers he did not deserve.

"How many?"

"How many what?" Ally frowned at him.

"Men. How many have you been with?"

"Are you kidding me right now?" she asked.

"Do I look like I am?"

Of course, he was serious, and it was starting to annoy her. "Do you see me asking how many women you've been with before me?"

"You did not ask, and I assume you already know I've been with quite a lot. My reputation with women has been painted far notoriously than I would want it to be."

"You're so arrogant!" She spat. "The fact that you still believe I did this on purpose makes me so mad right now," she exclaimed, raising both her hands in disbelief.

"If you've been with other men—"

"I told you! I never had sex with them! The second guy I've ever let touch me was in senior year high school. He made it as far as touching my breasts before my dad sent him away with his tail between his legs. The last one was just a selfish lover who wanted me to do things I was not comfortable with, and I stopped!" She breathed harshly before she continued silently. "Are you satisfied now? Have I given you a worthy explanation to earn your trust? I want to leave now." She walked towards the bedroom door, having had enough.

"I'm sorry."

That stopped her, but she did not look back.

"I haven't had the best experience with situations like this."

She stayed rooted in her spot, not saying anything.

"I'll admit, I was shocked… and then I got angry that you might have taken advantage of how much I wanted you." He sighed. "Please, look at me, Ally."

She slowly turned to face him and saw pain in his eyes. The series of events that has happened tonight might have brought out something he tried to hide. It might have triggered his anger. She wanted to ask, but they both had enough of upsetting each other in one night. She moved closer, leaving a good distance between them.

For a long moment, they did nothing else but stare at each other.

She saw the man she had been attracted to since the night they met, standing a good six feet tall with brown hair now sexily tousled and dark and long lashes shielding his beautiful greens. His body was moulded perfectly with smooth, well-proportioned muscles and a chiselled face that she was sure made just about every woman get drawn to his charm.

"What now?" she managed to ask after sorting out her thoughts.

"Stay."

Why? she wanted to ask, and maybe she should have just to know what he was thinking, but she did not. Instead, minutes later, she found herself tangled in his arms once more on his bed, still fully dressed and letting a shirtless Xander lazily stroke her arm.

"You have classes tomorrow, right?"

"Hmm."

"I'll drop you off at your apartment early in the morning. So stay the night."

"Hmm?" She turned her face to look at him.

"You don't want to?"

"It's not that." She managed to shake her head as much as the little space between them could allow. "Besides, my class tomorrow is in the afternoon."

He was staring at her, willing her to continue. She knew if she agreed, it would be their first night together. She was itching to ask him what they were—what she was to him and what she was to expect—but she could not. She did not want him to think she was pressuring him. It was just one week, anyway; they had time to define whatever was going on. With that thought, she smiled at him.

"Okay."

That one word she gave him with all her heart confirmed she was giving in to whatever she was feeling for him, that she was willing to delve deeper and deeper into what little he was ever going to give her.

He went back to stroking her arm, slowly gliding it to the more sensitive parts of her body. He was starting to arouse her completely, making her heart beat faster. "I wonder what you thought about sex after that horrible experience you had."

"With you? Who said it was horrible?" she said, laughing.

He swatted her bum playfully. "Now, I've just been bruised. Was I horrible? I did not get that message when you had me locked in your legs and would not stop moaning. *Don't stop.*" He teased her, trying to mimic her voice in the throes of passion.

It sounded terrible to her ears, but it was so funny the way he said it. They went silent for a moment, both of them keeping their personal thoughts to themselves, until he looked at her in concern. "Did I hurt you?" he asked.

Ally knew what he meant, and honestly, he had been less than gentle, but those thoughts ceased to dominate her mind right now. All she remembered was the way he had kissed every part of her and how he used his hand to take her along with him as their skin fused together, and she still glowed from the pleasure.

"I feel fine, though, I feel more than fine actually". She hoped he got the message.

"Well, it's a good thing I get to erase your horrible first experience."

She laughed out richly. Was he forgetting he was her first real experience?

"I'm guessing you'll be giving me a better experience?"

He looked at her smiling, and she knew he got the message.

"Oh, why Miss Storm… I thought I already did that."

"Did you?" She teased back.

"Come here. I'll be more than happy to refresh your memory."

She squealed when he suddenly gripped her hips as he towered above her with a huge grin on his face. He passionately found her lips and reminded her of how their lips were better together before moving on to her neck. Xander got rid of her clothes once again. True to his word, he did refresh her memory, and more, all through the night.

It was certainly a good thing she only had one class the next day.

***

Weeks had gone by. Three weeks to be precise, after that night, and it has been a month now with him. Ally could not be more content in a relationship. What they had was not defined by any label yet, but she was with him exclusively, and she wanted to believe the same of Xander though there was no reason to think otherwise.

He made her happy, the sex was great, and she was always smiling with him around and thinking of him when he was not. Laurie had told her days before that no matter what she did, she was already hooked—only a tiny step away from declaring she was in love. Would that be so bad, though?

Her mother was still against her decision, and that had left a dent in their relationship no matter how they tried to ignore it. Xander's father was the same, she had heard, though she had not been fortunate to meet the man.

As a college freshman, trying to juggle school and being with Xander was not easy. There were a couple of times when he would be free from business and not travelling, but she would be neck deep with school activities and vice versa. Whatever time they both created to be with each other was less than they hoped for. Though Xander showed his displeasure about the whole thing, he still managed to make their time together something memorable.

That was what it was. Every moment with him was extraordinary so far.

If she had not taken years to study hairdressing before deciding on a major, she would have more time with him now. She smiled at the thought. No, she did not regret her choice. She had a natural talent when it came to hair styling, and she had taken a step to explore it.

Plus, if she had taken another route in life, who knew if she would have ever met Xander?

"I'm out." Trish's voice cut in through her thoughts.

"Enjoy your weekend," She said to her roommate.

Trish was off to see her boyfriend, and she would probably be doing the same if Xander was not away on business.

Was Xander her boyfriend? No, but at least he was her man. He had once suggested getting her an apartment close enough to the campus for their privacy. She had turned down that offer, but then he had brought out the idea of getting her a car instead so she could get to his place faster when needed.

Both suggestions made her feel exactly like what her mother and the papers referred to her as—his mistress, a fling, just another girl out of many. The words had left a bitter taste to her mouth so she was not going to indulge them.

She did not care what people thought of her, but it got her thinking for days what Xander really thought of their relationship. What was his reason for being with her? Still, she was not confident enough to face him and ask.

Before it all gets too crazy she would, she promised herself.

***

"It's been weeks. You started with her just like you did with Barb."

Xander turned his furious eyes to his assistant.

"Don't give me that look. You know I'm right. You're so lenient towards her. It'll end up a disaster."

"I told you never to mention that incident again."

"Well, give me a reason not to."

He dropped the file in his hand, slamming it on the table. "Is this really about that?"

"What else?" Julia shifted her weight to her left leg.

"You tell me, Julia," He asked, his eyes fixed on hers.

She let out a small laugh. "If this is about my feelings, I think you made it clear it's a lost cause."

"Then why keep making this about it? She's not Barb," he said stiffly, trying to get his point across.

"Are you in love with her?"

"What?"

She saw the answer she wanted in his eyes. He was not, but why did this one feel different? Why did she feel certain unease whenever she saw or heard Alicia Storm's name come up?

"Then why is this different? It's just how you were with—" She stopped herself before she could mention Barb's name again.

"I'll say this once. Stay out of my personal business. If you can't, find another job. I've had enough of you dictating to me what I'm supposed to do with Ally."

She took a pause, calming herself and trying to remember that the man in front of her was her boss right now, not a friend or her ex-lover at the moment.

"I'm sorry."

She did not doubt that he would replace her if she continued with her rants. Nothing was getting to him. Maybe it was time for her to stop and accept that there was no way she could get him into her arms again. There would always be another chance when he was done with *her*, but she was afraid that might not be anytime soon.

"I don't need you to be sorry. I need you to be professional."

"Right, and you will get that henceforth."

He took his eyes away, but she doubted if he believed her words. The professional Julia he worked with was great at what she did. She was confident about that and knew that was the reason Xander kept her around him. She was efficient and made the every business days, bad or good, easier to handle. She was excellent at what she did. Firing her would be a setback, but she was not irreplaceable.

How many times did she try to remind herself of that?

She knew that, but then, she also knew the real reason Xander kept her around was because he had misunderstood the conversation her old friend, Mandy, had with him. If Xander thought she was suicidal because of her feelings for him and he felt a tiny bit of responsibility for her because of that, she would take it.

She never corrected what he thought but at the same time, she did not think it changed anything with him either.

"But I'll say something… as a friend."

"I don't want to hear it."

"Tell her. It's only fair that you tell her what you expect and how it ends."

***

A frown emerged on Xander's face as he remembered his earlier conversation with Julia.

Though he did not like that she mentioned it, he remembered that he had refused to discuss his expectations with Ally a month ago because he was sure she was going to end it. He knew he had to do that now, though. All week, he told himself he would get to it, but he was not ready to let her go, and accepting that fact was like swallowing a bitter pill down his throat. If Ally chooses to end things, he would have no choice but to let her. He had never begged for a woman's company—except for one, and he remembered how that ended. He was not about to put himself in that position again.

Damn, that woman. With the scowl on his face still prominent, he knew it was time to make things clear with Ally.

***

If she had accepted the car he wanted to get her, it would have made things easier. At least he wouldn't have to worry much about her whereabouts. At five four inches, Xander knew Ally had more energy in her to make up for what she lacked in height, but that would not cut it for him.

He could not deny the pleasure he felt when she was in his arms. He desired everything about her and would never have a thing changed. Her skin had a deep glow to it which he never failed to worship with his mouth whenever they had sex, and when they were not, he had no restrain over his wandering fingers. Her breasts were always full in his palms, and he loved stripping them off her bra, loving the way they usually spilled, ready for feasting. She had hips that could make a man go crazy even when clothed and an ass that always followed his command during lovemaking when he held on as he drove into her...

No way! No more of these thoughts, he told himself.

He just showered minutes ago. He looked down at a part of him he had just woken with his thoughts and groaned. He was expecting her any minute from now. He could not take another shower. There was no time for that. He just had to calm himself before she arrived.

Minutes after walking it off and going through his mails, he was successful at calming his throbbing need. He heard the door and knew she was here. She was the only one he was expecting this evening since he had cleared the rest of his day to be with her.

It was distracting seeing her walk towards him in a peach dress that pronounced her every attribute he had just been thinking about. The colour complemented her skin though he loved red best on her—the colour that forbade him from keeping his hands to himself.

"Hi." She greeted with a kiss.

He kept it short unlike before.

"Is something wrong?" she asked. "You sounded urgent on the phone."

"We need to talk."

He saw the tensed look on her face and knew he should not have started like that. He could only imagine what was going through her head.

"What about?"

Normally, when she arrived in his apartment, she would drop her bag and whatever she had with her, but right now, she held on to her bag tightly and took the couch two seats away from him—like she was ready for whatever he was going to say and be out the door any minute. He did not like that.

"We need to make certain things clear."

"I'm listening."

This time, her face was void of any emotion, only deepening the frown that was starting to form on his face. What the hell was she thinking he was going to say?

"I absolutely am not the marrying type—"

"I know that," she cut in.

Her answer somehow angered him. Was she going to listen to him or believe every crass word said and written about him?

"And I'm not a father material," he continued.

She remained silent.

"I don't know what you want or expect from this but... I'll never change myself to be the perfect me that you might hope to see."

"Then what are we doing?" She finally responded.

He feared that it would come to this. Seeing Ally set aside her bag, he felt relieved. At least she was not preparing to be out the door.

"You've said what you want to say. Now listen to mine." She stood from where she sat.

"How did you conclude that I've made up an image of an ideal you?" She made the slowest steps towards him. "I don't expect a ring from you, and I certainly don't want to burden you with something you don't want."

He questioned her with his eyes.

"A baby," she answered. "What if protection fails? What do I refer to you as? Who do you say I am when people ask? Are you… are we supposed to be seeing other people?"

"No!"

She never ceased to surprise him with her answers. He had never expected her reply the first night they met and now, she completely beat what he thought her reaction would be.

*

Ally stopped in front of him and almost smiled at his outburst. Why he looked surprised, she could not imagine. He could give her ultimatum, and she could not? She was glad he created this opportunity for her to do what she had been afraid of.

"No to which question?"

"The only man you're allowed to be with is me."

"And you?"

"I'm not seeing anyone else. It's just you. And what do you mean when people ask? You're my woman."

"I think the world knows that already."

"And?"

"I—" *Your woman sounds like your mistress,* she wanted to say. This was her opportunity to voice out her concern. Would it go wrong if she speaks her mind? Would he get angry? Well, at least it would make things clearer between them.

"If people see me taking my girlfriend out on a date, it shouldn't be—"

"Girlfriend?"

"You'd rather be referred to as my mistress?"

Maybe Xander knew that it bothered her, that the gossips have been affecting her lately. Now, she was certain hardly anything passed him by when it came to her feelings and their relationship. It probably was why they were having this talk in the first place. He must have suspected that she liked him a lot more than she tried to show or admit. Of course, he would have guessed.

"And I'm your man… your only man."

She laughed, and he pulled her towards him. She fell on him and would have winced at the impact, but the look on his face remained the same.

"You think it's funny?"

She shook her head, still laughing.

"I'm not joking, Ally. I'll have the head of that man who dares to look twice at your direction."

"Then why don't you keep me in here, you barbarian?"

"Should I?"

She kissed him, but he did not respond. She felt a small smile forming on his face before she took his bottom lip in her mouth, sucking on it lightly.

"You should see your face. I could say green isn't your colour"—she said, referring to his jealousy—"but that would be a lie. Your green eyes drive me crazy."

"Really?"

She nodded, despite the fact that she had said it before. He loved hearing it.

"You're sure they're the only things that drive you crazy?" He just loved flaunting the fact that he was gorgeous in every way and loved to hear her admit it. "Want to know what about you drives me crazy?"

She nodded again.

"Before that, though, I should answer your question earlier. We take precautions. We should both be protected, just to avoid any mistake."

"But what if it fails?"

She just sounded like a woman who wanted it to fail, but she hoped Xander did not translate it as that.

"It won't. I'll introduce you to a friend tomorrow."

"Friend?"

"He's a doctor. Don't worry. Jay's a good friend, and you'll be comfortable with him."

She understood.

"I can't give you marriage, Ally, and I don't want a baby. I'll *never* want a baby."

She was shocked at his statement. Never was such a strong word. Was she comfortable with this? No, but she could go with it for now. It was not like she wanted a baby right now either, and she had not really given marriage some serious thought at this point in her life.

CHAPTER 4

Two months.

What do you do when you hit the two months mark with your millionaire boyfriend... or was it billionaire? As Ally had come to know, Xander was a self-made millionaire, but if he inherited his father's business and wealth, he could become a billionaire. But for some reason she did not understand, Xander refused to be put in his father's spotlight. He was more than capable of making his own money, he said.

This was quite a big deal to her. She had been in a relationship that lasted seven months before—but that was in high school when she dated Peter at the age of fifteen. This was different. She was not the big-chested girl who was experiencing puberty anymore. She was an adult in a relationship with a man she cared about, and it was not just any man. It was with Alexander Cross—the man who had everything and wanted nothing from this relationship.

Just a month ago, they laid out their expectations of each other and what they had going. She was staying faithful to all that was said between them, but he never said anything about love.

Love. She sighed inside, trying not to make sudden movements to wake him up. She turned to face the man beside her and just stared at him, taking in his features. She had fallen in love with him.

She had doubted it at first, but now she was sure of it. It was something totally out of her control though somehow expected. So when she eventually came to terms with it, she had not been shocked or surprised, just cautious.

Ally did not know what would happen to her heart if and when Xander decided to end what they had going on.

The month had not exactly been a smooth ride for them, not with both their parents giving their opinions and the media giving various versions of their relationship. Her mother hated her relationship with him—or was it Xander she disliked? Her mom never made that point clear enough whenever she insisted she put an end to her 'infatuation.' And his father... She closed her eyes at the memory of last night. Though it was not news that Xander's father did not approve of his son's 'fling,' listening to him say it to her face had been frightening.

The man was one or two inches taller than his son and definitely had a larger build. The grey suit he wore fitted to his body almost to the point of bursting. Both father and son looked nothing alike except for the green eyes. They had not been welcoming on his father, though.

Xander had arrived unexpectedly in the middle of his father telling her to stay away from his son and to find something productive to do with her life.

"Go find a man that would respect you as a woman." Those were his exact words.

It stung, a lot. Ally was not sure if it was because of the way he had said it or because, deep inside, she knew it might have some truth to it.

Xander had asked her to go to his room, leaving the men to exchange words. Father and son had not been gentle with words, and she had no reason to eavesdrop when she could hear every word said.

After his father left, the atmosphere had been a little tense, but Xander had assured her that they were alright. He was not listening to the crap being thrown at them and so should she, he told her. He got what he wanted: a promise from her that she wouldn't change her mind. Xander had added an arrogant statement just to prove his point:

"It's over only when I say it is." Typical Xander. He probably did not find it as offensive as she had.

She knew he did not say those words out of disrespect, but what did that say about their relationship? Could she really ignore his twisted and arrogant way of saying and doing things? She could not even understand what he truly meant.

She remembered her conversation with Laurie two days ago, and it still unsettled her gut in the strangest of ways.

"Let's meet for lunch. You're either busy with school or with that sexy man of yours these days. It feels like years since I saw you. You can do that right?" Laurie said on the phone.

"Yes, Laurie but—"

"I know. You have to get back to whatever it is. I just want to know what's going on with you."

"Give me the time and place. I'll be there."

Laurie was right. It had been a while since they met. She had a feeling it had to be her mom asking for this, but if her mom was so concerned, all she had to do was talk about it with her. But she always made it obvious she did not care about her relationship with Xander except when it involved a breakup.

She made it to the small restaurant minutes before their scheduled time, and Laurie walked in on the dot, looking stunningly beautiful as always. They exchanged greetings, and when they got settled, a cup of coffee was placed down for both of them.

"Spill it. Is he keeping you against your will?"

Ally laughed. "I've been attending classes, haven't I? Besides, we haven't seen each other for two days."

Laurie twitched her mouth before raising an eyebrow. "Look at you sounding like a neglected bride. You said two days. Don't make it sound like you've been separated for two years."

"Is that what it sounds like?"

"And more. I hear you hardly stay in your apartment. Are you thinking of moving in with him?"

"What? No. I only stay over whenever he's around and I'm less busy with school. Did Trish tell you that?"

"You think I need hot gossips about you from Trish? I only need a click on the internet. You're a hot topic."

"I try to avoid reading those things," she muttered.

"Well, you can't. The fact that Alexander Cross is dating a freshman is better gossip than a thousand tickets to fame."

"I don't want that."

"I know, do they?" Laurie gave a resigned sigh. "What are you doing, Ally? Are you sure about this?"

"At the moment, yes."

"That's a stupid answer, but okay, I'll go with it. Are you happy?"

"Yes."

With that, Laurie perked up immediately. "I needed to hear that before I told you."

"Told me what?"

"What I found out!" Laurie shifted her body forward, moving closer to her as if telling her a secret. She did the same. "It seems he's crazy enough about you. You're the second woman who's made it to two months with him."

She relaxed back in her seat and stared in disbelief at her cousin. "That's what you needed to tell me? Where did you hear that from?"

"A credible source. But still, these things aren't news. You truly never take a peek at what is said about you two?"

"Only when I accidentally come across it. Are you checking up on him?"

Laurie frowned. "What do you take me for? I've got my concerns. I don't have that much free time. I recently met this guy. He's a socialite, and somehow, Xander's name came up, and when I realised he knew your boyfriend, I poked for more answers."

She kept silent.

"Tell me you don't want to know."

"I don't want to know," she muttered monotonously.

"Yeah, right."

She did want to know, but then again, she did not want to find out about things that might not be true and start overthinking her relationship with Xander. She liked what they had.

"Are you drifting off on me right now?"

"Sorry." She smiled as a hint of red started blooming on her cheeks.

"That smile is dangerous. Are you in love with him? Have you accepted what you two are?"

Ally kept quiet once more, not knowing what to say.

"Oh, wow! That was faster than I predicted. And what about him? Have you told him?"

"What? I can't. He does not want that sort of commitment. It'll complicate things. You should understand me better."

"Why? Because I have sex with them n' leave them?"

"I didn't mean th—"

"You're right, but I've always made it clear from the start, and it's clearly understood between my partner and I. No expectations, Ally. You? You don't want that. You never will. We are different. I take different lovers when my body feels like it and don't care if they do too. Can you say that about yourself? Will you be okay if you knew he had some other woman? So don't tell me about complicating things. It already got complicated when you decided to stake your heart in it." Laurie took a deep breath and spoke in a calmer voice. "If you're not ready to tell him, then don't. You shouldn't spread yourself all out. Not now."

"What do you mean?" she asked curiously.

"Tony talked about a woman he dated for five months before it got ugly. Said it was no news, anyway." Laurie waved her hand in dismissal. "He was pretty into her from what I heard before she betrayed him." She finished in a low voice.

Betrayed Xander? Ally had never heard of that. Laurie's voice cut her off from her own thoughts.

"You have to get past those five months before I can be confident about sending you all out into the battlefield." It was said so casually that she wanted to laugh at her cousin.

"Are you serious?" Ally asked, smiling.

"Do I look like I'm kidding? By the way, I'm starving." She said the last part more to herself and called for a waiter to order their food.

She paused for the waiter to leave before she continued. "I'm not going to build my relationship on a past one."

"No one's asking you to build anything. Here's a fact: he's notorious for taking women only weeks at a time. That woman lasted five months, and it got ugly! Aren't you the least bit curious why? You need to avoid that."

If Laurie put it like that, it did make sense, but she was not going to ask Xander what had happened. He would know she was listening to gossips, and besides, he had never been comfortable talking or hearing about Laurie. She guessed the first impression had a lasting effect. She had asked him about that before, but Xander had only replied that there were just certain people you meet and dislike without a reason.

She was the one left in a tight spot. The people she cared about were not getting along.

Their food arrived, and a few minutes later, Laurie asked out of nowhere. "So, how good are you in bed with him?"

She went into a coughing fit and tried to control her spasm. Laurie extended a glass of water to her, which she gratefully took. "What was that about?"

"Pssh. Anyone would think you don't even know the meaning of sex, which is impossible, considering who it is you're dating."

"That's totally none of your business!" she said, bewildered. She never told Laurie about her unfortunate night with Xander where she found out she was actually

new at something she thought she was not. Laurie would only have more to say to that, and she had already put that past her. Since Xander had never talked about it after that night again, she saw no reason to bring it up herself.

"Fine. If you say so. I'm just saying since I know you had practically no experience in that department before you met him. It's either he has taught you things, or you just leave all the work to him, because let's be honest… one time sex at fifteen and a hand job does not exactly make you a pro."

What sort of an evil, witchy temptress was her cousin? But Laurie was not in sync with her inner cursing, and she just continued.

"The man has been tagged notorious in bed by thousands of women. It may seem like I'm pushing, but you should keep him interested. Don't just let him love your body. Love his, too."

Ally had not been able to shake off Laurie's words. It had been on her mind since she heard it, and when she had found privacy in her room, she had reluctantly googled different articles on how to keep a man interested sexually.

Bringing herself to the present, she watched the man sleeping beside her. She could stare at him all day. She lightly traced his lips, nose, eyes, and chin with her fingertips, content with the act. Still treading carefully in order not to wake him, she lightly grazed his stubble. She had previously confessed she loved it on him when she spotted the slight growth.

Xander had admitted he ignored it in between balancing his workload and trying to get back to her. She loved the look on him, and she remembered the way he teased her with it when he kissed her, eliciting uncontrollable laughs from her.

"If you love it so much, I might just keep it unshaved."

Surprised, she looked down at him, but he still had his eyes closed.

"Hmm…" He hummed.

"How long have you been awake?"

"Just now," he said, his voice raspy from sleep.

It was a nice start to their day, and she thought it was now or never after chickening out last night.

"You're still staring," he said.

Instead of giving him a witty reply, she looked down at the sheets wrapped around their nakedness and slid her hand under it. She loved this man. The bolder she got, the more she got nervous and excited.

Excited. Admitting that to herself made it seem easier to do.

"Hmm…" he murmured approvingly when she caressed his abdomen.

She slid her hand lower, and when it made contact with the piece of him she was searching for, he froze.

That made her stop, but she left her hand where it was. She was not expecting this reaction. *Is this bad? What am I to do now?*

The specimen put on hold in her hands gave her the answer. She felt him grow, and she cautiously moved her fingers when he said nothing. It looked like she was doing better than she had first thought from his unsteady breaths and incoherent murmurs. She knew Xander had his eyes on her, and she made an effort to face him just to feel more connected to him and maybe tap some courage and encouragement while she took the initiative.

It turned out to be a big mistake.

For a moment, she saw the look she wanted on his face, and in seconds, it was gone. He looked at her like he just caught himself enjoying something wrong. He brushed her hand away lightly and suddenly got out of bed, not attempting to cover his jutting manhood.

"What the hell was that?" he demanded.

"I—I..." She stammered, looking down at the standing ovation she got from the lower part of him and back to his face. He looked like he was enjoying it a while ago. What was the problem? He could touch her but she could not?

"I need to get to work. Get ready. I'll drive you to your apartment, or you stay if you want to," he said, walking out of the room.

What was it just now? What had she done wrong?

CHAPTER 5

Ally dropped on the couch, unaware of Trish's eyes on her.

"Trouble in paradise or exhaustion from too much loving?"

"Huh? Is there anything like too much loving?" *More like no love*, Ally added to herself.

When Xander had blatantly rejected her and left his room, she was left so weak, she could not move from where she had been. None of her research had prepared her for such a reaction. When he came into his room, showered and ready to dress up, that was when she came back to her senses.

There had been no time for her to take a shower, so she moved about, still in a daze, for her clothes. She had awkwardly picked up her things with one hand while she clutched the sheets to her bosom with the other. She had felt too embarrassed to even shed a glimpse of her flesh. The silence had been suffocating, and she had not been bold enough to see if he was watching her or not.

On the ride from his apartment to her place, the only words said were, "I'll call later."

Should she have said something to that like, 'When? Will you? Are we going to talk about what happened?'

No way. She hoped they never talked about that. It had to the most embarrassing moment of her life. Laurie would have a field day with this—that was if she knew, but she was not planning on telling.

She had just wanted to give him what he has been giving her. Xander appeared to be a man who would want that, but she must have been wrong… gravely wrong for him to react like that. She should not have made assumptions but rather asked or talked about it.

That was a lesson learned for another time—*if* there was another time.

She felt hurt; she could not deny that. He had made her feel like a child, treating her like that.

She yawned out loud and saw the frown on her roommate's face.

"I'm tired," Ally said as an excuse, forcing out a smile.

"Looks like it. What were you doing all night?"

Trish frowned again, and Ally guessed her roommate's thoughts. Love troubles. But it had not been just that. The stress of her daily life must finally be getting to her. The only thing she could do at that moment was take a shower, get some rest, and wait to see if he called.

***

Julia had watched her boss stride in this morning with a taut look on his face, and it had not gotten any better with the day. Something was bothering him. If his snappy and rude comments to his staff did not spell it, catching him drifting to his thoughts did.

Was it that girl? Was he having problems with her already? Well, at least she got him hooked for months—something she had been suspicious might happen from the onset. She remembered the night it all started and knew Xander had looked more intrigued than interested by Ally.

"If you keep this up, you might as well dismiss your whole staff."

"Not now, Julia. I want to be alone."

"I have left you alone. You look like you needed that, but it's getting on everyone's nerves. Mine too, which makes working with you today a pain in the ass. Work it out. Do something about it, whatever it is."

She left him to think about it.

***

Was he not trying? That was all he had been thinking about… Ally, what she did this morning and the way he had responded to her touch. Hell, he bloody reacted like she had some kind of infectious disease.

Xander knew he handled it all poorly. He knew that, but she just caught him off guard. He just could not understand why she thought she had to do that after two months of being together. Was she paying attention to whatever nonsense was said about him? She could have come across or heard something; it could be her roommate... or her cousin. He never liked that one.

He had to talk to her. No, they needed to talk. He would apologize and get that insecure look off her face. He had watched from the corner of his eyes how she scrambled about trying to get herself together this morning. He should not have shut her out. He made a big mistake.

He was sure she did not know what effect she had on him, and though he was trying hard not to show it, it was a losing battle. What she did this morning… Oh, man. He groaned, dropping his pen and resting back in his chair with his eyes tightly closed. She had no idea, absolutely no idea.

His languidness was over as he sat up and found a way to make things right. He called for his assistant.

"Yes?" Julia approached him and waited while he scribbled something down.

He handed a note to her. "I want this note delivered with a bunch of red roses to this address." He gave another note to her.

"Just as I thought." Julia did not bother keeping the words to herself. It was loud enough for him to have heard.

***

It has been three and half hours since she received the roses and call from Xander. He had called to ask if she received the flowers and the note. She had, but she was not sure what it was about even though the note had been self-explanatory.

I'm sorry. Have dinner with me, and we'll talk. I'll pick you up at seven.

Typical Xander, not giving her a choice.

With a double light coat of mascara, a bold touch of red lipstick, dabs of loose powder, and a light blush, she was satisfied with her reflection. She tamed her unruly waves in style with pins, something she knew Xander disliked, but she made that choice for herself.

Barely ten minutes before seven, she was ready. She was dressed in a knee length, plain red dress with a sweetheart neckline. The thin straps held her ample bosom, allowing a decent view of her naturally tanned cleavage. The dress was not as figure hugging as she would have originally opted for, but she was playing it safe. She was not sure what to expect tonight, considering the events of this morning, so it was no use wanting to dress up for him or encouraging him.

Wasn't she doing the exact same thing, though? Xander loved red on her, after all. At least she had made her choice on that.

Five minutes before seven, the doorbell rang. She left a note for Trish, letting her know she was out.

"Hi," he said as she opened the door.

"Hi."

She knew what Xander was thinking with his eyes boring into her hair. If only their morning was not so awkward, she would have laughed at his reaction. It was even funnier seeing his stiff face, trying to hold back his words.

They made it to dinner without a word exchanged between them. Surprisingly, the silence was not suffocating.

An employee came in view and led them to an elevator. Silence still hung in the air, and when the elevator stopped, a rooftop came in view.

It was a magnificent setting.

The next thing she would have done was gasp at the sight, but her dazed brain could not manage to get a sound out of her. When she heard his voice, she turned to face him. He was smiling at her, and she closed her mouth. He looked satisfied, probably at the sight of her gawking.

The table for two they were led to was romantically set up, and she looked in awe at the beauty and serenity of it all.

Was this all for her? She could not believe her eyes.

"Do you like it?" he asked after drawing the chair and letting her sit down.

"It's beautiful."

"It's a new addition to the restaurant. I'm told we're the second customers to use it. It's quite private."

She looked around. They were alone now. "Did you book the whole of it?"

"Yes. We needed to talk."

He did not have to go to such lengths for them to talk. She almost scolded herself for wanting to blush. The rooftop looked like it was created to accommodate five guests at most. Though it was on a rooftop, there were glass walls that shielded them from the night air, which could be opened wide depending on the customer's choice. The intricate designs looked awfully expensive, and everything seemed too delicate to touch.

A table here must be expensive, let alone the whole floor. She could only imagine people as rich as or wealthier than Xander and how they lived their daily lives. She almost always got a glimpse of his life, alright, but she tried to stay away from the excessive parts. But sometimes, that was just impossible.

Like tonight.

She wondered why he had to go to such extent. If they needed to talk privately, they could do it at his place. Well… they both knew how that might end up, and he must have been serious enough to want to clear the air.

Silence ensued again as their food was served. "Eat. We'll talk after," he said.

Good way to make me more nervous, Xander, Ally thought.

The meal was so satisfying, she almost forgot why they were here. She felt so full now. She went way beyond her limit, greedily feasting on everything laid out before her. It was a good thing she wore a dress that was not sticking to her every curve; she could already feel her tummy bulging out.

It took a few minutes for the table to be cleared, leaving only a bottle of wine and their glasses, but she just needed water for what was to come, so she requested for it. She did not need anything else messing with her head. She already had enough wine, and Xander right in front of her was enough to do the job.

"What happened this morning," he started talking when they were finally alone once again "was not what it seemed like. My reaction was..." He sighed.

"You were surprised?" She offered the word he probably was searching for.

"I was shocked. As you must have noticed, I was more than willing for you to go on. Hell, you probably had no idea what you were doing to me. I wanted to be selfish enough to not stop you."

"But I wanted to. Not stop, I mean." She quickly added.

"No, you didn't want to do that." A frown appeared on his lips once more. "I saw the look on your face when you looked at me. You were unsure... like you were afraid of something."

She had been unsure and afraid. That was because she was insecure of what she was doing. It was a first for her, and she was too conscious if she was doing it right. She was afraid of what he might think of her boldness and how he would take it.

"Someone must have said something to you. Perhaps, you must have read something nasty about my previous relationships."

Something nasty? Was Laurie right about his tall orders when it came to women and his bed?

"I wanted to, Xander. Whatever look you saw on my face was just me being scared you might hate what I was doing… or maybe even me for that matter."

"Ally…" he said, looking her in the eyes. "Remember that guy you told me about?"

What guy?

"The one who wanted you to do things you weren't comfortable with."

Todd.

"I didn't want you to think you had to do something you weren't comfortable with for me."

If this were any other time, she would say Xander was in love with her, but she knew better. But that had to mean he cared, right? He had been listening. He had listened and remembered.

"Anyone would know what you were talking about. You did not have to give me the details. You don't have to do those things. I'm okay with what we have."

"Xander—"

"And listen now because I might not get to say them again. I like what we have. There are so many things about you that drive me crazy already. You're smart, honest about us, easy to talk to, and great in bed. If you're any greater, I would probably be signing my own death wish."

She laughed at that.

"Well, thanks for the compliment, but when I tell you I want you in that way and more, I mean it."

It's the time to be bold, Ally thought.

"That other guy was a tool. It is not the same with you." At that time it had been more like an itch she wanted to scratch, and Todd had been there. It was a relationship out of convenience. He was an attractive man and someone she was familiar with.

"Good. 'Cos I hate that it's because of me you're dressed this way tonight. Do you know how bad I wanted to turn you back and get you changed into the bold and sexy woman I've come to know you as?"

"I know. The frown on your face was fun to watch."

"Really? Guess you were trying to appease me with the colour still." He smirked before standing from his chair, walking towards her and finally squatting beside her. "It didn't work, though," he said in a lowered voice that sounded so sensual to her ears. His hand found its way to her hair and got rid of every pin securing it. "Better."

She grinned. Oh, boy. She was in for it. If he was doing things like he had been doing all night, how was she to control her feelings?

"So you're saying we could be more adventurous? That's what *you* want?" he whispered, his gaze boring into hers.

"I believe I do. I'd want that," she replied huskily, not even meaning for it to come out of her mouth that way.

Xander captured her mouth in a hot kiss and stopped only to whisper. "And I don't think I could hate you as you are now." And his seducing lips found their way back to her trembling ones.

***

What more could a girl ask for at the moment?

A ring? Maybe that was overrated. A promise? That was a thing created for temporary ease of mind which eventually got broken. It has never been reliable.

What then?

Right now, Ally was just happy with the man she was in love with. Four months together, and she would not have it any other way. You could say it was too good to be true—she heard that a lot, anyway, but what did she have to lose from not looking back? Besides, when you've got your crazy best girl cheering you on, who could put a damper on it all?

Laurie had been wonderful. She avoided getting too involved in her relationship but also let her know she was there for her. Silly girl had called just last week to remind her to keep pushing to the five-month mark, something the media and articles out there reminded her of.

She had not seen Xander in three days, though. He had business in Tokyo, and she had two tests to focus on.

The attention she got from dating a man like Xander triggered her mom's reprimands, his father's disapproval, and college students wanting to talk to her more. She had even been approached to join some sororities, not that she ever considered these invitations. She was not sure how to cope with more coming in, especially from the entertainment industry. It was scary for her when Laurie had said something about getting her own agent soon. She felt like an ordinary girl turned celebrity overnight when she has always considered herself socially passive.

It was all distracting, but she managed to not let it consume her. Xander was aware of it, and he never failed to remind her to never listen to gossips about them and for her to just do her own thing.

Since that night they talked about what she wanted two months ago, he made sure to let her set the pace to whatever she was comfortable with in and out of bed. The communication had turned out to be better and the sex… mind blowing. If things continue this way and their relationship stays decided by both of them, she could not see where things could go wrong. He had not been with any other woman in the four months they have been together, after all.

He was supposed to be in the country now. He called last night about an early flight and wrapping things up at the office first before seeing her. She would have loved to be there, but she had a second and final test this morning. She had a good feeling she did really well and planned on surprising Xander at work. Maybe they could go home together from there.

Home—she was so used to that word now that she always tried to control its use in front of him, not sure how he would react to it. Xander's persistence on her moving in should have given her a clue, but she could not be so sure.

She thought of confirming Xander's presence from the most reliable source in his office, but she had a feeling that his assistant was not too fond of her, and she tried to avoid crossing paths with her as much as she can.

She had eventually recognized Julia as the woman who approached her and Katie on the night she had met Xander and was not blind to miss the unpleasant look she got from the woman whenever she was with Xander. She ignored Julia every time. There was no use telling Xander that his assistant might be jealous of her.

She was not sure it was the reason, anyway. And so, she planned on making her visit a surprise.

It could turn out disappointing if he's not there, Ally thought as she flagged down a cab.

***

"You look tired, you should get some rest. You're going to be swamped with more work in the next few months."

"I'm fine. You were working too, so you should get some rest. I'll need you at your best."

"You did most of the work while I just sat through the deals." Julia dropped the file on his table and walked behind his chair, resting her manicured fingers on his shoulders before he could protest. She was giving his stiff shoulders a massage. "You're working yourself too hard. *Relax*," she said, kneading her hands on his still tensed shoulder.

Xander gently moved his shoulders away from her reach, and she sighed.

"If I had other intentions, I would have made it known in Tokyo. After all, we shared the same room."

"Don't make it sound like we shared the same bed."

Julia laughed. "Ally sure has made you serious."

He did not make a comment. Of course, they had only been in a room together when work required it.

"What if… what if I was not your assistant? If I never took the job, would you have wanted me?" she asked mischievously, trying to make light of the subject.

"Where are you going with this?"

"Just answer."

"I never get involved with my employees."

"Then I'll quit."

He looked at her. Her tone might have been serious, but she had a smile on her face. "Give me two weeks' notice then," he plainly said.

She laughed as she walked away to stand opposite him. "Like I said, you're too serious. And am I that dispensable?" She raised an eyebrow in question.

He could guess what she was trying to do. Julia was expecting for them to start where they left off when she applied to work for him. Maybe that might have eventually happened if she was not working for him or he had not met Ally.

Ally. That woman, though he tried resisting, had him wrapped around her finger, but she could not know that though she was not capitalizing on him whatsoever. He believed it was one of the things that made her different from the other women he had been with. Lissa might also be an exception, but what made Ally different from her was her singular affection for him. Ally only wanted him and no one else.

And he liked it that way.

He was satisfied with her. He did not want any other woman for now, and it was an easy decision to abide by. Flirts and seductresses, no matter how skillful in their art, had no effect on him. People wondered when they would end it, but they would have to wait a while. He did not know himself, and at the moment, it was the farthest thing from his mind. What he had been thinking of, though, was calling to let her know he's back, but he was not sure what time her test was meant to end.

"So, should we await wedding bells?" Julia's voice continued to pester him.

"Yours, I suppose? Being with Ally is great, but it's just fun. I'm never getting married to her or anyone for that matter. You've always known that."

He saw her smirk before laughing out loud. She answered his question. "And would I wed myself?"

"Dom is willing to be that man."

His best friend, Dominic, had always liked Julia since the four of them, including Jay, knew each other back in college. Xander had always been too arrogant to give in to Julia's obvious attention towards him, but he disregarded Dom's feelings, and gave her what she wanted. No doubt, it had been what it was to him—a brief fling. They might have just been in their late teens at that time, but still, nine years on, he was sure that Dom's feelings was the same and genuine.

"He's not the man I want, though."

He stood from his seat and stood in front of her. Julia was a friend and a damn good assistant, but he had to draw the line till it sunk in deep for her. They were never going to be what she was thinking or hoping for. He had made that clear even before Ally showed up. Any clearer, and he would be forced to take stronger measures.

He cursed the day he found out she attempted suicide because of him. He never talked to her about it because he honestly did not want to deal with any more problems. Not when he had a girlfriend now.

She raised both hands in surrender as if she knew what he was thinking. "I know. No more of that."

"No, you don't know." He slid both his hands in his pocket. "What we had is over. Eight years. Forget it and be with a man that truly wants you. You're a beautiful woman. Don't sell yourself short. Move on, Julia. I have."

"What's wrong with knowing what I want? I can't control who I like, but I can control my feelings, and I have. Let me one thing, and we'll never speak of this again."

He saw the serious look she wore turn desperate by the minute.

He watched as she stood on her tiptoes and slowly raised her head to meet his, giving him time to protest if he wanted to, but he stayed rooted to his spot with his hands still in his pockets. She found the back of his neck with her fingers and immediately landed her lips on his. She made all the effort in kissing him, but when she realised there was no interest on his part to return it, she pulled back with a disappointed look on her face.

"Obviously, you did not find whatever you were looking for. If this scene or discussion ever rears its ugly head again, you'll have to look for a new job."

If such a thing would happen again, he would not hesitate to fire her, and he knew she understood that. Xander was certain this time.

***

Meanwhile, in Julia's office behind Xander's slightly ajar door, Ally was trying to catch her breath.

She managed to get her feet into the elevator, taking a ride down. Disoriented, she tapped her foot impatiently, wanting to get out of the building before someone recognised her presence. The sudden ringing of her phone jerked her out of her trembling mind.

Xander was calling.

CHAPTER 6

"Where are you?"

"I'm done with my test." It was not an answer to the question, but she tried to compose herself. She could not let her voice give up how shaken she still was from what she had heard.

Hey, I thought we were having more than just fun together, she had wanted to go in there and ask upfront.

Was her earlier conclusions about their relationship too early to make? Moreover, that woman... she did not like her at all. Was Julia going to quit? Ally had heard her say that before Xander's words about marriage.

She knew he was not interested in that, but hearing him say it in such manner was a slap in the face. It burst the bubble she had been living on, and the cruel reality was suddenly clear to her. What was that woman trying to get out of him, anyway? She was not sure what brought on the conversation, and she did not have the guts to stand there and hear more of it. Was that part of an assistant's job these days?

"Where are you?" he asked again and it was at that moment that the elevator's bell chimed.

She raised her head up to look at the lady that entered and returned the greeting directed at her.

"You're here?"

She could have deceived herself that he sounded happy, but he probably was not.

"I suddenly don't feel good. So, I'm heading back. I'll see you—"

"You're leaving?" There was a pause between them, and that was when she knew he must have realised something was up. "I'm coming down there. Wait for me."

Before she could even attempt to try and stop him, he cut the call. She gave a short sigh. How was she supposed to act just barely minutes after she heard that he did not think much of their relationship? They had never had a major fight before. Well, there was the first one…

Not really. That was more of a misunderstanding.

He came downstairs and gave her a long look that unnerved her, not saying a word other than dropping her. She watched his back as he walked in front of her, just as sure as she knew his staff must be looking at them.

It made a silly thought run through her head again. Had she chewed more than she could swallow by dating this man?

Not a word was said as he drove, and she thought she was better off staying at her apartment. Nothing had changed. He still did things that were satisfying to him, expecting her to agree. Her tears threatened to fall.

"What's wrong? How was your test?" She had ranted about how much she prepared for the test. Did he think that was what bothered her?

"It was good," she replied flatly, devoid of any enthusiasm.

"Are you really feeling sick?"

She did not give him a reply. She knew Xander was watching her closely, probably finding her attitude strange.

"I'll go get some rest."

***

Xander concluded that something was bothering her, that much was obvious when he tried to read her back at the office. That or she was really coming down with something. He knew no matter how tired they both were, Ally always made an effort to enjoy their time together after days of separation. She had not even asked how his trip went. He gave her some space by keeping himself busy in his study.

He called Julia to tell her he was going to take a while getting back to the office. After getting some work done, he stretched his limbs, suddenly tired, hungry, and in need of a shower. He went into the bedroom only to find her curled on her side—a position he had left her in—with her eyes closed. That worried him. Something was truly bothering her. He was going to get it out of her, though.

He did not want to wake her, but he could not resist a kiss to her forehead either, so he did, very gently. His back was barely turned away from her when he heard her voice.

"What are we, Alex?"

"Alex?"

She said nothing and earned a sigh out of him. He never dealt with this side of the women he got involved with.

"What do you mean?" he asked.

"You have to be right, anyway," she continued. "I know what you think about marriage, babies, and this relationship, but... are we just having fun? Is that what this is? I'm just fun to you?"

Every sentence came out monotonously.

"Where did you hear that from? I told you not to listen—"

"Should I not listen even if it's coming from you?"

Immediately, he understood.

She had been there. How much did she hear? He had to tread carefully because she obviously misunderstood his words. He watched her slowly sit up and another sigh escaped him. Was he really going to do this? Indulge a woman's concerns about what their relationship should be?

"How much did you hear?"

"How much did I have to, to understand what you meant?"

"Okay, listen."

"If this is what it is, what I am to you, we should end—"

"Damn it. Listen to me, Ally. I care about you, okay? I thought you knew that. I thought you understood me."

Yeah, he was going to do this, as unbelievable as it sounded to him.

"I thought I did." She looked at him, and it slapped him in the face to see how pained she looked. His stupid choice of words must have hurt her more than he imagined. "I can still get out now. I'll be okay with that. You owe me nothing. We—"

He joined her on the bed and held her hands. "I need you to come to your senses and listen to me." She averted her eyes away from him, withdrawing her hands, but he was not allowing any of it. He pulled back her hands in his but released one of them to turn her face back to him.

"Julia and I dated back in college." He saw the way her body froze at his this and realised maybe he should not have started with that.

"It wasn't even that. It was merely a fling." He tried to amend.

She looked like she was thinking about something before a frown appeared on her face. "And what is it now?" She sounded irritated.

He was getting the woman he knew back. "Nothing. I don't see her at all if that's what you mean."

"She works for you."

"You know what I mean." He sighed, and a short silence hung above them.

"Why are you telling me this? What has this got to do with us?"

He had to watch what he was about to say. He was not sure if Ally had heard and saw the whole conversation, if she knew about the kiss.

"Julia… I wanted her off my back. She has this idea that we might get back to starting where we left off."

"What?"

"I don't think that way. It'll never happen. That's what matters."

"What are you saying?"

"What you heard me say must have come out all wrong, but I did mean what I said about what we have as being great. *You're* fun—the most fun I've had in my life for years now."

"Being regarded as fun does not sound so great right now. I heard what you said, Xander. I understand not getting married being part of the deal. I agreed to it. But if you think what we have are all fun and games, I'm not sure I want to keep having your kind of fun." She withdrew her hands, successfully this time.

He frowned. "Deal? There was no bargain. We wanted each other. We desire each other. The chemistry has been there from the beginning. We care about what we have."

"Really, Xander? I'm not denying the obvious, but you want this, you want that, and I'm just supposed to go along with it. That's more like your own deals."

"I have never forced you to agree to any of it."

"Yeah, when you leave me with no choice! It was hard to say no when I was attracted to you and a lot harder than you can imagine when I've fallen—"

Ally stopped herself before she could spill the beans, a whole bag of it. He was not stupid. He had a good guess about the rest of the sentence. He was not going to ask about it.

"So what are you saying?" he finally asked.

"We need to break up."

She said it calmly.

"You're joking, right?"

She got up from the bed.

"Tell me why I should agree to this stupid suggestion of yours," he said, trying to control how he was really feeling.

"I've been giving you reasons. Were you not listening?"

"Oh, I was," he replied, starting to be angry. "But all I've heard is a woman telling me I have been making all the choices for her and forcing her to be with me!"

"That is not what I'm saying," she gently replied.

"Then tell me. What do you want, Ally? I'm asking." He challenged her, and she seemed surprised by his question.

She gave him a sad smile. "You know this is the first time you've ever asked what I want."

Xander always had control in his past relationships, and that was how he preferred it. He wanted to have the upper hand in everything. He did not leave room for more claws to dig deep into him. He would have wanted to say he regarded Ally the same way—after all, she was a woman. But he did not. She was the second woman to ever tell him it was over, and honestly, he was experiencing a different kind of pain than the first one. It was deeper, much more raw.

"I don't want to let you go, but tell me what you want." Maybe they could compromise. Was he trying to manipulate her decision? Of course, yes.

"Why?" she asked.

"What?"

"Why don't you want to let me go?"

"I like knowing you're here. I love having you in my bed. You make me smile and make the stress I live with every day of my life seem lighter. Though you drive me crazy—everything about you drives me crazy—I'm willing to pay the price. I find myself thinking of when I'll be with you even when I'm working. I wouldn't have another woman replace that now."

He was telling her the words he knew might help his case, but there was some truth to it.

Then she burst into sobs. "You're a really bad guy."

"What did I do now?" He wrapped her in his arms, and she did not put up a fight.

"I hate you."

"No, you don't," he replied.

"Yes, I do." It took a while for her to calm down. Soon, he found a way to have them both on the bed with her quietly tucked in his arms.

"What do we do now?" he quietly asked.

"Give each other some space."

"I don't want space."

"I want to be sure this is what I really want, that I want to be with you without regrets or blaming anyone. I just want to know what being without you will be for me… that I'll be able to handle my decision."

"So you're asking to fake a break-up?"

"Separate."

He groaned. "I don't like this." He sighed, brushing his hands down her skin. "My fate lies in your answer. How long will you be torturing me?"

"I'm not sure."

"We're not losing contact, are we? I want to talk to you every day."

"Then there's no point to any of this if we do that."

"I can't see you, I can't talk to you, I can't touch you... if I can't hold on anymore, can I come knocking?"

"If I say it's okay."

He was letting her take control. He was letting her tell him what to do. But it was not just any woman; it was Ally. She was not a selfish woman like all the other ones he let into his life, and he was trusting his instinct on that.

"Fine."

"What will you do about that woman?"

Xander knew who *that* woman was. Ally did not bring up the kiss, so she must not have seen it. She was bringing up separation because of the words she had heard him say, and he could not imagine what else she would be suggesting if she knew about what Julia did.

What she did not know would not hurt her. He would leave it like that.

"Julia is no problem. I made sure of it. If she weren't one of the best at her job, I would have shown her out." There was no need telling her what he feared Julia might do. It was not her business to worry about.

There was no need to tell her more details. It had meant nothing to him. He was sure Ally trusted him.

"Do you trust me, Ally? I need you to."

"I do. I just need to be sure I trust myself."

***

Two weeks.

Two torturous weeks and he was acting like the world was on fire. Why would he not when he had been away from Ally for that long? He was cracking at the seams and not sure how long he could hold on. If she did not call any time soon, he was going to barge into her place to get her back before the end of the week.

Julia had not made a single remark to annoy him lately, not when there was obviously something up with him and Ally.

Why was she taking this much time like she had all the time in the world? Was he really that easy to forget?

"I can't do it anymore." He found himself repeating those words on the receiver.

He had absentmindedly dialled her number, and now, he was staring into thin air, regretting this poor decision. He was going to wait until the end of the week. Why couldn't he just hold on for a bit more? He was left wondering if he had just ruined things for himself.

"I-I was about to call you," he heard the voice he missed say in a soft tone.

He decided to go along with it like he had not been sulking and was not affected by it.

"About what? This crazy idea of separation?"

"Yes. It's been two weeks, and I don't know any longer if this is for me. You were right."

A short pause followed.

"I want to be with you, Xander. You don't know how many times in the past week I struggled with calling you. But I couldn't. I suggested this after all."

He listened well as she spoke on.

"This isn't forever. I know this. You're clear on what you want, and I can deal with that. The days without you have taught me that I'd rather have some time with you than nothing at all and live to regret it.

Her words caught him short of whatever it was he intended to say.

Somewhere along the line, she said, "What am I to do after we're over?"

He was not sure Ally realised she had said that, but he did not like the sound of it. No, he was not thinking of that, and so should she. All he knew was that he did not want to waste any more time apart over something stupid.

"H-hello? Xander?"

He must have been out of it for a while.

"I need to hear you tell me to my face."

There was no point saying more, and he cut the call.

***

Xander knew the sensible thing to do was to slow down. He was being too presumptuous. What if she was not at her apartment? There was only one way to find out. He got out of his car and knocked on her door.

Ally looked shocked to see him standing in front of her. It had only been barely ten minutes since he called with his office number. He must have recklessly driven over because the drive from his office to her place should take at least fifteen to seventeen minutes free of traffic, and her face said the same.

"Alex, you should be careful while dri—"

He captured her mouth in a searing kiss, swallowing the rest of her words and skillfully searching for what he wanted, and groaned in content when he found it.

She kissed him back with the same passion, if not more.

"I will get used to you calling me that if you keep at it," he said when they finally broke the kiss, still cupping her face firmly with both his hands.

"What? Alex? You like it?"

He lifted her to straddle him, and she crossed her legs behind him, something she knew would drive him crazy. She held on to his nape and made contact with his straining erection, not letting go of the rhythm she found, while he held on tightly to her perfect bum and back.

"Ally." He groaned. "You're driving me insane. Do you know how long I've waited?" He kissed her again. "How long *we've* waited?" he said, referring to his object of arousal.

"I like him when he's at his full potential," she managed to say in between their kiss.

"I like him more when he's *working* at his full potential."

She laughed at his proud statement. "Arrogant idiot," she muttered before kissing him again.

"You're the only woman who calls me that and can get away from it."

"Then I should take advantage of this position more often." She grinned, and he searched her purely happy face.

How had he gone for weeks without seeing this look?

"Where's the bedroom? Tell me, or I swear I'll have to take you right here."

This was going to be the first time they would be using her room—for anything, actually. He had never considered hanging out at her apartment and had never considered hanging out at any place of her choice really. It had never been an option, but maybe he had to make a few changes to make her happier.

"Thank goodness Trish is out. What would she think of your behaviour right now?"

He had no reason to bother about someone else, and he still would not have if her roommate had been around. He frantically walked them towards where Ally pointed him to.

"Alex," she moaned when he landed her roughly on the bed.

"I love hearing you call me that, and I'll let you know how much when you scream it while I'm inside you."

Discarding their clothes within seconds was the only patient thing he did after that. There was nothing patient or gentle about him, and like he promised, for the first time, she did scream his name.

***

"Did I hurt you?" Xander asked softly, an hour after ravishing each other's body for the second time.

The first time was something Ally had never experienced before. Xander had been rough, but she knew what she wanted and did not object to it.

The second time had felt like an apology, his way of making it up to her. He had taken the time to pleasure her—or better said, torture her. She could not remember ever being so vocal and demanding during lovemaking. It was, indeed, a good thing they were alone.

"If you did, I'm not sure I noticed." She smiled.

He kissed her passionately. "Will you move in with me?"

Was the ever arrogant Xander truly asking her that? She found it strange, but she could not deny that she liked it. She felt Xander raise himself on his elbow to stare at her, and she started laughing instead.

"Do you know how strange this is?"

"I'm learning to consider what you want."

"Should I, though?" She playfully considered. She had no doubt left now, so she might as well go all in. It did not matter what people said or what Laurie would think as long as it was what she and Xander wanted. He was right. She needed to put them first before the opinion of others.

Her response got stuck in her throat when he kissed her bare shoulder, tangling his fingers in her hair. "I lived with my grandfather until I started college."

She was surprised. He had never shared anything about his family with her. He never even liked talking about his father though she had seen the man a couple times.

It was sudden, and she was not sure how to respond.

"My mother abandoned me and left me with him, my grandmother left him a long time ago, and the girl I cared about in high school thought it would be fun to take advantage of my feelings. I was even dumb enough to fall for that mistake a second time when I saw her again. She's a really crazy woman."

"You loved her?"

"If that's what it was. Women that mean something to me always end up leaving a significant scar on me."

"That's why you don't trust women," she quietly said.

He sighed. "I love my grandfather, but I hate that his wife made him weak. I see the way he looks when her name comes up. I never want to be that way. No man should be that way. Now, they can't stand each other."

"What about your father?"

"He found me when I was in uni. I did not even have an idea who he was before that. He told me how my mother ran away with another man, taking me with her. Obviously, he struggled with it for a long time, searching for as long as he did. Now he hates her, and I think sometimes he sees her in me. If you did not notice, I look nothing like him except for the eyes."

"Yes," she whispered, lightly touching his eyelids.

He held the hand and lightly kissed her fingers.

"He came to me and told me I was his heir. Honestly, I had no problem with it. I was having fun, and suddenly being a rich man's heir overnight was a big plus. I grew out of it, though, when I saw that I was just another chess piece to build his fortune and most probably his revenge. He involved me in his business, and I went ahead right after university. Later on, he employed my help to triple his profits. I never felt comfortable after that, sitting on Dad's money, and I made sure I earned my own money—my first million. Since then, I haven't looked back."

"Where's your mom now?"

"I have no idea."

"Have you tried looking for her?"

"Why? She didn't want me, so what would I do with her?"

"Ask questions. Hear what she has to say. I've always believed in listening to both sides of an argument."

"Well, this is no argument. There's no excuse for a mother abandoning her child."

"If you put it that way, but there could be a number of reasons people—"

"Are you my shrink now?"

She smiled. "Hmm… do you need one? And that's harsh of you to say that. Psychiatrists and psychologists actually help people."

They heard a door shut close.

He changed the subject. "We should take a vacation to one of my houses."

"Vacation?"

"Italy. Have you been to Italy?"

Ally shook her head. "I believe the only country I've ever been to is Brazil and that was with my parents. We went to see my grandparents. My father was Brazilian. I was seven, though, so I can't say I remember lots of things about Brazil."

In truth, Storm was not supposed to be her surname. Her father had taken his American mother's maiden name instead of a father's who had abandoned him and his mom.

"So we should do that during your summer holiday."

"Don't you have businesses to manage?"

"Are you saying no, Miss Storm?"

Who would say no to a trip to Italy?

"Ally?" Trish's voice drifted to her room. "Are you cooped up in your room again, moping about your boyfriend? You better get out of that room before I get in there."

"So you've been moping," Xander said, teasing her.

But her mind was elsewhere. She was sure they left the door unlocked, and if Trish barged in—

"Ally—"

She went under the sheet as Trish came in and saw them.

"Oh!"

"Hello." She heard Xander say and tuned out what Trish might have said. She felt the sheet being lifted off her head after she heard the door close.

"That was so embarrassing!"

"No, it wasn't," Xander laughed.

"Easy for you to say when you won't be the one that's going to be teased about it."

"Then we might as well give her more to tease you about."

"Don't you dare, Alex!" she said in fits of laughter as he pulled her under him.

He did dare, though.

***

Ally jumped from the bed immediately when she heard Xander's car leave. He had been called by one of his security men saying that an issue urgently needed his attention. He apologized since they planned to spend all day together. He got a lot busier since that week started and had mentioned it had something to do with a new partnership his company made with a Japanese firm.

He worked hard to make the day free for them only for him to be called again.

She was relieved, anyway. His absence kept him from noticing she was uncomfortable around him for the past week. It had been three weeks already since she moved into his apartment. The media had a lot to say about that, so did her mom and his dad—people who did not have the slightest right to stick their nose into their business. The only people who agreed with her were Trish and Laurie.

She walked into the closet she shared with Xander and dipped her hand where she had hidden something amongst her clothes. She had been extremely discreet securing it, asking the help of a much older nurse. The feeling of what she might discover was giving her an unpleasant feeling in her gut, but she needed to be sure.

She could not walk into a hospital or pharmacy. He would find out, as would the rest of the world. It seemed everything she did these days was for the whole world to gossip about.

She sighed in fear as she stared at the pregnancy kit in her hand. She felt a tear run down her cheek as she realised how grave the next few minutes will be for her life.

She had to get it together somehow. She moved from where she was and followed the instructions. After a few minutes, she breathed heavily and nervously waited for the result.

It was time. She picked up the pregnancy test and checked—nervous as hell.

The stick she held did not sympathize with her. It was positive. She did not know why, but she started to cry, and not long after, she began to heave. Rushing to the bathroom, she puked her guts out, unable to stop the tears. She was pregnant.

I'm pregnant! She did not know how long she sat there for, but the last thing she expected was to see him by the door.

"Ally, what's wrong?" He ran towards her and held her in concern.

I am so stupid.

"Do you need to go the hospital? Hey, sweetheart, talk to me," he said when she did not reply.

She tried to control the tears but failed as his eyes turned frantic. It finally dawned on him when he stared at what she held in her hand.

She was so scared to look at him and just covered her face with her palms, repeatedly shaking her head.

"How?"

CHAPTER 7

"How?" he whispered silently with a face drained of emotions.

Ally could see the disbelief in Xander's eyes, but she knew what they both saw was correct. This was no joke. She was truly pregnant.

He stood up, and she did not have to look up to see the anger radiating off him. This was all going wrong. She was not planning to let him find out. More accurately, she doesn't have *any* plans ready. She had not thought that far before she got caught.

"Are you pregnant?" she heard him ask.

Her continuous sobs must have given him the answer to his question because he walked out from the bathroom.

To her, it had been hours since Xander walked away, but in truth, it had only been minutes. Then she heard a loud crash in the room, shaking her out of her troubled thoughts. She shakily stood up, supporting herself with the tub, afraid of what she might see. She took cautious steps to the bedroom, and just like she feared, she saw Xander like she had never witnessed him before.

His jacket was on the floor, tossed there without an ounce of care, and his white shirt was tucked out messily. She looked at where he was staring at and saw the source of the noise. In his rage, he had thrown something at the mirror on her vanity table.

He was angry and distraught.

"Why?" She heard him well though he had said the word in a near whisper.

She felt his pain, and she wished she could take it all back and undo her mistake. She could not see his face with his head turned away, but his bent posture as if in defeat and his stiff shoulders was enough to give away what he was feeling. He looked like he was not breathing at all, but she knew better.

"Why?" He repeated, his voice full of venom.

Not once in their whole relationship did Ally think he would use that tone on her. He faced her, and immediately, she recognised the look he had. It was the same face he made when he talked about the women who had hurt him and made him put up his defences.

"Alex…" The tears had stopped as if they saw something more frightening and worth being locked away from.

"Don't call me that," he said through gritted teeth.

Whatever was she to say to make him listen?

"You'd better start by letting me know who the father is because it can't be me."

"What?"

"You've been on the pill for months! How can it fail now?"

At first she thought he implied she had cheated on him, but when he mentioned the pills, she understood what he meant. He was right.

"There's—"

"I told you I didn't want a baby! You knew that. Why would you do this?"

"It isn't my fault."

"It isn't? So it's my fault then?"

"Why are you being selfish?"

"Selfish?" he exclaimed, mocking her with every bone in his body.

"You act like I made this baby on my own. You get to not use protection, so the blame solely falls on me because *I'm* the one supposed to take care of it?"

"Don't be dramatic! I know a deceitful woman when I see one, and that's what you're being right now."

She fell silent. Was this going to be their first real fight? She did not think it was going to be all bed of roses, but she was not prepared for this. They would get through it, she assured herself.

"How long have you known?"

She was hesitant to answer, but she did not want to rile him up more than he was at the moment. "I was suspicious, but I didn't want to say anything just in case it turned out to be something else. I had the test this morning just to be sure."

He scoffed. "If you think I'll tell you this is okay and plan a wedding, you're mistaken. I'm not marrying you."

She was appalled he would think that of her right now. She couldn't place sole blame on him, though. A lot of women must have tried to use him before. She needed to make him understand—preferably, when he was calm enough.

"That's not what I want," she told him.

"Is it not?" He smirked wickedly. "Tell me you haven't thought about it. Tell me you haven't fantasized about your perfect you and me. Tell me you haven't fallen in love with me!" He raised his voice slightly at the end.

"You know how I feel about you, about us, but I would *never* use this the way you're thinking. I've never thought like that... and if you knew I loved you, why didn't you say something?"

"You think—"

She was not finished just yet. "Just for the same reason I could not tell you. So respect me, and don't make it sound like it's the worst thing I've ever done in my life."

"One of them," he said, looking at her belly.

She sighed. This was going nowhere. All they would do was exchange hurtful words, some that might be too late to take back and forget.

"I'll let you calm down. We should both calm down before we say things—"

"You're the *worst* of them all."

He was comparing her to the women of his past—his mother, grandmother, and the first girl who broke his heart. He despised them all, and now he loathes her more than any of them. What could she say for him to believe her?

"I wanted to hear the words from you. I wanted somehow to believe this had to be a mistake, that you were different, that you would not use my desire for you to make a fool out of me." He ran his hands into his hair, something he did when he was frustrated or angry about something.

She stood there, staring back at him, too stunned to defend herself.

"Not once did you defend yourself and count this as a probable failure, an unwanted outcome out of a hundred." Xander faced her squarely. "You did this on purpose," he said with finality, staring hard at her.

"What?"

"Admit it, Ally, damn it! You stopped taking the pills."

She was dumbfounded. Her eyes must have given something away. He stared at her in pure disbelief. His face contorted into one of disgust, and before she knew it, he was walking out on her.

"No, it isn't that way. Let me explain." She ran to him, standing in front of him as she held his arm, trying to stop him from leaving.

"Explain? Unless you start explaining what a lying, manipulative, and deceitful bitch you are, I don't want to hear it."

His words made her eyes sting again. Who was this man? He was nothing like the man she had foolishly let herself fall for. Thinking back, Xander was only gentle to her when things went his way… when their time together was all happy and fun and everything is great under the sheets. She must have been in her thoughts for too long because the next thing she knew, he had jerked her hand away from him and walked out.

She was still in the same spot when she heard the sound of a car's engine blaring and speedily driving off. She realised she had messed things up, and she had to do something to convince him, but now was not the time. The whole encounter was getting to her. Her legs gave out, and she tried to draw in deep breaths to her starved lungs as she sat there, heaped on the floor.

What have I done? she asked herself.

The tears let themselves out again. She was aware of the intimidating man's absence, and she was left feeling empty—desolate.

CHAPTER 8

No matter how Xander tried to see it, the same thing kept replaying in his head. Ally never denied his accusation, but why was it so hard to accept that she was capable of manipulating him like that?

What was she hoping for, that he would declare his love for her? Hoping it would be different with her? That being crazy about her meant he would be happy about a baby? That he would be a different man and commit? He did not even want any of those things! He told her that right from the start. Did she think five months with him was enough to get what she wanted?

He had gone back to his office, hoping to bury his anger and resent in his work, but instead, found himself drinking alcohol, something he hardly did during work hours. How deep had he allowed her into his life for him to only notice now? It was like a band-aid had been forcefully removed from his already bruised skin.

He was hurt, angry, and burning—burning inside for trusting her. He knew he should not have. He told himself several times that she was no different, that she was still a woman, after all. But he did. He did trust her. Damn it! He trusted her.

There had to be some sort of explanation, something good enough to justify her actions. What was he thinking? No reason could be good enough. There should not even be a reason for what she did.

"I thought I told you I don't want to be disturbed!" he said through gritted teeth, roaring it out like a lion.

Julia did not seem shaken by his tone. A look of concern masked her face as she drew closer towards him.

"What's going on, Xander? You left the office looking like a man in love and barged in like you just caught your wife in bed with another man."

Was she taunting him? He looked up at her and could not see her eyes revealing anything. All the same, his assistant was not what he needed right now. He needed to be alone.

"I won't repeat myself, Julia. Get out or get another job!" He could not handle another woman and her antics right now.

His tone and words got her attention, and though she hesitated for a moment with shock plastered on her face, she eventually left him alone.

He meant it when he said he wanted to see no one and no calls directed to him. He needed to think about what to do and not let another woman believe she's got Alexander Cross where he vowed never to be.

***

"Laurie…"

"Are you crying?"

"What am I going to do? I m-messed things up. He's so mad right now. I don't think he'll ever forgive this. I never intended for this to h-happen. It's all—" Ally's words came out jumbled, rushing out with her tears.

"Whoa, slow down, Al. Calm down and tell me what's going on. Where are you?"

Ally tried explaining everything to her, but Laurie had to soothe her with words before she could understand anything she was saying.

"What should I do, Laurie? He hates me."

"I'll think of something, but you have to calm down, Ally. It's not just you now; you have a baby to think about." Laurie could not help but think this was somehow her fault. She wanted to help, but maybe she had gone a little too far this time. She had to ask. She needed to know.

"Ally? Um... you did not take my advice, did you?"

She heard Ally sigh softly. "I thought about it, Laurie. I wanted to. I was tempted to, but I could not go through with it. I could not do that to him. I love him."

Laurie gave a sigh of relief. "For a moment there, I thought you went along with my crazy idea of hooking him."

She was glad it did not turn out that way. Why had she given that advice in the first place? She was glad Ally did not listen to her this time around. She had fallen for that wretched woman's trick, someone who she later found out was Xander's assistant.

"Let me talk to him."

"Laurie—"

"I know he does not like me, but I'll make him see reason. He has to talk to you. You said yourself that he cares about you, then both of you have got to sit and talk through this. It isn't something that will disappear if you ignore it."

"Yes, but—"

"All I need you to do is pick yourself up and feed that little one. Take a shower too if you haven't."

Ally let out a very short laugh, and that was good enough for her at the moment. She would go see that arrogant man and that woman—someone who's conieving plan Ally did not know about and did not need to. She would confront them, and that way, kill two birds with one stone.

Hopefully, she would not have to kill anyone.

***

"It's you."

Laurie turned to place a face to the voice. Good, just the woman she wanted to see, but not right now. She needed to see a certain man before her.

"I need to see Alexander."

Julia raised an eyebrow. "What for? Don't tell me you're here to—"

"Cut the crap and don't pretend you don't know who I am. I saw your face in the paper. You purposely sought me out knowing who my cousin was, so it should be my line to say you want a clear path to seduce Alexander Cross. I suspected you at first. Trust me when I say I know when a woman is interested in a guy. But then you threw me off with that talks of Alexander Cross' other women and my cousin's relationship with him. You chatted on and on about your boss's life to me, pretending not to know about my relationship to Ally."

More and more eyes were being glued to both of them, and she could see Julia was not comfortable with the sort of attention they were getting. Julia grabbed her arm and led them inside an elevator after snapping at two men who dared cross her path.

There was nothing for her to feel uncomfortable about. If Julia was planning on killing her to keep her from talking, at least there were more than enough witnesses who saw her get dragged in. Besides, she was sure she could take on the skinny bitch if it came down to that.

"What are you doing here?" Julia hissed under her breath.

"Like I said, I'm here to see your boss."

All of a sudden, there was a smug look on her face. "It's about her, isn't it?"

She frowned in anger.

"Relax, it's not like it was hard to guess with the mood he's in."

Julia crossed her arms over what she assumed would be fake bosoms. *What a witch!*

"If you're sure you can dip your head in that inferno burning around him, fine. Your incineration." She shrugged.

Alexander Cross was the last person she would be intimidated by. It was no secret that he did not like her much, and honestly, she could not care less about that. The only reason she tolerated his presence if she had to was because of Ally. There was no reason to put her cousin in a difficult situation. She already had enough going on with her mom because of the man. And now that the same man was trying to make things more difficult for her, she could not just let Ally's soft nature handle it.

"What? You weren't able to seduce him out of his misery?" She lashed back at Julia, satisfied with the look that appeared on her face. The elevator came to a stop, and they stepped out.

"What are you waiting for?" Julia taunted when she came to a stop.

She should never have fallen for this woman's tricks when she appeared before her at the cocktail party. Looking back at it now, it seemed like she had been perfectly sought out. It was not easy for a woman to fool her, but Julia successfully did, enough for Laurie to classify her as a viper.

"Which way?"

She went into the room she was directed to without knocking, and what she saw was the last thing she expected. Ally was right, he was not taking this too well. He's resorting to alcohol in the middle of the day with a disheveled look that certainly was not his style.

"What the hell are you doing here? Came to finish what your cousin started?"

"And what did she start?"

She almost pitied the guy right now seeing she would not want to be in his position either. Really, what would happen if she got pregnant by one of her lovers? That was never in her plan. *Not all plans work out*, she thought. A vivid evidence was right in front of her. Still, he had no right to spit harsh and unnecessary words at either her or Ally, and she would make him listen.

"You need to talk to her. I just spoke to her, and she sounded hysterical."

"So you know all about it? Of course, you know all about it," Xander answered his own question.

It sounded like he was mocking her, but she ignored it. "She told me what she could say amidst her distress."

"Distress?" he laughed mockingly. "She knew what she was getting herself into."

"Ally isn't the kind of girl who would do this on purpose. You have to listen to her. So what if she was on the pill? What is hundred percent certain these days? If you wanted to be thorough, why didn't you do your part and wrap it up?" She moved in closer, not taking her eyes glaring eyes off him.

"Admit it, you're selfish. You think continuous use of pills have no effects on women? You wanted no hindrance to your fun, and you got something extra in return. In the end, it's not just her baby; it's *yours*, too. Face it. It's not going to disappear even if you ignore it."

"I never liked you," he said spitefully.

"I don't particularly like you either, but Ally does. If you care about her, you'll give her a chance to at least explain."

He was not saying anything, and she believed something she said must have gone through his thick skull. It better had. She walked to the door, confident she achieved what she came for.

"Also, you should get rid of that monster working beside you." There was no need to further explain. If he were half the smart man he was said to be, he would know who she meant.

She only had one stop left: to go see Ally and calm her down.

***

Ally tried to stay calm and hopeful, but it was not working especially when she hardly got enough sleep… if she did sleep at all.

It's been two days since Laurie had come to her and assured her things were going to turn out fine, but it did not. Since that morning, she had not seen Xander. He never came home, and he was not picking up her calls. She has been trying for several hours now, and it wasn't even going through anymore. She was worried.

Laurie had said he had not been in good shape. Where was he sleeping? It was not like she had to worry he would be on the streets or squatting someplace; he was a man capable of providing the utmost comfort for himself whenever he wished.

She had called his office yesterday, but she was told he was busy. She tried getting out of the house to get to class, but she had felt sick and stayed home instead. Laurie had checked up on her again yesterday and called several times just to make sure she was fine. Her cousin had even wanted her to leave the house, not wanting her to be alone, but she wanted to wait, just in case Xander showed up.

She was scared even if she could not admit it to anyone out loud. She wished she had her mom right now, but she was the last person she felt she could confide in now. Even though she knew she had Laurie, she still felt alone. She needed Xander. Seeing him would at least put her at ease.

She thought about all that has happened in the past few days; one bad decision, one horrible mistake, and here she was, paying the price. If Xander was not going to listen, who would? Her mom? The press? People who have been waiting for all this to go wrong? She had school, still a freshman planning on taking her first-year exams soon, and now this? She was a twenty-one-year-old girl who was not sure about her future yet, and now she had a responsibility for another life—a responsibility to take care of someone else's future.

It was true that she never planned this. Why would she when she had something great going on with him and still had years of college ahead of her?

She had hoped she was going to be one of the lucky ones. Obviously not. She should go to the hospital to know how far along she was just to be sure she let this happen… that it was partly her fault. All of a sudden, she started panicking again. If Xander were to appear in front of her now and ask for an explanation, what would she say? How would she explain her stupidity and ignorance? It was eating her up. She had to tell someone. She had to tell the only person who would not judge but listen.

"Ally, I'll be with you in a while." Laurie's voice came through immediately after she picked up the call.

She fell silent, and Laurie had to ask again. "Ally, is everything okay? You're not feeling sick, are you?"

She spoke eventually, slowly and almost inaudible like she was drained of her source of life. "I stopped taking the pills, Laurie. I stopped. It's my fault. What do I do?"

There was silence at the other end, and she could only do one thing as she steadied her irregular breathing and held tightly to the phone with her eyes closed.

Hoping.

If only she could wish all this away.

CHAPTER 9

Ally was going crazy waiting for Xander's call. Four days have gone by, and she was yet to know where she or their relationship really stood. She could understand that he was still angry, but distancing himself from her would not make this go away.

After making that visit to the hospital yesterday to confirm how far along she was, she had the faintest hope in her that the pregnancy was not as a result of her mistake. Though she knew she was still partly to blame, she assured herself that Xander would understand.

So why did she froze when she got to his office building? Right after she left the hospital, she took a cab to go see him and try to explain things. After two minutes, the cab driver had impatiently asked if she was getting down or not. She wasn't, and he drove off.

She looked down at the untouched plate of food before her. She did not know why she even bothered to cook since she had not been able to get much down in her for a few days. Laurie had said she looked weak. She *felt* weak.

She heard some rustling at the front door, and her heart soared. Getting on her feet, she moved to the door, expecting only one person in her mind. "Al—" She stopped herself before she could complete the name he seemed to loath now. "Hi."

He walked past her to the bedroom they shared only four nights ago. He dropped the bag in his hand and got rid of his clothes one after the other until he was down to his slacks. She watched him do all that without interrupting, hoping he would at least look at her.

Xander walked to the bathroom and closed the door behind him. She picked his discarded clothes slowly, trying to make time go faster, but she was not slow enough because he made sure to take his time in there, and she waited.

He eventually came out dressed in shorts and a grey tee. She sighed inwardly out of relief. The clothes he chose meant he was staying. They could talk. They would work it out.

"I thought you would be out by now."

Shocked by his words, she stared at him with mouth ajar.

"What happened to you?" she heard him ask again.

He must have finally seen her and what she looked like. It was not her finest moment, maybe the worst he had ever seen her, but she could care less about that now. The last thing she had given thought to in the last few days was her appearance, and even now that he was noticing it, she thought it made no difference because, despite the fact that there was a hint of concern in his question, contempt was dripping in his voice.

"Is that what you want? For me to be out of here?" she managed to ask.

He refused to answer.

"Are we going to talk about this at all? Just let me know what you're thinking."

"I thought I made things clear the last time we talked, and you did for me too."

"It isn't what you're thinking."

"What am I thinking?"

"That I did this on purpose to trap you or whatever you think is the reason."

"Only you would know the reason for that, Ally."

"And I do! Only if you'll hear me out." She breathed heavily, already drained. She could not go on shouting, and he must have noticed that as he looked at her skeptically.

He fell silent.

She sat on the bed, holding on to the sheets tightly with downcast eyes.

"The two weeks we were apart, I stopped taking the pills. I did not do it on purpose. After a few days, I forgot. We were not together, anyway. That afternoon you called, it was unexpected, and what happened after certainly wasn't my plan. I was not exactly in a position to think about anything. It was only when I saw the pack and noticed the quantity left did I realise what I'd been doing... or had not been doing." She eventually looked at him. "You have to believe me. I did not plan this."

"How can you say you forgot? And you failed to mention it when you found out?"

"I was scared, okay? I knew what you thought about commitments, and I just hoped I would be one of the few lucky ones and get saved from my stupidity."

"But you didn't, did you?" he said sarcastically.

"Stop making this sound like my fault. I didn't make this baby alone."

He pointed a finger at her and took a big, angry stride towards her. "Don't even go there! If you want to guilt me into accepting this, you're mistaken."

"What are you saying?"

He gave no reply.

"Say something, Xander! Guilt you into accepting this? I waited days for you, called you, tried to talk, to apologize, but you're beginning to act like a boy who got his ego ripped."

He laughed in contempt.

"Stop it," she whispered.

He did not hear her.

"Stop it!" she said more firmly, and he did. "What do you want me to do? Just tell me. Say what's on your mind. I'll listen."

"Nothing. Nothing I can think of." He suddenly looked drained.

"That's not good enough." And it truly was not good enough for her. She needed to know. She needed to know Xander could move past his fear and help her embrace hers, that they could do it together.

"Why is that? You made the decision on your own to keep it to yourself, so why don't you make another without me?"

She could not believe what he was insinuating.

"Laurie was right. I shouldn't have—"

"Laurie! Have you ever thought maybe that cousin of yours led you into this on purpose?"

"Laurie led me into nothing. She's been nothing but helpful. The only one—"

He snickered. "Maybe she's there just to get you out of the way."

"What?"

"Stop being naïve, Ally. Your cousin isn't exactly a great example of a healthy relationship."

"That does not define who she is. Wait." She stood up. "How did you know that.. .about Laurie? I never told you."

He slipped and got caught, and he tried to defend himself. "So what if I had her checked on? I don't trust her."

"Why would you do that? *I* trust her." Laurie would be mad if she ever found out. She hated people getting into her business, especially her private life.

"What has she been telling you? Did she convince you to get yourself involved in this mess?"

Now, it was her turn to laugh, but in disbelief this time. She needed some energy to keep her going, but Xander was doing so well at draining the little she had left.

***

"You're a friggin hypocrite. This mess? And isn't that what you did with women before me and what you're doing now? You took one after the other at your convenience. Is that not what I would be too? Another girl in your past?"

Xander frowned. What the hell did that mean? Was that what she thought about him all the while they were together? Did she ever trust anything he told her?

"Then maybe I went for the wrong cousin since she's exactly a female version of me like you so rightly pointed out." He was not sure why he said that. It might be because he was angry at her, but he knew deep down, he had not meant it.

He saw as Ally stagger on her feet and rest her side on the edge of the bed.

"Please," she whispered softly. "Please don't do that. I know you're angry, but don't hurt me with words like that."

There was evidence of distress on her face and body, and he wondered what she's been doing for the past four days. He was concerned, but he could not show it. He could not give her a reason to think it was okay; that any of this was okay. It was stupid to have uttered those words to her, for hurting her, but he was so angry he did not know what to do with what he was feeling or where else to channel it.

He thinned his lips, pushing other stupid words out of his stomach, and walked out of the room before he do more damage than he could repair. Then again, did he want this fixed? Could it be fixed? They were questions he had no answer to as he started walking out.

"Three weeks," he heard her say and stopped, his back still to her. What the hell was she saying?

"I'm three weeks along."

He stiffened as it went through his every nerve, and as soon as he freed himself from the trance of her words, he walked out.

***

The moment Ally woke up from a two-hour sleep, the only sleep she could get throughout the night, there was no sign that Xander was home. After the harsh confrontation they had yesterday, he had gone into his study, and she assumed he looked for another room to sleep in. She looked at the time. Four twenty-seven a.m.

She groaned at that ungodly hour. Not long after, she started heaving and made a quick dash to the toilet.

I couldn't go on like this, she thought when she finally stopped puking and felt a little better. Right there, she made a decision as she continuously rubbed her tummy.

Xander had broken her heart. There was only one way to make things go back to the way it was. But first, she had to get out of this house. She had no reason to stay her anymore.

She continued to rub her tummy to feel better. The little gesture was quite soothing to her.

***

By late afternoon, Ally had achieved all she had planned for the day without involving anyone—including Laurie. She had moved her things out of Xander's house and was ready to move on to her next plan. She made the decision, and she was standing by it… or so she thought.

Moments ago, she swore to not let anyone change her mind, but now, here she was on her mom's front door, ringing the bell. Maybe deep inside she wanted someone to change her mind. Why else would she be in front of the one person who could easily change it? The truth was, she missed her mom, and she needed to hear from her that it was okay. Maybe her mom would understand.

Honestly, she had not thought twice about her decision. If abortion was really the right thing to do, and if it will put everything back to the way it was, she'd do it. She was convinced it was the solution for everyone—for everything.

"Alicia?" Her mom looked genuinely surprised to see her.

Mother and daughter were not on the best of terms, and she knew her mother would like to know that she had been right about Xander. She was not planning on saying anything, though. She needed her mom. Her parents were the ones always there for her through thick and thin.

They had each other when they had to visit her father's family, the Cruzes, in Brazil. Being called the wife and daughter of a prodigal and illegitimate son behind their backs was hard, but they managed to get through it. It had always been the three of them, and now that her dad was gone, it was only her and her mom. What she needed now was that feeling, and she just needed to know she still had that.

She followed her mother to the kitchen quietly and took a seat. They were quiet for a moment, and Ally noticed how busy she must have been in the kitchen with utensils and ingredients lying everywhere. If she were home, she would be helping her mom out. Regret was starting to seep in, and the last thing she wanted was to cry in front of her mom.

"How are you, Mom?"

"Good. You?"

Not good. "Fine."

"Is something wrong?" Her mom paused for a moment to look at her closely. Maybe she thought her being here was unusual because whenever they disagreed on something, she usualy made the first attempt at reconciliation by calling.

"I just wanted to see you. I missed you."

"I miss you too, and you're welcome to see me anytime, baby. But that boy you keep around you—"

"Mom, please. Not now."

Her mom sighed. "You look awful. What have you been doing to yourself?"

She lied. "Tests, exams... school stuff." She stood up to pour herself a glass of water just to avoid further questions. It worked, but not for long.

"Are you sure, Ally? You look pale and thinner."

She froze behind the fridge.

"Just stress." She adjusted the funny voice that came out of her. "I had the bug recently... It's nothing." *More lies.* "Mom…" She said softly, not sure if she should tell her.

"I know you don't like me saying this, Ally, but that boy would do nothing but hurt you in the end. Men like that are conceited and only think about themselves. He's a stain to you. All that's said about you infuriates me. You don't know how much I wish you weren't with him. You'll only have yourself to blame when it all ends. All I could do is wait and watch, and that kills me."

Well, there goes her answer. There's no way she could tell her now.

She spent the rest of the day with her, lying that Xander was on a business trip and she was taking a break from books. Funny enough, she consumed every food she could find in her mother's kitchen, and her stomach agreed with it. She actually felt sad knowing she would not be having this for a while.

***

"You can't be serious, Ally. Don't do this. It's not right."

"I have to. I have no choice."

"Are you insane? Of course, you have a choice. You're going to give up on all that you've strived for because of him?"

"That has got nothing to do with this."

"Don't make me... ahhh!" Laurie groaned out, frustrated.

"I don't—"

"Don't say you don't have a choice. Please stop saying that. Do you want me to call your mom?"

"I wasn't going to say that, and you can't bring mom into this. I don't want her to find out."

"If you think I'll support you on this, you're crazy. If I need to smack some sense into you, I will."

Laurie had been trying to talk Ally out of her decision for the past thirty minutes. She had hurriedly appeared in front of the apartment she shared with her roommate, Trish. God bless the girl for pointing her concern to her; she was grateful about that. If Trish had not asked her to come, she would have not found out about Ally's decision to have an abortion.

She had found out just by the slightest chance, and she was grateful for that.

It was insane the more she thought about it because it was unlike Ally to ever make such a decision. Yes, she was in love with Xander and was trying to do what she thought was best for him, but she was certain if Ally was in the right frame of mind, it was not what she would have wanted. Could her cousin think of herself for once?

"Is he making you do this?"

"I told you, he does not know."

"Ally, come to your senses. I understand you want to get rid of your baby and you're not ready to be a mother, but you have your mom. I'm sure she will understand."

"She won't. She hates Xander."

"So? It's *your* baby, too. A part of our family. A part of you."

"Xander... I love him, Laurie. He does not want this baby. Besides, I have school; it's my first year! Mom might not forgive me, and even if I do have the baby, it would be a mistake. Many people would wish it was not born."

A resounding slap echoed in the room, and shock registered on Ally's face.

Laurie saw the deplorable state her cousin was in. Ally was just a shell of herself, and god knows what she must've been feeling inside. Is this what love got to offer her? What Ally needed was someone who loved her, and she could give her that even if right now, she believed it was not the kind she has to offer. She had no choice but to try and bring her back with a slap. At least she hoped she did.

"You want to talk about forgiveness? Start with the words you just uttered. *Who are you?* Why do you get to make others choices for them? If you get rid of it, will it bring Xander back to you? Will that make him fall in love with you? If it does, will a part of you never resent him? Will you never resent yourself? And what does that make me if I let you go through with it even if I know you'll eventually hate yourself for it?"

Ally burst into tears. "I didn't want you to get involved."

She took her in her arms and wrapped her with all the comfort she could give. "Obviously. I owe Trish a big kiss."

"I'm not sure she would like that," she said in between her tears.

"She will have to." After a while, she asked, "Better?"

Ally nodded, still in her arms. "What do I do, Laurie? I did not plan this. How do I fit a baby into my life?"

"If you want to keep your mom in the dark for now, I'm with you. You have me. And forget about him. Please, Ally. It sounds impossible now, but you have to try. When he's come off his high horse, he'll come begging. But please… please, Ally, don't go behind my back and make that mistake. Promise me."

"I promise,"she finally said after a long pause.

***

"Let's take a break."

"You take one if you need it."

Julia sighed, probably tired from working for days on end.

"Ten minutes," he said and muttered something incomprehensible. Xander knew what they were all thinking, but he did not care. He had to take his mind off the situation, something he was too afraid to face, and yet he could not stop thinking about it.

He was going to be a father. Ally was pregnant with his child.

It was easy to admit that to himself, but saying it out loud brought shudders to his body. There was no proof he could give love to someone else. Could his flesh and blood be any different? He wouldn't know. He never had a good example.Why was it so damn hard to accept?

He was being a coward, and doubt was starting to haunt him.

He was afraid, but Ally was scared too. He was ignoring her—abandoned her, leaving her at his house after spitting out those harsh words even though he very well knew she was feeling ill. Now, he does not know how she is doing. He lost count of the times he picked up the phone to call her before cowardice set in. Whenever he remembered the way she looked so weak, he would pick up the phone again only to put it back down and bury himself in work, self-hate, and alcohol.

He wanted to let go, but how?

"*Relax,*" someone whispered in his ear, and he did.

He let his guard down, and Julia must have sensed this from his lack of rejection.

He should not let this happen, but he was tired of thinking. He wanted to let it all go just this once. Just this once, he would pretend Ally was with him and that it was all great like it was months ago. If the woman behind him was the only option, he would take it. Xander was not sure how things had progressed this fast, but Julia had somehow made herself available beneath him.

The only way he could block out her moans was pretend she wasn't even there. But she was, and she was right under him. She meant nothing, *this* meant nothing, and that was all that mattered.

"This means nothing," he managed to say in between pants.

"I-I know." She gasped when he tugged at her black skirt and raised her left thigh roughly. She tried to touch him back.

"Don't." He was not about to have fun or enjoy what she would give. He was just searching for a way to let out all the anguish.

Are you sure about this, Xander? his conscience aked him. If things got back to normal and Ally were to know, what would he say? If he did this, it would mean cheating on her. Though he never had to worry about those things before, it felt absolutely wrong, and he could not understand why the hell he felt so guilty.

All these questions swirled around Xander's head, but only one woman got her answer as she stared at the man she was in love with entangled in another's arms.

Ally turned to leave unnoticed by them, clutching her heart in her hands.

CHAPTER 10

The last few days, Julia watched her boss stride into his office with stiff shoulder like every other part of him. As his assistant, she always had been a victim of his moodiness. Everyone who crossed path with him has been, but she could not help but think she was getting the larger chunk of his anger… especially since what happened between them two days ago. Now he treated her less of a trusted assistant, and their friendship seemed long gone.

But she could not say she had regrets. He had used her, and she was willing. Was it not what she had wanted all along? Of course, she did not want to be used, but she wanted to get close to him, and she thought it was enough, but it had not been the same as before. He was different. Whatever passion they once shared was missing now.

She eventually found out about what was going on with him. It was not that hard. He avoided leaving the office, and when she tried talking about Alicia, he flipped out. She was surprised the other woman had the nerve to step beyond the line when she knew just how much Xander opposed marriage and children. Betrayal was the best word to describe it. Who could blame Xander? Alicia did take advantage of his affection. She must have thought she could get away with it. Ha! Even Barb could not.

She would have liked to say she had the last laugh, but she clearly knew by what happened two days ago between Xander and her, he did care about Alicia.

The mailman brought her out of her thoughts. It was an envelope, and there was no mistake as to whom it was addressed to. She signed and looked at it, wondering what was inside.

Then again, there was no need to wonder when she could find out.

***

A knock came on his door. Julia was there. It must be important; it better be. He was not to be disturbed for petty reasons in his state now. Five months ago, he thought he had everything right; that in every situation, he was in control. Back then, his ego was something that could not be easily brought down, but it all shattered around him all because of one woman.

Xander stared one last time at the white gold necklace he had in his hands laid out in a red velvet box. Its neatly cut diamond pendant would have been perfect on her dainty neck. He closed it before placing the box behind one of his drawers.

Before this whole mess, he had every intention to surprise Ally with it on a special dinner. He had purchased the jewellery because he wanted to see it on her every day, to know that she had a reminder of him on her always. It was a foreign feeling for him, something he had not felt in all twenty-seven years of his life. He could not give her anything before that because she refused his every gift, believing that accepting them would make her his mistress.

What exactly had he had with Barbara? He thought he knew it all, but Ally's absence and the situation of it all were close to driving him crazy.

He looked up and saw Julia walking towards his table. She laid a white envelope in front of him, and he looked down at it. The handwriting was familiar. He looked at the woman in front of him, and he knew, just like she did, who it was from.

"Was she here?" he asked in a quivering voice he barely recognised.

She shook her head. "Delivery."

He nodded stiffly but was not sure why she was still standing there. Did she have another message for him? "Anything else, Julia?"

"No."

He did not believe her; he knew she was waiting just because she thought she had the right to. Not today. He felt a sense of dread, and he was not about to let anyone witness his reaction from whatever was written inside.

"Leave me," he said, leaving no room for protest.

As soon as the door closed behind her, he hurriedly ripped the paper out of the envelope. It was barely a one-page letter from the woman he once cared about. Shit! From a woman he probably still cared about, a woman whose presence and words brought a sense of awareness to every part of his being and eventually toyed with his sanity, who finally proved to him that women were really full of deceit.

There was no use prolonging the inevitable. He impatiently skimmed through the letter, holding his breath.

"How the hell did she find out?"

What the hell did that mean? Was this a permanent end to them?

Alex,

I'm sorry I messed things up between us—for you. Maybe I'm solely to blame, and I've accepted that. But I've had time to think about it, and you should know that I'm not sorry any of it happened.

You are really not giving me a choice in all this. Mom is mad as it is, your father is spiteful enough, and you've been indifferent—if I can call it that. You refuse to talk to me, and whatever it is you have with Julia just made things clearer for me. I now understand what you've been trying to tell me all this time with your absence and silence.

You're free, Alex.

You have made it clear what you wanted, and I have made my decision. I'm having an abortion.

Don't bother with whatever you might be thinking. I honestly don't want to know. If you're slow on that, it means I hope I never see you again.

A.

He abruptly stood up from his chair.

"Oh, hell." He groaned the words out as he ran his hand through his hair and his other hand tried hard not to crush the paper in it

Abortion? She has to joking!

Just when he had spent the last few days trying and struggling to accept it all, dreaming of it and imagining what it would be like, she was deciding to get rid of it? He stood up, marching straight towards the elevator. He had no time to worry what his staff would think of his behaviour.

Ally blamed herself for the situation; he made her feel that way. If she went through with getting rid of the child, Xander knew he would blame himself for the rest of his existence for turning out to be the exact kind of parent he had always loathed.

***

The first thing Xander did was drive to the house they shared to try to stop her. He had a feeling he was already late, but he needed to confirm. On his way, he called the head of his security and barked instructions to check everywhere and anywhere she could be, starting with the hospitals first, and to make sure they stopped her. He did not care how.

He rushed into the bedroom as soon as he skidded into the driveway. His shoulders sagged when he saw evidence that she already moved out. It seemed like she had left the house days ago.

What exactly had he been so mad about? How the hell did he let things get to this point? How the hell could he wish away his misery while things fell apart around him? All these questions plagued his mind.

After a few moments, he finally heard his phone ringing. He didn't know how long he had been standing in the middle of the room dazed. He saw the caller ID and smiled. He got the information as fast as he needed it, and that was what he liked.

"She was at City Hospital, but that was two days ago."

"What?" He did not want to expect the worst, but then, he realized two days ago was when he was stupid enough to accept Julia's offer. Had she been there? How the hell did she found out? Did Julia tell her? He would not put it past his assistant.

"I need you to keep looking, and when you find her, call me. But before that, find out what she was doing at City Hospital."

Another option was to check her apartment, but he knew the best option was Laurie. He confirmed her address and drove straight over there.

***

"I should laugh in your face and spit at you." Laurie angrily spat as soon as she saw Xander on her doorstep.

"Where's she?"

"I'm not sure what she had me deliver, but it damn well looks like a wake-up call for you. Too bad it's a little too late."

So Laurie had posted the letter.

"I don't have time for this. Where the hell is she?" He barged into the house.

"You won't find her here."

"Where then?" He moved within inches of her.

She crossed her arms. "Now I see why she wouldn't tell me either. I don't know. She's gone, and it's entirely your fault."

He heard what she was saying, but it all just wouldn't register. "What about the baby? Did she… is she—"

"I told her not to go through with it. I thought she listened. it seemed like it. Ally thought her final decision rested on seeing you only she came back looking like the grim reaper made a visit. I've never seen Ally like that. What the hell did you say to her?"

Nothing, absolutely nothing. It must have been what she saw. Now he was certain she had been there that day.

"I kept asking, but she would not tell," Laurie continued.

He sighed, running his hands through his hair. His men were yet to call with any information, her cousin had nothing useful to give except reprimand him for something he already knew was his mess. If she truly went through with it, why was she hiding?

What do you think, Xander? He asked himself, knowing he had one clear answer to that.

A phone started ringing, and it was Laurie's. He waited for her to pick it up, but she was not moving. Instead, she shifted stance, letting him know she wanted him out of her apartment right now.

He was not leaving. He was not stupid. It could be her. It could be Ally calling.

"What else do you need?"

"If you two are as close as Ally always insisted, why would she not tell you where she was going?"

"Maybe because she expected *this* would happen, not that she thought you cared that much anyway."

Xander winced.

"She said she was taking some time to clear her thoughts and would be back before exams. She wanted to be alone; that's all she told me. I did not expect her to disappear."

Disappear was a strong word to use; he knew he would find her. It was what he's gonna do when he sees her that's bothering him. Is Ally hiding evidence that she might have gone through with it? If Ally was now without his child, what could he possibly say to ask her forgiveness and explain his cowardice? For letting her shoulder the huge burden and cheating on her on top of it? He doubted she was going to want him anywhere near her at this point.

The blasted phone kept ringing.

"Pick up the damn phone."

"This isn't your place to give commands. Get out."

He frowned at her, but Laurie gave him the same expression. He stepped out.

What was the use of his money and name if he could not find a Ally and his child?

***

Laurie made sure he was out the door and far from it before she picked up the call. "Hello?"

"Are you busy?" Ally's soft voice asked.

"Ally…" she said in both resignation and frustration.

"I'm fine." She was not even sure if Ally was trying to assure her or convince herself.

"Where are you? Come home. If your mom finds out, she's going to have my head."

"It won't matter when she finds out."

"That's not true, and you know that." Ally wasn't giving in, and she stopped asking. That did not mean she would stop trying. "You were right. He was here."

"Hmm."

Laurie sighed. She knew something happened, and she was going to get it out of that bastard somehow.

***

"HOW CAN IT BE SO HARD FINDING ONE WOMAN!"

Paul, head security, did not flinch at Xander's booming voice and banging fist on the table.

The door opened, and thinking it was Julia, Xander started to shout at her, not even looking to see who it was. It was someone else. Xander rubbed his right hand on his forehead. He did not need this now.

"I see it's true."

He signaled for Paul to leave them. They had a conversation to finish. "What are you doing here?"

"Tell me it isn't true that you're rotting because of a girl."

Rotting? Is that what he looked like? "I don't have time to argue with you."

"Neither do I, but when they alerted me on the headlines that would be gracing the tomorrow morning's papers, I had to create the time."

What was he talking about?

"Are you going to run the business down because of your foolish emotional dramas?" His father must have heard about that deal he lost. Nothing passes this man.

"You're just like your mother," he said, irritated. "Foolish sentiments that would get you nowhere. It's a good thing that girl left before I could take her out just like I did your mother."

His father knew about Ally too? Did he know where she was? What if... Wait. What did he just say about his mother?

"What did you just say?" Xander stared right at his father, looking to see if he could draw anything from his face, but the man had his hard look sitting right on his face. "What do you mean just like you did my mother?"

CHAPTER 11

That question kept replaying in his head, and he could not get it out, but the reply he got only made it more disturbing.

"Acting righteous does not suit women like your mother and that girl you were using. They know what they're getting into from the start, but then you see them asking for more."

When he demanded a better explanation, his father snickered at him and told him to get it together. Well, he tried. Getting it together was the least he could do for three weeks now since Ally disappeared. His father had been able to stop the prints from publishing the recent turmoil in his life, but he knew he had too much going on for all of it to be ignored by the media.

They had picked up on Ally's absence, and the questions he was asked left him feeling more helpless. At one point, he even welcomed the attention, thinking gossips would give him a clue as to where she was, but was futile since his men were yet to provide him with the news he wanted.

He soon found out his father has been blocking his every effort to get information on both his mother and Ally. His father had people interfering even before Ally had disappeared, and now he was keeping him from finding her. He hated that his father was more powerful than him and could dictate his life as he wished. He had always known his father as a cold, hard-hearted man and had never thought of him otherwise. And now he had enough reason to believe that there was more to what happened between his parents, something his father was not telling him.

That was why he was here today.

He had not stepped in here for a long while, but he had to be here for some answers. This man was the only reliable source he knew. After years of stopping himself from listening to all his grandfather said, here he was now, standing on his doorstep, eager for information.

"When you said you were coming in a few minutes, I thought you were pulling one on me."

Xander walked towards his grandfather, the old man was the only reason he managed to keep it together when he was younger. "I wouldn't do that to an old man."

His grandfather let out a big laugh. "Nothing old about me, boy."

He pulled him into a hug, and Xander, at that moment, acknowledged to himself how much he missed the man. He let himself be swallowed by the lifestyle he has been leading and has turned into a shallow man with each passing day. He should have had at least the decency to face his grandpa like a man.

"You look like you've got lots to let out," his grandfather told him.

He did, but that could wait till he has showered. He took his bag from Paul and dismissed him with the car.

***

Xander felt more relaxed as he got out from the bathroom. He looked around the house. There was no sign of his grandfather.

Nothing's changed, he thought as he looked around. With a towel still in his hand, trying to get his hair dried, he walked into the bedroom he used as a teenager. He threw on a t-shirt and shorts from his bag and went to look for his old man in the only place he thought he might be.

His grandfather was seated out the porch with a beer in hand. His guess was right.

Noticing his grandson, he asked him to join him and handed him a bottle. Though the night was chilly, Xander barely felt it as both of them stared into it in silence. His thoughts were in a jumble, his mind unsettled, and his feelings unbridled. He had a feeling that all this time he has been banking on a principle that was all wrong, and he hoped to understand some of it tonight.

Imagine how a few words could change one's life. His father's words certainly did that to his.

"What's on your mind?"

"Tell me about Mom." He looked at his grandfather who was still staring out into the distance.

His grandfather sighed, taking a swig of his beer before he looked straight at him. "When I read the things written about you, I somehow knew you still believed what you wanted to. I didn't want you to end up like that man of yours, but you wouldn't listen."

Xander knew that already. He just wanted to know what he failed to hear years ago.

"I'll tell you about your grandma first. I know what you think of her… of our relationship, but there are… There's something you need to know. I cheated."

He was shocked. That couldn't be true. His grandfather's heart was broken by his wife, and it had always seemed like he was truly in love with her. If he cared that much, why would he cheat?

"I cheated on my fiancée with your grandma."

"What?"

"And that resulted to your mother."

"So, you're saying you were never in love with grandma?"

"Not really. I cared about her, but it was an arranged marriage. We thought we could make it work, but not once did I feel for her as much as I did with Beth."

Xander assumed that was the fiancée's name.

"What happened between us was honestly a mistake. It was a reckless night." His grandfather let out a sigh. "Your grandma always said I was never going to be over Beth, and maybe that's why she looked for affection someplace else."

"She was in love with you? Grandma?"

"I don't know. I never really got to look at her—or anything she did. If she was in love with me, my indifference snapped her out of it."

"Why didn't you tell me?" He felt like he was living a lie, thinking she cheated on him as his grandpa pined away for her when the truth was the exact opposite. His grandfather was actually the one longing for another woman while he ignored his wife.

He took another mouthful of his beer before he continued. "Not only did I ruin two women's lives… I also ruined my daughter's, too."

Xander's eyes narrowed.

"Your mother... all she saw while growing up was a dysfunctional family. The first time I noticed your mother growing up was when she met your father, but by then, I couldn't do much to stop it." He chuckled bitterly to himself.

"Why?" he whispered into the cold night air.

"I had no right!" he said out loud, anguish laced in every word. "That's exactly what your mother told me. She asked me questions about her life, and I could not even give an answer to one." The old man's shoulders shivered. "I took up the role of a father when my daughter turned eighteen… a useless father at that. I couldn't even protect her."

Those words hit home for him. It sounded awfully familiar. He did not know if his unborn child would be a boy or girl, but he had been a lousy father for not acknowledging him or her. And if Ally had gone through with getting rid of the baby, he had lost the chance to redeem himself. He couldn't even protect the baby from his own selfishness. Not knowing if the baby was alive or not was eating at him, destroying him slowly inside, and he knew that.

"Do you regret it?" he asked.

His grandfather turned silent for a while, but he obviously did from what he was seeing. It seemed like his grandfather had bottled up his feeling for too long. Now it became clearer to him why he tried so hard to set him straight and instill so many principles on him.

"I saw myself in that man, and I couldn't stop it. It felt like I was being punished. Your father was a bastard who got her pregnant and abandoned her."

"What? How can that be? He's always said that she left him… and me for another man."

The deep set lines on his grandfather's face deepened, but not because of the years he has lived but from anger. "That's the story he's been telling you? She left him, of course, but your mother never abandoned you. Not in the way you believe she did." He scoffed. "What a coward. Your father seduced your mother at twenty-eight, proclaiming a love he knew she yearned to experience when he was already married and had a son."

This was all news to him. He had a brother somewhere? Where was he? How did his father manage to keep him in the dark for so long, and how come he was the one running their companies with his father if he had an older brother?

"Where are they now? Do you know?"

He sighed and averted his eyes. "I think that's where I failed as a parent again. When I found out, I threatened to expose him to his family. Perhaps, he loved his family, or maybe he just feared what the truth might do for him. He promised to stay away from your mother. I don't know what went wrong from there. That night, your mother came home shouting how I never loved her and why I wanted to see her unhappy. Whatever that bastard told her is still unknown to me. She left home, and I never saw her until she came on my doorstep months later, pregnant and with your grandma in tow. She found out about his lies, and said something about his wife seeking her out."

"She was threatened?" Xander asked.

His grandfather shook his head. "No. I don't think that was it. It was strange, but she said his wife thanked her instead and told her to get away from him as fast as she could."

"Why?"

"I don't know the story to that either."

"Where is she now? Mom… where is she?"

"I don't know."

Xander frowned. He has hit a dead end.

"Your mother left you in my care when your father threatened to take you from her. He found out about you. She did all she could to get you out of his reach even if that meant staying away from you to stay off his radar."

He remembered the night his mother appeared after years being away. They thought he was asleep in his room, but he heard their voices. He crept to his door, unnoticed by them, and heard his grandfather asking what was going on and what his mother had said after that.

I'm leaving. I'll have to be away for a while. I can't take Alexander with me, but you'll take care of him, won't you?

Xander took it the only way a thirteen-year-old boy who felt abandoned could: bitterly.

His mother always called him by his full name, Alexander. He resolved himself to forget about her if she could do the same with him. He never wanted to be called by that name again, and so, took the shortened form of his name. Luckily for him, it stuck. Anything other than Alexander.

"Why ask me now? What changed?" his grandfather asked, but he just took a gulp from his bottle, knowing real well what changed.

Ally and his child... if he still had that, but that was no story for tonight.

His grandfather must have sensed his hesitation. "Don't be fooled by that man. He never cared about you or your mother. He wanted you just because he lost his heir and his wife to a car accident."

The words brought a dreadful chill to his spine.

***

"Finally!" Laurie breathed out as she picked up the phone on its first ring. She has been expecting it all week.

"Hello to you too, cousin," Ally said slowly.

"You've got to stop doing this to me, Al. You're killing me here. As much as I love taking the bitch role for you because of that idiot, your mom is the bitch leader." She put a hand to her mouth and calmly added, "Sorry if that's too much for the baby."

Ally chuckled.

"I'm serious, Al. Call your mom. She's mighty worried. If she had not heard it from me that you were okay, you would have the police on your ass right now. Besides, she insinuated the last time she was here that she might just move in just to catch you call." Laurie shuddered at the thought. She loved her privacy too much.

"Sorry, Laurie."

She sighed. "I understand sweetheart, but what are you doing? It's been weeks."

"Like you said, I don't want this baby taken from me. It's mine now. To him, it's dead. I want it that way."

Ally's words kept her mute for a while, and it scared her. She was doubtful of her cousin's state of mind, but she was certain she needed someone with her. She did not even know where she was, and the stubborn girl was not budging. It was frustrating her how it was all turning out.

"I can come stay with—"

"No, it's okay. I need to do this on my own."

"You don't have to do any of it on your own. You can't escape him forever. You might as well shove his ass up his mouth right now."

Ally chuckled again.

"I'm serious, Al."

"I have a plan, Laurie. I just have to see how it turns out. It might seem like I'm running, and maybe I am, but I really don't want to let his presence affect my decisions. I need time. I still love him, and I know that's not going to fade away soon. I just need to know how to deal with that and move on."

She let out a breath. "I love you."

"I love you, too. Thanks, Laurie, and please tell Mom I'm okay."

"She doesn't understand. Should I tell her you're preg—"

"No!"

"Okay."

"Mom will just go to him and start spilling things I don't want to clean up after. Besides, she'll probably babble on about me still being pregnant."

"Okay. Call me? I need to know how the baby's doing and how you'r doing."

"I will. Thanks, Laurie."

"All for my godchild. So, you know, you better not be giving my title to some new bitch you just met."

"Laurie..."

"Language, I know. I'll be better with my words."

"Um... there's someone at the door. I have to go."

"Okay."

"Call me. I mean it, Ally. Don't make me wait this long next time."

"I promise."

***

There was no one at the door. In fact, Ally was not in the house she rented. If she went on any longer on the phone with Laurie, her cousin would know she was having a little trouble breathing well and that she was actually in the hospital… especially when the doctor came in a moment after.

"Hello, Ally. A little trouble breathing again?"

CHAPTER 12

Xander was yet to confront his father. He needed more information before he could take action, but it was extremely frustrating that all he could do for now was sit down and wait for something... *anything.* He put Paul in charge of finding out about his mother and Ally, but that has produced nothing so far.

Since he recently found out about his mom, Xander really did not expect to get a feedback soon, but whenever he had to think about his talk with his grandfather, all he felt was an emotion he never thought would come to haunt him. Shame.

All the while, he resented her and his grandmother when he could have done something. And now he felt helpless and at a loss at a number of things.

How good would it have been if he had Ally with him at this difficult moment? She had always been a great listener, and he clearly remembered the time when she had suggested he listen to his mother's reasons and just like always, he had been a stubborn man. But there was no use to thinking about it. If he had not screwed up her trust in him, he probably would not have found out the truth about his mother and the secrets his father kept.

It has been a month since Ally disappeared, and he could not imagine the pain she must have felt to have gone to this extent just to be away from him. He had to be a darn good record breaker at making mistakes because it seemed like he brilliantly pushed away every great relationship that could have been, single-handedly.

There has been no news about Ally for the past few weeks, and he had come to realise that his father's influence was far greater than his. He knew there was no way of getting to the bottom of things unless he finds a way to get his dad's men out of the way. Paul had talked with him about a plan he hoped would work for them. Despite all this, he still instructed Paul to have men on Ally's cousin at all times. If there was anyone who could lead him to Ally, it was her. He was not buying her story that she had no idea where her cousin was.

He knew in his gut that Laurie knew something. If they were anywhere as close as Ally always claimed and she didn't know, she would be on his throat and giving him hell. He was desperate but not stupid.

He knew he was the last person Laurie would want to be in the same room with. She disliked him, and he did not particularly like her either. However, he was starting to wonder why that was the case. He assumed it was when he found out she had no qualms with taking men whenever she wanted, but was he any different from Laurie? He treated women just the same way. Ally pointed that out back then.

Another option he had was to face Ally's mom, but he would be the most stupid man on earth if he did. Even before all this, the woman had been against his relationship with her daughter, and he knew meeting her before he talks to Ally would be a big disaster. What would he say anyway? There was no excuse for what he did. If he decides to blame his past experiences for his actions, it would only prove to everyone that he was the kind of man who held on to the past and passed on blames.

Then again, all his past turned out to be a big fat lie. What has he been holding on to all this time? He knew he had a lot to make up for—his mom, grandma, and Ally. Maybe if he hadn't met Barbara again, he would be in a different position right now. He remembered when he first met Barbara in high school.

Barbara was a senior then, and despite the fact that he had no interest in dating or scoring girls—his mother's abandonment still making him bitter towards the female kind—he had been attracted to her. His friends had egged him on, but he thought talking to her was impossible. Plus, there was the fact that she was older than him and obviously more experienced.

But a party had made it all possible.

After reluctantly agreeing to tag along to a senior's party, one sober night for him quickly turned to a wild, drunken one, and he found himself with her. He was not sure how it had come to be, but he did not refuse fate, which he thought it was at the time.

On that night, he gave his virginity to his first crush, and for a while, he forgot all about his mom. But it all came crashing down when Barbara said that she forgot all about it, blatantly dismissing that night as unremarkable. She had made fun of his *tool* in front of their friends, saying that his face would have been worth it if not for his lousy member. He was awfully embarrassed.

Thinking about all that now, Xander was sure that was the only reason he approached her at the restaurant when he saw her again years later. What he did not know then was that it would bring an even uglier memory for him.

His arrogance blinded him from reason. Even when he saw that she was with someone, he wanted to make her see that he had more than a face to his name now—a new surname well worth billions.

She sought him out not long after, and a relationship formed. He thought he was doing it just to get back at her, but there was one thing he could not deny: he was still attracted to her.

Barbara was flawless, a woman of rare beauty. She was a seductive, leggy blonde with the perfect face and proportions. He was so deeply invested in her that he discarded every other woman he had by his side. And when she got pregnant, he had planned to take it a step further—only to find out in the cruelest way possible that the guy he had seen at the restaurant with her was the father of her child.

He was her on and off boyfriend for two years, and she was secretly cheating on him with the douche. After that, he totally blocked out everything about women. She had turned crazy, stalking him to get back together.

When Ally told him she was pregnant, everything came back… everything he was not prepared for. He remembered clearly every word he said to her. Deep down, he knew it was his, but he had been a coward and ran away.

He might have lost the only truth in his existence because of his stupidity: Ally's love and his child… if he still has any of them.

It was all frustrating doing nothing, and his patience was wearing thin. A man of his status should get what he wanted when he wanted it, but it has already been a month, and things were not going his way.

"Boss."

He looked up to see Paul in a dark suit looking no different like he always did. He had a brown envelope in his right hand.

"And?" he asked expectantly. Paul was well aware of what he was asking. It was always the same thing.

"We're still looking. But you might want to see this." He collected the envelope, searching Paul's face as if it would reveal what was inside.

As he tore the envelope open, different thoughts flooded his mind, and he was allowing himself to drown in it. Whatever was stated on that envelope would reveal who he was.

He barely noticed Paul giving him his privacy until he heard the door close. He opens the contents of the large, rectangular, brown parcel, and the first thing that caught his eyes was pictures of his mom. She looked exactly like he remembered in most of them, but the others just got him wanting to cry at the state she was in.

Sprawled right in front of him, on his table, was the past his father had tried hard to hide from him. He stared at a picture of his father and his deceased wife with their son, his would-have-been big brother.

All the information he had in front of him told him about the past but nothing about the present. Just what kind of a man was his father? What kind of state was his mother in now?

This was nothing close to what his father had fed him, and there was no better way to confirm things than asking the man in question. What would he say? Would he admit he only married the woman for her inheritance? That he was just a replacement son and his mother was his idea of fun? Would he admit he was just a sick old man who never knew how to love anyone?

Somewhere in the document, he found out that his mother had not stepped into the country since the last time she reappeared. Whatever reason she was running from, he was going to take it out of the way.

He could not put it past his father. After all, he had more than admitted it when he claimed to *'take her out.'* He was going to start putting things the right way, and he knew exactly what to do. He was done letting his father use him.

The door opened, and he saw Julia come in.

"What's all the fuss about? Everything okay? Paul was looking moody." She focused on his face. "Well, better than how you're looking right now."

"I have to go." He stood from his chair, putting back all the pictures and documents in the envelope.

"What's going on? What's this about? Where are you going?"

"That's none of your business. I'll call to tell you what to do. I'll need—"

"Of course, it's my business! I'm your assistant."

He looked up and saw the frown on her face. She still thought they had more than a business relationship. It was his fault alright, but maybe if he cut that off, it would be one less problem for him. Then again, he could not be bothered with it right now. Bringing in someone new to replace her would not be the best move for the company. He still had a responsibility to the company no matter what.

"This isn't business. It's personal, so it makes it none of your business." He went back to what he was doing and getting other things he needed to be packed.

"Then it's about *her* again? You're still looking for her?"

He sighed. He had no intention of repeating the same things over and over. One stupid move and Julia's foolish hope of having him shot through the roof once more.

"Not that it's any of your business, but this is about my mother."

"Your—"

"And I want no comment from you."

She gave him a sad look. "I still like to think we are friends."

"It would do you a lot of good if you quit thinking that. What we had is over, Julia. Accept it, and you'll be able to move on."

But I don't want to move on, he could read that on her face.

He brought out his phone and called Paul to get ready to move as soon as Julia left his office. He needed to start making his plans now.

***

Right outside Xander's office, Julia was panicking and nervously biting her nails. She had the look of a slimy little liar about to be caught in her lies. She was on edge.

She got a glimpse of what was on those papers on Xander's desk, enough to make her assumptions. What to do? There was only one person she could ask for help, but going to him was as good as saying goodbye to any hope of getting Xander back. But not if she played it right.

"What am I going to do?" she whispered to herself.

***

"See you on Monday, Alicia."

"Bye."

Ally pushed open the door of the salon where she worked and embraced herself against the warm jacket she wore on that chilly evening.

It was Saturday, and the day had been great. There had been a fairly good amount of customers and the ones she attended today loved her work. She got no complaint—except from that brunette who looked at her like she had met her somewhere before and had done something really wrong to piss her off. Everyone applauded her work on the girl's hair, but it did not make her any happier.

You can never please everyone, after all.

It was a good thing she was free for the rest of the weekend at the local hospital. She worked there on days she was not in the salon, and it was not as stressful as she initially thought. It was not as big as the ones they had in the city, but it was the most reputable in town. Ally was sure no one had an idea that she was pregnant save for the doctor who usually attended to her. She had asked him to be discreet… at least for now.

It was a good thing she was not showing obvious signs of pregnancy just yet. No one but her could see the little bump on her belly for she avoided wearing tight-fitted garments—clothes that would make

Xander scrunch up his face. She always found it funny when he had that face on.

She caught herself thinking of him, a smile playing on her lips.

Who was she kidding? She was in love with him, and that was not going to go away anytime soon. That was the only reason she was in this small town. Well, there was her mom. She did not want to hear her say, 'I told you so.'

No one seemed to know who she was here or who she had dated, and that was fine. There were no paparazzi, which was great. It was not a long walk from the salon to her home, and she was there in no time. She saw a bag sitting in front of her apartment, picked it up, and saw packets of sweet and sour candies inside.

She smiled, knowing who it was from; this was the second time he did this. Accepting this might seem like encouraging him, but she could not resist these things, and he got her the best ones too. The women at the salon thought she was crazy for saying no to him because, according to them, he was every girl's fantasy. She had scoffed when she heard that, thinking to herself how they would describe Xander if they saw him.

Mike was twenty-seven, an olive-skinned, well-sculpted, brown-haired man with light blue eyes. She saw him almost every day since he was a doctor at the hospital she worked at. He was the only one who knew about her craving for sweet and sour things. He caught her with a box, and he just assumed she loved them. Unfortunately, she was still not over a particular green-eyed man. So, though she knew how hot, attractive, and sweet Mike was, all that did not make her lose it one bit. In fact, she was thinking of coming out with it and telling him she was pregnant with another man's baby to put him off.

She dropped the bag on her kitchen counter to get out of her clothes and change into something more comfortable. Her apartment was quite cozy and more than she expected to find at a fairly good price. It had everything she needed: a living room, a dining room-cum-kitchen, a bedroom, and bathroom with an empty storage room. She loved it and was getting used to it. It would just be her and her baby… and maybe later, a very persistent cousin and soon-to-be aunt coming around for a visit.

Her gaze went to the paper she had been keeping on her dresser for a few days now. She almost forgot about them. She sighed. She did not want any problem. Knowing that Xander's father found out where she was staying was scary, but she was not going to let that affect her.

She really could use having someone around to stay with her while she went through all this, but she did not want to bother anyone. Laurie had insisted, but Ally knew it would only be for a short while. Her cousin had a life of her own, and she really could not picture Laurie living in this quaint town. Besides, if Laurie came over, her mom and Xander might be the next people to show up at her doorstep, and that was what she feared the most.

It did not seem like Xander's father knew about the baby because he did not say anything about it. It surprised her that Xander had not come barging in here despite what Laurie had told her.

Forgetting about all that for now and the fat cheque that sat there, she walked out to get something to eat. However, before she could get started, there was a knock on her door. She went to see who it was and saw a woman she had never seen before. Ally felt something familiar about her, though. She just could not pinpoint what it was.

"Can I help you?"

"Alicia Storm?"

She eyed the beautiful, sophisticated woman in front of her. "Yes? And you are?"

The woman gave her a bright smile, and a soft gasp left Ally's lips.

That smile. She has seen it before. That smile was a hard one to forget, and she had only seen it on one face until now.

"I'm Liliana Rose. Liliana if you like. Alexander's mother."

CHAPTER 13

"Okay. Spill it out."

Laurie and Ally had been talking for a few minutes now, and Ally just knew there was no way she could escape her cousin's interrogation. Laurie was that smart.

"What?"

"I want to know what's on your mind. Every second you say something to me, I can feel your hesitation. Does it have something to do with the baby?"

She realised there was no point in lying. If she could not tell Laurie, there was no one else to tell. The truth was, she was not even sure what to make of the situation. Why did Liliana come to her and not to her son? The woman did explain that, though—sort of.

Xander's mom, Liliana, seemed overwhelmed when she had invited her in. She said she wanted to know all about her son, but why come to her? She was confused, wondering how Liliana knew about her. She did not know where to start. Saying what she had heard about her from her son was not an option. The few things Xander had told her were not exactly nice words to spill to the woman. Her presence made no sense to her.

The encounter only gave her more questions. If it were this easy for his parents to get to her, why was he not here yet? Laurie said he was looking for her, but did he really mean it?

"Now I know something's definitely up. Is it the baby?"

"No. It's…"

"Come on, Ally, spill. I would come kick you in the rear to get it out of you, but I don't even know where you are."

"Xander—"

"The idiot found you?!"

"His parents did."

The other end of the line went dead. "His parents?" she exclaimed after a moment of silence.

She had no intention of telling anyone about his father's visit since the man wanted it that way. She slipped. Perhaps, because she was preoccupied with her thoughts.

"I thought his mother was dead or something close to that. His parents aren't together, are they?"

"Definitely not together, and she is definitely not dead." She explained to her cousin everything she knew about Xander's family. There was no point holding anything back at this point. Laurie was her only ally at the moment. Besides, she was family, a sister and her best friend.

"ALICIA STORM! How could you hide all that from me?"

"I didn't want to complicate things."

"By not telling me? Things *are* complicated." Laurie sighed, probably trying to wrap her head around all she just heard. "Oh, girl, you've got yourself involved with a shitty family."

"I know," she mumbled under her breath, but not loud enough for Laurie to hear.

"Are you seriously okay, Al?"

She smiled. "Honestly, I'm fine."

"Then tell me where you are," Laurie demanded immediately before she could be interrupted. "Are you honestly still going to tell me it's because of your mom or that idiot? I'm not them. Don't you trust me to keep that a secret? I just want to see you. I've been going nuts whenever you pop into my mind. We could skype, but you've decided to adopt this ancient means of communication. It really bugs me when I start imagining things… and they aren't lovely."

She sighed, understanding she was not being fair to Laurie. She was trying to shut out the life she knew, but it was impossible—not if they came looking for her anyway. Just so she could avoid the gossip, she got herself a phone that could only make and receive calls, and yet Xander's mom had turned up out of the blue to see her.

"Xander's mom said—"

"Think of your own mom. Jeez, Al! Did you think she wouldn't care? I'm close to getting a sore butt. She's always up my ass!"

Ally laughed.

"You think it's funny? That's because you're not the one being hounded."

Before she could give a reply, she heard a knock on her door. "Hold on, Laurie. Someone's at the door."

She got the door and was surprised at who it was. He was the last person she hoped to see at the moment. He was supposed to be out of town.

"Mike."

"Mike?" Laurie's voice blared in the background.

"Hi." He gave her a charming smile. "Bad timing?" he asked.

"Hmm..."

"Who the hell's Mike? Are you dating?"

Mike must have heard Laurie's voice too because he looked at the phone in her hand.

"Come in. I have to take this," she whispered on the receiver.

He closed the door behind him as she walked further into the room and out of Mike's earshot.

"I'll have to call you later, Laurie."

"Who's he?"

"Mike, my boss."

"At the salon?" Laurie asked in disbelief.

Oh, shoot! She did not tell Laurie about working at the hospital, too.

"Ally?"

"He's a doctor. I have to go," she whispered, turning to see if Mike was anywhere near. She saw him still standing in the middle of the room waiting for her. He was not even looking towards her direction.

"Is this some kind of role play? Your *doctor?* I bet you're the nurse." She could hear the teasing tone behind her cousin's words.

"That's dirty, Laurie. Not close to that. *Ever.*" She kept her voice low just to avoid Mike probably overhearing her.

"Oh, please. Is he hot?" she eagerly asked.

"Bye."

"Fine. But don't think you're off the hook. The next time you call, you better be spouting an address, and that's soon."

"Okay. Bye, Laurie."

"See you soon, Al."

Ally went back to Mike.

"Hey," she said when she reached him.

"Hi." He gave a bright smile.

Wouldn't Laurie love to see this? Mike was a truly attractive guy, and you would not have to look twice to confirm. He probably was the same height as Xander, and though they had different features, she was certain women would find Mike incredibly good-looking in a heartbeat. He had a close to perfect body, currently covered in a checkered shirt with rolled up sleeves and jeans that showed off his firm thighs and butt the women in this town couldn't stop raving about. All that said, she had never thought of checking them out. She was still unable to find other men attractive. Only two words were the reason for that: *Alexander Cross.*

She gave him a smile in return, hopeful she had not revealed her thoughts somehow. She led him to the couch, inviting him to sit. "I thought you were out of town."

"You thought right. I got back earlier than expected."

"Thanks for the candies, by the way."

"My pleasure. I don't need to ask if you enjoyed them."

She nodded eagerly. She could not deny she found them delicious.

"But I could offer you more than that."

She looked at him wide-eyed.

Mike caught the look on her face, and he was quick to reconstruct his sentence. "Oh, no. No! Shit, I don't mean it that way."

She chuckled.

"That came out wrong. Of all the ways to say it..."

She was laughing silently at his embarrassment.

"I just meant proper food. Dinner."

That stopped her. This was the right time to tell him. It would be better if she told him about the baby than say she was not interested in dating him, right? The guy deserved the truth.

"Am I that bad?" he asked her when he did not get a reply.

"What?" Realising what he meant, she clarified, "It's not that. You're a really attractive man."

He grinned. "Good to know, but?"

"I-I..."

"I don't want to be just another attractive guy or doctor to you."

"I'm pregnant!" she blurted out.

Oh, boy.

Did that come out right? She did not mean to say it so bluntly. Her eyes must have been asking the same too because he started to laugh.

"You should see your face right now," he said.

"Sorry, it's just..."

"I know."

"What?"

"I'm a doctor, remember? I knew the first time we met. It would be an insult to my profession if I didn't," he said light-heartedly. "Besides, you make it easy for people to detect, or maybe it's just me. I always find myself staring at you."

"Staring?"

"I don't mean that in a creepy way, believe me. I'm attracted to you. Sorry if it's a little too obvious. It's insane, I know. All this time, I knew you're pregnant, but I still feel the same way."

"You do?" she asked silently.

"Was that the only reason you've been avoiding me? Because you're pregnant?"

No, Ally thought. She did not see him the way he wanted. Deceiving both of them would be unfair. She was not yet over a certain man.

"If it is—"

"It's not," she interjected.

He nodded slowly. Was he accepting the fact that she was not interested?

"The baby's dad?"

"Y-yes."

"Is he still in the picture?" he asked, searching her eyes.

She shook her head.

"Then, go out with me. Forget that I've been trying to ask you out for now."

Her words got stuck in her throat. *How can she ignore that?*

He quickly added before she could react. "Just dinner. No pressure, I promise. 'Cos I have a feeling it might be the only thing I'm getting. Well, that's of course if you say yes."

It *was* the only thing he would get *if* she said yes. What was the harm in one dinner, though? So she agreed, only to feel uncomfortable and guilty when a grin appeared on his face.

Seeing him out the door, her eyes widened. She saw Liliana on her driveway, slowly approaching where she stood.

"Your guest?" Mike asked, looking surprised.

"Yes."

She could not imagine what Mike must have been thinking. The classy lady and her shining, black luxury car and well-suited chauffer sure seemed out of place. She would have to ask Liliana to tone it down a bit. Catching everyone's attention was the one thing she did not need right now. Thank goodness it was a Sunday and she did not have to work.

What was the woman doing here? She told her all she knew about her son. Did she think she knew more? Sure, she and Xander had a lot of intimate moments, but they were mostly apart for weeks on end. She did not even invest that much into knowing him more, blinded by her feelings for him.

All her questioning only made her realise that their relationship had been riddled with gaping holes from the very beginning.

"Ally…" Liliana greeted her with a bright smile.

"Liliana!" She greeted back.

Weird. She did not know how to introduce the two people standing with her to each other.

Hey, Mike, meet my baby's grandma. Liliana. Here's Mike, my boss I just agreed to go on a date with.

That would be awkward.

Thankfully, she did not have to do anything. Both just exchanged some sort of acknowledgement, and Mike left.

She led Liliana in, the woman's constant smile unnerving her.

***

Maybe it was the cheap wine Ally offered that had Liliana's expensive bum in a mess. All she heard the woman talk about was her son.

"Alexander this... Alexander that... I wish Alexander were… If only I had made a different decision, Alexander would..."

She was close to telling her to find Xander and explain to him all she was telling her. If only it would not sound so rude.

"Why tell me this?"

"I can't exactly approach his flings and tell them who I was. But you"—she looked straight into her eyes—"you're different."

But I was just a fling too, she wanted to say.

"How would you know? Was it because I lasted longer with him?" She snapped. Not that it mattered now. She ended up as one of his women in the end.

"I don't know what happened between you two but—"

"That's right. You don't!" she shouted.

Seconds later, she almost bit the tip of her tongue, realising what she had done. She did not mean that. She was embarrassed to meet Liliana's eyes. Instead, she reached for the jar of sweet and sour candies in front of her, popping three pieces into her mouth and chewing on them to distract herself.

"Ally…" Liliana softly spoke.

Ally was forced to face her.

"I'm grateful you've invited me into your home. You owe me nothing. I honestly don't know why I'm here either. I constantly had my son checked on. I wanted to be a part of his life, and it's the only way I knew how. I was not about to rely on what the papers gave me. In the pictures I got, he appeared truly happy when he's with you. His smile felt sincere. I would like to believe so. I feel like you're the only chance I got to reconnect with my son."

"I'm sorry. That just came flying out. I didn't mean to snap. I just get cranky most times." She rubbed her tummy unconsciously. "Though I try not to take it out on people, talking about Xander is not something I can handle yet."

She kept on talking, but when she looked at Liliana, she realised she had not been listening at all. She was looking around as if she was searching for something. She watched Liliana's eyes flutter from the glass of orange juice on the coffee table and the jar of water beside it. She then fixed her gaze on the jar of candies.

"Do you want some?" she asked hesitantly, unsure of what's running through the lady's mind. She could not have guessed the truth, could she?

"Sweet and sour candies. Not particularly a weird preference, but I craved some of those when I was with Alexander." Liliana looked down at her stomach. "You're pregnant, aren't you?"

Ally was surprised. She was not even showing yet. She knew this woman for how many minutes?

"You know…" she heard Liliana say. Of course, she knew. She was the pregnant one. Then Liliana gasped. "Does he know?"

It was far more complicated than that. If she explained, it was not like she would walk out the door and go talk to her son about it. Mother and son had not been in touch for years.

"He—"

The loud banging on her door stopped her. She sure was more popular with visitors recently. She frowned as she went to get the door.

She opened the door to find a man with dark, cropped hair and molten, dark eyes boring into her. He cocked his head to one side. She was not sure what he was thinking about. Who was he?

"Where's she?" he asked in a rich tone of pure male sexiness, his voice as sinful as the body it came from.

No way. She could not... This was the first man every part of her body agreed was attractive since Xander.

"Theo?" Liliana's voice cut in as she came into view behind them. "What are you doing here?"

"What are *you* doing here?" the man asked, his gaze directed at Liliana.

"Do you want to come in?" Ally was forced to ask. She did not like the little reunion on her doorstep. Her question made him look back at her, and he was searching her face.

"Who are you?" he asked, looking back at her.

How rude! He was in her home. "Who are *you*?" She threw his question right back at him.

"He's my son," Liliana's voice cut in.

CHAPTER 14

"Now, who's she?" the idiot asked again with folded arms, staring with dark eyes on her face. He was assessing her, and he was making it so obvious.

Did arrogance run in Xander's family? The gorgeous one standing on her doorstep certainly had that in his genes. Perhaps, he was thinking his looks or whatever else he had going on for him allows him to ask all the questions in her house.

"Theo, I thought you were on a business trip?"

He should be thankful Liliana was quick to show up before she threw him out; she certainly meant to do that.

"I am," he answered, taking his eyes off her.

There was a pause before Liliana spoke again, narrowing her eyes at his supposed son, "Were you following me?"

Reluctantly, he took his eyes away from Liliana, casting them to the ground. She could not help but check out his features, wanting to see what he might have in similarity to Xander.

"Ally…"

Nothing. She searched so hard, but there was absolutely nothing. When she eventually heard her name being called, she almost flushed red with embarrassment.

"Are you okay, Ally?" Liliana asked.

"Hmm? Yes! Yes, I'm fine."

"Ally…" She heard the man beside her testing out her name, but there was no way she was looking at him again. She was yet to recover from her earlier embarrassment. Instead, she faced Liliana.

"Do you want to take this inside?"

"I think we'll just go somewhere else instead of troubling you with our—"

"We might as well have our talk here. Obviously, whatever you're about to tell me involves her, and she seems important to you to have had this hidden from me."

She knew he was looking at her, but she was not falling for the bait. She was going to avoid looking at him for as long as she needed to.

Liliana heaved a sigh. "I was not hiding anything. She's Alexander's girlfriend."

"Ex-girlfriend." She was quick to correct it.

He stepped in, and she closed the door behind him. She was interested to know what was to be said. Obviously, Theo knew he had a brother, but she was sure Xander had no idea that he did. Then, on the other hand, maybe he did know but never told her about it. She couldn't help but keep on finding holes in what they called a relationship.

Theo looked somewhat older than Xander; more muscular and taller. That could not be the case, though—unless Liliana had a son before Xander.

"Ally?" Liliana called again.

When she heard her name, she looked at Liliana who seemed concerned. Were they saying something?

"Is she always this way? Always zoning out?" Theo said.

She put herself together and sat down, facing both.

"So, you're Alexander's woman?" Theo added.

"I'm nobody's woman."

He smirked. "Don't worry about the details. The papers do that well enough for you. I wondered at first, but you actually look better in person."

Was that supposed to be a compliment? It sounded like an insult to her, coming from him. Must've been from that ridiculous smirk on his face. Ally opened her mouth to voice out a comeback, but she found herself speechless. She closed her mouth and turned to face Liliana, silently asking help.

"Theo, you've come to speak to me. Leave Ally alone," Liliana said softly.

Good thing she picked up on that.

"You should have told me." Just like that, he put on a more serious face, facing Liliana.

"I did not know what to expect. Besides, you're rather busy with the company."

"Father's death does not mean I get to ignore your life. I thought we were in this together?"

In that exchange, Ally saw the deep understanding they had for each other. She sat back and just listened.

"Do you know what you had me thinking? I thought it was someone else."

"A man?"

He shook his head. "I honestly did not want to think that far, but you had me so close to thinking that."

Liliana smiled. "Is that why you had me followed?"

"I could not guess what you were thinking. I had an idea it had something to do with Alexander but never imagined you with her. I just knew you had something to hide." Liliana rested her palm on his hand. "You did not tell me she was important to you. I would have helped."

"I'm sorry."

"What do you intend to do now?"

They could have taken this outside if they were going to be this way. They were at her place. Why were they ignoring her? Theo had insinuated it had something to do with her somehow, and she wanted to know what. Ally faced them again and listened in to their conversation.

"I'm not sure. He was in town. I almost ran into him but..." Liliana sighed. "I'm glad I didn't. That—" Liliana jerked her head towards her direction.

Oh, now, she remembers I'm here? She commented on her head.

"Alexander's father was here, right? Why? What did he say to you?" Liliana asked as a concerned look mixed with something Ally could not recognise clouded her face.

Should she tell them the reason for Mr. Cross' visit? She looked between the two people seated in her house, and her gut told her it was okay. She could not explain it, but she wanted to trust Liliana at least. Besides, she had already told Laurie about it. What was the point in trying to keep it from them? They looked anti-Xander's dad anyway.

She told them all about the man's unexpected appearance in her home, his threats, and his demands of her to take the money he offered and stay away from his son.

"He's such a bastard." Liliana seethed in anger.

"So you took the cheque from him?" Theo blurted out.

That felt like an accusation. She faced him and frowned in reply. "What was I supposed to do? With the look he had on his face, I knew he was not going to back off. It's not like I wanted his money, nor do I have any intention of spending it."

"Don't you have a family?"

"That's none of your business."

"Well..." Liliana interrupted in a high-pitched tone. "Theo, what do you think?"

"That just means I have to get to work." He stood up, and Liliana followed him.

"What do you mean? Do you have a plan?" she asked behind him.

"I've always had a plan. That's why you should have come to me the moment you decided to meet her."

"Then, you'll need all the information I have."

"I doubt there's anything you know that I don't already," Theo said, but Liliana just shrugged before excusing herself to get something in the car.

"Excuse me, but would you stop referring to me like I'm beneath you?" Ally said the minute they were left alone.

He smirked. "Wouldn't you like that? No worries. I like it when my woman is on top."

Surprised at how twisted he turned her words, she shot back. "I wouldn't dream of it."

"Coming from the woman who's obviously been drooling over me since I came in sight."

Unbelievable! This man was even more arrogant than Xander. She did not think it was possible before.

Any more of this one, and I might actually... Actually what, Ally?

She was kidding herself. He wore arrogance well. She was just irritated at herself, trying to understand why in hell she found the guy attractive.

"So far, my only thoughts of you is that you're rude. If you're expecting me to fuel your grandiose sense of self, find some other woman, *Theodore*." She scoffed inwardly, seeing the blank look on his face. Perhaps he was not a fan of his full name. She gave him a serving of the smirk he kept dishing to her earlier.

He smiled. "It's Theopolis. I find nothing wrong in what you just called me, though. I'm Greek, sweetheart." He finished with a smirk.

Ugh! Talk about having the last smirk.

***

The call he just received from Paul could not possibly infuriate him any further than he already was.

Only it did. Finding out that his father has been relentlessly blocking his every attempt to investigate was more than enough to send him into another fit of anger. He should fire his team, but he trusted Paul. He was losing it each day though, getting all the same news every day.

He has had enough already. He would get his answers directly from his father.

Xander did not want to deal with his father until he had the facts, but the man was leaving him no choice but to open his dirty closet. His father made a mistake by involving himself in his relationship.

His father never liked Ally. To him, she was just another distraction for his son. The truth was, he never once thought of Ally as a distraction.

He messed up, and sorting it out was taking longer than it should. Maybe he should have tried harder. Maybe he was just scared to face her—and what facing her might mean for him.

But he missed her terribly. He was an arrogant, selfish, and thoughtless fool who had made this mess for himself. He ached for every part of her. He needed to have her beside him and know she was near and not hating him.

"Your father's here." Julia interrupted his thoughts.

He nodded, dismissing her. Packing what little evidence he has gathered so far, he put all other things on the back of his mind—including Julia's quietness the past few days which was so unlike her.

He walked towards his father's office and thought of asking why he had gone MIA for days. There was no business overseas to take care off, and it made him suspicious. He did not trust the man. He never did. He had just been overeager to accept a parent that wanted him and the package that came along with it. He had been resentful of his mother, and over the years, he never really connected with his father either.

Not bothering to reply to his father's secretary, he barged into his office.

"I see your senses aren't the only thing you're losing these days. Where have your manners gone?"

"Where is my mother?"

He waited, studying his father's reaction to get something from it, but he barely twitched a muscle.

Instead, he looked down at the papers on his table and casually spoke. "You hate her," he said it like there was nothing to discuss further.

"No, don't start with that crap. I'm done being fed of your lies. You made me hate her. This horrible story you have going on about how she left you— and *me* for a richer man."

"I *made* you hate her?" He laughed. "That was all you. Whatever I told you is the truth, not that I needed to make you believe it."

He dropped the envelope he had in his hand on the desk with a thud.

His father stared at it. "What's this?" he asked, turning to him.

"Why don't you check it out, Dad? I'm sure it isn't anything you don't already know about." He was turning impatient to hear his father start talking, but he was taking his time searching through the contents. Then he watched him drop them like it meant nothing to him.

"The moment you went to visit that old man, I should have known you would do this."

"My grandfather? Were you... are you having me followed?"

"If you have nothing else to say, leave my office."

"You're the one who needs to say something to me."

"Would any of it matter to you now?"

"Your past means little to me. It's finding my mother and the woman I love that matters. I won't make the mistakes you made." Xander banged his fist on the table. "Stay out of my business."

His father let out a laugh. "Love? They both left you, and I can tell you they're quite happy with a life without you."

"No. *I* left them." He started hating his mother and let her go when he could have believed his grandpa. He let himself drown on his father's lies and what his own paranoid mind had created, and his lack of trust sent Ally away. No, they did not leave him. He made them leave.

"Your mother is happily married to a rich man. She's where she's always wanted, and she's even got a replacement for you!" he said with so much venom.

"Maybe. If that's true, you're just angry she was able to achieve all that without you despite all your efforts to ruin her. I'm sure you're burning in frustration."

His father shook his head. "You'll understand me soon. You can never trust women. It's how this starts. I paid her off, and she was quite eager to take that choice."

He froze at his father's words. "You bastard," he said slowly and angrily. "Where's she? Where's Ally? I swear if you touch—"

"Did you hear me? I paid her off!"

"I don't believe you. She'll never take your money. I know her. I trust her."

Again, his father laughed at him. "You look pathetic right now. Just like your mother."

"Do you ever regret what happened to your wife and kid?"

His question shocked his father into silence.

"Right here." He searched for a paper amidst the ones on the table and raised it to his father's face. "It says right here that the 'accident' might not have been an accident. Did you do that?" He watched as his father's face contorted into different expressions before finally settling on anger.

"Whatever you think of me, I cared about them."

"I doubt you know what that means. I'm warning you. Stay away from them, and get your men the hell away from my search. It won't be just one son you'll lose, but two."

With that, Xander walked away from his office. He must have looked a sight to the employees who came his way. With the raised voices they might have overheard from earlier, it was a matter of time before the gossip started to spread.

He did not bother going to his office or calling Paul. He walked to his car with a burning determination and drove as fast as he could. A lot of horns and curses were the last things he could be bothered with.

He had arrived. He sighed, killing the engine and looking at Laurie's front door. He got out and banged on the door.

"What the hell!" He heard from the other side.

"You?" Laurie said with disdain when she opened the door. "What the hell are you doing on my property? I'm giving you—"

"I know you know where she is."

That shut her up.

"Tell me, and I'll be out of here."

"I'm expecting some—"

"Please. Tell me."

"Tell you and what? You go running off on your high horse and cause more damage?"

He barged into her apartment, taking a look around as if he would find what he was searching for if he looked closely.

"What do you think you're doing?" She closed the door behind her and faced him. "Get out, or I'll call the cops."

He ignored her and fished out his phone. He called Paul and started giving him instructions on focusing the search solely on Ally—this time, with no excuses. He was sure his father would heed his warning. His father will not be faltered by any threats, but Xander knew his father needed his heir more, and that was one thing even Cameron Cross could not force his son to be if he pushes his buttons any more than he had.

After ending the call, he faced Laurie again. "I'll find her eventually, but you can make it sooner by telling me where she is."

"I don't know where."

"I don't believe you. There's no way you haven't been in contact."

She folded her arms, staring straight at him. "I Don't Know Where She Is," she exclaimed, making sure to emphasize every word.

Though she tried to look strong, he noticed her defensiveness and was more certain than ever that she was hiding something.

CHAPTER 15

Back at the salon, Ally was going to lose it. She's been receiving a disconcerting look from that woman for the past hour. She could understand that the brunette was jealous, thinking she was going to steal 'her' man. Truly, it was understandable, but she has had enough of her spiteful looks and snappy comments.

"Ignore her." Helen, her tall, dark-skinned boss with a fierce attitude, stopped her from reacting. "She's been after the doc the minute he arrived in this town. It's no secret to anyone. Getting all the attention she's always wanted from the doc? Girl, I'd say she thinks she has the right to hate you."

I haven't even gone on that date I promised him, Ally thought to herself. What would she do then if she knew about that?

"Well, she can have him. I don't want him, and I really do not like the way she's talking to me."

The gossips started when she was new in town, and the confrontation with the stuck-up brunette at the salon only made it worse. She was most likely the originator of the rumours, at least that was what the women at the salon said. And to think she was successfully keeping her pregnancy a secret? Oh, the pandemonium that would arise when people finally knew.

"The hot doc is interested in you. That's something everyone in town with a damn good pair of eyes can see."

"But I'm not," she said loudly and looked up to see the witch watching her. She sighed and walked away from Helen, wanting to escape her laser-like stare.

She went into another room to find something else to pass the time since she was free of customers at the moment. Sorting out hair products that were already sorted seemed a better idea than being out there.

"I think you're more suited for Michael. Tiffany has always been a..."

She looked up to see Mel, a part-time employee at the salon who was born and bred in this town. She looked young, probably her age or younger, but she rarely spoke to her. She was a pretty girl if you looked closely. She had black eyes and a pert nose but had full pink lips which Ally was almost certain was bare of added colour. She had a surprisingly fair skin compared to the tan and dark skin so common in the town. If only Mel dared to do something to her hair and stopped putting it in a tight ponytail all the time, she would definitely be one of the sought-after women in this town.

"She's just not as beautiful as you are. She's never nice."

"Uh... Thanks."

Mel managed a smile. "Are you American?"

Surprised at the question, she realised what Mel was trying to ask. "Yeah, born and bred." She wanted to be more specific and say New York, but she was not ready to give any hints about herself. "My dad was Brazilian, though."

"Was?"

"Yeah. He passed away."

"Sorry."

"It's fine."

After a few seconds of awkward silence, Mel engaged herself in something else, and she did the same. Barely two minutes later, Mel spoke again.

"That explains your looks, I think. Do you speak the language?"

Ally smiled. "Not really. I can only manage a few words and sentences in Portugese, but I understand fairly well."

Someone called Mel's name. A new customer had just arrived. For a Monday evening, there was quite a good flow of customers.

"Sorry about your dad," Mel muttered before she left.

She was, too.

Maybe if she had her dad here, he would have put Xander straight like he did every guy in her previous relationships—and she would not even be in this town.

The chatter from the other room came to a halt as though everyone in it went mute. Ally moved her legs to check what was going on, but before she could take a step into the room, the murmurs started. She eventually realised what was going on and looked in the direction all the women had their heads turned to.

The black car certainly grabbed attention, but it was very obvious it was the man standing beside it that got their fancy. Muffled whispers errupted from the crowd when he started to walk towards Helen's salon.

So much for keeping a low profile.

What great luck would she have if he was actually here for someone else! But she had none of that, it seemed, as he came in and stood right in the room staring at her.

All heads turned to her, and she caught Helen's curious look before she turned to Theo's direction. Having no choice, she moved towards him. He could have at least dressed formally like he always did.

Instead, he had to choose casual today in a pair of slacks and an open shirt revealing his neck and a glimpse of his taut chest.

Talk about something else for the ladies to gossip about.

She wrapped her hand on his forearm, and he went along, allowing himself to be pulled outside. Good for her because there was no way she could have dragged such a well-built person by the arm.

"How come you don't own a mobile phone at this age?"

She had a good reason for that.

"What are you doing here?"

"I wouldn't be here if I could talk to you on the phone. It was useless calling your place knowing you would be here."

She tried controlling her breathing. She could not lash out. She knew better than to start an argument, knowing well enough that they were being watched.

"Quit trying to look like you're not angry. It doesn't suit you."

"What are you doing here, Theo?" she asked again.

The week after he first appeared on her doorstep, she had seen him around, constantly pestering her. However, the week after that, he never showed up again. She thought she would not have to see him again, and had not even bothered to ask Liliana about him. It has always been on the tip of her tongue, though.

"Apart from seeing where you work?" he replied, taking a look inside the salon again.

"Are you serious? I can't have people talking about me. They'll think you're another man trying to get my attention." She had enough gossip about Mike.

"Am I?" He smirked and moved closer, making her move back. A few more steps and she almost tripped, landing in his arms. "Careful. You wouldn't want to give them the idea that you are falling for me… or in this case, because of me."

His face was too close to hers, blowing warm breaths that caressed her face. Instantly being aware of the muscles holding her, she let herself out of his grasp. "Stop doing that."

"What?"

"You know what." She gritted through clenched teeth, taking her eyes away and dusting off the non-existent dirt on her dress.

He folded his arms and watched her. "You're attracted to me, and it bothers you. For some reason, you can't accept it. Probably because of Alexander?"

She looked up sharply at him, shooting him a frown, but he only had a smile on his face. A smile, not a smirk, and it unsettled her even more. There was no way she was admitting anything to him when she was not ready to admit the situation to herself. Before she could say anything, he spoke up.

"I'll be going to New York tomorrow. Is there someone you would like to get in contact with?"

"It's really none of your business. He might be your brother but—"

"I was talking about your cousin... or your mother." He lightly shrugged with a suddenly expressionless face.

Liliana must have said something about Laurie and her mother to him. "Uhm... Well, I do have something to give Laurie if you don't mind."

"I asked, didn't I?" Before she could say anything else, he added. "I'll be at your place tonight to get it." With that said, he got in his car, and it dramatically drove off the same way he had arrived.

It was a good thing she would not be working at the hospital that night. She was considering Liliana's advice about quitting her night job especially because she was getting some help from the older woman. She had subtly tried telling her to stop coming around too much, but she was not sure how subtle she could sound and not come off rude or unappreciative. Liliana's presence made her uncomfortable. She was acting more and more like a mother-in-law, a word she knew she should not be thinking about. That could never happen. So she had resorted to distancing herself and thought of Liliana only as her baby's grandma.

Besides, how do you stop a woman who is determined to experience her grandchild's existence at the next doctor's appointment?

She sighed and braced herself for whatever was to happen as she walked into the salon. As soon as she dared to put her face up, several eyes hungry for information met hers.

***

Ally was wondering why she gave Theo that answer earlier today. After all, she could speak to Laurie over the phone. Feeling quite unsure as she scribbled her message down on a piece of paper, she soon threw that thought out when she imagined Laurie's face reading the address on it.

A chuckle came out from her. "Oh, I miss you, Laurie," he said out loud before carefully picking up another paper and thinking for a while.

She had decided to write her mother a letter. This one was necessary. She would much rather do it on paper than on the phone.

She thought of how worried she might be. Her mother was probably wondering why she decided to keep her in the dark. She explained everything in the letter—a decision that was not easy to make. So what if her mother gets disappointed? Perhaps, she would say, 'I told you so.' What if she had followed her warnings from the start?

A lot of what-ifs ran through her mind as she wrote her heart out, on the verge of tears, but she could not guess what her mom's reaction to it would be.

***

When Ally heard a knock on her door at around eight-thirty that night, she knew who it would be.

It was him, alright, but she could not understand his sudden change of attitude. He refused to come in and told her to just go and get what needed to be delivered. She but had to ask him. "Is everything okay?"

"Do you think it's a good idea I come in? If you believe nothing will happen, then I will."

She was not expecting that reply and could not come up with one either. It was not like she had any intention of jumping him—but what if he did? What would she do then?

"I am attracted to you, but I'm not going to make a move on you knowing you have a past with my brother. There's still unfinished business between you two. That will be like piercing my mother's heart."

If only you knew you, Liliana, and the baby are evidence of his presence in my life.

"Besides, how do I call him brother if I refer to you as my woman?"

She looked at him wide-eyed and agreed with him.

Come on Ally, think straight. This guy was thinking too far ahead of himself. She should not be thinking about this. She could lie and say Theo reminded her of Xander, but they looked nothing alike. This might just be her body's reaction. He was Xander's brother after all.

What she was feeling with Theo around was absolutely incomparable to what she felt for Xander. Even now, she still found herself thinking about him; she was still vulnerable to him.

"New York will tell if I get to invite myself in without your permission." She heard him say.

She looked at him, unable to unravel the meaning behind those words. And he left, leaving Ally watching his back for a while.

"But I'm pregnant with his baby. You don't know that, do you?" she said softly into the night.

***

For the past week, Julia has been hearing about the fight Xander and his father had weeks ago circulating in the office. Rumour has it that the feud was making the son quit the family business. She would have believed it if he did not show up for work. Since he returned yesterday after a three day's leave, he has been neck-deep in work and was seeing an international businessman who's supposed to come in later in the day. The meeting, if it turned out well, was going to be huge for Xander, and she was doing all she could to make that happen for him.

She knew Xander and how he thought—at least she still knew his mind as a businessman. The fact was she hardly knew what was going on with him anymore. Sometimes, she wondered what she was still holding on to. It felt like the Xander she once knew did not exist anymore, and it was not difficult to guess why—Alicia Storm. It hurt to know he saw something in that petite girl that he never found in her, and it hurt more than anything because she had feelings for him she never had for any man before.

"My father's still not in his office?"

"No."

Like his son, Mr Cross had been away from the office for three days straight now. She remembered how five days ago, she had gathered the courage to face the man. He was the only person she could turn to if ever Xander finds out what she had been keeping from him. It seemed like a good idea to come clean to him at first, but if she told him she threw away his mother's letters, she was not sure how he would react—especially now that he was searching for her.

Xander hated his mother then, and at that time, she thought she was doing the right thing by him. Thinking clearly now, her decision had been the worst. It seemed like she made a lot of those whenever he was concerned.

She thought that getting an ally in the form of Xander's father will help her find a way back in his arms, but the cold-hearted man was quick to let her know that she was no better than a lay for his son.

"What time does this guy arrive?" Xander referred to the papers in his hand.

"In a few hours. Why don't I get you something to eat? I'm sure coffee is the only thing you've had all day."

He ignored her comment. "I don't see the file from the last business deal we made in Hong Kong here. Are you sure he was the one?"

She rose from her seat to stand beside him, bending to sort out the pile of documents in front of him.

***

Xander expected her to go back to her seat after she had pointed out what he needed to see, but then he felt her hands on his shoulders. He certainly needed a break from the pile of stress mounting on him, but she was the last person he wanted any sort of contact from. As he was about to voice out his disapproval, someone came in.

He felt Julia's hands slide away from his shoulders as the three gave each other brief assessments.

"Excuse me, who are you?" Julia asked politely.

"I would have introduced myself if someone had been outside expecting me. I'm Theo Christakos."

"We were expecting you in a few hours."

"I suppose," Theo said.

He finally saw the man in person. Xander knew who he was and his strength in business but had never crossed path with him in whatsoever way.

Julia walked professionally to Theo's side with a charming smile, directing the man towards him. They exchanged a firm handshake, and Julia excused herself when she was told to leave.

He looked at the man in front of him. Though Theo's interest in partnering with him had been sudden, he tried to figure out the guy. He was one of the few businessmen in the world with a name worth more billions than his father's. He was curious though as to why Theo Christakos chose his company. Men usually sought out Christakos for a business deal, not the other way around. He knew that because he almost fell into that category once before backing out at the insistence of his father.

***

After about forty-five minutes of talking business and trying to establish expectations for a possible collaboration, Theo suddenly asked an unrelated question.

"Are you married, Alexander?"

He looked at him, trying to see if it was a genuine question. "Call me Xander. No. Are you, Theo? I can call you Theo, right?"

"Of course. I'm not married. Then I would assume the woman beside you earlier—"

"She's just my assistant." Xander cut him off before he could finish his sentence. He got the feeling that he wouldn't like the guy. He proposed this meeting, and he came to him; so why was he all over his personal life like it was his business?

"I just like to know who I'm dealing with."

Who was he kidding? He knew Theopolis Christakos probably ran a background check on him—or maybe he left out the personal aspects of his life like he requested Julia do.

"We're not dealing with anything yet," Xander replied.

"Yes, of course, but wouldn't you agree that knowing you personally can help me make a decision about you professionally? You are a businessman; you know what I mean."

"My personal life would not be a good beases for your decisions."

Theo nodded slowly with a smile. "Call it coincidence, but this deal is similar to my... an acquaintance of mine."

He tried and managed to hide his frown. Theopolis Christakos was coming off strange to him. After all the information he had on file about the man, it felt like he was missing a vital piece. The man did not sound like expected.

"I can't get involved with her because of some issues she had with the man she dated before. If I did, it would turn out messy. Not just for me, but for her. I know that of course, but the idea of pursuing her is still tempting."

Who the hell told that kind of story during a first meeting? He did not even know the guy at all, but he did try to understand what he was getting at. He tried to relate Theo's story to their business, and he understood Theo was probably a man who did not like sticky situations. He did not want that either, but what was the need for the metaphor when he can come out with it straight?

"I assume your father will be involved?" Theo asked after some time.

"No."

Theo raised an eyebrow, but he had no intention of elaborating on his reply. Now he was more certain Theo knew more about him and his company.

"Fathers…" Theo murmured.

He was aware that Theo's father recently passed. It was news considering their status in the business world. He did not know the man but felt it was polite to give his sympathy. "Sorry about your father."

"He was a man who spent his years well with little regrets. I have my mother, though. She's lost a child before, but I'm sure she believes in getting back that piece of love soon."

Again with that kind of talk. He was told that this man was a stone-faced, hard, and unemotional man when it comes business deals, but he was not seeing any of that. "Sorry about that." He was not sure why he was saying sorry. It was all about politeness for him.

"Oh, he's not dead. Just... distant," Theo replied, staring right through him. "Sometimes, it takes a while to know that what you've been searching for is right in front of you."

He did not like the uneasy feeling he was getting from this man. Could he be interested in something *beyond* business? It could not possibly be that, he thought. His mobile phone rang. Seeing who the caller was, he excused himself. "Hello, Grandpa. Is something wrong?"

"Alexander, your grandmother just called me. Your mother contacted her."

"What did she say?"

"She did not elaborate. All she told me was that your mother is doing everything she can to get back here."

"Here. You mean..."

"Probably the same thing I'm thinking Xander. I wanted to let you know just in case you can do something to help her."

"I understand." He looked towards Theo who was patiently sitting and waiting for him. "I have to go now, Grandpa. I'll give you a call later."

Just as soon as he ended the call, his phone rang again. It was Paul calling.

"We found her, boss."

"*Her?*" He was not sure who he wanted to face right now, but the words Paul spoke gave him great relief. Was it his mother or Ally?

"Ally. We found her."

He held his breath as his heart thumped wildly. He gave him instructions and to meet him downstairs. He then promptly gave his apologies to Theo, and they both walked out of the office and into the elevator, ignoring Julia's questions. Not wanting to lose the deal, he discussed with him an alternative schedule if Theo was still interested.

"I wouldn't want to miss out on a possible great partnership." He assured him.

As they came out of the elevator, Xander turned to face him. "Just like you said, my personal life could, after all, help you make your professional decision. This is important to me."

"Family?"

"You could say that." It was definitely about family.

"I could work with a man who puts his family above work," Theo said, and both men shook hands.

Paul came around and opened the door for him.

"You never know, we might see each other sooner than expected," Theo said.

Firing up the engine, Paul questioned him withouting turning to face him. "Boss, do you know that man well enough?"

"Today was our first meeting. Why do you ask?"

"That's strange."

"What is?" He asked from the back seat.

"That man was in that woman's house yesterday evening and this morning."

"What woman?"

"Ally's cousin, the one you have us checking up on: Laurie."

"What?"

"I'm sure it was him."

"Could he just be one of her lovers?" he muttered with scrunched eyebrows.

"That was what I thought and did not report it to you. It might not just be a coincidence," Paul replied.

And to think he thought Theopolis Christakos preferred men, one possible conclusion from the way he had been looking at him back in his office.

Inside, he doubted the idea of Theo being Laurie's lover. It was just too much of a coincidence. Theopolis Christakos shows up personally with a business deal they never got around discussing and instead made strange references to a woman, his father, mother, and a lost brother. He laughed at himself. He was thinking way beyond the line. There was no way Christakos could be that knowledgeable about his personal life and know about his long lost mother. Besides, Theo's story was not exactly the perfect fit for his life.

"Boss, did you hear me?"

"What?"

"There was no abortion record about her in the hospitals you asked me to check up on."

He sighed. He tried to think positively about it every single moment since he received that letter. He firmly believed Ally would never have the abortion no matter how upset she might have been. But then he would ask himself if his foolishness had not driven her over the edge. He had put her through a lot.

He would know soon. In a few hours, he would have his answer. Theopolis Christakos was another matter to be dealt with later on.

CHAPTER 16

"Katie! Enough right there. Get back to work."

She was standing in the corner of the shop where she could not be easily spotted, spying on her aunt who was obviously not in the best of moods. Even the cheery girl scampered away with a sullen look at the tone her aunt used.

"What the hell, Ally. See what you're about to make me face?" she whispered silently to herself.

She already knew what her aunt would want to talk about: Ally and her situation. When she found out that Ally had sent a letter to her mom, explaining everything in it, she grew mad at her. She has been pushing Ally to tell her mom from the start, but she never listened, and now that she finally did, it had to be on paper. She could not imagine the shock and anger her aunt must have been feeling to know what her daughter had gone through without her knowledge.

Laurie had a sharp tongue, but today would not be a good time to use it. Before long, she was spotted by her aunt's light blue eyes. It was almost like she had been expecting her to show up. She had no choice but to approach her.

"Aunt Carla..."

She received no form of greeting in return. Instead, her aunt instructed her workers to get back to work and entered a small room she used as an office. She followed, gently closing the door behind her and timidly turned to face her aunt.

"Why didn't you say something to me?" Aunt Carla finally said with a sigh.

She wanted to reply, but the defeated look on the woman's face shut her up. That was so unlike her aunt. Aunt Carla was just like her sister—her mom, from whom she definitely inherited her sharp tongue. Ally got her soft spoken attitude from her father.

"I would have expected a hint from you—*anything*." She looked up at her. "Even when you tried not to out her out completely, you always gave me a sign to let me know I was missing something."

"I'm sorry. Are you angry?" Of course, she was. She rephrased it. "Are you *really,really* angry at Ally and me?"

"I'm so angry right now, it feels like I might die from it. I'm angry at myself, Laurie. Can't you see? I pushed my daughter away. I said nasty things that made her run from me."

She wanted to console her aunt. It was not her fault. But, nasty things? Her aunt must have sensed her silent question. Her aunt sighed again. She was sure doing a lot of that.

"She never mentioned it to you?" She rubbed her forehead with one hand. "I kept saying to her how she would regret being with that boy."

She would laugh if the situation were different. Alexander Cross was far from a boy, but with his foolish actions, he might as well be one.

"I practically told her she would come back to me broken and I'd say I told you so. I guess when that happened, she just did not need more of me rubbing it in her face. It was no secret I hated their relationship."

Yes, that was something neither her nor Ally could figure out why.

"Oh, no." Her aunt sounded like she just figured something out.

"What?"

She stood abruptly and made way as Carla paced the small room. "The last time she was home..." She had her fingers in her lips and froze for a moment as if confirming something in her thoughts. "She must have been pregnant then. She looked so fragile, and she ate a lot. She was pregnant, and I failed to see it as I stupidly ranted on about him!"

Even I would think twice about telling you, Laurie thought but held her tongue. That was Ally, alright. If it had been her, she would have shut her mom up and make her listen to what she had to say.

"You have to tell me where she is, Laurie."

Laurie looked back at her aunt's expectant eyes. "I really don't know, Aunt Carla. She wouldn't even tell me. All she says when I ask is she's fine and would be home soon."

"Well, that's no good. I want to see her, and damn it, Laurie, if you know and you're not telling—"

"I swear, I don't," she said with a straight face while crossing her fingers behind her, silently asking for her forgiveness.

"If I have to call your mother to make her ask—"

She raised her hands. "Really, Aunt Carla, if you're bringing Mom into this, you should know there's no reason for me to lie." The last thing she wanted right now was her mom using the situation to spend a few weeks with her.

"If only she had not promised in that letter to forgive me if I don't meet up with that boy…" Ally knew what her mom was capable of doing. She would have gone and raised hell on Xander. "Tell me you at least gave him shit when you found out what he did to my baby."

"Oh, I gave him shit alright. Lots of it that he fears my presence now." That was not entirely accurate, but whatever to ease her aunt's mind at the moment.

"Oh, he'll have one more to fear. He'll regret the day he messed with my family."

Prepare yourself, Alexander Cross. She snickered in her head.

***

Laurie breathed in some fresh air as soon as she was out of the shop. There was hardly anything she could have said to make the situation any easier on her aunt, but after making a reluctant promise to contact her whenever she heard from Ally, Laurie was a free woman, for now.

She dared to lie even when she had been threatened of her mother's involvement because she knew she was going to be out of the state by tomorrow. If her mom did come hounding at her doorstep, she knew she would be a long call away, expressing her regret at being away for business—which by the way, wouldn't be a regret for her in the least. There were only a few people she just could not handle, and her mother was on the top list. She loved her mother, but she was so frustrating most of the time.

As she threw on her shades to protect her eyes from the blinding sunlight, she thought of things to buy before travelling to see her cousin and godchild with a bright smile on her face. And at that moment, she remembered what that cousin had just put her through and fished out her phone from her bag. She checked the time on her wrist. Ally must be home right now.

She started to walk and spoke immediately as she picked up.

"Do you know how pissed I am at you right now?"

"Sorry?" Ally asked with uncertainty.

"Sorry? I assume you know why you should apologise more convincingly?"

"And I assume you're about to tell me why?"

"Come on, Ally. Your mom was heartbroken, and I should tell you she blames herself for everything." There was silence at the other end. "I'm not telling you so you can start to over think things."

"No. Liliana's with me right now."

"Oh." *The woman seemed to be everywhere*, Laurie thought.

"Yeah, but not here in the room with me."

She could hear the change of mood in Ally's voice and wanted to distract her from it. They could talk about the depressing things when she was with her. That was tomorrow, anyway.

"So I saw the yummy hunk you sent for me. Thank you so much by the way for making me hot and bothered throughout the night," she said teasingly.

Ally chuckled. "What? Theo?"

"Yeah, he told me what his full name was but Theo stuck. Though yummy, he was one arrogant piece of an ass."

"I said that too. But I didn't say an arrogant piece of... you know, put it the way you have. He's so much like his brother."

"He has a brother? Well, well… maybe that one will suit me better." She heard Ally cough at the other end. "Are you okay?"

"Yeah, fine. Just…" Ally trailed off, obviously trying to get her voice back.

"Taxi!" She hailed a cab and gave the driver her destination, frowning into the phone as she continued to talk. "Are you okay?" asked again.

"Yeah, it's just that... He's Xander's brother."

"What? That *asshol*e? They're brothers?"

"Yes."

"In what way? Those two look nothing alike. Well, except for their horrifying asshole trait."

"Laurie..."

"Yes. You admitted to it just now. Are you sure?"

"That they're brothers? Well yes, they share a mom. I think that tells it."

"Haha, smarty. Well, the guy at my doorstep yesterday looked older than your Xander. He may be adopted or something unless you're saying she had a son before Xander. Or maybe he's just one of those guys who look more mature than their age."

They continued their conversation for a while until the taxi stopped. After paying the driver, she got down and promised Ally to have every conversation possible when they see each other the next day.

"Do you need me to bring anything along?"

"No."

"Okay then, bye."

"Bye."

She cut the call and stepped into Xander's office building. There was something she needed to do before she went shopping. Meeting the receptionist at the front desk, she came out disappointed. Xander was out for the day.

***

Ally wanted to correct Laurie when she said 'your Xander.' It might just have slipped out. She did not think Laurie was a fan of Xander at the moment and would have any reason to refer to him as that.

She thought back to what Laurie had said. Maybe those two were not blood-related? She never thought of it that way. Well, she could ask Liliana who was presently in her kitchen.

The woman could not stop cooking all she could when she fleetingly mentioned she felt like having a homemade meal while in her room, searching for what to wear to her 'date' tonight.

At first she thought of wearing something less flattering so as not to seem like she was encouraging Mike for something that will never happen. However, Liliana suggested she dress up a little to not crush the man's ego any more than it might be. Somehow, Liliana had gotten her to confess about her date tonight and all about Mike. Surprisingly, she was not judgemental and even gave her some pretty good advice. She was glad Liliana was around today. On the other hand, it could just be because of the great mood Liliana seemed to be in. Her smiles and enthusiasm would have been infectious if it were not so confusing.

Her phone rang, and she expected it to be Laurie again since it was just her and Liliana who had her new number.

"Hello, beautiful."

She paused as she let the tingle that travelled through her body at the sound of Theo's voice settle down.

"Hi." Her voice came out softer that she wanted. He was not even supposed to have this number.

"Surprised? There's nothing else to do here except work. Maybe in another circumstance, I would have found myself company, but that's just not working out my way."

Company? Did he mean a woman? Why was he telling her? She turned her weight on the bed, unsure why his words got her on edge. He was not hers, and she was not his. Why did his words make her want to tell him not to do it?

This was crazy. She knew the guy like thirty seconds ago, and he was Xander's brother. It did not even feel appropriate, but her head and senses always said otherwise.This could easily get out of her control, and it felt like it was already.

"Company?" She faked ignorance.

"I know you understand what I mean." She picked up the breath Theo let out. "I know I promised not to pressure you until the situation here helps me decide, but tell me I'm not crazy for thinking this isn't just with me."

You're not crazy, she wanted to say but could not. She knew nothing about him except the obvious she found out in the past weeks. Admitting whatever it is she felt would be like getting with Xander all over again.

"This is crazy."

"It is."

"We spoke like five times when you were around."

"We did? And here I was, thinking we spoke six times."

Was he making a joke out of this? She did not find it funny. The fact that she might just be attracted to Xander's brother was not funny to her at all—especially since she was pregnant.

"What are you doing now?" he asked.

She was grateful that he was not forcing it. She had to somehow figure out this complex feeling she was ignoring. "Your mom's here."

"I know. She said something about seeing you today. What about you? Obviously, she isn't beside you right now."

"I'm trying to pick a dress," she said without thinking.

"What's the occasion?"

She went mute, unconsciously biting her lower lip. "I… I have a date."

"Date?"

"Hmmm, hmmm."

"With who?"

"Someone you don't know."

It was silent until she heard him ask, "Is it serious?"

"What? No! This is just a one-time thing. I told him that, and he knows it. So this is just like a friendly date." She rushed out the words, trying to let him get the picture of the situation.

"A date is a date, at least in the view of a man who wants you. He likes you, right?"

"Uhm... Well, that... We talked about that."

"You're so naïve."

"Excuse me?"

"Do you even know this guy?"

Who was he to tell her what to do or not? "Well, yes. He's my doctor."

"Your doctor?"

Ally groaned in her head. She definitely was saying too much in the heat of the moment. She did not want him to find out that she was pregnant, and she knew what the reason was, of course. She knew at the back of her mind that Theopolis Christakos might stop being attracted to her. But was it not a good thing if he lost interest in her?

"Why would you need a doctor in that small place you just moved to? Are you sick?"

No, just pregnant. "I'm not sick. I'm a woman."

"You're going out on a *friendly* date with a man who has access to touch any part of your body?"

"He does not have access to anything! How did you get this number, anyway?" She desperately needed a change of topic.

He let it go though his voice sounded like he was still angry about it. "Well, you do own a real phone! Mom gave it to me, told her you would want me to have it as you gave me some errands to run for you and you would want the feedback."

"So you lied your way into getting my number out of her?"

"That's how you see it. And don't you want feedback?"

"I already got one."

"From that cousin of yours, I suppose?"

"Laurie."

"Good, then." He did not seem to care. "Do you also know who else I saw?"

"I'm sure it's no one that has anything to do with me."

"At least I knew one more thing about you. You love hiding from your problems. It was easy to guess on our first meeting, but the way your acting now just made it conclusive."

"It's not—"

"I have to go. Enjoy your date." He hung up before she could get another word in.

What was he so mad about, anyway? They were not together. They were not friends, and were only acquainted for a week or so.

She huffed out and heard a knock on her door. Liliana poked her head into view and asked if she has decided on something to wear. With Laurie and Theo's call, she had not come around to look for it.

Anyway, she already knew she had nothing suitable. She had not packed any evening dresses when she left New York because she never imagined she would be in this situation. Liliana stepped inside and insisted on helping.

At least someone was eager about tonight for her.

***

"Is there something else you need, sir?"

"I'll call when I need something."

Xander barely gave the hostess a look. He did not have to do so to know she was disappointed with his answer. After his messy breakup with Barbara and before he met Ally, most, if not all, flight attendants on his company private plane offered themselves willingly, and he took some of the offers without hesitation. They were there to ensure his comfort, anyway. He did not see the trouble in it since the hookups were just on the plane.

It had not been a difficult arrangement since he made sure those women were delivered expensive gifts after their *engagement*. Two of them even made it clear they were good with just the sex and wanted no gifts, but he was not a fool to fall for that. He was smart enough to know what to avoid. They wanted more of him which would have eventually made them clingy.

Paul was seated two seats away from him, looking professional as always, but there was no point in asking questions now. He was tired, anxious, and gravely needed some sleep. The past few days had required his all: he had spent two days away from work with his grandfather and the last few days working at the office, trying to catch up on what he had left behind. His father's sudden disappearance did not help him either. Yesterday, he had finally sat together with his grandmother and they had talked.

His grandmother made things easier for him to understand, telling him all she knew regarding his mother's absence—actually, disappearance was a more accurate word. Each side blamed themselves for the misunderstanding, but Xander knew his grandmother only tried to help take the guilt off him.

It did not matter. He had already accepted his mistakes. They talked for a while, apologising to each other for the time lost. Then his grandmother asked if he did not want to find his mother immediately, but he told her there was something important he needed to sort out first.

Sure, hearing all those stories about his mother made him want to find her more, but that would have to wait for now. He had something more urgent to attend to: Ally.

Perhaps, she needed him more.

He wanted to tell them about Ally, but there was no time. His grandmother already had a good guess of what it was all about, though.

***

Stress caught up with him, and Xander had dozed off before he knew it. But he only felt more like a wreck when Paul woke him up to prepare for landing. A car was awaiting their arrival, and Paul got the door for him. He took the backseat, and his trusted employee took the front.

There was no way he could be this nervous, but he was. He had not prepared a speech or something to help him manage the confrontation, something he wished he did, but it had to be done. The car drove up to a house, an abode much too small to be comfortable in, he thought.

Ally could not be living this way all this time. Xander could not believe his eyes.

He wanted to confirm if they were in the right house, but he hesitated, knowing his employees were waiting for him to take the next step.

He took a deep breath in, trying to steel his resolve to do what he was there for. But before he could summon up the courage, he saw a familiar figure coming out the door.

He would recognise her anywhere, despite her obvious weightloss and sullen skin. The shiny vehicle caught her eyes, and he watched her tilt her head in curiosity. He eventually made up his feeble mind to get off the car and saw her facial expression change, morphing into anger and disgust.

"What the hell are you doing here?" she shouted with an agitated voice.

"Ally—"

"You have no right to be here. This is my life now. You made your choice, Xander. Go back to it."

"You're my choice. I see that now, and I'm so sorry for abandoning you and our baby. I love you."

She laughed at him, mockingly and bitterly. "*Our* baby? *Love*? You shut me out when I said those words. Those were the things you lost along with me."

He looked down at her midriff. There seemed to be no sign of life in there. It was too flat. Maybe she was not showing yet. Maybe it was all a hoax.

"I made the decision you obviously wanted me to make. I had the abortion."

"No. That's not possible. You wouldn't…" He looked at her belly again as if it would suddenly grow. "No. No…" he repeatedly muttered as he staggered back. He was not sure what was happening, but he felt everything shaking around him.

It was not supposed to be this way.

"Boss!" Paul's voice called out to him, and he was shaken into reality.

He looked up at his head of security who was looking at him with a slightly confused face. He composed himself and sat upright. It was just a dream, and he was still on the plane; he must have fallen asleep in the midst of all his thoughts. Paul informed him that they were arriving at their destination in a few minutes. He readied himself and made sure this time, everything was for real.

He could not help but look out the window and think of it all—of something, in particular, he had said in his dream.

I love you.

Those words also came out on their own when he confronted his father. He had tried pushing it back for the longest time.

Did he even know what that meant? Was he sure? He once said that to a woman before—to Barbara, but what he had felt for her was too different to what he felt now. Then again, it was not a matter of knowing or being sure for himself but being able to convince someone else that his feelings ran that deep.

He ran his fingers through his hair and gave the stubble on his face a light scratch, hoping as hell that things were not as bad as his dream.

***

It was eight p.m. already, hours after trying to find a dress and speaking to Theo. She was not able to ask Liliana if Theo was blood-related after all with the woman fussing around her.

Ally was in her room, looking at herself in the small mirror, thinking that her outfit was over the top. She had been doing so for a good few minutes. She was not sure where Mike was taking her, but she was sure there couldn't be a place around town sophisticated enough to match her dressing, but she could be wrong.

She should not have let Liliana take control. She was given the dress after she admitted she had nothing in her closet that could do the night some justice.

Liliana's enthusiasm had been suspicious at first, but she thought less of it when the older woman admitted that something wonderful had happened to her that day. What that was, she never said.

Liliana just could not stop the smile from showing, and she was happy for her. The woman was passing on the emotion to her a little too strongly. The gorgeous black dress was a strong evidence.

"Raul will drop you there, and you can have the night to yourself," Liliana said as she entered her room with a big grin.

"Is there something you aren't telling me?"

"No, darling."

"You know what Mike's planning, don't you?"

"What? Of course not," she quickly said and left her room, but within seconds, she turned back. "You look beautiful, but you're running late." And she disappeared again.

How can that be not suspicious? She's rooting for another man in my life.

Then again, maybe it was just her. She could be thinking too much. Ally grabbed the last thing she needed—her purse—and was out the door and in the car as fast as Liliana could make her.

She said a quick hello to Liliana's driver who was an older man.

"Hello," he replied in a thick accent.

An hour ago, Mike called and apologised for not being able to pick her up and sent a cab instead. She would have been perfectly comfortable in it, but Liliana had other plans and called Raul. Whatever all this fuss was about, she would know in a few minutes.

When the car stopped, Raul informed her they had reached the place and that he would only leave when she was received as ordered by Liliana. She looked out the window, but she did not see anything that looked like a restaurant.

"Miss Ally?"

She looked at him, slightly embarrassed. "Oh, thank you, Raul."

She got down and cautiously walked through the only walk path she saw, looking around for any sign of Mike. The place looked like an old garden of some sort, and she could not help but think it would have been a spectacular beauty once. She saw bright lights illuminating a corner, and quickened her steps, turning towards the spot.

When it came into view, a gasp left her as she took in the sightbefore her. She immediately understood why he had not come in person to pick her up. There was no way he could have managed it all on his own. Maybe this was what Liliana had been hiding.

The garden looked like something conjured from a perfect romantic movie—with a table for two in the middle, candlelight, flowers, and food. She even spotted a familiar box of candies carefully placed on the side. She let out a small laugh at his thoughtfulness. A pregnant woman can be unpredictable when it comes to her appetite, and those goodies calmed down her insides really well. Mike was the only one who knew that and Liliana, of course.

She heard footsteps from behind her.

"Mike! This is beautiful. How did you—" The words died in her mouth, shock and anger contorting her face. "What are you doing here?"

"Ally…" Xander breathed out.

That was the only word that drifted through the silent night from the last man she expected to see.

CHAPTER 17

Her name was all he could utter as he stared at her that cold, silent night.

Out of the many things he wanted to say, that was all he could get out. Xander felt relief wash through his bones, overwhelming him. He was grateful she looked nothing like what his dream had made up.

The one thing Alexander Cross wanted at the moment was to hold the woman in front of him in his arms so tight never to let her go—never let her get hurt and never give her a reason to stay away from him.

"Ally..." Too bad that was the only thing he could manage to get out of his lips when he wanted to say so much more.

He badly needed assurance that she was okay. She appeared to be doing well. Maybe she was better off without him.

Had she thought about him like he had in the last two months? Did she have sleepless nights like he had? Had she considered coming back? Would she consider forgiving him if he came crawling and bleeding, begging for a second chance?

His thoughts rooted him to the spot, but they immediately evaporated when he saw her turning the other way around, walking away.

Not again, he thought.

"Ally, please. I just want to talk."

He heard her scoff. There was no attempt to slow down or stop on her part.

"I know you hate that I'm here, but if you would just calm down and listen..." His words fell on deaf ears.

He caught up to her and held her arm, halting her steps, but she refused to look at him still. She tried to jerk her hand away, struggling with her breathing—something he realised was a little too fast and deep.

Oh, no. That tool of a guy warned him about this.

Turning towards the garden, he curled his arms on her back, supporting her. This time, she made no objections, probably having no strength for that. All the way back, he supported her weight with his as he led her by the arm.

She was still trying to catch up her breath as he sat her down on one of the two chairs and crouched right in front of her.

For a long moment, he said nothing to her. He was afraid to touch her in fear that he would only worsen the situation. He wanted to give her comfort and not the opposite.

She took one long breath, finally steadying her breathing, and for the first time, he let himself look at the part of her body he had once refused to acknowledge.

"What are you doing?" she asked.

He slowly took his gaze away from her abdomen to her eyes. Though the lighting was dim, she looked radiant, shining beautifully as the candlelights captured her face. "I..."

She subtly wrapped her hands around her stomach as if to protect their child from him. It was not so obvious in the body-hugging black gown she wore, but it was there—a tiny bulge. He would not even know it was there if he didn't look close enough.

She was breathtaking as always as she sat on that chair a little crouched. Her face was as flawless as it ever was. Her golden brown eyes that hid behind her dark lashes looked away, but her tempting red lips only lured him in.

She went to tuck a strand of hair behind her ear, and he wanted to do that for her. She looked as beautiful as he remembered, and he felt jealousy stir up inside him, knowing she made that much effort for another man.

"How do you feel now?"

"Better. Enough to be out of here." Just then, she attempted to stand.

He stopped her.

"What do you think you're doing?" Ally asked.

"Making you listen."

She scoffed at him again, this time, staring at him with brown, irritated eyes.

"Oh, I was not aware all it takes is brute force. I should have hired some since I was not capable of that."

Xander understood where she was coming from. He had not given her a chance to explain then, so why should she do the same?

"I know you hate my guts right now. You're pissed I'm here, and you probably wish I never appeared in front of you again."

"Spot on, Cross." She was using his surname; she must be terribly pissed. If it were under different circumstances, he probably would have smiled at that.

"I need you to hear me out."

He was not sure where her strength came from, but she sprung up from where she was seated.

"I've had enough of this. I'm not sure what you're on, Alexander Cross, to think you have any right to be here and demand things of me."

"I'm not demanding—"

"And did you say hear you out? You absolutely have no right to say those words to me," she snapped. So much for trying hard to look composed. She was angry, and he could see that.

She was about to say something else, but she held back, walking away once more.

"Where are you going?" He matched her pace, trailing one step behind her.

"It's none of your business."

"It's late. At least let me drop you off."

She stopped and turned to face him. "Look around. This is a small town. I'll be perfectly okay walking back to my house. And stop talking like what I do is still your concern. You should remember that we're over."

That left him speechless.

He looked at her and saw no hint of softness in her eyes. She meant her words. Though difficult to accept, she was the same woman who had her acting crazy months ago. He knew he was to blame for the situation.

She thought her words finally sank in and turned on her heels. But he was not letting this opportunity slip by.

"I know you're still pregnant with my child," he said in a quiet voice enough for her to hear through the rustling of the leaves.

She turned to him, and he could not tell if it was anger, fear, or sadness that crept in on her face. Perhaps, it was all of it.

"I know you never had the abortion. You must have written that to make me stay away—to hurt me like I did to you."

She lunged towards him, pounding her balled fists into his chest as if her punches will make him feel all the pain he has been putting her through. "You don't get to spout nonsense to me! You hear me, Alexander Cross? Not now, not ever again!"

He tried holding her hands but was unsuccessful. He avoided trying to be forceful so as not to hurt her.

She eventually stopped and faced him sternly. "I'm sure you got the wrong woman claiming to be carrying your child. She isn't me. Go back to your mistress. Maybe you'll find what you're looking for there."

"I know you saw me that day, but I did not sleep with her."

She could only laugh—a very fake one, mocking him.

"Julia isn't my mistress. I told you that."

"You're one arrogant bastard to have the guts to say all that to my face," she said with disgust. "You did not sleep with her? So your bare ass and her raised skirt were just you two trading bottoms?"

"I…. I couldn't do it. I DID NOT DO IT." He emphasized his last sentence, hoping to make her understand.

"So you're saying nothing happened?"

Something did happen that day, but he would be stupid to admit that at this moment.

His hesitation must have answered her question. "Like I said, go back to your mistress. Oh, wait! That was exactly what I was to you too, anyway."

"It wasn't like that with you, you know that."

"Do I?" She moved closer, never losing eye contact. "Then tell me exactly what I was to you."

He was not going to back down from that challenge.

"I'm not sure if what I'll say will give you more reasons to hate me but, Ally, you are the first in a damn long time to make me want something permanent with a woman. It might sound rehearsed… but shit, I've been thinking of what to say to you over and over in my head."

Caught off guard, she just stood there, moving her head a little in denial.

"That first night I saw you, I wanted you immediately. Though I tried to convince myself of the contrary, it was not just your body I was attracted to. I was confused. I just could not place why… why I could not get you off my mind and what was so different about you. I would have known if all I wanted was to spend a few nights in bed with you. Without my consent, I started having selfish thoughts—to have you just to myself and keep you. It was crazy that I had such thoughts the moment I laid my eyes on you. I wanted to keep you."

She looked like she did not believe a word of what he just said.

"You were the only woman I was crazy about, the only one who gave me a new perspective on things. You meant more to me than I gave away, and that scared me deep down even when I couldn't fully admit that to myself. I have been such an ass to you. I knew you loved me, but I let my arrogance feed on my past experiences and made a fool of myself."

He paused when she finally looked away from him and took a seat on a bench not far from them. Xander went to stand but crouched in front of her instead, realising he would rather have her see what he was feeling.

If this woman still loved him, she would realise that every word from his mouth was true— unless she could not forgive his mistakes. Not that he was expecting smooth sailing when he came here, but he at least expected to see some sort of reaction from the woman who once loved him.

He hoped to see some sort of reaction from a woman who maybe, somehow after all his mistakes, still loved him.

"I screwed things up for us. I was a coward, and I should have dealt with my issues without shutting you out completely. When I read your words about the abortion"—he saw her eyes finally resting on his—"it scared me out of my wits. I was going to be that parent I've always detested all my life; a father who really did not care about his kid and like a mother who abandoned her responsibilities."

Did she get it?

"I did not want to be that parent. I don't. And that opened my eyes to a lot of things." He shook his head in thought. "You won't believe how much it changed me. I realised I wanted it all. All of it... I still do."

There were a lot of things he wanted to do right now: hold her, assure her, convince her, and tell her he loved her, but he knew it would be inappropriate and foolish to say that to her now.

"Keep me?" That was the first thing she muttered as she shook her head lightly. "I'm glad you did a lot of soul-searching while I was away, and I did too. It's great you know what you want now, but you're mistaken if you came here expecting your words to dull my senses. I stopped wishing for your understanding when you referred to me as the worst of all the women in your life, a bitch who was intent on trapping you from the start. Hearing you referring to this innocent baby as a mess in your life hurt like hell, Xander."

He sighed. He remembered his words all too clearly and wished for a miracle that she did not. "Ally—"

"And you know what? I stopped giving a shit about you when I saw you having sex with your ex in your office."

"I wasn't... I did not—"

"How confident could you get? Door's open… doing your act for anyone to see."

"I didn't mean—"

"It meant you did not care. You did not give a damn!"

"Ally, please—"

"You know what? Maybe you were right. Maybe we were never suited for each other. I was not your type of woman, and I was too ignorant to care then. Me being pregnant showed a side of you that I would never date—a man I would never want to be with." She sighed, not meeting his eyes. "It doesn't matter to me if you stay here or wherever else you go. Just stay away. That shouldn't be hard for you."

What could he say to that?

"Please, I want to leave here," she said through the heavy silence.

"I'll take you."

It was late and the night had gone a lot darker, so she did not object.

Xander expected her to ask how he found her, but not one question was asked. Both of them preferred the tense silence that hung in the air as they walked to the car and drove to her apartment.

Though they were both seated at the back, the wide space between them was a clear indication of how far apart they were for two people who were once intimately close.

"Just so you know, you gave up your rights to this child when you left me to make the decision on what to do with it. We have nothing in common except for our past, and you should respect that."

She opened the door, but before she could get out, he spoke as firmly as she had, "I'm not giving up on both of you."

She did not face him and got out.

He watched her get inside the house and waited for a few minutes before giving Paul the confirmation to drive them to the hotel.

***

Paul wanted to say something, but whatever it was could wait. Paul knew him well enough to not ask questions when he was in that state. He let him be as he found his way to the room he had booked earlier.

Xander, tired and defeated, decided to take a shower though he knew no amount of water could wash away his regrets and fears.

Thanks to Paul, he found out a lot of things about her life during the past few months. He knew where she worked, who she talked to, where she lived, and the guy she was apparently dating. The events earlier that day kept replaying in his head, keeping him longer in the shower.

He had a distressing encounter with an eager brunette that afternoon. She was willing to give him information, claiming Ally had forced herself on her boyfriend, a local doctor by the name of Mike.

Of course, he did not believe her lies. Even Paul saw through them. But he did draw something from her claims: there must be something going on between this Mike guy and Ally. His jealousy would not let him settle his thoughts. He wondered what kind of guy Mike was, what he looked like, and if Ally was truly interested in him.

He was a doctor, after all. He must be a good catch for that brunette to be all over the place accusing her, definitely some guy if Ally let him anywhere near her.

Xander was restless.

He had all intentions to approach him like a gentleman, but seeing the guy interact with different people for a few minutes made it known to him that he was a people person. He obviously had some sort of charm, seeing how the ladies reacted when he approached or talked to them. His features were a great plus too.

So what if he looked like he had it all? This guy could not have it all. He could not have Ally if he could help it.

Agitated by his thoughts, he found himself going straight to the point, and the men finally came face to face.

"Excuse me. Mike?"

"Yes? What can I do for you?"

"Alicia Storm works for you?"

Mike looked at him skeptically until there was a glint in his eyes. "Who's asking?"

"Obviously, I am."

He smiled. "So? What's it to you?"

"Important. Very important, that's what it is to me."

They stared each other down.

"You want to answer the question now?"

"I think I have an idea what this is about. Let's take it somewhere private."

He looked around and noticed a few stares directed at them.

Mike led him to his office. It was so small compared to his best friend's back in New York.

"She did work here, but she cut back on that since she had the salon."

Xander knew about her working there, and it made him wonder. Perhaps she was so short on finances that she had to take on two jobs.

"You didn't know that."

"I do actually." Only a few hours ago, he thought.

"Then you're not here because of her?"

"Why else would I be here?"

"To check out the guy who you probably want to have it out with?"

"Are you dating her?"

Mike chuckled. "How well do you know her?"

"Excuse me?"

"I'm not sure if it's because she's not attracted to me or if she's just been too hurt to get herself involved with anyone again. It could be both." Mike shrugged, fixing his eyes on him. So Ally had refused to go out with him. "Now I'm just her doctor."

Doctor? Does that mean?

"She's pregnant?" he swallowed his ego and asked.

"You're the baby's father, right?"

"I am," he proudly replied.

He had quite a long talk with Mike, asking about Ally's health, the baby's, and everything associated with the pregnancy.

Though the guy barely gave him details, he thought Mike seemed to be a decent guy, sincerely thanking him after. At least he could give the guy that.

On his way out, the doctor called him back. "And hey." Xander turned to him. "You might want to take my place tonight."

He explained everything about the friendly date Ally and him were supposed to have, and got a frown out of Xander. Mike seemed amused and had the guts to tell him he was only helping because he obviously looked desperate and she needed the closure.

Closure? No one was giving anyone that.

He exited the hospital and boarded his car once more but not before being warned about Ally's hyperventilation—something that happens whenever she's anxious.

He seemed like a cool guy, someone he would probably befriend in some other life. If only Mike weren't attracted to the only woman he wanted.

And that was how he took Mike's place.

It was not a surprise that he was the last person she wanted to see, but he was not staying away, neither was he giving up. He just had to find a way to make her know that.

Feeling the torrent of water raining down his body one last time, he turned the shower off and finally stepped out of the bath, hoping there was not another man in her life who could make his plans go south.

CHAPTER 18

Ally was moody, hungry, and angry, and she was blaming it all on hormones.

Don't pregnant women conveniently use that excuse? And maybe rightly so. Or maybe it was the fact that she had woken up four times through the night with thoughts she just could not shake off.

Why the hell did he have to show up now? She was so close to forgetting him, so close to forgetting why she even moved places.

She was on that path, and she believed she could do it. But now he was here, saying words she would have jumped into his arms for not so long ago.

She flung back the cover and dragged her tired self into the bathroom to try to look less like she was feeling. There were lots she would have to face today: the salon with the many customers coming in and Liliana, who had texted her late last night about going to check up on her after work and asking her about the last night's date.

She still found the woman's interest weird. She could have sworn Liliana was hoping she got back with her son and especially when she found out about the baby.

What was she to say to her now? How could she tell her that Xander was in town? She would probably be the reason those two finally meet if they both hovered around her so much.

She already has a lot on her plate. And not to forget her crazy cousin who was due in town today and the man who proclaimed he was not giving up on her. She was here to breathe a little, right? God forbid her mother adds to the equation and show up too.

Shake that off, Ally, she warned herself. *You don't want to attract your thoughts to your doorstep, right?*

Done brushing her teeth, she looked in the mirror and wondered if she should do something to her hair—not that she ever really gave much effort to it before. She had tried a number of times and given up. Once, she straightened it, and it took less than two hours for it to start returning to its original state.

Her father had seen her struggle with it and told her the way it was made her look beautiful and that it was part of what made her Ally. She smiled at the memory. Of course, she suspected that her father only said that because she was his daughter. It was what fathers were supposed to say. So it meant so much more to her when Xander confessed to loving her hair and always wanting it free.

It would be nice to pull it in a ponytail or a messy knot once in a while, though.

One would not believe her hair woes considering how good she was with fixing other women's hair. She just never got around to take her time with it and eventually stopped bothering.

But he loves my hair just the way it is.

She shook her head, opening her mouth and making funny sounds as if that would help ward off her thoughts. That was not her common sense talking. It could not be. It was the ignorant side of her. Common sense dictates she should be sensible enough to forget about Xander.

"Think straight, Ally," she told the image staring back at her through the mirror. She took off her oversized T-shirt and went into the shower.

After a quick wash, she still felt more tired than she expected. It was tempting to ask for a day off. She would have to call in sick, though, since they were unaware of her pregnancy or at least she hoped they were.

Naked, she looked at her baby bump in front of the mirror before she heard knocks on her door.

She took a clean oversized white tee with 'SUNSHINE' written on it and put it on, ignoring the fact that she didn't have a bra. Since last week, her breasts were finding underwears a bit itchy. She took her panties and black shorts and put those on too before seeing to who was at her door, shouting for the persistent person's patience.

Unbelievable, she thought, looking at who stood in front of her.

"Surprise!" With a charming smile, she raised her bags with both hands. It would have been infectious, but she was not feeling up to it at the moment.

One moment, she would act like a mother, and another moment, she's just a sophisticated, high-class woman, a fine lady someone like Ally could not possibly be seen with. But right now, she looked like a giddy best friend who's got time for gossip, a trait she saw more often with Liliana nowadays.

"Liliana."

"You must be hungry." She let herself in.

She let Raul in, who carried Liliana's purse and a shopping bag. Liliana did not go shopping this early in the morning, did she? She was about to thank him for last night when the ball of morning enthusiasm that is Liliana cut in. She was finding it hard to believe she was a mother of two twenty-something-year-old men, or maybe just one; she had not gotten around asking about that. She should.

"I had this dream last night that you would need me to prepare you some breakfast and pamper you."

"You did, didn't you?" she asked sarcastically.

"Thank you, Raul. You can be on your way."

Raul dropped the purse and bag on the sofa, and after she thanked him, he curtly let himself out, leaving her to face the woman who was acting weird. Well, weirder than usual.

"You aren't going to work today," she said, walking towards the kitchen with the bags in tow.

"I'm not?" She followed after Liliana. "I still have groceries left, you know?"

Liliana turned to look at her. "You don't look like you have any intention to anyway. Come on. Go sit and watch TV. Relax. I'll feed both of you."

She was still deciding on that since her shift was in the afternoon. She stood still for a while, watching Liliana unload the ingredients in the bag, trying to see if she could guess what was going on. She got nothing.

"What's in the bag?" She referred to the one on the sofa, pointing to it.

"Why don't you see for yourself? It's for you."

She did and was surprised at what she saw. She did not expect Liliana to get something like this for her.

"You like them? You mentioned once that they were the only things you felt comfortable sleeping in. I've only seen you in one of them." Liliana raised her voice a bit from the kitchen so she could hear.

"Two, actually, but thanks."

She looked at the oversized tee-shirts. They were six in total. She could imagine Liliana's face as she picked them out, having fun with the words printed on them. She raised one of them up, amused at the prints. One has 'I'm Sexy and You know It' printed across it with a winking eyed and long, thick lashes.

"Really?" she asked, looking at where Liliana was keeping herself busy.

"Yes, really. It's a small store and one of the few good ones. Besides, you're beautiful—an attractive pregnant woman, and it should be noticed."

But she did not want to be noticed. That was better kept to herself. She did not want to have to explain anything to Liliana this morning.

"That's because I'm not the size of a whale yet."

"Even when you get to be, I'm certain you'll still have that glow. When I was pregnant with Alexander, I was a mess. My skin was all blotchy, and I was crying over things that weren't even sad."

She laughed. "That's hard to believe."

"Why?"

"Because you look great. Perfect, in fact."

"Well, it was a different situation at the time."

The mood shifted a bit, and she was sure Liliana remembered something sad. What must have happened to her during that time?

"Thanks for these." She raised the bag. "And I'm so hungry."

"Right on it. And don't forget to call in sick."

Ally smiled. Maybe she needed that after all.

"See? I'm a psychic. You do need me this morning after all."

***

After a satisfying meal of crunchy pumpkin spice parfait coupled with some muffins and orange juice, Ally let out a large burp.

"Excuse me. Sorry."

Liliana laughed. "I'm glad my grandchild agrees with it."

"Hmm." She rubbed her stomach.

"What do you think of crab salad sandwich? Though it depends on your seafood craving by lunch."

"You're making me lunch, too? How come you're so good at this? Where did you learn to cook?"

"Aegeus made me go for it. He insisted I had the qualities for it even when it was clear I was not a very good cook," she said with a smile.

"Aegeus?"

"Theo's father."

"Oh, right."

Before she could ask the question she wanted to, Liliana continued. "It was at a time I had a lot going on in my life. Apart from having Theo to take care of, I needed something else to focus on."

She watched Liliana gently sipping from her glass of juice.

"I never got to make my son a nice, hot meal, you know? I only learned how to cook a decent meal after I left him. I was not much of a mother to him."

"Why did you leave him?" That came out without any thought whatsoever. She was glad it did, though. Xander had always spoken with contempt about his mother, and she wanted to know Liliana's side of the story.

"You're a mother now. Would you not to do anything to protect your child?"

She could not answer that. It made her think of what she almost did. Was she any better?

"Even if that meant staying away?" Liliana added.

"I-I'm not sure."

"There are things much easier said than done." Liliana looked intently at her. "I know you don't like talking about my son or our relationship. I see your hesitation whenever I ask, but… does he hate me?"

"I-I wouldn't use that word. Xander rarely speaks of you. To be honest, he only talked about you to me once. I'm sure he just did not understand what you did and why, and that's what you should be explaining to him."

She contemplated on telling her how the date went—*who* turned up for the date. Should she let them meet? Was it in her place to do so?

"So? You haven't told me how your date went."

A slight ridge formed in the middle of Ally's brows. Was this woman truly a psychic?

Liliana smiled. "Why are you frowning? Do you find it weird to discuss such things with me?"

"Actually, what I find weird is you encouraging me."

"And why not?"

"Cause I believe some part of you still wants me to get back with your son."

"That so? Well, that would be a perfect picture, the father of your baby together with you, but I've once been in love and betrayed to know what you're feeling right now. Though he's my son, I can't force you to be with him if you don't love him anymore."

Was she still in love with Xander? She was not sure. She was hurt and angry, but it was undeniable that she still had strong feelings for him. She stopped being the Ally who was crazy in love with him, but she knew no matter how much her anger suppressed it, she still cared. She did, and she knew that was something that would not disappear in months.

Liliana said something about loving and betrayal. Could it be Mr. Cross? What had he done to her? What happened between them? Did she love Theo's father?

"Love can be tricky. What I thought I had with Cameron felt real. It felt like the best addition to my life. Even at the times when I think I knew what went wrong, I just don't see it. Was I too blinded by love? Was it there all along? Somewhere deep down, I knew, but I just did not care if I at least had him."

She was talking about Xander's father. He was the man she had been in love with and had betrayed her. She could relate with Liliana. It was almost like she was describing her relationship with Xander.

"It felt sincere, though. He made me happy, but now, here I am without it. In fact, it's the reason I'm here today." She finished with a sad smile.

What exactly was she doing with her own life? Ally wondered. Where did her plans before she met Xander go? Is this where she imagined being at the age of twenty-one? She was going to be twenty-two soon with no definite plan for her life.

How could she let herself drown for Xander—so much so that nothing else had seemed important?

Liliana sighed. "I think we had a lot of sour talk after a good meal. You should get some rest. What were you doing last night after the date? You still look tired. Did it go well or not? But don't worry, you can talk to me whenever. I won't push."

She was truly tired. "Thanks."

Ally walked into her room without another word, and just as her back hit the bed, she drifted to sleep.

***

She woke up to the smell of freshly baked cookies. She stretched out her limbs and saw that she had been out for hours.

Two twenty-three p.m., the wall clock said. It was well worth it, anyway. She felt a whole lot better, and the irresistible aroma got her grinning.

"Someone's hungry," she said more to her baby, rubbing her stomach. She went to the kitchen to catch Liliana all laid-back and singing. Ally smiled. "You don't have a bad voice."

"Ha! You're awake. Great. Just in time for some snacks. What do you think of these? Chocolate chip cookies."

"I think they look great. They're calling out to me."

"Then you should be nice and answer to them." Liliana put some on a plate for her.

"Thanks." She bit into one and commented on how good it was.

"You look relaxed now."

"I feel better. What have you been doing?"

"Cleaning, baking—"

"What?"

"Don't look horrified. I can do those things," Liliana said, looking amused.

"You did not hire any help? But..." She looked around her and saw the change in her dinky home.

"It was no big deal. It's a small task."

"You didn't have to."

"I wanted to. And..." She saw Liliana's hesitation but encouraged the older woman to go on. "If you don't mind, I would love to spend the night here."

"What?" But she was quick to add. "I don't, but is everything okay?"

There was a loud knock on the door.

"Hmm, I'll see who it is," she said, her words muffled by a large chunk of cookie she stuffed in her mouth.

She opened the door to see someone she expected much later in the day. She had not even gotten around to telling Liliana someone else was going to be spending the night.

"How's my favourite baby?" Laurie bent to give her stomach a rub.

"I'm up here." She pointed to her face.

Laurie looked at her with a serious face. "Oh, I literally meant the baby."

Ally frowned.

"What's got your panties in a twist? I would say get laid, but that's out of the question since you already made a nine-month situation of abstinence." Laurie smiled brightly and winked.

"Haha," she said swallowing the last bit of cookie.

“Come here,” Laurie said, and the cousins held each other in a tight embrace. “Thank God.” She heard her cousin’s muffled voice.

"And who's this beauty?" Liliana dropped in beside them.

"Wow," Laurie said as she stared at Liliana and then back to Ally. "You weren't kidding when you said she's really beautiful. More than I imagined, actually. I thought you were being nice with your words. Hate to say it, but I get where the dickhead got his looks from."

Liliana was too amazed to speak for a moment before a smile appeared on her face. Ally was shocked her cousin would say that about Xander in front of his mother.

"I would say any man who hurts this beautiful girl right here has a nut or two misplaced," Liliana said, smirking. The woman had no qualms with it, it seemed.

"I like you," Laurie told her.

"And I'm sure I wouldn't have a problem saying the same about you."

"Laurie, meet Liliana, Xander's mom. Liliana, Laurie, my cousin." She interrupted just to keep them from talking too much on a subject she would rather they not poke into.

"Sheesh cuz, invite the girl in, take her bag, show her to her room. Welcome her."

"Sheesh, give a girl a break. She's pregnant," Ally muttered.

Laurie raised her eyebrow at her.

"She's been in and out of that mood for a while now," Liliana commented.

What mood? Everything was good with me. They have to be exaggerating things.

"I understand that. But still, my godchild is strong. So move your lazy ass and don't blame it on the poor kid," Laurie said at her cousin's pouty face.

It was obvious that Liliana and Laurie would have no problem bonding, far from what she expected. She was irritated further when she heard Laurie say something about a girls' night. She groaned inwardly. That was not a day she signed for.

Maybe she really was having mood swings.

Ally expected one other person to appear, and she sure hoped that one would be telepathic enough to not show his face today. She was not sure she could handle it especially with Laurie around, and not to forget, Liliana.

"And oh, Ally, please call your mom soon so she'll stop threatening me with mine."

"Your mom's around?" She followed the women into the kitchen.

"No, and hopefully it stays that way," Laurie said, diving her hands into the cookies.

"Stay away from them!"

"Holy shit." Laurie stared at her cousin in shock. "Back off, bitchy Al. I didn't come all the way here to face this side of your pregnancy mood swings."

"They're *my* cookies."

"Says who? Last time I checked, you don't know how to bake."

"But they're for the baby." She gave her a sad look.

"Oh, nice one, Al, but I'm not buying it." Laurie put a hand behind her ear. "Hear that?"

"Hear what?" She frowned.

"The baby saying it's okay for the godmother to have some."

"Come on, ladies. There's more than enough." Liliana interjected.

"Yeah, don't be selfish, Ally. There's more than enough." Laurie smiled, biting into one.

She just smiled back before putting her tongue out at her cousin.

***

"You asked for me?" Julia asked as she stepped into Cameron Cross' office.

"I want you to tell me everything you know about my son, his mother, that girl he was sleeping with, and the business deal he's about to make without my consent."

Julia looked doubtful.Why did he want to know all this from her? She was sure he knew everything already. He was so demanding as if getting answers out of her was unquestionable. She had questions of her own; who was going to answer them?

"It will be wise for you to answer truthfully."

Left with no choice, she started telling him what she knew. There was no point lying to the man, anyway. Was there any reason to lie at this point?

To her, Cameron Cross was a scary man, and she was not prepared to be on his bad side.

She told him all she knew about Xander for the past few months, and the only thing he seemed quite surprised at were the letters she never delivered to him.

"Where are they?"

"I disposed of them."

"What was written in it?"

"I-I never opened them."

"That's a lie. You're the sort of woman who likes to own something over my son. You want him even if you have to get that by playing the you-know-him-best card—your idea of protectiveness.

"I love Xander," she boldly replied.

Cameron laughed at her. "You wouldn't know what that is, Julia."

"And you would?" Julia bit back without thinking. The intimidating man in front of her had no business mocking her feelings even if it involved his only son.

She should not have said that to him. She could not make that mistake again talking that way to her boss.

He smirked. "What was in the letters?"

"I honestly don't know. I only read one out of the three I received over the years."

"What did it say?"

"Just a message to Xander that she missed him and regretted how things turned out the way it did. She loved him even if he might hate her. She hoped he would let her explain someday when they met." She exhaled and saw a frown mar the man's face. "Yeah, the content said something around that," she added.

He sighed. "And the girl?"

"Alicia? After Xander had found out about her pregnancy, he ended their relationship."

She watched Cameron Cross go silent and looked like he was thinking hard about something.

"Stupid boy," Cameron muttered. He picked up his phone and talked to someone to get a plane and car ready. He stood up, packing some things. "And I hear the Christakos boy was here. Xander had a meeting with him?"

"Yes."

"His enemy walked right into his home with his consent."

"What does that mean?" she asked, curious.

"How does the stupid boy do business these days? His head is so screwed up, he could not even get more information about who he's dealing with?"

"I did that for him. Theopolis Christakos is one of the richest—"

"I know who he is. Your research must have stopped before you found out that they're step-brothers. What exactly does he pay you to do?"

"What?"

***

"That can't be right. Are you absolutely certain, Paul?"

"I confirmed from the neighbours. She's been visiting for weeks."

"How?"

Xander looked at the pictures again and saw the same person: his mother.

Was this right? The picture was taken this morning.

His mother knew Ally, and Ally knew who his mother was. He was sure his mother must know who Ally was to him. If not, what else could be their connection? Unless there was another good explanation for this.

This was an unexpected turn of events, and he was not sure how to approach it. He came here for Ally, hoping to face his mother later and now, the two people he had wronged most and was scared to face were in the same place.

He had wanted to give her space after last night and show up on her doorstep later in the evening, but this revelation stunned him. Right now, he did not know what to do.

Facing Ally now meant facing his mother, too. Ally hated him, and he was not sure what kind of resentment his mother had towards him.

Something was ringing somewhere, and he could not figure out what or where until Paul's voice interrupted.

"It's your assistant."

"Ignore it."

It stopped ringing, and a beep sounded.

He continued looking at the pictures and stood to pour himself a drink when Paul spoke again.

"She says it's urgent. It's about your father... that he knows."

What did that mean?

Raising the liquid to his mouth, he gulped the content and felt a slight sting in his throat. Just then, the phone started ringing again. He nodded at Paul, giving him permission to answer it and put it on speaker.

"Why didn't you—" Julia started.

"I don't have time for idle chats, Julia. Speak."

He heard a sigh. "Your father was really scary today. He asked me all sorts of questions about your life."

"Why is that new? He knows everything."

"I don't think he did. Well, I couldn't exactly lie since he threatened me. But since I don't know where you are, and you still refuse to tell me—"

"Julia." He was not in the mood to listen to her rambling.

"It didn't matter to him, anyway. It seemed like he figured out where you are."

"Good for him."

"Not good, Xander. At least for you."

"And what does that mean?"

"Xander?" she asked softly.

"What is it?" He really was not in the mood for this.

"Are you with your mother?"

"How? My father knows?" Now he was concerned.

"Your mother tried…. b-but I thought you hated her… so I t-trashed away all letters…"

Her words jumbled together, and he could not gather what she was trying to say. He looked up, and by the look on Paul's face, he knew he was not the only one in the room who had a problem making sense of Julia's words.

"What?"

"I'm sorry. You need to know."

"Slow down. I did not hear a word except for letters. What letters?"

"Of course, you didn't." She was silent for a moment before resuming in her usual tone. "It doesn't matter. Just take care of your business... and there's something else I think you should also know. Theopolis Christakos is your step-brother."

"Where is that coming from?"

"Your father. Your father told me."

CHAPTER 19

Ally could not deny that she had a great time yesterday with Liliana and Laurie. It had been a great way to de-stress herself. Once, during the night, she even wondered how great it would be to have Liliana around when the baby was born. Then her thoughts drifted out of control, imagining Xander to be around them also—with her and the baby.

She had just finished getting into her dress and noticed that her efforts to hide her baby bump was failing. Did her tummy grow overnight? She realised she could not keep hiding behind her clothes forever. What dress could hide a nine-month pregnancy when she gets to that? And what would happen when the baby arrives? Would she be hiding her baby too? She stayed away from the city and moved to this small town to avoid the press that was all too eager to invade her privacy, but here she was still hiding herself.

"Wow."

She looked up to see Laurie peaking her head into her room, hiding her body behind the door.

"You look pregnant."

"Thanks for stating the obvious."

"You know what I meant to say." Laurie let herself in. "Is something wrong?"

She hid her face away from her cousin, pretending to be busy getting ready for work.

"Ally?"

She looked up. There was no point going in circles when it came to her persistent cousin. "I don't know," she said with a defeated look on her face.

"Hey, hey." Laurie moved closer, wrapping her arms around her. "Tell me," Laurie calmly said.

She was glad she had Laurie here with her. In Laurie's arms she realised she was not doing right by herself—or her baby.

"What am I doing, Laurie?"

"What do you mean?" Laurie turned so she could see her face.

"What am I doing? I left New York to be away from a lot of things, and those things are catching up to me. I don't even have any plans for my baby. I'm hiding from my mother when I really, really need her with me."

The waterworks were about to break the dam. Down the pit of her stomach, the urge to vent out all her feelings and sorrows fought for release, fuelling the tears even more. It was a fight she already lost.

She sniffed. "The support I've had apart from you is my ex-boyfriend's mom and an ex who suddenly shows up to confuse me all over again. How crazy can that get? I'm in this small town, Laurie, and I thought I had it figured out. But now? I don't know. If I stay here, what is here for me? If I return home, what do I go back to? I don't want some mean strangers following me and writing about a twenty-one-year-old who fell in some hot, rich guy's web."

"Ally, calm down," Laurie said when her breathing started to pick-up.

In what felt like thirty minutes but was probably three, her breathing turned normal.

"I haven't even shopped for baby clothes." For whatever reason, the words made her sad.

"Sweetheart, you haven't shopped for baby anything."

"Tell me I'm not stupid."

"Of course, you're not. You were hurt, and you needed space, you wanted to protect the baby. It's been months, and now, I just think you're trying to run from New York. Your mom needs you just as you need her, and I'm sure from what I learned about Liliana yesterday that she isn't going anywhere. And take it from someone who's been at the receiving end of your ex, I don't think he's going anywhere either."

"You're supposed to say things that'll calm me and assure me that I have things under control."

"And I've just told you that. You *are* in control, Al. Every other thing or person surrounding you is just your support. It's your life, your future, and therefore your decisions. The question is what do you want to do?"

They stared at each other, both probably expecting a reaction from the other.

"You're right. I need to decide." She picked up her bag.

"What are you doing?" Laurie asked.

"Going to work. And tonight, decision making."

Laurie gave up, folding her hands and staring right at her. "You bet. I don't leave until two days from now, anyway. Just know you have me to deal with."

She was tempted to roll her eyes, but a tear dropped from her right eye, and she wiped it away before her cousin could see it.

Deep down, she was happy Laurie was here. She walked out of her room, and Laurie followed behind. She turned to say something but saw Laurie already going at her breakfast—the meal Liliana had prepared before leaving for something that urgently needed her attention. She already had a mini feast herself this morning before getting ready.

"I'll pop by over there later," Laurie said after swallowing the bits in her mouth.

"Excuse me?"

"You can't expect me to stay in here until you get back. I'm sure there aren't sights worth seeing around here. So my dear, expect my awesome presence in that salon."

She chuckled. "Do you even know where it is?"

"You said you walk there. I guess it's either the nearest salon from here or the only one in town."

"Why do I have a feeling you meant that in a mean way?"

"It's the truth. I mean, how do people manage living life here?"

"It isn't as bad as you think. It's nice and peaceful."

Laurie shrugged. "I'll see you."

"Okay, but remember, no one knows I'm pregnant."

"You think? They'll definitely know about that," Laurie said, referring to her stomach. One would be blind to not notice.

"I just had a big breakfast. Later."

She closed the door behind her and breathed in the fresh air. The sky was clear, and it appeared to be a beautiful day. Laurie was right; she needed to make her decision. It was not just about her anymore.

Tonight, she would take out all her cards and lay them on the table.

***

She had barely walked twenty steps when she saw him. His body rested on his car with both hands hidden in his pockets. He was looking straight at her. Though her insides stopped working for a moment, her legs continued moving.

She did not like the fact that she was still vulnerable when it came to him. But Ally knew that whether she found it difficult or not—regardless if she wanted it or not—she needed to be strong enough to tell herself and him what she wanted concerning her life and the baby.

She did not want to ponder much on all the things he said two nights ago, but she clearly could not forget that he said he wanted her—them. He was not giving up? Everything would have been better if only he reacted half as determined from the start.

With only a few steps away from him, his body straightened, and his hands pop out of his pocket.

She could be civil, at least she wanted to be. It was too early to start exchanging words. She did not want a repeat of what happened in her room with Laurie. If she bared all she had in her in front of this man—a man she was still unsure how she truly felt about now—she knew she would lose it, and the last thing she wanted was to lose it in front of Alexander Cross. Once was quite an experience.

He cheated on you.

That thought crawled its way to her whenever she thought of him… whenever she saw him. She still could not get the image of Julia under him in his office and what they were about to do out of her head.

She stopped and faced him. It would be better to know why he was near her house this morning than say nothing at all

"Hi," he said softly as if any other tone might break her.

How long has he been standing here waiting for me? "Hi," she replied. She saw a shadow inside the car and assumed it was the driver.

He must have noticed the shift in her eyes. "It's only Paul."

She faced him again. "What are you doing here?"

"I wanted to see you."

"Now you've seen me."

"I thought maybe we might get breakfast together."

"I already had breakfast." Her replies were monotonous. She knew there was some other reason. He looked like he was almost scared of asking her, and she was not going to push.

"I'm sorry if I came on too strong the other night. I know I was the last person you expected—"

"We said all we had to say." She cut him off.

This was not helping either of them. It felt like they were going back and forth, and it made her wonder if this was the sort of relationship they were going to have from now on.

***

She had said all she wanted to say that night, but he still had a lot to say—to add and to give.

"No. I meant every word. I'll do what it takes to make you believe in me again." *Love me again*, he wanted to add. He watched her slowly shake her head in disagreement, her unbound hair moving freely, just as he loved.

No on said it would be easy? He made her go through the difficulties alone. So hell if he had it easy for himself. He would be more concerned if she did not care and forgave him just as easily.

"Stop staring."

He looked up to see an annoyed look on her face. He was not sure what she meant until he saw her do it again and wrap her hands around her tummy.

Had he been staring?

"You look..." He had so many beautiful words to describe her, but none was coming forth.

"I know I look big." The frown was still etched on her face.

Was she referring to her weight? Because he was not seeing it. Almost nothing changed from how she looked months ago. He then realised what Ally was thinking. If it mattered to her what he thought of her, then she must still care for him, and he was ready to use that.

"You look beautiful." His words did not dispel the frown on her face. "I wasn't staring because… I didn't realise I was doing that. I just... It's the first time I'm really seeing you growing." *With our baby.*

She turned away to leave.

"Ally."

"You look like you have nothing important to say. I have to get to work."

"I can drop you off."

"I can walk."

"But I do have things to say. You might not want to hear them, but I'll be here until you do, wherever you are, whenever you want. I'm here because I need you to know both of you can rely on me. I'm not going anywhere, Ally."

She shook her head. "Listen to yourself, Xander. It's like you're offering to be my donor after death. What use is it of?"

"I'm really sorry. I probably will tell you that for the rest of my life."

She said nothing and walked away.

He did not try to stop her. He knew he had to put his words into action; he was just not sure how to start. Winning her back was proving to be the toughest thing he had ever had to do in his life.

"Sir."

He turned to look at Paul who had his body out of the car with his mobile phone in his hand. "I just got confirmation that your father is here."

"Then let's go. I'm sure he's expecting the welcome since nothing goes over his head."

With a nod, Paul got in to start the car, and he followed. His father's presence was not going to destroy the two relationships he's found here and intended to rebuild. He would do what he had been coward enough to avoid—protect them.

***

Xander was out of the car as soon as Paul drove them to The Purcell Hotel which was without dispute, the best hotel close to the town. He was not sure where he was supposed to meet his father, but before he could get into the elevator, Paul and one of his men was beside him, probably the one who gave him the information about his father.

No words were spoken. While waiting for the elevator, Xander was aware of the pair of eyes watching him, but he ignored it. He did not care if the woman recognized him or found him attractive. As soon as the elevator door opened and a couple came out, the woman smiled at them. He was not sure about the two men with him, but he did not bother returning the smile.

"Your father's waiting for you," Paul said as the elevator closed and it was just them.

"Isn't he?" he replied mockingly. "Tell me he did not force his way into my room."

"He booked the room opposite yours."

He huffed. The first day he arrived at this hotel, the best rooms, according to the receptionist, were apparently the three rooms on the top floor. All three were the most expensive in the whole hotel though the price was not half as high as the best ones in New York. One of the rooms had already been taken. He occupied one, and now his father booked the last, but he would make sure his father was out of this town as soon as possible.

He walked out of the elevator and to the door of the room opposite his and knocked. Immediately, it was opened, and he looked up to see James, one of the men who worked closely with his father. James gave him a nod and walked out the door, closing it behind him. He had never been friendly his father's employees, but they respected him, and he acknowledged them in return. James and Bill were the only ones he knew by name who worked for his father.

Cameron Cross was sitting on one of the two chairs placed around a round table in the room, a suite not any different from his. A glass of alcohol was sitting in front of him along with some papers lying on the table. Xander was sure his father was aware of his presence as his eyes briefly scanned around the room. Nothing was out of the ordinary.

He halted his steps in front of his father, sliding his hands into his pocket. Did he really know this man he called dad? Was there a genuine father and son bond between them? His father kept many secrets. He carried a frown with him everywhere, and he was sure he has never seen the man truly smile or laugh.

Not once since his father introduced himself to him had he seen him with a woman or heard of one associated with him. He knew it was impossible that his father was without female company, though. He was a man, afterall—a man who could compete with most guys in their thirties and forties. He had facial features any woman would fancy. That, Xander was absolutely sure about. The green eyes he inherited from him was a winner with the female kind.

"Why are you here?"

His father gave him a pointed look. "Show some respect. I'm your father."

"What father keeps stalking his son?"

"Stalking?" He watched his father laugh, mocking him. "Don't flatter yourself. We both know why I'm here."

"Then let's talk about that." Xander moved closer and drew his hands out of his pocket, resting them on the head of the chair in front of him. "Let's talk about how you made sure my mother stayed away from me and how you pulled your strings to make sure she could not step foot into this country. Why the hell would you do that then lie all about it?"

"I see you have better sources this time. She's remarried; was, I guess. And I hear you're collaborating with your step brother, only he was right in front of you and you never figured that out. I know your head's been out of sorts the past weeks, but letting your guard down like this?"

He knew his father was mocking him, baiting him in fact, and he frowned at that. His father was only trying to avoid the question. Honestly, he was less concerned on why Theopolis Christakos approached him and so assigned the task of finding out about him to Julia. Besides, he had not asked for his personal information. There was no way Julia could have gotten a deeper search back then. That kind of thing was Paul's job.

Thinking about it now, all Theo had said in his office somehow made more sense. The mother Theo referred to was his own mother, and his brother was none other than him. His mother never gave up on him if he remembered clearly what Theo had said.

"All your life, you've craved that deep, meaningful connection you did not have with your mother. No wonder you could not see the snake of a woman you were crazy about and get rid of her. I had to do that for you."

What was he talking about? *Ally?*

"Barbara was it?"

So his father had been the reason he never heard from Barbara again. He took a seat. What does his father know? What was he hiding?

He gave him that mocking laugh again. "And that girl came around. Despite me telling you to break it off because she'll end up being like the other women in your life, you ignored me, and the opposite happened. You ran, scared of something you've never experienced with a woman before."

"Are you here to throw my past at me? You better stay the hell away from her. I'm warning you, Dad. Ally's not one of your games."

"Obviously, you're here for her. It must have been quite a shock to find your mother here too."

He was angry. He still could not figure out his father.

"I heard you've made me a grandpa, too. That's something to look forward to, I guess. So don't worry. I have no further business with the woman you claim to love."

"I love her."

"Hmm. Does she think the same way? She must want nothing to do with you if she took my money. Now I understand why. You should count yourself lucky, I suppose. At least she did not run away from you with your child even when you told her to."

He did not need to be reminded of that. "You keep repeating that she took your money, but tell me, has she cashed it? I'm sure she took the cheque to get rid of you. You've never liked her, and she was smart to know it was the only way you would let her be. I trust her."

His father smirked at him, and he felt like punching something. He was not getting anywhere with this man.

"What happened with your first wife and son?"

"First wife? I never married your mother."

He gritted his teeth. His father was trying to make him angry on purpose, it seemed.

"I take it that you have enough information already since you were so eager to confront me in my office," his father coldly said.

"I want to hear it from you."

For a moment, it felt like his father was not going to speak anymore, but he finally did.

"It was an accident."

"That's what it was said to be. Was it?"

"If you have a question to ask me, be direct, son. I taught you to be a man."

He was not sure what his father taught him anything, but he knew what he got from him: resentment and a hard exterior. Having Ally in his life somehow opened him up to the truth.

"Did you have anything to do with their deaths?"

His father casually stood up. "We should sit and swap stories soon, or should we do that now? You think I had them killed?"

"It was her parent's money you lived on. You had another woman hidden, and she found out and was mad about it. And the car that crashed was yours."

“Even if what you said is true, why would I kill my son?"

"You had not planned him being there?"

"I loved him."

Xander went numb at those words. All his life, he never heard his father use that word.

"He was my son, afterall."

He felt different emotions run through him, but he could not process any of it. "So I'm his replacement?"

He could not even explain what he was feeling and why. He did not care what his father thought of him. He was a grown man who would have his own family soon. Why would his father's thoughts matter to him?

"You can never replace him." He took his jacket on the bed, put it on, and started buttoning it up.

He swallowed the hurt and anger he felt and said in a low voice. "I don't understand why you hate my mother so much when it was you who put her in that position. What do you see me as? What do I mean to you?"

"I hate your mother. I hate your mother for betraying me."

"Betray?" he whispered.

"Whatever I did then was for her own good, and at the first chance she got, she fled."

What the hell happened years ago, and how was he to understand if his father was not saying things clearly?

His father was already at the door.

"And, Alexander." Cameron waited for him to turn around.

"Just as you can't take William's place, no one can take yours." The door closed behind him, leaving him to stare at the emptiness.

William… that had been his name. He would have had an older brother named William. What would he call him if things had turned out differently? Will? Liam?

Had his father just said he loved him indirectly? Just who really was Cameron Cross?

CHAPTER 20

Laurie's appearance at the salon that afternoon had not only turned heads and left mouths open, according to her, a few hearts had flipped on her way there.

Ally could only roll her eyes and smile when she told her that. But she hardly had time to do that with an overehear Laurie setting up for the night and their movie time. They had gotten all sorts of junk food at the local mini mart, all Laurie's treat. It was for the better since Liliana had called to apologize that she would not be turning up for the night, promising to meet her at the doctor's the next day instead.

She rubbed her belly, thinking about tomorrow. She had an appointment with Mike to know if everything was good with the baby. She was not sure if she wanted to know the sex of the little life growing inside of her yet. If only she had someone to share this experience with. The feeling that she should decide on such things with Xander, or at least get his opinion, was always there, nagging at the back of her mind.

But what did all that matter, anyway? He lost all his rights to the baby the moment he showed her just how much he hated the life they made together.

Laurie was right. She should make up her mind on what she really wanted.

"What's with that smile on your face? What are you thinking?"

She looked up to see Laurie walking into the living room with the bottle of red wine she had bought earlier and a glass jar of water.

"Tomorrow, I'm going to see this little nugget again and how much he has grown," she said, rubbing her stomach in circles for a little bit longer.

"And I'll be there," Laurie said, sitting beside her with her legs crisscrossed. "And he?" She poured herself a glass of the red wine and turned to face her cousin, sipping it.

She shrugged. "That just came out. I still haven't decided if I want to know."

Laurie raised a brow. "Or you're just hoping you have a mini version of that stupid hunk in your oven."

"What? No. No, I wasn't even—"

"Hate to break it to you, but have you seen our familia? Traffic of girls!" Laurie spoke with finality as if anything else would be impossible. "You know from our mom's line, the last record of a male in the family was like a *thousand* years ago. So that's like ninety-nine point nine percent probability of a girl."

She smiled. "That's quite an exaggeration, but I understand where you're coming from. The fact is I did not make this baby alone so that theory might be wrong, and I'm sure it doesn't even work like that. What if the baby genetically leans towards Xander's?"

"Why are you thinking too much about this when you can go for the real thing?

"Can I?"

"What are you scared of?"

"I'm confused. I don't know if I want to risk my sanity again."

Laurie sighed and gently said, "I can't believe I'm about to take his side but listen, good cuz." Laurie shifted to face her. "Alexander Cross loves you."

She stared at her cousin with wide eyes. "Says who?" She wanted to laugh at Laurie's words, but she just could not.

"Says Laurie Callahan who's always right on these things."

"Always?" She smirked playfully.

Laurie stuck out her tongue. "Mostly right, but the point is I was there when that butthole wouldn't give up looking for you."

"Language, Laurie."

"I try," she said not really apologetic, looking down at her stomach.

"It could just be him being mad. He's always been an arrogant man, so maybe he was just stressed that I did something he did not approve of."

"Quit rambling, Al. I know what I saw."

She sighed. "Still, even if any of it were true, I don't know if I want to be with him anymore." She turned to Laurie, and silence ensued. She could not see a reply in her cousin's eyes. "You think it's a stupid thing to say?"

Laurie shrugged. "I've never been in love. You have, so it's like you're telling me it's no big deal… That it happens, and when it does, you might as well undo it whenever you want."

She opened her mouth to speak, but when nothing came out, she closed it again and looked away from her cousin.

Laurie sipped her wine. "So, you don't love him anymore?"

"It's confusing."

"I want to hear it. And don't tell me your confusion has something to do with his brother. Your smarter than that."

"Theo?"

"Tell me I'm wrong. Tell me that you're not attracted to him."

"He's a very attractive man," she replied defensively.

"This is about him?" Laurie stared wide-eyed at her. "Are you serious, Ally?"

"I haven't even said anything!"

She stood up with one hand on her hip and the other one expressing her emotion, flicking it around. "You don't need to."

"When did you become a fan of Xander, anyway? You don't even like him."

"Stay on the topic, Ally. This is about *you* and a stupid thing you're thinking of doing." Laurie said, pointing her finger at Ally for emphasis.

"I'm not thinking of anything."

"Well, we agree on that. You're not thinking—at all."

"Why are you getting so worked up on this?"

"Did he... have you two been...?"

"I'm pregnant, Laurie, with another man's baby. That's disgusting. I would never—"

"See where your dirty mind takes you? Who's asking that?"

"Sure, you weren't."

"Actually, I was not. I just wanted to know if you two have been flirting with each other or agreed to date or something or maybe kissed."

She could not call her encounters with Theo flirting. Sure, she knew he was attracted to her and she might be too, but she did not act on it. Thank goodness he was not around to remind her of what she was avoiding. If she told Laurie, would her best friend understand? It sounded to her like her cousin and best friend was getting soft towards Xander.

What had Laurie seen in Xander's eyes to make her believe in what Ally was finding hard to accept?

"Say something, Al."

"I might be attracted to him, I think."

Laurie stared at her and sighed in defeat. "How strong is this attraction?" She sat down again beside her.

"I'm not certain," she said almost in a whisper. "You know, Laurie, Xander was the first man every part of me lost itself to. Nothing made sense with him, yet everything did. I had never even felt that way with other guys, even those we've said we would go to bed with without a second thought. Xander redefined everything for me, and that was fine with me because I wanted no other man in my life. I couldn't imagine a life without him in it."

She stared into nothingness as she spoke, reliving all those moments in her head.

"Then I overhead the conversation he had with his assistant. He assured me he was just getting rid of a jealous woman who could not have him, and I believed him. Then I went on and made a mistake of not taking my pills. I got pregnant and... and he got *so* mad, he became a different man. He put me through hell, and you know how horrible a mother I had become because of that. I was so lost that for a moment, I thought about giving him what he wanted just to have the old him back—the Xander I fell in love with."

She looked at Laurie and saw tears streaming down her cousin's face.

"You remember how I came to you and suggested an abortion? I was that horrible, Laurie, because of a man. I was too consumed in him that if you hadn't helped me realise, I would have killed my own baby."

Now the tears were free, easily flowing out without restrain from both their eyes.

"You wouldn't have. You're not that kind of person." Laurie hugged her side to her, wrapping her left hand over hers. "You wouldn't have." She repeated, trying to convince her.

"When you told me he loved me, do you know why it's hard to picture? I see him with that stupid ginger head, getting it on with him right in his office for anyone to walk in on."

"What?"

"I can't switch that off. I've tried. It hurts me when I shouldn't care anymore."

"He cheated? When was this? You didn't tell me."

"It was enough reason to stay away."

"That was why you left."

"It was my wake-up call."

"That bastard."

Instantaneously, she put on a smile. "It shocked me when I realised I felt something for Theo. Sure, it's not comparable to how I feel about Xander, but it's stressful denying it's there. It's not much, but still, he's the second man to make me nervous when he's close. To be honest, Laurie, I don't know what it is, so I just assume it's attraction that'll wear off."

"How do you feel for Xander?" Laurie repeated her words. "You still love him?"

"I know I still care about him. Do I still love him? Probably. Do I hate him? Yes. So you see, I'm a ball of confusion, and that's the last thing I should be, considering I have a life to nurture now."

"Sorry."

"Why's that?" There were no more tears as she faced Laurie.

"For going off on you earlier and not understanding."

"Is there a way to be mad at you?"

"If you ask me, I think you should just stick with a drama-free guy, like the doctor."

"Mike?" Ally shook her head. "Not for me. Besides, did you see his *girlfriend*? The one you noticed was weighing me with her eyes at the salon? She's the possessive-obsessive type."

"The brunette with the wrong shade of foundation plastered on her face?" Laurie squeezed her face.

"Tiffany, yeah. I think she's actually quite pretty." She chuckled.

Laurie only huffed in return. "You're always nice with words."

"Thanks, Laurie."

"For what?"

"Everything. For being there. For being here."

"It's not just me. You've always been there for me too, you know."

She nodded, knowing what she meant. Laurie had once been in a dark place before, and she had been with her every step of it all.

"You're right. It's time to make a decision about my mom, Xander, what I want, and what I need to do."

"And.?"

"I'll decide on them one by one, but for now, I'm sure I want to have my baby around family, so I'm coming home."

"That's great."

"I just have to wrap things up and decide on a few things before then."

"Well, make it quick because I freaking miss you." Laurie squeezed her affectionately again.

"I missed you too, Laurie."

"I think we already had our movie night."

It was already late, and the only thing touched on their snack buffet was the red wine and the jar of water.

She laughed. "Worst movie night we could have, a movie night without actually watching a movie."

"If I stay here, I would probably doze off before the second scene," Laurie said.

"Then go sleep it off. I urgently need to pee," she replied as she stood up.

She was in her oversized tee anyway with just her panties and no bra. It was comfort and convenience all the way for her.

***

Ally spent half the day at the salon, and for almost the whole time, Laurie had been stuck with her. She was meant to get off work by twelve since her doctor's appointment was at one o'clock. Laurie came in at the salon a lot earlier than their agreed time, dressed to haunt hearts. She needed more fun while she was here, she said, and turning a few heads was right up her alley.

She was dressed in a little white dress, the backside revealing just a little more than her cleavage was. The skirt of the dress was flowy but short, revealing what a great pair of legs her cousin had in those brown wedges. Laurie, whose blue eyes were captivating enough, further accentuated her features by holding back her dark hair with a tiny gold band.

She was finally thinking on things she wanted to do with her life, but Laurie leaving tonight would put a damper on her mood. She had Liliana alright, but it was not the same as having Laurie.

She smiled to herself, thinking of the many times Liliana's presence had been an absolute blessing. She had to thank her for always being there. Ally did not think she had done that yet. She probably might do that when she showed up at the hospital.

Liliana was supposed to be here with Laurie, but she had called in that morning saying that something urgent came up. She would be running a few minutes late, but she was definitely not missing the appointment.

It was not going to be a big deal with her if Liliana missed it, anyways. She had Laurie with her. But once again, she could not keep the thoughts she had last night from creeping in; Xander was close. What if he could be there with her? Well, not for her but for the baby.

"Let's get out of here. The atmosphere in here is stifling," Laurie silently told her as she walked towards her.

"Okay." She was not blind to miss the judging eyes directed at them.

Laurie opened the door for her as she said a quick goodbye to Helen and returned Mel's smile. When they got to the car, she apologised to Raul for the ten minutes delay, but the man just brushed her apology away with a smile and gave a slight nod when she told him they were good to go.

All she wanted to think about for now was the appointment, so she barely conversed with Laurie who was obviously still pissed about how people around here did not know how to mind their own business. After they got off the car, Raul informed them he was off to get Liliana, assuring her that his employer would make it. She thanked him

She hoped she could stall Mike until Liliana arrived.

The hospital was fairly crowded, and unsurprisingly, Laurie had eyes on her—both curious and appreciative stares. Making a beeline to the reception to confirm her appointment, she was led to a room where she was told her doctor would be shortly. She lay on the bed waiting while Laurie took a seat beside her.

"Are you nervous?" Laurie asked.

"Am I?" She sarcastically asked in return. Sighing, she gave her cousin a half-smile. "This is my first visit with family to check on how the baby's doing. If anything goes wrong, it'll all be my fault. I've been somehow... in many ways, negligent."

"Cut yourself some slack. It's your first, and you were in a pretty shitty place." She knew it was Laurie's way of trying to make her feel better.

"It's no excuse. I'm sure many have been in shittier situations." She returned her cousin's little joke, letting her know she was okay. It was probably just a bundle of nerves messing with her.

"Where's the doctor, anyways? Isn't he supposed to be here? He's the hot one, right?"

"I never said he was hot. And yeah, it's *Mike*."

Laurie scoffed.

"There's still a few minutes to spare. I would like to stall him if Liliana isn't here yet."

"You're one lucky girl to have her as your mother-in-law."

Her phone rang, distracting them both.

"She is not my mother-in-law," She said as she fished around her bag for her ringing phone.

It was Theo.

Why was he calling? It's been a while since she heard from him. There was only one way to know.

"Hello?"

"Remember when I said New York will tell if I get to invite myself inside your apartment?" She heard the deep voice undisputedly belonging to him, and it only confirmed she was affected by it—if she ever doubted his influence over her.

"Theo."

She looked up to see Laurie signal with her thumb towards the door and mouth something she could not understand. Ally gave her a slight nod and bit her lower lip in apprehension as the door closed.

She was not sure she would like his reason for calling.

"Where are you?"

"Um..." If she mentioned the hospital, he would want to know why, and she did not want him to know, at least not yet.

"I..."

"Perhaps I should just be straight and ask why you are seeing a doctor."

"What?"

"If you still can't answer that, then maybe I should outright ask why you never once mentioned to me you were pregnant." Theo's voice had a hint of anger in it.

"Maybe because it was none of your business?" She defended.

"Really? That's all you're going to say? I wanted to... You know you should have told me."

Maybe she should have. She just never thought he needed to know. It was not the right time. All the same, he would have eventually found out. She knew all her excuses were just for her own selfish reasons.

"I'm mad, and I don't know how to deal with it. I don't even know what I'm mad at, really. That I'll have to stay away from you or knowing I can't have you eventually…"

Silence.

"Say something," he said after a while, the hurt and pain never leaving his voice.

She did not know what to say. She could not think of anything to say.

He sighed. "I should probably give up, but I never take the easy way out." He chuckled. "I guess I'll know from your face what you can't say now when I see you."

"I'm sorry." The words came out without her thinking about it. She did not know what she was sorry for.

"Well, I'm not. Not yet. I'm glad my mother told me before the situation became uncomfortable for everyone. I know what it means to her to have found Alexander and be with him again but..."

She tuned out every other word Theo said. The only thing she could focus on was that Liliana found Xander. Maybe she just got it misunderstood.

"Has Liliana been in touch with Xander?"

"I don't think so, but you know he's right where you are, right?"

"Yes, but does Liliana know this too?"

"Of course. The only thing she wants is to make up for her mistakes and have Alexander in her life."

"So she knows."

There was a bit of silence before Theo spoke up. "I can almost imagine the wheels in your head turning, sweetheart. I'm sure whatever my mom told or withheld from you was not meant to hurt you in any way. She adores you. Trust me. I know."

"What about deception?" She asked.

"My mother isn't capable of that. Whatever you're thinking, talk to her first and hear what she's got to say. I have to go now, beautiful. I'll see you soon."

From the moment he cut the call to the moment Laurie came in, she had different thoughts swirling in her head. She suddenly felt like an idiot.

"Okay, did we all miss the childbirth because you look pissed? Who forced it out of you?"

She saw a cup of what she assumed to be coffee in Laurie's hand and guessed that was what she went out to get.

"Liliana," She replied, frowning.

"Chill, sister. That was meant to be a joke. You still look pregnant, and I don't see a baby around."

"She lied to me."

"Who? Liliana?"

"Of course, Laurie. Who else do you think?"

"Calm down and tell me." Laurie took a seat beside her.

"I don't know what the truth is yet, but I think she knew all along where Xander was and how he's been in contact with me."

"Then wait to ask her what the truth is. Besides, what's the big deal if she did know all that? He's her long lost son after all."

"It's not about that. It only makes sense now; the pampering, attention, dressing me up for that dinner, and who knows what else? It just feels like she's been with me only because of Xander."

"Well, it makes sense," Laurie said. Seeing the frown directed at her, she quickly added. "But I'm sure it's probably not the reason- or only reason. You should just ask her."

"I will," She said as the door opened. Mike came into view and gave her a big smile.

"Hi, Ally. How are you today?"

"She's pissed off right now, doc, and you've only added to it by keeping us waiting." Laurie faced Mike before she could reply.

Mike looked at his wristwatch and looked straight at the brunette. "I think I'm right on time."

"It's fine, Mike. You are right on time."

In the mood she was in, she wanted to tell Mike she was ready for her ultrasound even without Liliana there but she could not deny that she actually did care if she went on without her.

"Um... Mike, can we just wait a little bit longer? I'm actually waiting for my—" She had never really thought what Liliana was to her. "—my friend."

"I'm sorry, Ally, but I'm busy. I think I can spare a few minutes, though. I'll be back in ten. If you're ready before then, just let a nurse know."

She immediately nodded. She was relieved, but by the look on Mike's face, it seemed like he was more relieved than she was. Just then, the door opened, and the last person she wanted to see was standing behind it.

The small room suddenly went silent. All three of them were waiting for her reaction.

"W-What are you doing here?"

She sat up straight as she watched Xander walk into the room, closing the door behind him. She glanced at Mike who seemed uncomfortable.

"You did this?"

"I should have told you," was all Mike said. "I'm sorry if you're pissed at me. He was persistent. He found out and insisted even when I said no."

She did not know how to react. If she was not doubtful of Liliana's intention with her at the moment, she probably would be glad Xander was present somewhere in a deep, unconscious part of her.

"How did he know about this?" Laurie asked. "Aren't you supposed to be a doctor?"

"I am a doctor," Mike replied, trying to hold back his anxiousness.

"Isn't there supposed to be some sort of doctor-patient confidentiality?"

"I did not give information that's a risk to my patient's health. I did not give him any, in fact. This is all him but if you don't want him here Ally, you just need to let me know." Mike defended.

"But it's a violation to her privacy."

While both Mike and Laurie continued to bicker, she matched the intensity in Xander's look. Their gazes held each other. She wondered when he and Mike became buddies and if this was for real. Months ago, he did not want a baby, and now he was in here for the check-up.

Xander showing up in place of Mike that night should have roused her suspicion. Even when Mike had called later that night to apologise for not showing up, she should have asked more questions. She had been too shocked to bother about placing the pieces together.

Now they fit.

***

Liliana already felt emotionally exhausted by the time Raul stopped the car in front of the hospital. Her unpleasant meeting with Cameron had drained her energy though she had tried to hide it in front of him. From the moment she received his call late yesterday evening, she had been out of sorts. It was the first time she faced him after years apart. So when Theo called to give her a heads up about what he talked about with Ally concerning Xander, she was not sure she could handle the younger woman being angry at her too.

She had to admit that she had not been entirely honest with Ally, but she did all she did without intent to hurt her. She cared about her, and it was not just because she carried her grandchild. Ally made her feel useful as Alexander's mother, and she has grown to care about the person that young lady is.

Stepping out the car, she assured Raul she was fine and could handle herself. She was directed to the room and right outside of it, she heard voices coming from inside.

Maybe she had the wrong room?

She looked up at the number again to confirm she was right. Room 2A. She opened the door and walked in. She had the right room alright. Seeing Ally on the bed and her son not far from the door was enough confirmation.

When Liliana imagined meeting her son again for the first time, she imagined a lot of things, and a small hospital room was not in one of them.

***

Mother and son stared at each other, knowing who each other was with the expressions on their faces, and before Liliana could come out of her shock, Ally spoke up.

"I guess I'm ready now, Mike."

"Ally..." Liliana walked towards her. "Theo called and told me what both of you talked about."

Her eyes went to Xander who stiffened at the mention of Theo's name. Maybe it was because his mother just passed by him without much acknowledgement.

Mike prepared for the sonogram while Laurie was busy glaring at him. They were all here for a simple reason, and it was already turning out to be something else a lot more messy. Honestly, it made the room a little stuffy for her.

"You can explain to me later," She replied.

"I just want you to know I would never intentionally hurt you," Liliana said.

She did not smile, and from the sad look on Liliana's face, the older woman knew she did not believe her words.

"Okay. Raise your top for me, Ally." Mike took his position, and everyone in the room silently moved closer to see what he was doing.

She had her eyes firmly fixed on the monitor. Suddenly feeling tenser, she realised it was the first time she was exposing her bump to this many eyes. She jerked slightly at the feel of the gel on her stomach and caught a couple of eyes on her, not missing Xander's concerned look.

"Just for a bit," Mike said. He placed the transducer onto her belly and moved it around. Their mouths were all sealed as every other part of their senses zeroed in on the images and sounds on the ultrasound screen.

She only took her eyes away from the screen for a brief moment when Mike started explaining what was shown on the screen.

"Is everything okay?" she asked.

"Everything looks perfect. Since you are in your first trimester, we still have to monitor you through the last trimester for both your health."

She just nodded. She would not be having that here, anyway. So she let herself be absorbed with the image of her baby again, savouring the continuous, steady beating sound that filled the room.

"That's your baby's heartbeat. See that?" Mike pointed at the image, showing and explaining to them the other parts of the baby.

"That's real tiny... and weird," Laurie whispered, loud enough for the room to hear.

Liliana laughed and said softly, "That's beautiful."

She could not tell what Xander was feeling. Unable to tear her eyes away from the screen, she could not look at him to see. A tear had already escaped her left eye when Mike confirmed that the baby was in good health.

"Are you crying?" Laurie asked.

She shook her head. She was regretful, but at the same time, grateful. She was happy that the baby was strong; easing her worries and regrets just this once.

Mike then told her the baby's sex was hard to determine at this stage, but she was not disappointed. Mike even assured her it was just one baby. She laughed at that.

"You can quit glaring at me," Mike said to Laurie as he wiped the gel off her stomach.

"You're so full of yourself for a small town doctor. Act professional. No one's interested in you, if that's what you think."

Liliana excused herself from the room when her phone started to vibrate, catching the eyes of her son before leaving the room.

"How would you know what I was thinking if that's not what you were thinking?"

Laurie glared at him again. "You're not my type."

"What kind of types do you go for?"

"Are you insinuating something?"

Ally felt eyes on her and immediately knew who it was since it couldn't be any of the two bickering at each other like kids. She looked straight at him and was unable to know what he was thinking. The only thing she saw in his eyes was warmth, and through Mike and Laurie's voices, they kept staring at each other.

"Who are you again?"

"Family," Laurie proudly said. "And you?"

"You can't work that out?"

"Are you calling me stupid?"

"Are you?"

"Ally, are you sure this Hollywood wannabe is okay as your doctor?"

Mike chuckled. "That's immature."

"You called me stupid."

"I did not."

Laurie was about to say something else, but Mike cut her off. "As much as you obviously find me attractive and our conversation entertaining, I have other patients to attend to."

Just then, a nurse came in to tell him he was needed elsewhere. Mike walked out but not before saying bye to her and silently exchanging words with Xander. Shaking everyone's hand but totally ignoring Laurie, he was out of the room in no time.

"I'll be outside," Laurie told her, looking angry. "Are you gonna be alright?"

"Yeah. It's cool," She replied, and Laurie bolted for the door.

"Hi," She said. Now left with Xander, she did not know what else to say. She went to get off the bed, and before she knew it, he was right beside her, helping her up.

"I can do it by myself."

He gave her space but still had his hand on her arm.

"What are you doing here?" She asked again. That one was left unanswered.

"I wanted to be here for you and our baby. If I had asked, you might have refused. I'm sorry if you did not like it, but I still would have made the same decision. It was not Mike's fault." He rubbed his hand on her arm, soothing her.

She sighed, and without knowing it, she leaned more into him. It took a while for the realization to set in, but when she did, she released her arm from his touch—almost as if she was burned. It might have seemed like she hated it, but she knew better. It felt good, *really* good, and it only made her body want more.

And that was when she realized what was happening. She wanted more of Xander's touch. It all clicked in her head.

Oh, no.

She was horny.

She shifted her legs uncomfortably and got out of the bed as the urge got more demanding. Xander, not realizing her predicament, moved back but had little space between them.

"We should talk. Tonight, at my place."

Laurie was leaving tonight, anyways, and she did not think she would have Liliana over today. She already made her decision, and he should know about it. It was about time to stop hiding behind excuses and petty reasons.

By then, her hormones would definitely be in check.

Right?

CHAPTER 21

Saying she was fine with this would be lying to herself.

Since the embarrassing discovery she had in the examination room, Ally had been restless. She felt better now, though, but knowing what or *who* was coming later tonight had her on edge once more.

Laurie caught on it after they got home. She had reluctantly told her cousin about it, and the brunette had a good laugh at her expense. *The sly fox.* That only infuriated and frustrated her more, and all her darling cousin had to say was to solve the problem herself since there was no way she would let a man do it given her condition.

How would she do that, though? She had never done so before. It was not that she had never attempted it. She just never got the pleasure it was supposed to bring and never tried again. Besides, how to pleasure herself was not a topic she was comfortable asking anyone. It was a lot better when Xander did it, anyway.

"No, no, *no*! Ally, stay on track," she chanted to herself.

Laurie had left for the airport an hour ago, and she was expecting Xander in thirty-five minutes as per their agreement. Laurie was driven to the airport, courtesy of Liliana's driver.

"I can see you off."

"No need. You should take some rest." She gave her a tight hug. "I'm glad you made the decision to come home."

She nodded in agreement.

Just as Laurie was about to get in the car, she halted to face her. "You could also consider letting Xander help you untie that *knot*." She finished with a wink.

Using Xander for her own needs? She could not do that—selfishly use him without attachment. No matter how much she tried to deny it, there was a level of attachment already. How could she sleep with Xander when he wanted them back together, when a part of her still cared for him, and he was the father of her baby?

She really did want to have sex, though. Xander would be the best option—if not the only one. She could not imagine being sexual with another man while she carried another's baby.

But it was so hard to not have sex-related thoughts when she was horny. All she could do was eat and, for a while, a few stretches. Obviously, none of that helped.

The only time she had not thought of sex today was when she had a brief talk with Liliana. She was angry not because of what Liliana had done but because she feared she would be disappointed at whatever Liliana would reveal—that she lied and purposely kept things from her. It even made her wonder if the past weeks with her have been real.

She cared about the woman. She knew that, and did not want their relationship to turn cold.

She remembered the events that occurred that afternoon at the hospital.

Liliana dropped her and Laurie at her apartment, and though Laurie tried to break the awkwardness in the car, it was still obvious that things were tense between them. She noticed Liliana's hesitation when she opened the door to her apartment and invited the woman in. She was not about to listen to her reasons outside her doorstep.

Ally did not like that; Liliana never did have a reason to be invited into her apartment before letting herself in except at the beginning of their earliest meetings.

Immediately, Laurie excused herself, and Liliana begun to apologise profusely for what she had done. She confessed to knowing about Xander's every movement—including that time when he showed up at her date. She did not ask how Liliana knew that, too focused on keeping herself from yelling, 'I knew it!'

She always found it weird that Liliana supported her seeing another man and her eagerness to know how it went the next day.

Liliana had promised to come around the next day, hoping she would forgive her and still let her in. She had thought about it and realised it was really not a big deal to be mad about—at least not enough to ignore her. Besides, Liliana still had to face Xander, and she could not figure out why she did not embrace her son at the hospital when it was what she wanted the most.

The knock on her door jolted her upright and out of her thoughts.

Xander was here.

She went about, hurrying to place her mini buffet away, but it was no use. The evidence of her solo feast was everywhere on the sofa and table. She smacked her lips together just in case she had a little bit of something hanging around. Wiping her hands on her oversized tee—this time, she had shorts and bra on—she turned the lock and opened the door.

Ally had deemed it unnecessary to look nice. She was after all in her comfort zone and had no intention of letting him mistake her purpose for calling him tonight for something more.

"Hi."

"Hey." She breathed out and invited him in.

She was not sure if he had taken the time to look good. It was not that Xander had ever needed the effort, but he looked fresh, clean, and out of his earlier outfit. He was in an ash casual shirt that fit snugly to him with the top three buttons undone and dark blue jeans.

His face was still unshaven, and she could not deny she had always liked stubbles on him. He wore it well. The feel of it on her fingers always tickled her and made her grin.

Closing the door behind him, she slowly but unconsciously checked him out when he had his back to her.

Those black sneakers… He had on a black and white cup sole sneakers which had always looked hot on him. She had said that to him once. It could not be why he had them on, though, could it?

She had to get her emotions in check. The least thing she needed was to jump him even if it was her body's top priority right now.

She realised his silence was because he was staring down at the mess she made on her living room. Yeah, she knew she should have cleaned that up.

Xander turned to her. "Did you have someone over?"

She walked past him and dusted the visible crumbs off the sofa. "I was hungry." She faced him to be more specific. "I suddenly had this craving that just wouldn't stop when I started."

He looked hesitant but then asked. "Do you have these cravings a lot?"

"Um, yeah. Maybe... Sometimes, I guess."

"Here."

She looked at his outstretched hand to see a pack of sweets she had not noticed on him. She slowly took it and saw what kind it was—sweet and sour. A smile threatened to form on her lips.

He swept his right-hand fingers through his hair, looking unsure. Someone did a bit of homework on her current state, she thought. But then again, it might just have been Mike's doing since it seemed like they were best of friends now.

"I didn't know what else to bring. I tried flowers, but the only decent flower shop around here was out of your favourites, and if I were to have them delivered, it would take—"

When did he start rambling? Ally thought. He looked less like the confident Xander she had always known.

"Thanks." She cut him off. "This is perfect." She raised the pack to him. "Just so you know, the flowers would not have lasted here, anyways." She would explain why to him soon.

She saw his confusion and promised to explain to him. She invited him to sit on a seat away from hers, ready to talk, but she knew that before she could talk to him about her plans, she needed to ask him about his mom. The mother and son's reaction back at the hospital were not right to her.

"Before I tell you what I intend to do, I want to ask you about Li—your mom."

"What about her?"

"Have you two talked yet?"

Xander shook his head.

"That's crazy. She's been all about getting you back and to be what she couldn't for you. Make up for the lost years, you know? I don't know what you still think of her, but... I think you should hear her out."

"So you two are close now?"

Close? Ally would think so. They did not share their deepest secrets, but still... yeah, they could be friends.

"I like her. I don't know the deal about the past, but she's a great woman."

"Yeah. Maybe she always was."

She faced him, but he had his eyes forward, away from hers.

"I found out a lot of things, Ally: my mother, my father, the truth about my grandparents, and about an older brother and a step-brother. I was living a lie. My mother did not abandon me because she did not want me; my dad made it seem so. And my grandma never left my grandpa for another man. In fact, he broke another woman's heart to set a mistake right, and he never did act like a husband or father when he should have. Everything I've always believed to be true was a lie. I set my principles on something that was far from what I knew."

Wow, Ally commented in her head.

"Yeah," Xander said like he heard her thoughts. "The only backstabbing female in my life was Barbara, but I was immature and stupid. Honestly, if I had not been arrogant and so obsessed with trying to prove something, I would have known she was no good."

He gave a sad smile.

"Turns out the joke has always been on me. I blamed the women in my life for all my insecurities, but the men were the ones to blame. They are cowards—and now, that includes me. I can't keep blaming others for my mistakes. I know I hurt you, and you'll probably never forget. Hell, I'll never forget what I did and almost made you do, but it doesn't mean I wouldn't keep trying until you forgive me."

***

I love you, was all that Xander wanted to say, but he was sure that was the last thing Ally wanted to hear. Besides, even if she did hear him say that, would she believe him? He was afraid of that. Since the moment he said those three words in front of his father without having to think about it, he knew deep within every part of him that those words were true and precious for him. He could not say when it happened or why he was finally able to admit it to himself and to anyone who cared to listen, but saying those words to the woman beside him scared the hell out of him.

In any other circumstance, he would have huffed at his own thoughts. *Alexander Cross afraid of a woman's rejection?* But Ally was not just any woman. She was the mother of his child and the woman he was in love with.

"Do you know what happened between your parents?"

She evaded all he just said about her forgiveness, and that did not go unnoticed by him.

"I don't have the details, but my dad won't tell me anything, and it's not like I can ask my mom."

"Why not?"

"I hated her for so long. I'm sure she must resent me in a way."

"She loves you and truly adores you. I'm sure she'll answer any questions you have. The first time I met her, every question she had for me was about you to the point that having her around was uncomfortable. She misses you."

"So she came to you and introduced herself as my mom?"

"Basically, yes. I didn't believe it at first because she was so beautiful and young. Then I noticed the striking resemblance especially with... with your smiles."

He unconsciously drew a smile on his face. He honestly did not do that on purpose, he told himself. He was here to make progress no matter how small, but his plan of being forgiven and trying to remind her of how good they were together was not getting into play yet. But at least they were talking without arguing or disagreeing. That had to mean something.

"There." She pointed out his smile, beaming herself.

That little moment felt natural just like what they used to have, and they stared at each other until he had to distract them by shifting in his position.

"I know my dad came to see you."

She nodded. "Did he tell you why?"

"I got the hint."

"So you know he offered me money?"

"He told me."

"I still have the cheque in my room. Please remind me to give it you before you leave. I never cashed it, and he must know that."

He did not reply. He was not sure why Ally did not just rip the paper, but he would do the honours himself. If he were feeling generous, he would do it in front of his father.

He missed this—talking to her. He wanted to tell her all he had discovered in the past months and share it with her. When they were dating, she listened to everything he had to say. Ally always had questions, wanting to know more about him, but he could not say the same for himself.

He, Alexander Cross, never took the time to know her well, if he did know her at all in fact. There were very few things he could actually say about her or her family. Shame clouded his conscience, and it was another way he came to realise that their relationship had been one-sided. He had taken a lot from Ally, but what did he actually give her?

Memories of the few moments she got to know at least one more thing about him crept into his mind: while they ate, when he had just finished ravishing her body, or this one time he obliged her and talked about when he made his first million in the shower, lazily soaping each other. What ensued after was one of the hottest sex he had ever had.

He needed her. He needed Ally back in his life.

***

So far, talking with Xander had not been as awkward as she had imagined, but she could not deny the awkwardness that emerged a couple times.

He appeared to be thinking, and she wondered whatever he could be thinking about. He seemed so distracted by his thoughts that he almost looked uncomfortable. His face said differently, though. He shifted in his seat, and her eyes bulged at what she saw.

Bulge was the keyword.

She swallowed. She did not just see that. Her mind only saw what it wanted to see. Yes, it was just her mind playing tricks on her. Why did she even look? Damn, hormones!

But then, like a magnet, her gaze was drawn to the sight again. It was just for confirmation, she told herself. This time, she saw it all too well—a little too well in fact.

He had to be doing this on purpose. If they were in the same predicament, it was only a matter of time before one of them jumped the other without protest. She had to say something.

"You have got to be kidding me." Her voice jerked him into finally paying attention.

"What?" he innocently asked.

"*What?* Are you serious?" She stood up, facing him. Just when she was doing great for herself, he suddenly decided to 'pop' a little situation—which was not looking little, by the way.

"What are you going on about, Ally?"

"That!" She pointed in the right direction, and he finally caught on.

"Shit," he muttered, looking down at his current predicament.

"That's what you have to say? Were you... I don't want to know what you were thinking of."

"If it's any better, I was thinking of us… of you."

It sounded to her like he was teasing her.

"No, that doesn't make it better." She could not believe this. This situation was getting sexually dangerous for her, and damn if she would let it be ground zero.

"Put that thing away!"

"Now come on, sweetheart. That's not fair. I just can't put *it* away. Besides, I didn't even know it happened."

"How can you not know? It's freaking part of you!"

"You can't blame me. It's just like if a boob's out and you aren't conscious of it until someone points it out."

She unconsciously looked down at her chest. He was not referring to her. "Excuse me. I'm sure I would know if one of my boobs came out of place... and it isn't like that."

He was teasing her, but she did not care about that right now. They had a calm conversation a moment ago, and now she was raising her voice, unbelievably frustrated. She was trying to avoid something, and it was like he was telling her to come at it.

"Let's just stop talking about boob and... and whatever it is!"

He smiled.

He was *smiling*! Was he finding it funny?

"I'm sorry if it makes you uncomfortable, but you know how it's got a mind of its own."

She remembered. She knew that all too well, but none of Xander's talk was helping a*t all.*

"*Alex,* come on."

That one word froze them. She was in disbelief, couldn't quite believe what she had called him. Xander jerked in response, finding that his southern member has developed a liking for it.

"Bathroom," he whispered.

She told him where it was, and then he was out of sight. She sighed and took a seat. That was embarrassing.

That was a big slip-up,but at least it got him out of the room. This night was not going as she wanted. She brushed her fingers through her wavy hair.

A few minutes passed, and she heard a voice behind her.

"I haven't been with anyone since you left."

She turned to see him standing behind her and forced her eyes to his. The last thing she wanted to know was how he took care of his southern region or if he did at all. Instead, she focused on his words.

There was no point running from this anymore. It was one of the reasons—*the* reason she invited him here tonight. She needed to act mature. She was going to be a mother soon. She should get it out.

"After I left the city? Because when I left your home, I'm pretty sure I saw you with someone else."

"I never did... I almost made that mistake, but I swear, I did not do it. I did not have sex with Julia. That's the truth."

"Then what did you have with her? What's the truth?"

He groaned out loud and admitted something she never expected. "I let her touch me."

Ally was stunned into silence.

"When I stopped, she insisted. I was frustrated and angry, and before I knew what she was doing, she was giving me a hand."

She chuckled sadly, turning her face away from him. "That's some sick way to play with words."

He crouched in front of her, and it reminded her of the night he first appeared before her after months apart, hijacking her date.

"Did you get off of it?"

"I wasn't... I'm sorry..."

That answered her question.

"I regret all that I did. I was an asshole, a coward who ran away from his responsibility and hid behind his past. I'm trying to be better, Ally. I just need you to see that."

Even if I do forgive you, I can't forgive myself, and being with you will remind me why.

"My plans will involve you seeing me around anyway," She muttered, casting her eyes to the floor. They were going to be in the same city, after all.

***

Xander knew she was evading the topic again. Did he hurt her this much to avoid even talking about it?

He was stupid for even thinking that. He remembered the way she looked that time he had just found out about her pregnancy. He had stayed away, and when he came home, she looked so weak and sick that seeing her like that had actually scared the crap out of him.

But still, what had he done? Stayed away, that was.

"Plans?" He was backing off for now, but he would not indulge her always.

"I've decided to go back home. I have to mend things with my mom. I want to have the baby around family. Maybe I'll think about school, or have that later and work. I came here to be alone, to think things through, and avoid being followed or have my every move monitored, but the gossip here is actually no better."

Was that why she talked about the flowers not lasting here? She's probably leaving soon, Xander thought. It was a good thing, if he would admit.

"Whatever you decide to do, I'll support you. I'll make sure you'll be protected. No one will come to you with questions or assault you."

"I mean... I'll have my mom and Laurie. And I'm sure your mom will be there."

After a few seconds, he caught her biting her lip, and a crease appeared in the middle of her brows. What had her deep in thought? She was so lost in it that she did not see the slow appearance of his frown.

And what did she mean?

He was the father of her baby—*their* baby. It was theirs. She mentioned practically having everyone's support except his.

Was he jealous of not having her attention right now? He realised he was.

"Hey," he said, gently stroking her arms. He had to touch her to bring her back to the present. He missed touching her. He always loved having her close and gently caressing his fingers on her soft skin.

"I'll be there too. I'll be there whenever you need me. I'm not going anywhere."

"Xander..."

He saw the shift in her eyes and the seriousness in them.

"I'm not getting back with you, Xander."

"Ally—"

"You're poisonous to me."

That shut him up. Those words hurt.

"You might think that's harsh to say, but it's the truth. What I felt for you almost killed who I thought I was. I was willing to be someone else for you."

"I love the way you are, the way you were. I never tried to change you."

"But *I* tried to change *me*. I was consumed with how I felt about you. Don't get me wrong; despite knowing how you felt about our relationship, I still believed in what I felt for you. I know there's nothing wrong in trying to please the one you love and doing things that make them happy. I wanted you to be happy, Xander. Your happiness made me happy, but... it turned out to be borderline unhealthy."

She closed her eyes and took a deep breath, like she was mustering enough strength to continue talking.

"I almost had the abortion, Xander."

He stared at her with disbelief in his eyes.

"I seriously considered it for you. I would have gone through it for you, to please you—to have you back. That person was not me. I would never have done that in a clear state of mind."

He could see the tears forming in her eyes. She looked so sad that he wished he could turn back time and stop himself from making her this way.

"I used to think I know who I was; my morals, the kind of woman I wanted to be. I had that image of me, you know? And no Xander, part of it wasn't a woman who made decisions like abortion just to get a man to stay.

"No." He held her hands, and she did not push him away. "No, I made those mistakes. I made you think like that. I'm the bad guy. You should not blame yourself. It's all on me. Blame it all on me, Ally. You are a good person, Alicia Storm, and I shouldn't have made you doubt that. You did not go through with it."

Her tears came down without inhibition, and he could feel every part of him aching at the sight. This was all his fault.

"Only because of Laurie. I would have done it if not for her, Xander, and I'll owe her forever."

And so will I, it seems, Xander thought.

"I tried so hard, Xander. I was trying so hard to hold on, but you let go."

Her tear soaked eyes focused on his painful ones as if the beautiful greens could provide the answers.

He knew that. Xander knew he messed up. In solitude, he had played different scenarios in his head of what she could have gone through by herself over and over again. But seeing her this way, his assumptions were no match for her pain. He had been a fool, a coward. *No more running. No more hiding*, he told himself.

"I know saying sorry and asking you to forgive me does not fix things, but give me the chance to make things right, to learn how to make things right for you… for us."

He looked down at her stomach, and he knew Ally understood what he meant. "I'll learn what makes you smile, laugh, sad, cry, and even angry." He wiped her falling tears with the tip of his fingers. "I just don't think I can do any of it without you in the picture, Ally."

He knew she was vulnerable right now, but all he did was wrap her in his arms, and she tucked herself into him. He did not get the answer he wanted to hear, but at least he could do one thing right for her now—even if it was just for tonight.

He knew his words would take time to sink in, and he was going to have to wait. But what else did he have on his plate? He could do that. It was, after all, a small price to pay if it meant he got a chance to be better for Ally and their baby.

CHAPTER 22

He was in the back seat of his car as Paul sat unmoving in the driver's seat, waiting to be told by his boss when they could leave. It has been forty-five minutes since they started waiting out there in utter silence. Paul knew better than to say a word to his boss.

Paul did attempt to do that on the first day, but Xander only repeated to him what he wanted. He needed to think.

As if sitting out here in front of her apartment could help him with that.

Since that night Ally cried her heart out before his very eyes and practically told him they could not be together anymore, he had replayed every conversation in his head to see if he missed something.

He had carried her to her room because she had looked so weak. There was no way she could manage it on her own even if she did try. He made sure she had gone to sleep before he left her side. That did not take much time at all, and he left to clear up the small chaos of snacks in her small living room.

It hurt him to know he was so clueless when it came to her pregnancy. It had changed her habits. Mike had fleetingly mentioned her craving for sweet and sour things, but he should not have to know that from a doctor who maybe, was just being sympathetic with him.

Done cleaning up, he checked up on her again before finally leaving, silently closing the door behind him.

He released a long sigh as soon as his body felt the seat of the car. It had been a long night, but Paul had not questioned him, even when he was told to wait a few minutes before driving… and even when the few minutes had turned into the whole night.

That night had been the start of his waiting and watching.

He always made sure Paul parked out of Ally's sight. This evening was the fifth night. His visits have been short and cautious, and he hated it, coupled with the fact that he was spending more time outside her apartment than around her.

"Let's go, Paul."

"Yes, boss."

Xander thought of what his next step would be. He understood where Ally was coming from and was willing to give her some space. She blamed herself for something she almost did, but he knew he had a big part to play in that. But staying away from her was a completely different matter from staying away from his child. If he walks out of the picture completely, it would be like putting the baby through what he had to experience with his own parents, and no child should ever have to go through that. No child should have to second guess the love of those that brought them to life.

So what if he wanted it all with Ally despite the fact that he had messed things up before waking from his slumber? He did not want another man in the picture. He did not want another man to take his place. Being selfless and letting that happen if it would make her happy would be the right thing to do, but is he selfish when he just wanted them as a family? That he wanted her and no one else?

As Paul drove in front of *The Purcell Hotel*, he was certain things between Ally and himself would be civil from now on, but to hell with being civil. That was for men who did not give a care.

He went ahead while Paul parked the car. He waited along with two strangers for the elevator to come down. Listening to the two chatting, he just had his hands in his back pocket, waiting for his stop. He looked up at the ding of the elevator, and the two men got out. As the elevator was about to close, he heard someone shout for him to hold it, but he ignored the voice. He just stood there, not in the mood to be nice.

He saw a leg in a green flip-flop stick out in the middle of the elevator doors, and a pair of hands stopped them from closing. A slipper fell off in the process.

He had to look at the person when he heard her mutter unclear words, probably directed at him. It was a girl, and she entered the elevator, putting her footwear back on.

She looked young from what he could see, even though he could not see her face well because her eyes were hidden behind dark shades. She was a slim, short, young girl in a black camisole and jean shorts.

Xander held his words. He was seconds away from bolting away out of this annoying girl's continuous murmur.

"That's it!"

He raised a brow when the girl faced him in a firm stance that was almost hilarious. She looked like she was ready to hit him. She had a hand on her hip, the other pointing a finger at him.

"Apologise to me, you rude and arrogant man."

For a small person, she sure had a lot to say.

He did not see what he should be apologising for. If he did, he would have done so. Instead, he ignored her as she continued ranting on how rude he was. Once the elevator door opened, he moved past her with one hand out of his pocket, casually padding to his room.

***

Xander settled in a comfortable T-shirt and jeans as he sat in front of the pile of documents he was yet to sort out. He had more work to wrap up after coming to certain decisions in the short period he had left New York.

He had already made arrangements to move out of his bachelor pad. Since he was going to be a father soon, he could at least provide a child-friendly environment and at the same time, child proof.

But inside, he knew that was just an excuse. He was planning to find a house more suitable for a family—a family with Ally and his child in it.

He also intended to wrap up all his businesses just in case he wanted to resign. Not that he has made a final decision on the situation as yet. He loved what he did, and he did it well. He just wanted to be out of his father's shadow with all that has been happening lately. He believed he could make his own path, but it would not be easy to start from bottom despite his experience and knowledge.

If he did decide to resign eventually, he had to let Julia know. All these would be in months' time, but nevertheless, he knew it was time for Julia to find a new job. He could at least recommend her to great companies. She is smart, so it should not be hard for her.

He knew Julia's presence was not a choice if he wanted Ally back. Ally never spoke again about what happened between him and Julia, and that bothered him. He knew he had a lot to make up for.

He rested his back to the chair, he could not concentrate.

He knew he could not get any work done if he kept thinking like this. Besides, he was meeting his mother in a few hours and probably would have another meeting with a brother in a few days' time. It's funny how things were. Just recently, he thought of how he would have had one, and now, he did. He just was not sure how he felt about this particular brother yet.

They had one thing in common for sure, though: his mother.

He had read the report Paul gave him on Theopolis Christakos. Knowing Theo had his mother's affection while he was left sulking and hating his mother for his absence was already enough reason to dislike the guy.

Was it immature of him? Maybe, but it was how he felt. The file suggested that both of them had a close bond—another thing he did not have with *his* mother.

He heard a knock on the door and stood to go check. It was Paul.

"Sorry, boss. There was a bit of misunderstanding downstairs, and I had to make sure it was taken care of."

If Paul was not elaborating, it was unimportant. If he said it was nothing of concern, then it was not. He trusted Paul. He was the only man he trusted besides his best friends and grandfather.

"I can't concentrate here either. I got nothing done." He sat back in the chair and rubbed his unshaven chin. "I just need you to make sure my meeting with my mother is scheduled as planned."

"Yes, of course."

"What about my father?"

"There's nothing going on with him. He's not making any move that we know of. He's still in New York, and like I said, he's been working."

He had heard about that and confirmed it from Julia. He knew his father arrived in New York four days ago and that he met with his mother before leaving. His father had been taking on work twice as he did before, and he did not understand that. What was he thinking? He had never once understood his father's mind.

"Is there anything else you would like to be done?"

He shook his head. "No. Just make sure it's all private. I'll call you if I need you. Hopefully, I can make my hands useful on something." He referred to the documents in front of him.

"Okay."

Just as Paul was about to leave, he remembered something and called his attention.

"It might be nothing, but I want you to check up on someone for me."

"Who's that?"

He frowned "I don't know who she is."

Paul concentrated on his face out of curiosity.

"It's probably nothing. Forget it. If I encounter her again, I'll have you check on her."

Paul did not seem convinced.

He smirked. "She was just some tiny girl I met in the elevator."

Paul boldly raised his brow at him and he understood. "I'm not stupid to get involved. She looked like a minor, anyway."

Paul nodded and just as he opened the door, he turned to his work, but when he did not hear the door close, he turned to see him speaking to a person he could not see clearly at the door.

"Boss?"

He was already on his feet before Paul called and saw the same girl from the elevator. This time, her light blue orbs were shining at him as her pearly whites happily showed itself in his presence.

He did not think she was a local. She did not look like one. She looked small and innocent, but on her face, she wore the look he was already familiar with. He had seen that look on the faces of women he entertained in the past. They wanted something in return for what they could give him. But the girl standing in front of him looked far too young. He took a wild guess and thought that she was probably eighteen or a just little older. But he could not rely on his guess and fall into a trap. The last thing he wanted right now was a scandal.

Paul's arrival could not have been timed better, he thought.

Paul was silent as he eyed the girl in front of his room. She looked harmless, but in Paul's line of work, everyone who got near his employer was suspicious to him.

They exchanged coded messages with their eyes. Paul gave him a slight nod before walking away. He already understood the situation.

He had enough to find out about her. She had to be in one of the rooms on the top floor since only the occupants there had access to the hallway that led here.

They were assured privacy when they booked the suite. He even had to request a key card for Paul because he was his personal bodyguard. Normally, only occupants were given access to one.

"Huh, did I make him leave? If you're busy—"

"You knocked on my door for a reason, right?"

"I was just thinking how we met with quite the misunderstanding, and I wanted to apologise because... can I come in? I brought this as a peace offering." She raised a small fancy bag. "It's hard to make peace with a stranger when you know nothing about them."

This girl had to be joking. It's only been hours since they met for the first time, and she was bringing him a gift and asking to come in? She was fishing for information, he knew that. Or perhaps she wanted something else. Her lame attempt to be invited in was actually painfully pitiful to him.

"You don't owe me an apology just as I don't owe you one. I'm quite busy, and your attempt to make things clear was not necessary."

She giggled.

Now he was concerned. This would be bad if she was underage.

"You sound like an old man. I bet all you do is work, work and hardly relax. Since...*you're not married?*" She continued without taking her eyes off him.

He should tell her about his woman and child, but he did not really see it as her concern.

"Just one drink." When she moved from her spot, he blocked the entrance with more of his body, and when she saw this, she gave him a full blown grin.

"I'm not asking to come in since I realise that probably won't happen. We can meet in the lobby. Definitely platonic."

She really was a pest who refused to scurry away, and her attitude was ticking him off. Before he spoke, she started to speak again. "Whenever you want then. You never can tell, you might find yourself in need of a little bit of fun."

She turned to leave and stopped in her tracks, drawing a smile once more. "By the way, my name's Sophie."

He closed the door behind him and looked at the bag in his hand. How had she managed to get it in his hand? He dropped it on the floor beside the door and would have Paul take care of it. She looked like she was interested in him, but he would wait to have Paul bring him information on her. He could not have a minor stalking him.

He heard his phone ring and hoped it was Ally calling him. Yes, he had her new number now. Just like what he thought, things were civil between them for now. He picked up his phone to see it was Jay calling. It had been a while since he last talked to his best friend. Jay knew all about what he was going through, and Xander had promised to update him on how things were going. He had forgotten about that.

"Hey, man," He greeted.

"What is it that I hear about Alexander Cross leaving everything behind for a woman? When the fuck did that happen? How?" His other best friend, Dom, spoke at the other end. Dom had been out of the country for a while, and he barely knew all that was going on with him.

Or at least he thought so.

"You have Jay's phone. Are you in New York right now?"

"Where else will I be, idiot? Jay couldn't possibly leave his work to take a vacation in France with me. What the hell, man? I hear about your predicaments from Jay, but you couldn't call to tell me?"

Actually, he did not willingly tell Jay everything. He just happened to be around. He was the one who prescribed Ally birth control pills and was one of the people he had taken his frustrations out on when he first found out about Ally's pregnancy.

"You were having fun pretending to be a French man. I did not want to spoil that for you."

"Yeah, Xander. No one beats you when it comes to lame excuses. I was done with work months ago, and you knew that. Now that I'm here, I expect you to tell me what's really going on."

He groaned, and heard Dom laugh. "I know you've squeezed it all out of Jay. Why do you want to hear me point out my sufferings?"

"You should have called to let me know, you know. I want to hear about this girl. I have to meet her."

"And you'll be doing more damage for me. You'll say stupid things, and I'll probably never see her again," He replied light-heartedly, knowing how much his best friend could spout ridiculous things when he starts. Dom was the funniest out of the three friends—not that he nor Jay were the funny kind.

"You're right, Jay. Xander's in love." He heard Dom say to Jay.

He never even mentioned that to him.

"Now I *do* have to meet this girl. Don't worry, man, I'll win her heart for you with my charms since I hear you've been making dick moves since you met her."

He groaned again. Either Jay said those exact words to Dom, or he was just translating it that way to piss him off.

Since the three became close friends in college, Joshua 'Jay' had been the serious one. He loved his books just as much as Xander and Dominic 'Dom' loved to party and pick up the women. But during the rare times that Jay made time to join them, the three always had a blast and made a lot of after party mess.

None of them were married, but now, he certainly was close to having a family. A surprise, since he never would have believed he would be the first one out of the three.

The three of them always joked around how Jay would probably be married with kids before he turned thirty and how Xander and Dom would play the rad, bachelor uncle role. But those two were focused on their career. Jay was aiming for his own hospital while Dom was an anonymous artist and a software programmer. Still, with the level of success Dom had, he could not stay in one place for a long period and still surrounded himself with women.

While he had also been a playboy, he never pampered or went soft with the women he slept with, unlike Dom. Dom actually made an effort to care about them.

"Seriously, man, how embarrassed can you make a woman get? Bringing her to your best friend for birth control pills?"

"It did not seem like a big deal. I trusted Jay."

"You know nothing about women. Obviously, you learnt nothing. I would not have left you all alone if I knew you would create this mess for yourself." Dom said, chuckling under his breath.

"Leave the guy alone," He heard Jay tell Dom.

"So, *Papa* Xander...?" Dom said, and his two best friends burst into laughter.

He cut the phone, and seconds later, it started ringing again.

"Aw, come on, man. Does it make you angry?"

"I have better things to do than listening to your stupid jokes."

"But I was serious. You are going to be a *papa*, aren't you? Besides, I just wanted to hear for myself if you love the girl." Dom's voice was calmer now, and he fell silent.

"Does it feel right?" Dom asked after some time.

"Hell, it feels more than right," He replied.

Dom chuckled. "When are you getting back?"

"Next week or before then. We just need to wrap things here."

"We? She's coming with you? Is she with you right now?"

"It's not like I have things in place yet. Honestly, nothing's working out for me. Sometimes, I let myself think I may never have it. It's just... civil between us now."

Civil...It was a word he was starting to dislike.

"You've got your best buds. You know how easy I win over women's hearts, and Jay can always give you the moral advice."

"What the hell does that mean?" He heard Jay ask.

"Dude, we all know you're the decent one amongst us three," Dom said.

It was true. For the most part of their years of friendship, Jay had set both Dom and him straight when they started crossing the line. Jay was great at making people see reason, and Dom was great with women—excellent, in fact. The only heart he knew Dom never won was Julia's. He never understood why Dom held on to his feelings for Julia for this long, but now, he was starting to understand how it feels like.

Being in love with someone was not something you just let go. He would make darn sure he wins Ally's heart by the time their child turns five.

They ended the call after half an hour or so, and Xander prepared to get in the shower. He would be meeting his mom in a short while.

***

Ally had been right.

His mom looked more beautiful than he remembered and really looked younger than her age. Looking right at her confirmed what the pictures could not tell him in a million shots. She seems to look different from their first meeting at Ally's check up.

He found his mother seated minutes earlier than the agreed time. He was a little surprised when Paul called to let him know his mother had arrived and was waiting where Paul had led her.

He had paid to reserve a rather small open space in the hotel so the dinner with his mom could be private.

Mother and son sat right across each other but were yet to say a word. It felt awkward for both of them until he took the initiative.

"I imagined something different."

His mother's face shot up when he spoke. She was not exactly looking him in the face when he joined her.

"I imagined a lot of questions and things we would talk about. For years, I had things I wanted to say to you figured out. But honestly, it makes no sense now. I hated you for a long time, and now I don't know how I feel about those things. I have just recently found out the truth about the past, but I still want to hear it from you."

His mom shook her head, speaking immediately. "I do have a lot to explain and to make up for. What I did, abandoning you, at that time it felt like I had no choice, that I was protecting you from my mistakes. But sometimes... most times, all through the years I've been away, I thought about my decision. What if...? What if...?" She looked at him. "Those two words were at the core of my regrets. I'm so sorry, Alexander. I should have been a better mother to you. Even when I didn't know how, I should have tried harder."

He could see sadness etched on her face. He was not sure what to say. His father never told him what happened. His grandfather was not sure about the details, and asking the woman in front of him, his mother, would be cruel in the state she was in. He saw the tears in her eyes pass freely, and she scrambled to wipe them away.

This was getting out of hand. If she continues crying, he will not be sure how to handle it.

"Perhaps we should just... Ehm—" He coughed out. "—get to know each other."

"We should?" His mom repeated.

That coupled with her teary face made him smile. Who knew those words would cheer her up instantly?

"There are lots of things we need to talk about, obviously."

"I'll tell you everything you want to know. What I want is to get to know you again. Be a mother to you... if that's okay." She said the last part as if she had just realised she might have been too forward. "But if it's not, we can... I can understand that. I'll just do what you want. Whatever pace you need—"

"Mom..." He firmly said to cease her rambling.

He watched his mother freeze at the word before turning wide-eyed. He honestly did not know what else to call her. A smile slowly appeared on her face as she swallowed back her sobs.

Xander was confused. Having two women he cared about cry because of him—even if this was for a different reason—was scary. He did not know what to do right now. It was easy to wrap Ally in his arms, but he was not sure how to handle his mom.

She looked at him with a tear-stained face and smiled. How could he hate her all this time? His mother obviously loved him. He stretched his hand and took hers on the table.

He had a lot to make right in his life. He had new responsibilities, and he was grateful for growing because of those two. He used to think he had everything going for him, but with his mother, Ally, and a baby in the picture now, he was looking forward to a new future.

He was not yet sure if and how he would be able to handle it all, but he knew it was well worth a try.

***

After few minutes of talking about the simple things, both could feel the air around them grow lighter—a yet unspoken understanding between mother and son. They would take it from there and see how their relationship gets mended. They still had a lot of missing pieces to fill, and Xander was sure he would get an understanding of what his father was hiding from his mother after some time.

She excused herself to freshen up.

He was happy. Her presence made him happy even though he was not sure why. Maybe it was the fact that he was looking forward to using the word 'mom' again after a darn long time. He took out his phone and sent a text to Ally with a smile on his face.

I met with my mom. Thank you.

***

Sophie watched both of them.

Was that the woman he was dating? He ditched having a drink with her for an older woman? Both of them looked happy in each other's presence, but she saw a relationship that was not convincing. They both looked unsure. It seemed that way to her.

She frowned. She really did not want to get into this kind of trouble again, but what was she to do? She was sick of hiding. She brought out her phone and searched for the contact she needed.

"Dave," she spoke as soon as it was answered.

"Sophie, where the hell are you? Tony is furious. He's threatening to cut you off his label."

She scoffed. "He can't do that. There's a contract."

"You know he can. So just get yourself here. Where are you calling from?"

"I'm protecting myself."

"Then you should not have had an affair with someone else's husband," Dave silently murmured, but she heard it. "These things happen sometimes. It won't be the end of your career, but *you're* the one making it a bigger deal."

"If everyone's criticizing me, you shouldn't too. You're my manager. By the way, I found something that will make it all go away. I found someone."

Dave groaned underneath. "You stupid girl. You're going to get involved with another man?"

She blocked the rest of his words out and continued. "He's rich, unmarried, and just what I need to block the hate on me."

"You really get on my last nerve, but I'll hear you out."

"Do you have a choice?" She laughed.

***

"Hello?"

"You sound dejected. Is something wrong?" Ally asked Laurie, concerned.

"Other than having an argument with Tony? There's a scandal with one of his singers. He was getting annoying, your name came up, and things just got out of hand."

"My name?"

"The idiot knows nothing about loyalty."

"Hey, what's this about?"

"You know Sophie Lane?"

"I don't think so. Should I?"

Laurie sighed. "You probably don't. She's a newbie. Apparently a talented one but a brat."

"Okay. And?"

"She stole someone else's man and went into hiding when the heat got too much. Tony said something about hate letters. No one knows where she is."

"*Okay*. What has that got to do with me?"

"He thinks she's somewhere close to Valley Top."

"Valley Top? Here?"

"Hhmhhm. I would ask you to contact me if you see her but you don't know her, and since she's hiding... *Ah!* Forget about it. Hearing her name all through last night was enough. I have this headache that won't go away now."

"So you had a fight with Tony," She said. "Do you like him?"

"Who? Tony? I'm sleeping with him... or was. I don't even know now. I wouldn't if I did not. Why ask?"

She thought Laurie might like Tony. She had not met the guy before, but she knew he was the same guy—the socialite Laurie talked about seeing around the time she started dating Xander.

That was a long time, at least for Laurie. She had never known her cousin to be in a relationship that long. Either her cousin was aware and ignoring it, or she simply did not realise she had broken her own rules.

"Hey. What about you? Have you gotten laid? You still won't tell me what you two talked about."

"I told you. We just talked. We're both clear on where we are. Things are good. That good really that we're coming together."

"Why would I want to know when you both climax?" She said nonchalantly.

"Laurie!"

"Ha, keep it down. I really don't feel good. I think I'm coming down with something."

"Then stop being dirty minded. Maybe you should visit the hospital if it's serious."

"I just need some rest. I haven't had sex in a while though, it can't be—"

"Seriously, Laurie, *get some rest.* Maybe it's time you need to be looked after. I'll be home in days."

After speaking to Laurie, a text came in on her phone. When she read Xander's short message, she smiled. She was happy for Liliana. *Good for you both*, she thought. It made her stare at her phone for a while before she gathered the courage she needed and turned her thoughts into action.

She dialed her mom's number. The voice at the other end made Ally realize it was time she went home.

CHAPTER 23

The first week back home, in her mother's apartment in New York City, Ally imagined she would feel awkward around her mother, and rightly so. It was so obvious that her mother watched every move and word she made. It had been exhausting by thc cnd of that week. It was starting to feel like she was living with a stranger.

So much that she had not caught her mom smoking and she wondered if it was because she decided to quit or the fact that she was now living with a pregnant woman.

For days, she played around how to approach the giant in the room but hesitantly withdrew every attempt she made.

Then it had happened.

The topic came up somehow, and her mother could not stop talking about the mistake she made on not paying attention to her daughter. Even when she insisted they should not talk about it anymore, her mother refused to oblige.

"You think I want to think about that? I hurt my baby girl. I did not put my daughter's feelings first... Instead, I was... I was thinking of myself. Your dad probably has been cursing at me since you left home."

"Mom—"

"I mean it, baby. I should have talked to you, maybe supported what you wanted with some advice and not criticize your every decision. He was what you wanted. You fell in love."

"Mom—" It was so easy for her to tear up right now. The last time she saw this kind of emotion on her mom's face was when her dad's sickness started to get worse. Knowing there was nothing they could do but spend the rest of his days together, reliving and creating memories broke their heart. And that was the same expression her mom was currently wearing.

"Ally, listen to me. Your father was not the first man I fell in love with."

Ally was confused. She assumed her dad was her mom's first love since that was all her dad had always sung to her. After all, all they talked about their relationship was knowing each other in their teens and getting married at twenty-one. Where and how did another guy come in?

She listened. She did not interrupt because honestly, she was curious.

She watched as her mom gave a resigned sigh as if she had no intention of letting her ever find out about this. "I met a guy when I was seventeen. I had just finished high school, and mom was willing to let Wendy and I go on this island vacation with some girls from Wendy's class."

Her mom smiled, and it was clear on her face that she was taking herself back to that moment. She could only wonder all the things her mom and aunt Wendy, Laurie's mom, did as young girls considering aunt Wendy was exactly like Laurie and probably more. She was aware that her mom was not exactly a softie. She was a very active woman, and it was no secret from who she had inherited her calm personality—her dad.

"It was not some place particularly spectacular. In fact, I had never heard of it, but one of the girls' families had some connection or something. Well, Wendy took care of all the details, and you know how persuasive and unrelenting my sister can be."

She nodded in agreement and smiled. She loved her aunt, but she sometimes agreed with Laurie that they had to avoid having her around. She was an unrelenting firestorm that would attach herself to everything she came in contact with and decide to make it her business.

"It was just two days after we arrived there, and I was unexpectedly having fun when I met him. He was like no man I had ever come in contact with." Her mom explained with emotion.

"He was good-looking but certainly not the most handsome guy I had seen. In fact, my sister wondered what I saw in him when there were more hot guys around according to her. I didn't think so. He had a charm that drew people to him, and most of the girls wanted him if he would have their company. I did too, of course, but I never imagined he would notice me. I was months shy of turning eighteen after all, and he was twenty-four."

She was seeing a pattern. That was almost the same gap between her and Xander's age. Now she feared she would not like where her mom's story was heading.

"Long story short, he did notice me, and I was flattered and hooked. Whatever I felt for him, it was neither planned nor controlled by me."

Her mom faced her with a smile. "So that's why I should have known better and supported you. But all I saw was history probably having a repeat with my daughter. It left a scar in me, and that's how much I know it would hurt if the same thing happened to you. So I just thought, how can I sit around and wait for that possibility?"

"What happened?" She wanted to know. She had never guessed such a thing could have happened in her mom's past.

Her mom sighed. "He never took me to their home even though it was no secret that his family was rich and famous in the town. I knew that.

He never talked about it, and I did not want to pressure him. I was a girl he met days before, anyway, and it was not like I was willing to meet his family too. I mean, I was seventeen."

She stretched her hands to hold her mom's, encouraging her to continue.

"Wendy warned me, but I was having the perfect vacation. It went on for three weeks, and one day, he wanted to cook us dinner, his favourite since childhood, and he was convinced I would love it too. We had gone to this popular shop that seemed like the only good one around. We were there, *shopping* for close to thirty-five minutes, laughing and joking around with just one ingredient in the basket, when this girl came up to us with a smile on her face."

Her mom looked right at her.

"I did not think the girl was a stranger from how they exchanged greetings. Their families had history, I guess. Well, he told me that after. I was shocked when unexpectedly, his fiancée's mother appeared beside her."

"Fiancée?"

She nodded. "Yes. She was his fiancée. Obviously, both of them knew ahead what was expected of them. He was engaged, and she was pregnant."

"Pregnant?"

"I did not need to be told, seeing the noticeable bump on her. The girl's mother made sure to point it out to me. I was not stupid to not put that piece in the puzzle. She was pregnant. They were engaged. It had to be his."

"Mom…" Ally felt for her mother. She could not imagine what that must have been like.

"I just did not understand why he had to do that to me. I tried wrapping my head around the situation, trying to create reasons why he deceived me. I was heartbroken, of course. I'd just been cheated by a man I gave my heart, my pride as a woman, and a promise of forever to."

"What?"

"He asked if I could love him forever, even though he was not sure anything of such kind was possible. Meeting me was already a blessing. He could have faith in forever if it were with me— so he told me."

Her mom shook her head with a sad smile on her face and she mirrored the expression only without the smile.

"I should have told you this before Xander came into your life. I saw him as another Pedro, and I feared you would be in my shoe."

"You still love him?"

"No," she said without hesitation. "Your father, bless him, made sure of that. I loved Pedro, but your father opened my heart again by sincerely showing me his. Mac showed me not all men are the same and not all love can be expressed the same way."

"You're saying despite all that happened, you still believe this Pedro guy truly loved you?"

She nodded. "Or at least I knew he was sincere about caring."

"Then? Did he give you a reason to why he did it? Why he lied?"

"What was the point? All I heard that day from him was that he cared about me and he was doing all he could to get out of the marriage. Besides, Wendy would not allow it. Then she found out from a local gossip that though no one knew about the engagement, there had been speculations that both families would probably try being one with a union. At least that's what was said."

"I'm sorry," She said.

"For what, baby? That was *my* experience. I know Xander is rich, famous, and attractive, but he's not hiding another pregnant woman from you. I did not like him, and I'm not saying I do now, but the truth is, I never tried to know him. It's clear he cares about you a lot but Ally, if it's what you want, I want it for you too. I need you to know that." Her mother held her hand. "I do not doubt for a moment that you'll be a better mom than I am to you."

Would she though? Was she ever be?

***

Ally took a gulp of water from the glass in her hand.

She still remembered very clearly the conversation she had with her mom two weeks ago. It happened after she came home with Xander three months back.

The conversation sometimes crept into her thoughts whenever she was alone. She was not sure if her mother had been trying to tell her something regarding her relationship with Xander. Maybe her mother might have noticed she was anxious about the baby's birth, and in her own way, tried to assure her that she would do fine.

When her mom found out that her relationship with Xander had turned rocky, she tried to be discreet, having them both under her watchful eyes. She never really asked her what and why, and Ally was grateful for that. Maybe someday she would be strong enough to disclose to her mom that she almost had an abortion. Besides, she realised that her mother refused to acknowledge much of Xander's presence. So it came as a surprise when her mom told her about her first love and heartbreak.

Surprisingly, during the past three months at home, her mom's attitude towards Xander was in no way a determinant of how she received Liliana. They got along well. So well, in fact, that both women shared interests they both enjoy; exchanging tips on cooking and taking turns watching her. It was not like she needed to be watched, but neither of the two women ever listened to her.

This day turned out to be a rare one because her mom and Liliana had a night out. She understood that was only because she was going out this afternoon and Xander was coming over later on. They knew she was not going to be alone.

She could finally breathe. Having a break from her mother and Xander's was freedom. She loved that they care, but they treated her pregnancy and not being with her baby's father a little too cautiously.

Talking about Xander, they have been civil the past months—a word she readily used when anyone asked. It was almost like they never had that talk, almost like she never said that she could not be with him and sobbed her eyes out and how he insisted he was not giving up.

He never talked about that again or anything regarding the two of them, and that was good for her. She did not have to dread his visits or be uncomfortable around him anymore. It helped.

They talked about the baby most of the time; her plan after the baby was born, for one. Whenever they tried coming up with names, it usually turned into a funny ruckus. They never agreed on any name. So he suggested that he come up with girl names while she thinks of boy names. They would then make a decision on their shortlist.

"It's going to be a girl." Xander would not shut up about the baby being a girl.

"I would like a boy."

She had always fantasised about having a boy for a first child, someone who can protect his little sisters or brothers, but now that she was pregnant, her six months' worth of wait was enough to know what sex she could start referring her baby as.

Another person she had grown to know better in the past few months was Theo. She did not know how things were like between him and Xander. She never asked either of them. It would be too awkward especially when Laurie had pointed out to her that Xander might know about her attraction to Theo.

She did not want to be in that kind of situation either, but her hormones and emotions were everywhere.

Was she still having urges? Hell, yes! But there was nothing she could do about it. It was something she had to bear until the next few months.

Whenever Xander was around her, the feeling just creeps in slowly until it became a full-blown thing. She assumed he must have an inkling of her predicament, but he never initiated anything. She was thankful for that because if he did, she honestly was not sure she would be in the right mind to think about anything else except her own needs.

Then there was that one embarrassing time when she and Theo were left alone in the house.

"I like you, Ally and I know you're attracted to me but I can't make your life any more complicated." He then walked towards where she stood.

Her senses had been out of whack that day. She assumed he was coming in for a kiss and prepared for that. She almost puckered out, thinking to herself how she would finally have her hands on a solid chest and a warm body. Just something, anything to take the edge off.

She had her hands on his chest which was much harder than she had imagined, and he rested one of his hands on her back, firmly supporting her weight as the other brushed lightly on her face. Her pulse went a notch faster, waiting for that one move from him and thinking, *this is it.*

That was when she felt his slightly cold lips on her forehead. *Forehead!*

He did come in for a kiss alright, but it was far from what she expected. It was just seconds longer than a short kiss on the forehead, and she knew what it meant. Just like Xander, he was giving her space. But the look she saw on Theo's face that day felt like a permanent one.

How did she end up from being a horny pregnant lady with two attractive guys to this hideously frustrating dry spell? It just made her more annoyed.

Theo saw the look on her face, but he could not have understood what she was really thinking.

Finally regaining a little sanity, she realised then that Theo was never really an option to satisfy her needs. She would have just used him. If only she were not pregnant when she met Theo.... She would probably have been out of control with him.

"If I kiss you, I would start something dangerous and hurtful. There's something I want more than to be selfish right now—for you to be happy."

Was she happy? Was she truly happy with the way things were for her now?

The only two people she heard nothing about were Xander's father and Julia.

At that point, Ally realised that she had drifted on her thoughts again and snapped herself from thinking too much, reminding herself she would be late for lunch with a friend if she kept it up. She needed the stretch. Besides, it had been a while since she saw his face. They only had the opportunity to talk on the phone. He was the only one she could talk to about the thoughts she sometimes had, thoughts that scared her. She was too embarrassed to discuss it with her doctor, not wanting anyone to think less of her because of it.

She got dressed in a floral knee-length dress and took a jacket just in case she needed it and was out the door.

The weather was perfect, and already, she was feeling more energetic.

When she opened the door to the restaurant, she easily spotted who she came to meet. His light blue eyes looked straight at her as he raised a hand. She smiled.

"Wow," Mike exclaimed, looking at her baby bump.

She hugged him as tight as her bulging midriff would allow.

"Did I keep you waiting?"

"Not for too long. You're lucky I actually spared the afternoon for you."

"I'm sorry. I decided to walk the last ten minutes over here. I needed it."

He laughed. "You look healthy—and round."

She chuckled. "You can say big. It's the truth. That's my mom's fault and Liliana's. I hardly do anything except take strolls, stretches, stir things—" She raised a finger to keep him from asking. "Don't ask."

He laughed again.

"The most effort I put into anything is eat."

"Well, it looks good on you. You look beautiful."

"And that's all they both tell me."

"It's the truth."

A waiter came and took their order.

"So, how have you been? I finally get to see your face. What keeps you so busy when you come here? It's not like you're here to work, is it?"

He shook his head and sipped on his water. "She really did not tell you anything about it," he muttered under his breath, but she heard it.

"She?"

Mike kept quiet. "Let's just talk about you and the baby. How have you been feeling? Do you still have those—"

There was only one *she* Ally could think of. "Are you talking about Laurie?"

Mike evaded the question, and as if on cue, their food arrived. He dug straight into it, but she refused to eat without getting an answer.

"Is something going on between you two?" She has been suspecting that her cousin was keeping something from her, but she had enough respect for Laurie's privacy to stop asking if she was not willing to tell.

"Am I right? Is something going on between you two?"

Mike gave in and looked her straight in the eye. "Obviously nothing if she has not said anything even to you."

"Is she supposed to say something to me?" She asked confused.

"She tells you everything about her, right?"

"Yes, except when it comes to her relationships. She always says they're not important and—" She stared wide-eyed at Mike. "Are you two seeing each other?"

"We were."

"Since when?"

"Two and half months."

"*Two and...?*" She exclaimed, putting down her fork.

Mike continued eating like it was no big deal. In contrast, she was surprised that the two got together. That was fast.

Two and a half months? How did that even happen? It did not even occur to her that they liked each other. Was it all just for sex?

"So what's wrong?"

"She's out of town, right?"

"Yes."

"She won't pick up my calls or reply to my texts."

"Did you two have a fight?"

"I'm not sure. She would not talk to me. She shut me out all of a sudden, and it would be better if I knew why. If she's trying to tell me she does not want me anymore, I think I should know why."

"Do you like Laurie, Mike?"

"That's why I'm dating her."

"Dating? You two are *dating?*"

Mike raised an eyebrow and looked at her as if what he just said was anything but strange.

"Does Laurie know you two are dating?"

"What are you getting at, Ally?"

"It's just... I've never known Laurie to...*date.*"

"I'm not the first relationship she's had."

"No. But Laurie does not get... attached like that."

"Did she tell you that?"

"It's how she's always been with relationships."

He paused for a while, dropping his fork. "Do you think she might have freaked out because I changed my relationship status from single to in a relationship on my Facebook? It makes sense since she would not pick my calls a day after I did that."

"Probably."

He groaned. "I only did that because of Tiffany." He groaned again. "She's been stalking me since you left. She would not leave me alone, claiming I'm single and free to chase. I should have told Laurie about it. I did not think it mattered since we were already seeing each other."

"Have you two really talked about what it is you both want out of your relationship?"

"Honestly? We've had a lot more sex than talk in the last two months."

"Okay! Sensitive ears right here."

Mike smiled.

"I don't need the details. But I think you should send Laurie a text, tell her why you changed your status—if that's why she's avoiding you. And don't forget to put Tiffany's name in bold. She does not like her. I bet she'll respond immediately. And when she does, you need to talk to her," She said, suddenly turning seriously.

"Thanks for the tip, Ally. I knew it was a great idea to meet you for lunch."

"Oh, so now you're just using me?"

He laughed. "What kind of gentleman would treat a pregnant lady in such way?" He joked.

She laughed and tasted her food. It was now unappealing to her.

"Do you want to get something else?" Mike must have noticed the sad face she made in front of her food.

"No. I suddenly don't feel up to it anymore." She was going to have an early dinner, anyway. But she can't tell Mike that. He might ask questions, and she did not want Mike or anyone else to think further into it.

"Is everything else good?" He asked, fixing his eyes on hers.

She knew what he was asking. He was the only one who knew. Not even Laurie, and she was sure Mike would not tell her, not even now that she knew they were involved.

"I think so. I haven't had weird dreams and having people around keeps me from thinking too much about it. But when everyone's around me, talking about the baby, I feel this sudden pressure on me again."

"I know you assured me it would be fine and you could handle it, but I think you need to talk to someone."

"Talk to someone?"

"It's not my field, and I'm not certain, but I think what you have is prenatal depression."

"What? I'm not depressed."

"Your thoughts are. And you're pregnant, and it's concerning your baby. I might be wrong, and it might be nothing, but I still would like it if you saw someone—someone who's better qualified in that area."

"Is that necessary? I really am not—"

"Ally," Mike firmly said. "Do you *want* this baby?"

She nodded.

"Do you *care* about this baby?"

She nodded again.

"Do you think this baby is lucky to have you as its mother?"

She hesitated on that, not answering.

"You doubt yourself, you blame yourself, and you don't think you deserve it. Believe me, it's unhealthy for all of you."

She opened her mouth, wondering who he meant by all, but not a word came out.

"Xander does not know about this. You can't be with him because you still can't break your own walls. How will you handle the one between the two of you? The guy thinks you won't give him another chance because of his mistakes."

She was aware that Mike and Xander kept in touch, but she did not know they talked to the point of having heart-to-heart conversations.

"You did not say anything, did you?"

"I promised you. We both know what you're going through. It does not feel right keeping it between us." Mike looked at his watch and sighed. "It's almost three. I have a meeting in thirty minutes. Come on, let me drop you off."

Before she could reply, her phone beeped. Meanwhile, Mike was settling the bill, and she used that moment to check.

"I'll be at your mom's in two hours. Don't worry. I had the best practice. Dinner will be perfect."

"Ally?"

She looked up to see Mike ready to leave. "I think I'll sit for a few minutes before leaving."

"You sure?"

"Yeah." She nodded.

"Will you give what I said a second thought? I'm available if you need to talk, always. You know that."

"I know. Thanks, Mike. It's really fine."

And it was fine. She sat back to do two things: reply to Xander's text—

"Looking forward to dinner. I'm sure you got it."

—and the other, to Google 'prenatal depression.'

CHAPTER 24

The past few months were a roller-coaster. It was quite a ride—at least that was what Xander fely. It was surprising how mature his mind had grown in all the events that happened. At the top of it all was that he was going to be a father. He never thought that chapter in his life would be something to look forward to with pride. But now, it is, and he got that because of Ally.

There were so many changes in just a few months: Julia was out of his life—professionally and personally; and he had a new business relationship with his father—only because his father was willing to bend his stiff ideals rather than see his son leave the company and be missing in his son's life, possibly forever. For some reason he was yet to understand, it meant a lot to Cameron Cross that his son inherits what he had. But it was not like the idea brought the two any closer than they were before.

Speaking of getting close, he had formed an unexpected relationship with Theo and Mike. In the beginning, he resisted because those two had their sights on Ally—or at least Mike did. However, Mike was now a friend he held in high esteem as he did Jay and Dom. All four of them got along well. He spoke to Mike more about his situation with Ally because he knew she was close to him and they talked often.

Theo, on the other hand, was a brother at arm's length. Brother… Yeah, that was a word he avoided using. It was weird to call Theo that, and he usually just called him by his name, not that Theo returned the courtesy. He was yet to decide if the guy was always trying to piss him off or just feeling brotherly whenever he addressed him as his little brother. Theo was a hard man to ignore because they were in a business partnership.

His presence was a constant reminder of what he never had with his mom. Whenever his mother tells him one of those 'Theo stories,' Theo always complements that by calling her mom. Fine, they somehow shared a mom, and the media and found that out and immediately sunk their teeth in, plastering his and Theo's faces on magazine covers and news. The headlines: "Two of the richest and most successful business bachelors, related."

He did not want to be called a bachelor anymore. He was in love, and he wanted that to be known. However, Ally had less paparazzi on her tail, and he could not risk her privacy. That was worth the silence for now.

He had stopped by the company headquarters this morning and was now taking the rest of the day off because of his plans with Ally. He was a bit behind, by the way, because Theo called in and wanted to go over something important that needed his very own attention. He grabbed his phone from the table and sent a quick text to Ally, letting her know he would be at her mom's soon. He could not resist adding a recent skill he acquired into the text.

She knew he was a horrible cook. He proved it the first day he brought her to his place, making a mess of the kitchen and scrap of what was meant to be their dinner, but now, he had lots of practice under his belt from his mom. She did not know that. She probably thought he was learning it from a cookbook or recipes online. He smiled when he remembered the look on her face when he came up with the idea of making dinner. She had looked horrified, but he did a good job of convincing her. She had warned him to remember she was pregnant, and it had made him burst into laughter.

Two more hours and he would be with her. He grabbed one of the three set of books he purchased and continued reading *Becoming A New Dad.*

***

Ally was ready for the evening, and as she walked towards the door to open up for Xander, she stared open-mouthed at the amount of groceries his hands held. He only gave her a grin as he passed by her into the kitchen.

"Should I be worried?" She closed the door and followed behind him.

He emptied his hands and faced her as she stood in front of the doorway. "This? You'll see I'm better at this than the last attempt I ruined on our first date." Xander rolled up the sleeves of his sweatshirt and gave her a smile.

She could only stare, still not convinced. She watched him for a while even after he asked her to go take a seat. So far, he looked like he knew what he was doing with a knife—at least there was no cut or blood yet. Apart from that, she was more comfortable around him, with just the two of them. At the moment, it was not awkward.

For a while now, he stopped constantly reminding Ally what he wanted. He was respecting what she wanted, and it was getting harder for her to forget why she fell in love with him in the first place and the possibility that she might still be—not that her mind gave her time to dwell much about it.

He looked towards her direction again and sent her a bright smile. It was not the first time Xander smiled at her genuinely in the past few months. In fact, she saw most of it during her check-ups whenever the doctor gave them good news about the baby's health. Every worry that she had would seep away for a brief moment before the doubts set in again. She would then wear that mask that said 'I'm fine, everything will be okay' when she really felt nothing like it deep down.

Right in her mother's kitchen, it was not just Xander's smile she found disconcerting. It was also his arms at work, his dancing green eyes that his green sweatshirt did well to bring out, and his—

The ringing of a phone cut through, making her realise what she was doing. It was Xander's.

"That's me," he said as his hands were dipped in what she assumed was mashed potato, among other things. He turned to her, seemingly realising the position he was in. "Please? Can you get it out for me and put it on speaker?" He nodded towards his front jean pocket.

She moved towards him and tried to use two fingers to bring the gadget out, but it was not working. The angle he was in was uncomfortable, and the stupid phone was placed too deep to get out that way. When he realised her struggle, he presented his full frontal view. His figure shadowing her small frame, she moved closer and had to use more fingers to get to the phone. It was almost impossible not to be aware of each other's presence. She could smell him and almost feel his body heat radiating. That was how close she was to him.

She hoped Xander did not notice the sudden change in her breathing. It felt like time stood still, the phone long forgotten. She had no idea what he was thinking, but she had her eyes on his chest and saw her other hand that was not trying to get into his pocket rest on the hard plane. She wanted badly to look up and see what he was thinking through his eyes, but she knew she should not. The phone had stopped ringing, and when it started up again, it startled her and she scrambled to get it out.

She saw the name on the screen—*Mom.* She answered the phone before shifting back a bit and placing it on speaker like he wanted. When

Xander started to speak, she excused herself. It was not because she wanted to give him some privacy but because she did not want to create time for him to react to what happened earlier.

She found a thing or two to occupy herself with since Xander refused her help. She needed to do so anyway. It was getting torturous to watch him, especially after that embarrassing display. She had imagined those hands doing something else and then, *that* had happened. Her hormones skyrocketed in his presence after she started becoming comfortable around him again. Giving each other pleasure had never felt like an itch that needed to be scratched. It was never a favour to satisfy the other's need, so why should it be different now? She knew it would be unfair to him, knowing what he wanted.

There was nothing much that could be concentrated on with Xander just a room away. An hour and a half later when she went into the kitchen to get herself some water, he looked really busy. He was the slowest cook she had come across. She looked around him and what he as doing.

At least what she saw was starting to look like food.

***

He noticed her come into the kitchen, moving around as if he would not notice her.

Xander was fine with that for now. He did not want to startle her and make things awkward. He would let it go for now. When his phone had started to ring the second time and broke up the moment they had, he almost got mad at his mother, groaning lowly when she told him she was calling to see how he was doing. It was the first time in a long time Ally had made contact first even if it was not on purpose.

That was progress, and he had his mom to thank for that—or otherwise.

He turned for a brief moment to where she was standing, and he noticed her stomach like he noticed every part of her.

As weird as it sounded, he was yet to touch his growing child. The closest he got was seeing that part of her during the check ups. The book he was reading advised that he do that and talk to the baby, but he did not want to spook away Ally's gradual trust in him. He noticed that she was still uncomfortable making contact with his skin. If she was avoiding saying anything about what happened earlier, it had to mean she was still uncomfortable.

He nodded his head, motioning for her to come closer, and raised a spoon towards her to have a taste of what he had cooking. He waited as she savoured the soup and saw her raise her eyebrows in surprise.

"Not bad."

"Yeah?" he said, pleased.

She nodded slowly, looking at him. "It tastes good. From a hopeless cook to decent! I'm impressed, Xander. What have you done to yourself?"

"You'd be surprised."

"So what's that?" She asked.

He raised an eyebrow. *She could not tell from the taste?* His mom told him she'd love it. "Really?"

"It tastes good, but I'm not sure what it's supposed to be."

He groaned a bit. "Are you kidding? You can't even tell from the look?" He moved out of her view to let her see.

She shook her head slowly.

"I swear I got everything right like she taught me." He was frowning, thinking of all his effort for the last hour and a half.

"She?"

"My mom," He replied without even focusing on her stance. He took a taste to see what he was missing. Everything he did was a step by step set of procedures he practiced for two weeks. It tasted the same. What could he be missing?

This had better not turn south for him.

***

Ally unfolded her arms slowly, catching herself.

Had she just been a little jealous at an unknown *she*? Thank goodness Xander had not seen that. She wiped the doubt away from her face. "So you got your lessons from Liliana."

He turned to look at her, probably confused at the mischievous smile playing on her lips.

"And you had this air about you like you made it happen all on your own. How many times did you practice, hmm?"

There was still a confused look on his face.

She got her glass of water and started to walk away. "By the way, the potato soup tastes great."

She was already out of there before it clicked to him. "You were playing me?" he asked loudly.

"Just finding out the truth," she shouted her reply for him to hear.

"Real smooth, Ally."

She heard him laugh all the way.

In the next forty-five minutes, Xander had everything down. It had turned dark by then. She was not shy to clear up her plate in front of him. The soup with yummy toppings was a delight for her stomach, and it almost tasted like Liliana's. In cases like this, it was always easy to use pregnancy as an excuse. She indulged herself with a bowl of ice cream after that. He did not seem to mind any of it as he looked happy, probably glad his efforts were not going down the drain after all. Her stomach took it all well. She noted that he avoided most things that usually made her throw up.

"Thanks for dinner," she said as they moved over to the couch.

"I'm glad you enjoyed it."

Xander sat beside her, leaving a safe distance between them. He glanced at her as she adjusted herself on the couch.

She knew he had his eyes on her. A lot of things had changed, but their awareness of each other could not be ignored. She knew if she wanted to confide in him, and this was the right time, the perfect moment—but could she? She did not want him to take the blame for how she felt; the nightmares, the anxiety, the fear of being a bad mother. She has conjured terrible imaginations of her child growing to hate her for what she almost did. She was afraid of being judged for it. Her mom was still in the dark about that, and as far as she knew, Liliana knew nothing about it either. It was just Xander, Laurie, and Mike who knew.

Maybe she needed the help. She had to think about the people who loved her. She had briefly read about prenatal depression, and it hit the head of the nail for her. She glanced at Xander who had his eyes on the movie playing on her TV. She bit her lip, finally making her mind up. She would give Mike a call tomorrow morning and discuss her situation at length. She was ready to talk to someone who would not judge or tell her it was okay when she knew it was not.

"We'll find out the sex of the baby at the next appointment." She randomly brought it up.

He nodded. "It's a girl."

She frowned. "You keep saying that."

"I've been reading this book..."

"You've been reading?"

"Uh, yeah."

"Baby books? On parenting?"

"Yeah, on being a dad. It seemed like a good idea. I'm ready, but I want to be sure I'll know what I'm doing when the baby comes."

It seemed he was more prepared than she was. Despite their awful start, it seemed Xander would love being a dad. That was what she wanted to believe.

"Have you come up with names yet?"

"No, not any that sounds right. You?"

"Two in fact. I'll just have to wait a bit to know if I'll be using any," She said.

***

Xander shifted in his seat a bit to look at her. "You know I'm not saying I don't want a boy, right?"

He wanted a girl like Ally, but if he got a boy, he would still be as happy. There was so much Xander wanted to do as a father that it was unbelievable even for him. The more he read, the more Ally grew bigger, the more he planned a future for them.

"I know, Xander. I think I'm hell bent on this idea of a big brother for my other kids."

Other kids? She wanted more. Maybe in a few years, he could grow with the idea... but the diamond question was: was he the man in the picture whenever she thinks about that?

The silence ensued. He kept his eyes fixed on the movie but was not really watching. The last time he sat through the end of a flick was when he was twenty-one. He was not a fan of this kind of movie and he definitely was not a fan of the space between them.

When they were dating, he never made them sit separately and would have her in his arms—his way of distracting her and making them do something they enjoyed together.

"I hear my mom is practically your roommate here."

"You can say that. I worried that those two would never get along. I even wondered who would ease things up here. Laurie would be perfect for it, but I also did not expect her to be around them always. Turns out I had nothing to worry about."

He would be the worst choice for that. Carla disliked him, and he was just getting to know his mother. He could not imagine the four of them in a room, including Ally.

"They act like best friends catching up on each other's lives. They bonded with cooking recipes and who knows what else. I love them, but I just wish they let me breathe."

"That bad?"

"I'm pregnant, not sick. Pick any day where you have someone shadow your every move, and you'll hate it, too."

He wanted to tell her that he would be the same as their moms if he were staying with her. He heard the concern in his mother's voice when she once asked if he had noticed Ally ever space out. She and Carla were concerned she might have something bothering her that she was not talking about. That may be the real reason they followed her around like she said earlier. Should he ask? If he did, what would he ask?

He let it go for now, but he had taken note of it and decided to be more attentive. That was part of the reason he was here tonight. He switched the topic, not wanting her to suspect he knew something about it.

***

Xander asked about her plans, but she was not sure if she should work towards getting a degree or work to support herself and the baby first. She knew for a fact that financial support was not an issue. Even if her baby did not have a rich paternal family, her mother, her cousin, and aunt would have been just as supportive. She just needed to know she was doing something right as well. It could not be all about Xander.

The paused movie was put on play again.

She knew Xander was not following the show, and it reminded her of how he used to always distract her before. She would really like to finish this film. She had started the first fifteen minutes with her mom and Liliana last night, but she had been too tired to stay awake longer. It was justifiable, considering the attention she got from the two women were a bit too much sometimes.

She missed Laurie.

"You don't have to sit through this, Xander. I'm fine."

"I can. It's just…"

"I doubt you're following a word said."

"I might have. You can't know that."

A smile escaped her lips. "Then tell me, what's the movie title?"

He frowned, trying to guess like it was the hardest puzzle ever.

She laughed at him.

"Remind me again?"

She was still laughing. "I told you twice already. 'The Age of Adaline.' Now, don't forget. You just might have to answer me if we *do this again.*"

There was no way she could have seen the cogs turning in his head when she said those words.

The movie was well into fifty minutes when the sound of sniffles gradually filled the room. She knew what it was like keeping a secret you badly wanted to tell but could not. The story only made her think about what she was hiding from Xander. She did not mean to, but it happened; the tears escaped her.

"It's just so sad that she can't be with him because of her secret," She told herself. It fit perfectly.

***

"Ally?"

Xander was not sure how to comfort tears caused by a work of fiction. He never did well around crying women. It always confused him, but this was almost funny. His lips turned up. She was crying because of a character in a movie.

"Are you laughing?"

Now he was smiling, but when he saw the deadly serious look on her face, he coughed it back in. It almost terrified the shit out of him. He had read about not messing with pregnant women. You know, hormones and all that shit.

"No. I—"

"You're laughing at me, of course."

"No. Sweetheart—"

"Have you even been following the movie?"

Why was she so serious all of a sudden? He had never seen Ally this frightening. He wanted to lie, but he had to back off on this one.

"I've been watching you follow it. Does that count?" He shrugged his shoulders, hoping she does not get mad at him.

She put the TV on pause and excused herself to clean her face.

He sighed. He had focused on a scene or two in the movie, and the guy almost reminded him of himself—a guy trying to win a woman's heart that had her walls up. He should know what it feels like. At least it was certain that the guy would get the girl at the end. That was how most movies go. And where did he stand?

She walked in and sat back before apologising. She did not need to. His mom had mentioned to back off when her hormones took charge. The film continued. The torture was almost over when he heard her say something that made him turn to her direction immediately.

"He's hot."

He watched her take a chance glance at his direction. His face asked the question his mouth wanted to. *Really? You find that hotter than the real thing? I have a better body than that.*

She bit a good chunk of her lower lip to prevent her from laughing at him. She found it funny? He was literally sitting with blue balls over here.

After the movie, where the guy *did* get the girl—Ally obviously pleased—he asked her to go rest in her room while he cleaned up the dishes. She offered to help, but he refused to let her be on her feet this late. She mumbled something about being like his mom, and he smiled at her cuteness.

He was washing the dishes and was almost done when he saw her figure standing less than three feet away from him. He looked at her, ready to reprimand her for disobeying, but she had an unreadable expression on her face, not moving from where she stood. She looked like she was contemplating something real hard. He rinsed his hands and wiped them dry to go see what was wrong, but she was in front of him before he could make his second step.

She had her hands behind his neck as she dragged his head down and planted her mouth on his. Purely on instinct, he had his hands on her waist, supporting her since she was on her tip toes.

Ally was kissing him.

It sounded almost surreal, but it was happening. It would be useless trying to make out one emotion from the many feelings swirling through his head. He felt her soft lips take in every part of his lips as she explored. It was urgent and needy, almost. He was not complaining, but he was curious. It was not like her, and if it was her hormones again, he did not want this to end as regret for her.

Six months. It had been six months and more since he had this. He missed those lips. He could go on tasting her. Consequences be damned. But when he felt her trying to get him to open up to her, he knew he had to stop.

He held her steady as she looked dazed, just staring at his lips. He put a slight pressure on her shoulder, and that was it.

She was brought back to reality, releasing herself from his hold and walking out of the kitchen.

He was frustrated. He at least expected for them to talk. She ignored the moment they had while he was cooking, and now she was going to do this? Not a chance.

He found her on the sitting room couch, not in her room hiding like he expected. She buried her face in her hands, and he went to sit beside her.

"I'm sorry," she said before he could start talking.

"I don't want you to be sorry."

"I understand why you pushed me away. I—"

"I did not push you away, Ally. You know I want you. I've always wanted you, and I'll probably always want you. What's going on? Please talk to me."

"I don't know why I did that."

He sighed. She had to know. She did know. She was just not letting it out.

He held her hands away from her face, asking for her to look at him. "What do you want?"

He knew; Ally must know that, but he needed her to say it.

"You know," she whispered.

"Tell me."

"I feel like I'm on fire, and if I don't do something about it soon, I'll explode," she finally said, watching his reaction.

'Will you not regret it? Are you ready for us? He wanted to ask that but found himself saying, "But is it what you want?"

She gave him a smile that did not reach her eyes. "It's my hormones. It has to be."

"Are you trying to convince me?" he said, smiling.

She returned and rested her forehead on his as she breathed out. She seemed more comfortable, touching him again. It looked like she craved being held right now. She ran her fingers into the soft hair that was now past stubbles on his jaw, and she closed her eyes to the feeling.

"I don't want to hurt you," she whispered.

She could not even if she tried.

He looked at her with their foreheads still touching, and she opened her eyes to see him tracing his fingers on her hands. "You could never hurt me, Ally. You're not that kind of person."

"Maybe I've changed." She brought her face closer, so their noses touch. "Maybe I'm not that girl anymore."

He could feel her vulnerability. Something was going on with her. Their moms were right to be concerned. "I see you, Alicia Storm. That's the woman I see before me. Nothing *will* change that. I've made mistakes, and I'll keep making up for that for as long as it takes. You are the mother of my child, and you'll always be the greatest change my life needed."

She shook her head as her voice came out so low, it almost matched the silence of the room. "I have forgiven you, Xander, but I don't know how to let go. How do I let go? I'm a mess." She tilted her head a bit, and their breaths mingled. Any closer and they would have a decision to make.

For Ally, her pulse was following the rhythmic pattern of her drumming heart. She had only a shot of resistance at this—a very weak resolve—while he tried to stay more in control. He had his brain to thank for putting up a good fight against his groin.

"Maybe it's better if we don't." She breathed out.

He was not stupid. She wanted this. Every fibre of her being was screaming it. Her touch was demanding it. What was she so afraid of? Hurting him? How could she? If they made love, he was not going to propose marriage immediately. He could wait if she wanted to start out slow.

Her resolve was so weak, she was not even letting go of him. And he was going to give her a way out of her hesitation.

"No. Take it. Take what you want. I won't ask anything of you."

Their lips brushed.

For a moment, neither of them moved. He knew this was not his call. It was all Ally's.

She withdrew her head from his and stared before slowly pressing her lips to his. What started unsure, slow, and cautious only took few seconds to turn hot and needy. They kissed like their answers were hidden behind it—like if they searched enough, they would both find what was missing.

Ally was straddling him now, releasing his mouth as both panted for air. His green eyes had turned darker just like his lips, and his hair was just like she remembered, disheveled and unbearably sexy. His eyes were locked on hers as she placed one hand on his chest while the other rested on his face.

"I need you."

CHAPTER 25

"I need you."

Xander allowed the words to settle in before he made a move. This was his Ally, the same woman who had caught his attention, attracting him to her without full comprehension why, the woman he had developed a strong sexual appetite for, and a woman he strangely wanted just for himself. But as much as he had been without sex for a while and how his groin wanted it, he knew this could not be that. Just as he had gone without it, he was sure Ally had too.

The last time this had happened to them was when she suggested time apart. He had taken her roughly at first then. Now, it was different. That moment had led to this—her being with a baby—and he had to be as gentle as he could.

He lifted her from his lap, carrying her bridal style into her room. She had his eyes on him the whole time from the moment she admitted what she wanted. He placed her softly on the bed and could see the rise and fall of her breasts. It was not just him. She looked like a woman about to have her first experience with a man. Perhaps it was almost like that with them. It was certainly a first for him to be with a pregnant woman—*his* pregnant woman.

He eased her out of her clothes, and she was willing to lift her limbs, making it easier for him. Had he said something about not seeing much skin before? Well, this was seeing much more skin than he thought he would just hours ago. He took a full minute to look at her; to map her beautiful new curves.

His eyes traced every inch of her skin they could get to until they made a brief stop on her breasts. They looked different than the last time he saw them—bigger and fuller—making him gulp back in the sudden rush of lust that came over him. He needed to take it slow, and so his eyes traced south to rest on her bump. Seconds ago, she had been bold, but now, she crossed her legs together and covered her bump as much as her small hands would allow.

He looked at her. "You look beautiful."

Ally swallowed, staring at him.

"You are beautiful." He repeated as his eyes asked for permission. He was not sure what to expect, but when she nodded, his hand immediately reached towards the part of her that carried their child.

He looked again just to be sure she was not going to protest before.

The feeling… The feeling of being a part of this, being a part of this creation overwhelmed him. This was what he could have lost, what he could have lived to regret.

"I'm sorry."

His head was bowed with his hand still on her stomach. He was not sure if Ally heard his broken voice. "I missed this."

She cupped his face in her hands to make him look at her.

"I missed the baby growing."

"You did. But you'll be there to see it come to this world and grow right?"

He nodded. He was never going to miss that; he had promised himself.

And for the third time tonight, Ally was initiating their kiss. Xander gladly accepted it, and as soon as their tongues meshed, she pulled away.

"Did you feel that?"

"What?"

"Here." She grabbed his hand and placed it on her stomach. Two seconds later, his eyes bulged at the movement he felt.

"That's our baby?"

She smiled at him, and her next words rushed out."I think he heard you. Oh." Ally gasped as a tear trailed down her cheek."This... it's the first time. When I never felt this, I was sure it was because of me."

Why would she think that?

He wiped the tear and cupped her face back. "Thank you, Ally, for so much." He connected their lips, and this time, they knew there wasn't going to be much talking.

She wanted this… and more, and he listened to her every request, every moan, especially when he started sucking on the skin beside her neck.

"Soon, baby, soon," he said under his breath.

His mouth traced down her collarbones and reached the peak of her breasts. He gave each one of them his utmost attention before drawing down and taking her buds in his mouth. What his mouth was too busy to do, his hands assisted. She could not contain her moans anymore, and she let herself go. She told him—pleaded, actually—what she wanted, and when he mentioned 'soon' again, she jerked his face up.

"Now!" she growled.

He grinned at her.

"And you still have your clothes on." She added.

He was about to rectify that, but her hands stopped him. She took off his sweatshirt and was going to do the same for his jeans, but when she saw it was too much hassle, she demanded he do it himself, making him chuckle. His footwear went off with his jean. Only his underwear remained. He saw her eyes rest on the very prominent object of his desire straining to get more freedom, and she reached forward to touch him. She did that for about ten seconds max when his hand stopped her.

"Sweetheart, you can't do that now. This will be over before we even start."

"Then we can start all over," she said.

His lustful dark green eyes and laboured, erratic breathing was enough evidence that he was trying to stay in control. He kept his head for a moment by shutting his eyes and telling himself tonight was more about Ally than his own desires even if her words were more than tempting.

He took her lips in his in a sweet and seductive kiss before laying her down gently. "Let me take care of you." He removed her panties, and the moistness of her womanhood was quite the evidence that she was growing impatient. He took care of that, trying to give her the first orgasm of the night without being in her.

"Xander!" She sounded frustrated.

He raised himself from her.

"Please. I'm not going to break, and you aren't going to hurt me. I want you."

He got rid of his last clothing and settled himself in between her. She was filled out gorgeously in so many areas of her body with all the things he took his time to do to her, but he could not deny that it was not just her body that was getting impatient. When he found his way into her soft feminine folds, they shared the feeling it created and their gazes locked in on one another.

The moment was not just about finding the desire they craved or the comfort they sought. It was that they found those things with each other, creating memories of old and new.

***

It had gone dark outside. The moon illuminating through the window of Ally's room was an indication of that.

When he came here, he had no idea he would have Ally wrapped in his arms after making love to her. What was with his attempt at cooking for her and ending up ravishing her? The first time they got intimate was almost the same scenario.

He looked down at the woman beside him. Her hair had fallen over her face as she shifted in her sleep. He held her closer to his chest as she lay on her side. What they shared moments ago had been great, but it left him feeling like a teenage boy. He was so scared of how to proceed, not knowing how safe it was or how fast was okay. The second time, he found himself flat on his back as she took control, being on top. She did not restrict herself, and that had made him find his release again. Hers followed soon after, as that did not stop her from going on until she got her satisfaction.

He was not sure what to expect in the morning. The night had been emotional, and it was possible only sleep that could clear away the sentiments by dawn. He was not expecting them to take off from where they left off tonight, but he hoped that at least something had changed—that it would spark a chance for him and a start for them.

He heard voices outside the room. The women were back from their night out. He was not worried about his mom, but what would Carla think? They still had a rocky relationship. The woman was great just like her daughter. She was not projecting her dislike for him towards his mother. It was the exact opposite, shocking not just him but Ally and Laurie too.

Laurie—the cousin he had disliked from the start. One thing he learned in all of this was to never judge a book by its cover. She turned out to be a great help for him.

The voices became quieter, but he was going to stay right here and face the music in the morning.

***

Ally was still fast asleep when Xander woke up. He placed a kiss on the side of her face before he left the bed. He picked up his boxers on the floor before he moved into the connecting bathroom to look decent for what or who he was going to face out there.

When he left the room, she was still sleeping. He never knew her to be a deep sleeper. It was just another thing that was different about her. The smell of bacon drifted from the kitchen, and he followed it. Carla was cooking.

Just once was he ever alone with Ally's mom, and that was during the month Ally had returned home. Carla had been clear that she was only respecting her daughter's wish of staying cordial, and if he was sticking around, he better make it the last time he hurt her daughter. He had been real clear on avoiding that, not that he has any intention of hurting Ally on purpose again.

Both of them never really had another conversation since then. This was not going to be easy. He expected the awkward morning with Ally, not her mother.

"Morning, Carla."

"Morning." She was not facing him.

He did not know what to say. He could not turn away now. He could not stay in Ally's room until she woke up just because he wanted to avoid her mother.

"Sit."

He stopped in his tracks and saw her put down a plate of bacon, toast, and eggs.

"Help yourself." She turned back to whatever she was doing.

He made a slow approach to the plate dished for him. "Thanks."

She said nothing. The kitchen had turned silent except for the sounds their hands were making. "The next time you make use of my kitchen, I expect you to clean it up."

The egg that was about to go into his mouth hung in the air. *Crap.* He had been warned about Carla hating seeing her kitchen in a mess. He did not get to finish the dishes when Ally kissed him suddenly last night.

"So something did happen between you and my daughter last night?"

He looked up to see her watching him, a mug in hand.

"If you want some, get it yourself." She raised the mug towards the direction of the coffee pot, and he got up and did just that. "So?"

What was he to say? It was a rather awkward topic to discuss with her. They did have sex, but did it change anything between them? He was yet to find out. "I don't know."

"Is that some kind of answer to evade the question?"

They were a few feet away from each other. "Honestly? I know you know what went on between us, but what I don't know is what it changed and what it meant." He went back to his food.

Carla let out a sigh. "You're a lot dumber than I took you for. How do you sorts get successful in business?" She murmured the last part, turning away at the indication that the toast was done. When she faced him again, she moved closer to where he sat eating.

"Like I told your mother, there is something going on with Alicia. I agreed to the whole dinner thing you proposed because Liliana believed you could get it out of her. How can you when you don't even notice?"

He frowned at her accusation. Was she telling him that he did not care? That he was not attentive enough?

"I've heard Ally cry once in her sleep. She dismissed it as a simple nightmare and withdrew herself. She's spaced out a couple of times when with Liliana and me. They are little things, but they are unusual of my daughter. I'm afraid if I approach her about it, she'll shut me off or just say that it's nothing as she always does.

"You're right."

She raised an eyebrow.

"It was there last night. I've never seen her space out, but there were meanings behind her words yesterday."

I forgive you. I can't let go. I'm a mess. I'm not the same girl anymore...

Every one of those words played in his head again. He was confused as well, but there was one person he could ask. He had to know something. Xander was almost certain of it.

"I'll find that out. There's someone who she's rather close to," He admitted, a little annoyed.

"Forget it if you're referring to Laurie. She—"

"Not her. There's someone else."

She scrutinized him before letting it go. "Whatever you find out, I want to know. I don't care what it is. When you do, I want to know. I feel uneasy. I won't be a useless mother again. I have to be there for her."

He nodded in understanding. Before she turned away, he called her. "And Carla?" He continued when she faced him. "I love her."

"What's going on?" They turned to see Ally looking like she was forcefully dragged from the bed. She looked groggy in an oversized tee and pyjama trousers. Her hair was left wild and sticking in all directions.

Did she hear his last statement?

"Is... everything okay?" He asked.

"You look tired."

"Thanks, Mom," she replied like it was obvious. "A bit though."

He did not think she did.

He looked at her as she dragged herself towards him. Carla turned away to find something to keep her busy.

Was it his fault? Had he taken last night too far?"

"Are you okay?" he whispered to her, hinting to her that his question was related to last night.

"I'm fine. Morning," she whispered back, looking away from him.

"Morning," he replied.

She stretched her hand to him, and he looked to see his phone with her. "It kept ringing." This was what woke her? He apologised, excusing himself.

"Don't say anything, Mom. Not while he's here," He heard Ally tell her mom.

She must think he was out of earshot, but he heard.

It was Collins who had been calling. Xander knew it had to be for a very good reason. If not, his new assistant would not have called him four times in the morning. He called back, and Collins picked up on the first ring.

"Have you come across any gossip this morning?"

Collins had a weird side to him, but he was not expecting that out of his mouth. "Collins?" He warned, and the boy got straight to the point.

"There's a story about you that came out this morning. I think you should get to the office and figure out what we have to do."

Not bothering to ask what it was about, he told him to get Paul in his office, telling him he would be there soon.

Xander came out ready to leave. He gave Ally a brief explanation, omitting the gossip because it might have her name in there too. She did not need the added stress. He was going to take care of it.

"Thank you for breakfast, Carla." Carla acknowledged his thanks with a ghost of a nod.

"I'll see you later?" he asked Ally.

"Hmm..." She hummed in reply.

He knew they still needed to talk. This morning would have been the worst time to do so, seeing as Carla sat right in the room. He kissed her forehead and was out the door.

***

"Breakfast?" Carla asked when they heard the front door close behind Xander.

"Yes, please."

She allowed her daughter some moment of silence with her food before she started to talk. "That's a first."

"What is?"

"You and Alexander."

"I can say the same about you. You served him breakfast."

"Well, he's never stayed the night before, has he? I did not come home to any kind of stench in my kitchen last night. So it must mean he got a plus for the dinner he made."

Ally kept silent.

"How was dinner?"

She was not sure what her mom was trying to pry off her. There was nothing to tell. "I don't know."

"Not what I want to hear you say. Just what is going on? Are you giving it a chance?"

"Xander and I had an agreement. There's nothing going on."

"You slept with him. It must mean something."

"Mom. Please."

Her mom wanted to say more but stopped herself. "I have to meet with a wedding planner this afternoon just in case you don't meet me when you come by. Call if you need me? It shouldn't take much of my time anyway."

She could see the frustration in her mom's eyes. Her mom must know something, and it was starting to eat at her. First Mike, then Xander last night, and now, her mom? How long did she think she could go on with it? She decided that she would not back out and gives Mike a call the first thing when her mom leaves.

It would be a step forward, hopefully.

***

Xander was met by Collins at the front of the company building and was joined by Paul in his office. He had been briefed by Collins on the ground floor and throughout their elevator ride. He was unfamiliar with the name Sophie Lane, who supposedly gave out the information about him, until Collins started talking about things that were unbelievably familiar to him. His time at *The Purcell Hotel* a few months ago stuck out in his mind. The *tiny pest* did this?

"I thought we took care of this?" He looked Paul straight in the eyes.

"So, you know her?" Collins asked, looking between the two men.

"If you're asking if I've met her before, then yes. A pest is what I call her."

"Is any of what she's saying true?" Collins bravely asked but immediately recoiled at the glare he shot at him.

"Paul, tell me what I'm missing here." He focused his attention back to Paul, looking angry.

"It was taken care of," He said confidently. "She was recently cut off by her producer, and last week, an article was published about her. I'm not sure why she got you involved. I want to believe it's for the attention."

"So? How is that my concern? I'm asking why my name is here." He raised the magazine, waving it in anger before slamming it back down on his table. He took a deep breath and rubbed his temple with one hand. "You know what to do, Paul. Find me answers and get back to me before you do anything."

"Okay, boss."

"What do you need me to do, Xander?" Collins asked.

"Get in touch with the idiot that wrote this bullshit without confirming the facts." He dropped in his chair. "I did not expect this start for my day."

"Rough night?"

"The opposite."

"Really?" Collins grinned teasingly. "Was it with Ally? Oh! You had the dinner thing? Did your practice come out any good?"

"Collins?"

"Yes?"

"How long have you been working as my assistant?"

"Two months and three."

"Exactly. I like you, kid. You're good, but don't make me get rid of your ass."

"Out of context? Sorry." He imitated his lips being locked.

He hired Owen Collins through Dom's recommendation. Xander had been hesitant at first, but the kid removed his doubts. Collins was a lanky kid that could almost pass for a teenager, but he was a twenty-one-year-old fresh university graduate who had a good business head. He was great with numbers though he acted his age or less of it half of the time.

He was the only one who called him by his last name, and when Collins met Ally, it was not hard for her to be charmed by his boyish banters. Ally connected with Collins, and the kid made it obvious that he was rooting for him and Ally to end up together. He liked Ally, and Ally felt the same about him.

"Does my dad know about this?"

"I don't think there's anything Mr. Cross does not know. So, yes it would seem."

He cursed underneath his breath. All was good just last night. It was barely twenty fours since he hoped for a new start, and now this. If Ally saw this article, the worst could happen. He should call her. She should hear it from him. He was barely hanging in there with what they had. He was determined not to let this little hiccup cut him off completely.

***

"Hey, babe. Miss me?"

"You don't know how much, Laurie. I wish you were here."

Ally had spent the afternoon at her mom's bakery shop. She helped out some, but the workload got much more than she could handle. Besides, it seemed no one wanted a huge pregnant lady around. Katie tried to get her to gossip just so she would stay still and relax. She felt unneeded there and left.

She stopped by a quiet-looking restaurant for some relaxation. And she was able to do so—until she felt someone was watching her, and the sudden clicks began. Out of nowhere, a man in suit took away the guy, no doubt a paparazzi, far from her. Xander still had someone watching out for her. The attention was still there but she sometimes feared that it would grow to an extent that she could not handle and would see her falling apart. There was nothing else to do, so she went back home. Her mom had been busier than expected and had called to tell her that.

Being alone only made her succumb to every thought she had tried to suppress, so she decided to call her cousin.

"Is this about the baby or Xander?"

"Forget it. How is—?"

"No, I won't forget it. It's obviously stressing you out. Tell me. You know I'm always here for you."

"I..." She wanted to tell her cousin all about her fears, but it was so hard to speak about. She knew Laurie would never judge her, and she should be able to talk to her about it, but she was scared.

A knock at the door bailed her out this time. "There's someone at my door, Laurie. I have to go. You still owe me an explanation about you and Mike."

"He told you?" Laurie groaned and murmured something incoherent.

"Is someone with you?" She asked.

Laurie ignored her question. "You can check who's at the door. It might not be important so we can keep talking." Laurie was not letting her off easy, she realised that.

She opened to see Xander standing there. "I'll call you back, Laurie. It's Xander." Laurie was saying something she did not get to finish before she cut the call.

"Why are you here? Something wrong?" He should be at work. He was in his suit and tie.

"Are you okay? I was told you had some guy taking pictures of you."

"I'm fine. That's why you came over?"

"Not really. I need to talk to you."

She let him in and closed the door behind them. It was late in the afternoon, and he was not supposed to be here. She hoped this was not about last night. She really did not want to get into that at the moment. She crossed her arm, standing, but Xander asked her to sit. "If this is about last night—"

"It isn't, but—"

"Good. I don't want to talk about it either," she said, keeping her voice down.

***

Xander watched her. Something was on her mind, bothering her. Did she know? Was that why she was acting cold? "Is this about the article?"

"What article?"

He searched her face. She truly did not know. They both took a seat, and he gave her the article's content and his side of the story.

"I did not want you to think I had a fling while trying to get you back." That was what Sophie Lane had insinuated in the article.

"I don't, and I honestly don't care about that right now."

The words she said just made something in him boil. "You don't care? We just made love less than twenty-four hours ago—*twice*."

"You said you won't ask for anything."

"I know what I said, Ally, and I'm not expecting anything, but we should at least talk about it. It must have meant something to you. You wouldn't have done that if it didn't."

"Why are we talking about this? It was just hormones." She was getting angry and frustrated. This was what she had been trying to avoid. "It's all because I'm pregnant!" She raised her voice higher.

"And? That has nothing—"

"It was nothing."

"Nothing? Ally, I love you."

She stood up, pacing the room. "You promised. Why are you doing this?"

"You keep pushing me, Ally. With you, I never know where I stand. I don't blame you, but I'm trying here, and it's like you don't see that… like you refuse to see it."

"But you knew. I made it clear," she said, dropping her hands in frustration.

He moved closer. "Tell me you feel nothing for me. Tell me you don't care about me at all."

She evaded his eyes. "Please leave."

He went silent, and she looked at him. He had an angry frown on his face. "I'm not leaving. You tell me what is eating you up. Tell me what has got you locked up like this."

She laughed mockingly at him. "You." She pointed a finger at him. "You made me this way. I let you, and I can't get over it. It was my decision, after all. I have myself to blame for always feeling worthless and guilty!"

He stared at her, shocked. "Is this about the abortion?"

"Don't say it!"

"You have to get over that. It's not your fault. Fine, blame me 'cause I deserve it, but how long will you hold it over my head? Forever? I made a mistake, Ally. No. I made *the* biggest mistake, but I had my issues too then. It's been more than half a year, and I'm trying to make up for that. I'll spend the rest of my life making it up to both of you cos I'll never forget it either. You think I don't think about the past? What I did? What I almost did?"

She looked like she would do anything to avoid this conversation.

"You're carrying my child. You and the baby mean *everything* to me. It's a lot harder to pretend I only care when I'm in love with you, Ally. You might not believe that, but it's not going to change even if you ignore it. So you can't say you don't care because I care about what is going on with you."

"You don't understand," she said, shaking her head while wrapping her hands around herself.

When he tried to move closer, she moved backwards, avoiding his touch. He let out a deep sigh. "Make me. I sure as hell need to."

"You said you wanted nothing in return."

"And I don't. What happened between us last night was not a favour from me. I wanted you too. I needed you too. I told you to take, but I'm not asking you to shut me out again. Say the words. What do you want from me because this is getting old?"

She ignored his question.

"Our relationship can't be the worst out there; the fights, the tears, trust, laughter, being stupid, hurting you, the unnecessary arguments... my faith in us..." Xander rubbed his face with his hands. "I know I have gone through the not so good parts with you, but I want to look back in the future and know we did that and came out having the great parts of it too. I want to know I can go through the bad and good and still have you."

She was gently sobbing now.

"Say something." It came out almost as a whisper. "Don't push me away. We can get through it together. You only have to trust me."

He had once asked her while they were dating if she trusted him, and she said she did. He was about to ask her that again, and he knew her answer will either widen the gap or bridge it.

"Do you trust me, Ally? We can make this right. I'm here, and I'm not leaving."

Maybe it was too early to expect that of her.

***

Her sob was the only answer she gave as she shook her head.

Ally had her head down. She did not know Xander had walked away until she heard the door shut with a bang. She let it all out immediately, leaning on the coffee table not far from her for support, unable to control the pain she was feeling.

I want to stop feeling this way.

Why did it hurt so much? It was hard to see the hurt and confusion on his face. He admitted to loving her. Xander *loves* her. That only made her cry out more.

Stupid girl, she thought to herself.

She turned her head and saw her phone sitting on the couch. She went to grab it and hastily searched for Mike's contact.

"Mike."

"Ally? What's going on?" He questioned with urgency, and she knew he detected the distress in her voice.

"I need help. I'll see whoever you need me to see. I can't go on like this anymore."

"Where are you?"

"H-home."

"Is anyone with you?"

"N-no."

***

Mike could only make it to her in a few hours, and that was too long. He needed someone by her side, someone she would be comfortable with. Laurie was with him at the moment, so asking her would be impossible. Her mom was not a good choice. He knew Ally might find it overwhelming. Xander was not an option either. He was the trigger, after all.

"Ally, I need you to calm down. How about I ask Gaby to come meet you before I get there? Will that be okay?"

"G-Gaby? Can she?"

She agreed, and he knew it was time that she gets all her fears all out.

A few minutes after he made a call to Gaby, Ally's current doctor, they both came to a decision and an arrangement. His phone started to ring, and he saw the caller id.

It was Xander.

What was going on really? He could take a guess.

After ignoring the first call to think, Mike called him back. Xander wanted to talk to him about Ally. When he told Xander he would not be available until the next day, he was willing to wait.

Well, finally, Mike thought. It was time for Xander to know.

***

It had been almost ten minutes since Xander took his place in his car, sitting motionless outside Ally's place. He did not know what else to do. Their conversation confirmed Ally was keeping something she's been dealing with on her own. He left to avoid his temper flaring up even more and taking full control. He felt useless and at the same time, angry. She was hurting; he could see that, but he did not know why. It could not be from what he did. Now he knew it had to be something else. She did admit that she had forgiven him.

All this had his head in a twist.

He was trying Mike's number, but he was not picking up. So when his name appeared on his phone, Xander picked up immediately.

"Mike, I need to talk to you. It's important. It's about Ally."

"What's going on?"

"I can't explain on the phone. When will you be back?"

"Tomorrow."

"That's fine. Call me when you do. I think I got something on what's going on with Ally. I think this is more than just what I did."

CHAPTER 26

"Are you okay?" Liliana asked, the woman she had miraculously found a friend in.

"I'm fine. I had work to put my mind off Alicia's absence. The worst that's been going on in my head is gone, and I pray that's over now. I mean, now that I know what's been going on with her, it just makes me so angry. Every time, *every time* I'm near her, you know? It was right there, and I didn't see it," Carla said, voicing out everything she felt.

"You saw it this time. We both did, and you were right to be concerned. Believe me, I see the look on my son's face, and I feel useless not knowing how to wipe it off him. At least you can be proud that you took part in the woman Ally's become. I can't say the same for myself. She's going to be fine."

"I know she will." She returned Liliana's smile. "I just want to start being useful for my daughter. If Mac were here, he would have handled it all better. He would have known in an instant and gotten it out of her or better yet, figured it out." She raised her wine glass, swirling the liquid around the glass as she fixed her eyes at the action. "She always confided in him with everything. I think that's where I failed. I didn't think it mattered. She had him, and I must have thought he was going to be there forever."

Liliana could see her friend getting into that zone. She was thinking of her late husband again. Carla had told her of how Ally's father had been diagnosed and how his death affected their family. Liliana wanted to take her mind off it and talk about something that would bring a smile on her face.

"You said you were going to show me pictures of Ally?"

That worked. She went in and brought out an album. The first picture in there was a younger looking Mac Storm and a baby girl. He held her so close with a big grin on his face. That was one picture of a proud father.

"Alicia's going to kill me if she knows I brought this out," Carla said, laughing.

"Why?"

"You'll see." Liliana continued to flip the pages, curious about what the next page will bring, and saw two hilariously adorable pictures of a young Ally.

Liliana laughed aloud. "But she looks cute."

"Oh, yeah? I said that too, but she won't hear any of it. She's tried so many times to tuck that picture away, but it always finds its way back there."

"I wonder how," Liliana said, giving her friend a knowing look.

The picture was of an eight-year-old Ally who had a missing tooth and a hair that looked somewhat like a bird's nest, in between being curly and tangled. A handful of that hair was extremely cut short as she pulled on it, facing the camera with a sad face. It seemed like she did not approve of the picture being taken with the close to tears look on her face.

"Her hair was a serious mess when she was younger. She always cried about being different, but Mac always found a way to appease her, saying it's what made her special and beautiful. Not that she believed him, anyway. That picture was when she tried to take matters into her own hands and almost chopped it all off. It was so funny, but of course, she did not think so. She was so angry. It was one of the few times I've ever seen her that mad. It was then that she made a decision to learn how to make girls' hair beautiful."

"And she's great at it now." Liliana had seen her at work one time with Laurie's hair. "Has she thought of going professional?"

"She wanted to get a college degree before thinking that far. She promised her father she would."

"Where was Mac from?" Liliana asked, seeing another picture of a man who had a close resemblance to Ally and her dad.

"He was half Brazilian and American."

"Oh, his father was American?"

"On the contrary, his mother was."

"And the name?"

"Mac took his mother's maiden name after his father's family refused to accept her and the baby. That was when she moved back to the States and raised him. Mac never talked about it much, but when Ally was seven, they contacted him, saying they wanted to meet him, the illegitimate prodigal son. Mac called himself that. We made a great family vacation out of it, anyway, so it wasn't a sour experience all through."

"What? Why?"

"They assumed he would be grateful being invited into the family. Turns out he's the only son his father had. He met his five sisters and..." Carla shook her head, remembering as if it was yesterday. "When they saw Alicia, they knew. Oh, believe me, Ally looks exactly like her great grandmother—Mac's grandmother. They had an uncanny likeness. Mac was not having any of that, though. He wasn't interested in the family, and he let them know that."

"Wow."

"Enough about me and the past. When are you going to face Alexander's father?"

"Isn't that in the past, too? Why do you ask? We have nothing to say to each other."

She and Cameron already agreed to stay out of each other's business. She was no more the teenage girl that was blinded by love or the young mother he could scare off anymore. Cameron knew that—especially when his dirty secrets had finally come out in the open. Besides her protests, Theo had made it clear to Cameron who he would have to deal with if he ever thought of overstepping his boundaries again.

"Don't you want to know what happened all those years ago? The truth? From what you told me, it seems like there's a lot of a gap to be filled between both of you."

"The truth was, he lied to me and used me. Whatever else is in between, I don't think it matters. I have things to look forward to now. I'm getting to know my son, and hopefully would be there for my grandchild." She cocked her head to the side a bit and scrunched up her face. "That makes me sound old."

They laughed. "You and me both," Carla said.

Carla stood to clear their dishes after trying out a new recipe they came up with together which turned out great. Liliana got up to help. They continued their small talk, mostly about their children and the past, when they heard the doorbell. Liliana offered to get it.

It was Xander.

"Mom."

"Alexander. I did not know you were coming over to see Carla."

"Yeah, I promised I would when I saw Ally."

"Oh, did you? Is she okay?"

"She is. I got to see her."

***

Xander has had a hell of a week.

He had been furious to know Mike knew such a big thing was going on with Ally and he never said a word about it to him. He even had the guts to lie about arriving the next day after his call when he came in that same day, taking Ally away before telling him and Carla what was really going on.

He had been so angry at the information, but it was dulled by Carla's sudden breakdown. Immediately, Mike finished explaining to them what her daughter was going through.

To know Ally had such a deep emotional trouble she was trying to come to grasp with alone was incomprehensible to him. He had no idea that whenever she talked about blaming herself for a couple things, those depressing thoughts were eating deep in her and taking growth. Maybe his words last week pushed her over the edge.

Mike told him it was not his fault. The truth would have revealed itself soon under any circumstance. Still, his words did not assuage his anger.

"Hello, Carla."

Carla wiped her hands clean and walked closer to him. She greeted him in return but not before using the word 'dreadful' to describe his look. He really needed to get rid of the beard taking over his face and take a good rest. The stress was taking its toll on him.

"How is she?"

"Fine. She looks good. She doesn't feel embarrassed seeing me, but she's still not talking to me."

It had not just been him. Except for Mike, Laurie, and her doctor, Ally refused to talk to anyone, asking some space to come to terms with what was going on with her. In the beginning, Mike had informed them that she wanted everyone to know she was sorry for making them worried and that she would see them only when she was not anymore acting like everything was falling apart because of her. Mike had tried to make the situation light and insisted it was Ally's way of saying it was fine, but he found nothing amusing about the fact that he could not see her and she was depressed.

For goodness sake, she was pregnant.

"Laurie calls me every day. I want to believe every word she says, but I know that girl will have Alicia's back anytime—even if that's to hold back on the truth."

His eye caught an open album in plain sight. He moved closer to take a look, flipping through them, unaware that both women were watching him. A smile bloomed on his face, and not until he looked up to ask a question, did he find them staring.

"Ally had a dog?" He stared at the several pictures of her and a brown Labrador. Both of them looked fond of each other.

"Ally loves dogs."

He did not know that. He continued flipping through the pictures.

"She had her for eight years. Paddy died three months before her dad started getting sick. That was one of the reasons I opposed your relationship at the start. She was getting too attached, and you were going to leave her at some point, anyway."

Liliana looked at her son who looked anywhere but at the women.

Carla was right. At the start, he assumed she was going to be just another chapter in his life that would eventually come to an end, but whenever he had her with him, he had found himself always wanting to prolong that so-called chapter.

"No matter how brave she acts, I still think it would break her heart. You were going to leave her just like she lost them. They were important to her, and you seemed important to her too."

"I would never do that now. I love her, and I'm not going anywhere."

His mom smiled at his determined words, while Carla just gave him a skeptical look. Time will attest to his words. When Carla's phone started to ring, she excused herself to receive the call.

"Are you sure you're okay? This must be tough for you too. You look tired," his mother said to him.

"I have to keep it together. If anything were to happen to her... I think I'll really lose it."

"Were you able to talk to her?"

He nodded. "Not much. She could not look me in the eye for more than a few seconds, you know? She's not talking to me. I don't know what to do for her."

"Maybe you should start with how you look."

He stared at her confused.

"You went to see her looking like this, didn't you? You look depressed yourself, Alexander. You can't go see her again looking like this. Let her know you're okay. I'm sure the last thing we want is for her to worry when she sees how anxious we are. You're wearing your heart on your sleeve, and it's not going to help this time. If you want to act macho, it's fine. But not this way."

Mike and the guys had told him to get a cut and shave, but he ignored them. It was the last thing he was worried about. He was meeting with them again tonight. Maybe he would take their advice, after all. He was going with Ally tomorrow for an appointment with her gynaecologist. At least she did not refuse that.

Carla came back before he could give his mother a reply. "That was my sister, Laurie's mom. She's coming to visit."

"That's great," His mom said.

Carla chuckled. "Oh, you haven't met my sister. She does not know about Ally's current situation."

"That she's pregnant?"

"No. What she's trying to deal with and my sister can be overwhelming. She wants to meet you." She looked straight at him but did not look fazed by what she said. Carla smiled, but it was not a pleasant one.

"My sister is someone you might want to avoid since every other person in the family tries to do that. She's always in everyone's business and very protective of Alicia. She's here for Alicia's birthday. She never misses it."

"Alicia loves celebrating her birthdays." Her voice turned softer. "It made me wonder when she never said a word about it. It seemed like she had forgotten all about it. She was always planning her birthday months before, no matter how she intended to celebrate it."

"That's about a month away," He said.

"Yes. The date never stopped those two before."

Xander thought Mike had been right about what Ally needed. He had to start showing Ally he was strong for her and the baby. Yes, he was worried and blaming himself, but he did not need to carry it around, looking pitiful. That would only add to her concerns. Thank goodness he came here instead of going back to his apartment. He knew what to do; a thought just came to him—something he hoped she would love. It could give them a fresh beginning; one without doubts or blames.

He left the women, planning to get a much needed new look before he met with the guys. Outside of his apartment, he saw men and women waiting to take his pictures and ask him questions. Two of the men Paul had stationed there stopped them from blocking his path. He heard their questions but ignored them. They were never going to keep quiet about Sophie Lane even when he had every crap written about him and Ally retracted. The damage was done.

The spotlight was now focused on his family again—something he really did not want around Ally especially at this time. Laurie said she never left the house except when she had to go to the doctorsfor her daily appointments. It did not matter; he already asked Paul to put some men on Laurie's place to watch their movements. No one was to get close to her.

That tiny girl was lucky she hid herself. Paul looked for her under his instructions, but she went under the radar. He later realised she was not likely to show her face anytime soon and instructed Paul to stop the search. He was not going to waste his time on her as long as she stayed away from him and his family.

He was quite surprised when his father asked if he needed his help to get Sophie Lane out of hiding. His father never asked him about things before, preferring to do things his way.

He knew what his father's search would do. He would find her and make her life miserable. As he had heard from Paul, the girl was at a low point already, and so he refused. He just wanted the attention and lies away from him. Then again, it was only typical of his father to still do something about the whole thing despite his reply. He was a man who did not like to be trifled with. Paul had informed him about how his father dealt with every person involved in that article except the dratted little girl.

He almost pitied what fate awaited her if his father ever got to her first.

He did not know where Sophie Lane was hiding, and it was better if it stays that way. He dropped his key and got out of his clothes before wrapping his lower region in a towel. He made a call to Collins, instructing him to make an appointment with William Fraleigh. He was taking steps to make him a family to Ally and not just as the father of their baby. He was going to show her why she fell in love with him before and why she could feel that way again.

***

"How are you feeling today, Ally?"

"Better. Lighter."

In the course of two weeks, she had gotten used to being in that beige room without feeling like the walls were closing in on her. Seeing the name on the door before she entered—Dr. Sarah Stack—also made her calm. It had not been as scary as she thought, sitting on that same olive green chair for the first time. Now, she was looking forward to getting things off her chest. She can talk about how she would be a mother without feeling guilty and anxious. She could now manage to talk about what she saw as her faults and how to let go of them and forgiving herself, knowing her love would more than cover the blemish.

The first days she was here, she had talked about the topic she had avoided all those times—the abortion she almost had, and how that had made her hate the woman she almost became. From there, she had talked about Xander, about her dependency on their relationship, and about her nightmares of her child hating her and people pointing accusing fingers at her. She did not spare a single detail, even confessing her troubling dreams of hurting the child accidentally because she was a careless and bad mom.

She was afraid of being a disappointment.

"I could not say it out. I felt embarrassed, ashamed, and guilty that I was sad about something I should be over the moon about. I'm with a child, and I'm supposed to be happy about that. That is what is expected. I have seen other pregnant women around me. They look nothing like me."

The middle-aged doctor assured her there was no set way to feel about pregnancy. "Every woman's body is designed differently. Do you know what any of those 'happy' pregnant women have gone through? Do you think it's all perfect? Nothing is ever perfect. It's okay to be anxious about your pregnancy, Ally. You are nurturing a life. It's a big responsibility."

She had talked about how her feelings have greatly affected her daily life. At first, she wanted to think it was all due to her being pregnant. When Mike cleared that out, it was still hard to accept something was wrong with her.

"Can you name the things you feel has been affected?"

"My relationship with my mother and with Xander of course. I've lost interest in the things I used to enjoy, I can't focus on making a decision, and I avoid people as much as I can—especially people who want to ask about my pregnancy. I am not an extrovert in every sense of the word, but I was never afraid to be in a crowd before. Now I am."

"From what you've told me so far, you were in a bad place with your mother and Xander during the time of your pregnancy. The fact that you did not have their support at that time must have broken you down. They were, after all, two of the people you cared about the most. It must have brought about the anxiety and negative feelings about your pregnancy," Dr. Stack pointed out.

"Maybe."

Thinking back, she knew the reason she had wanted to go through with it was to get Xander back. It was better that way anyway since her mother never approved of him. Getting rid of the baby had seemed like a win-win situation.

Dr. Stack further explained to her that what she felt did not make her a bad mom or a bad person, and she did not have to suffer for it. Her being there to see a specialist was a step to change all that.

She believed she had gone far since then in accepting who she was, what she did and the things that happened in the last few months. She listened on to Dr Stack speak.

"I would like you to engage in all the things you've been running away from."

"Like, what?"

"I want you to stop trying to be perfect. I want you to go out, have fun, and interact with your friends and family. Take enough rest and try to go easy on making decisions."

She nodded slowly.

"And about Xander?"

Ally had not really explained what she felt for him. "What about him?"

"I understand he's going to be there, but you should know that you don't have to make life changing decisions at this moment concerning you two. It's okay to have him by your side, helping out and supporting you. Do you feel comfortable with that idea?"

She nodded.

"At this moment, I want you to embrace all the help and support you can get. You should remember you're not in this alone."

Before she left for the day, Dr Stack asked if she might be interested in meeting expecting mothers and those who had just given birth to hear and learn from their experience. "You'd be surprised," she said with a smile.

She promised to give the doctor an answer the next day and walked out of the office feeling more relieved and happier than she's ever been in a while and saw Laurie waiting outside for her.

"Everything okay?"

"Everything's great," she said with a smile, and that answer made Laurie extremely elated. She knew what her cousin was thinking in that moment—that she was acting differently from the Ally that Mike had brought to her weeks ago.

She had been afraid of herself too; that she would completely lose her rationale.

As they fastened their seatbelts, Laurie reminded her who she was meeting today. "Xander will be waiting at the hospital. You ready to face him? Just you two alone? Can you handle that?"

"I think so. I have to," she answered. No more giving in to her fears this time.

Laurie did not try to get any more from her on their drive to the hospital. Through the convenient silence between them and the low music playing in the car, she enjoyed the afternoon air. It felt like she could breathe again—and that was meaning it in more ways than one.

It was not hard to spot Xander outside the hospital. He stood tall in his dark suit, and he looked... different. As they walked closer, she could see that he had gotten a cut and shaved off his beard. She would miss it, but it was starting to make him look like a caveman. She smiled inside. Not that she would have complained about it. As long as it was not long enough to make braids out of, she was fine with it.

He must have taken some minutes off work because he still looked just as he would on a morning ready for work.

"Oh, that guy's smitten. See the stupid grin on his face just in your presence?" Laurie said in a hushed tone as they approached him.

She failed to keep her lips from smirking as she playfully jabbed Laurie on the side. "He might hear you. Stop it."

"I should leave you two alone. I might get hit by the obvious sparks flying around."

"Laurie..."

"Or is it the hormones again?" Laurie faced her. "Oh, you took care of that," she said with a glint in her eyes.

They were close enough for Xander to have probably heard it. She tried to scowl at her cousin in embarrassment. Laurie stopped and gently put her hand over Ally's. "You sound like the girl who was embarrassed at the mention of Alexander Cross and sex in one sentence. I'm happy you could get over this, Al."

"Me too." She was getting there.

***

When Xander saw them approaching, he brought his hands out of his pockets and could feel his pulse racing. She looked good in that red gown that embraced her new curves, trailing down to a flowy skirt that moved along with her movements and the gentle sway of the afternoon air. She had on a sleeveless jean jacket and a pair of red sandals and left her hair free just as he loved it. Seeing her made him remember the pictures he saw at her mom's, and it brought a smile to his face. She looked beautiful.

Laurie suddenly stopped her to say something. They shared a hug, leaving him to wonder what was going on between them.

"Hi." They all exchanged greetings. He barely gave Laurie a second glance.

"Well, to avoid getting burned by this obvious electric atmosphere, I'll take my leave now."

He looked at Laurie, confused. She left after he promised to drop off Ally at her place. They walked side by side inside the hospital, and after confirming her appointment, they had to wait for her doctor to come in.

"How are you?" He had been thinking about this for quite a time. He wanted to ask how she was doing with her therapies, but it needed to be in a good way. In the end, he realised there was no way he could make it sound better, so he had just blurted that out.

"Good." She nodded. "Um... you got a cut."

"That obvious?" He ran his hand through his hair and chin.

She smiled. "I don't think your old look was hard to miss."

He smiled back. Just like his mom said, she had noticed.

"Um..."

"What is it?" he asked, not wanting her to hesitate to ask him anything.

"I was thinking on my way here if it would be okay if we could keep the sex of the baby a secret for now?"

That was a surprise to him. They had talked about knowing about it today weeks before. He was not sure why she had a change of heart, but he did not see a hint of sadness on her face.

"But if you're not okay with it, it's fine. I want it to be our decision."

He liked the fact that she included him in something concerning the baby.

“It’s fine. It would be a good surprise, anyway.”

They only had about three months to go. It was not that much wait, and who knows what else could come as a surprise within those three months?

"And, can we talk after? There's something I need to say to you."

Xander could see a change. Ally was not anymore the woman who was always hiding and avoiding conversations that had anything to do with them. She has been talking more and more, initiating a lot of things today. She seemed more confident and relaxed. Whatever she had been doing in the last two weeks was causing a great improvement. He was sure his mom and Carla would be glad to know this.

All this does not mean he liked the fact that she wanted to talk. He did not know what it was about, after all. His experience with that has never been favourable to him. Before he could ask what it was about, the doctor came in with a large smile, ready to show them their baby's growth.

CHAPTER 27

There were days when it felt like you could reach up and touch the sky. All you had to do was just raise a hand, and it was right in your grasp. Those were days where you literally felt like you could do anything you set your mind to.

At the moment, the day felt like that to Ally as she traced every move of Xander who went to get her ice cream from the small shop in the park. She was deliriously happy. It was not like she had everything in place for her. Not everything made sense yet, but it felt like it was going to.

She wanted to talk, and Xander wanted to hear it after her appointment because she agreed it was important but not urgent. He made a call to Owen—or Collins, like Xander always addressed his assistant—to tell him he was going to be a few minutes behind. He offered for them to go somewhere of her choosing where they could talk. She was in the mood for ice cream and a walk, and here they were.

She watched him as he stood in line with the kids looking up at him and some adults just plainly staring. He probably looked out of place to the kids with his clothes and height, and the adults might just be shocked that a very attractive dapper man in a suit was standing in line to get ice cream. She watched in amusement as Xander looked down at the kids who found him the most fascinating thing at the moment. He gave them what looked like a smile from where she sat and said something to them that made them all nod.

She continued watching as it got to his turn, observing his exchange with the man at the counter, and felt the baby kick. That had been happening a lot lately. She rubbed her stomach, slowly looking down at it with a motherly gentleness.

She had quite a journey in the past few months and have learned a lot from it. She was still taking part in it in a way as she was still coming to terms with the woman she turned out to be. She was grateful for where she was now; something she could not say before. She was now grateful for the help she got, for the love of her family that surrounded her but she took for granted. All that makes her feel alive now in every sense.

Deep in her bubble, she missed Xander approaching.

***

"Here."

She looked up to take the cone from him. "Thanks."

Xander took a seat beside her and did not miss her hand resting on her stomach as she tasted the cold, creamy dessert in her other hand.

"Everything okay?"

She nodded. "The baby's been kicking a lot lately."

"That's normal?"

"That's normal, Xander," she answered with a smile.

They both directed their gazes to nothing in particular, watching random things in front of them.

"How is the company doing?" Ally finally spoke up. The ice cream was half consumed by then when he looked at her hand.

He stared at her. The last time Ally asked him anything related to his business was when they were dating. She had always wanted to hear about his day even when she did not understand more than half of the things he said. It felt like years ago.

"I might have read an old article about a problem... and Theo mentioned—"

He interrupted her before she could go further. "It was nothing. It was an exaggerated piece. Everything's great though I have more work on my shoulders. I don't know what's going through Dad's head. It's too early to tell, but I think he's passing on more control to me."

He faced her. "The company's at a great place, actually." He relaxed his hunched pose on the bench. She did not need to hear that working with Theopolis Christakos had some major advantages in the business world.

He tried to mask the sudden urge to frown at the thoughts that came to his mind.

Theo. Theo and Ally.

Months ago, he had to keep his insecurity in check after noticing a rather obvious thing. He never talked about it to anyone in fear that someone would know his nights and days were spent overthinking, having wild imaginings about those two. He was not deaf to miss the fondness in Theo's words whenever he talks about Ally, and he certainly was not blind to the way she acted around him. That was more than three months ago, and he was not sure if the two of them were still in contact.

Now, he was.

What was he thinking, imagining that another man could take his place in her life? And to think that he suspected his brother?

"I'm sorry," She said. He looked confused about it, and she elaborated on it. "I'm sorry for pushing you away."

She did not have to apologize for that. The face she had on was neutral—no sadness, no frown, no crease on it whatsoever. It made him a bit apprehensive on where this talk might be headed. Her emotions were easy to detect and make assumptions on, but the lack thereof was unsettling for him.

"I know how much you tried to get me to open up to you. You always tried to talk to me, and I kept saying no in many ways. You tried to mend the mistakes, but I just…" She trailed off, shaking her head.

"Ally—"

"I loved you. I really did... and I never regretted any of it." She looked at him as he stared right back at her. "I don't regret falling in love with you, Xander. Yes, a lot did happen in between, but I have to admit it was never all about you like I might have made it seem. Dr Stack made me realise a lot of things that I closed myself to. Honestly, you were not the only reason I felt the way I did for a while. If I never assumed I was alone or let my emotions take control, I'm sure it would be a different story. The truth is, I never did well with losing the things that matter most to me, and I guess losing you was a bit too much to accept."

She paused. "I know I've said some things I can never take back... I said some nasty things to you, but it was the only way I could avoid dealing with any of it head on—keeping you away from me. That was what I thought, anyway. The problem was never you, though. It was just easier to keep believing it was. But that was no excuse, right?"

He knew he was the one who said unforgivable things to her when he found out about her pregnancy. He remembered that well. There was nothing she had said to him that seemed out of line.

He got robbed of his voice, not knowing what he should say. It did not seem too bad, though, because a gut feeling of his told him to just listen. It seemed Ally had more to say.

The silence and the chance to take in all that was said took over. Neither said a word for a while, and by her next words, she had finished the contents in her cone.

"About the other day..." She let her words drift off, hoping he knew what she was referring to.

The other day? Her pause and glance at him before taking her eyes away revealed what she was referring to.

Oh, they were going to rip the bandage off that topic now? It damn well be what he wanted to hear—what he *needed* to hear.

"For using you—"

He snapped his eyes at her, but she was not looking at him. "Stop," he said.

His commanding tone returned her gaze to his.

"That night did not feel like that. There was definitely something there. I'm not asking you to admit it right now, but don't say it meant nothing. It meant everything to me, Ally."

"You're right. It did mean something to me. I would not have done that otherwise. But can I... can we just focus on the baby for now? Together?"

He did not know what to make out of it. Was she saying they could not be together or that they should put off thinking about it until the baby was born?

"What are you saying?" His tone was calm, the complete opposite of what he felt. She just admitted to having feelings for him. What was she holding back for? Going back and forth with each other on their feelings was a real damper on his mood.

"I want to retrace every step I missed." Her hand lifted, resting on her stomach. "I've deprived myself of that from the beginning, and I don't think there was a day I truly basked in this pregnancy. Even now when I think about it, it's still scary, but I want to focus on being a mother before anything else."

He rested his back to the bench, seeing the composed look on Ally's face. He got the message; she was asking for him to back off for now.

But until when?

What Ally said made some sense to him, and he should be happy she was getting over all she put herself through. But couldn't she focus on doing that and them? Realising that his thoughts were a little selfish, he swallowed a lump down his throat and decided that yes, it was fine with him. Well, not exactly fine, but he could respect her decision.

Not a word she had said would change his plans. While she focused on being a mother, he decided he was going to continue building on their future as a family. He was not taking the easy way out.

Raising his head up, he asked a question that would let him into Ally's mind—even if it was just for a few seconds. "You're not saying no to us?"

"I'm not saying no. Just...not now."

***

Mike squinted his eyes, covering his ear that was closer to Laurie who was currently screeching her head off.

Ally just sat opposite them, smiling at Mike's reaction. She was not surprised. The news got the not so good side out of her cousin.

"I can't believe I'm just knowing this now. She did it on purpose! She kept it from me."

"She isn't showing up until a week from now, you know?" Mike said.

Laurie frowned at him. "Of course, I know. That's too short to form a plan. I can't tell a lie she'll believe by then. I can't even get out of it because it's going to be Ally's birthday. She probably has it in mind she's staying with me." Laurie turned to her and tried to give an adorable, pleading look. "Please, Al, live here till my mom leaves so she can stay with your mom. That way, they can catch up on sister things. I'm sure they have a lot to talk about."

She smiled, knowing that was just a lame excuse from Laurie to avoid her mom. "Aunt Wendy isn't that bad."

Laurie gave her a matter-of-fact look. "Um, you are the only one who thinks that... and maybe dad." She grumbled the last words.

She had always had a close relationship with her aunt. She had been around a lot when she and Laurie were kids—until that divorce between her and Laurie's father. Aunt Wendy did not take the divorce well, deciding to move away to 'find herself' like she heard. Her aunt had been out of contact for years save for a few letters and postcards that simply told the family—and a very worried Carla—that she was okay and alive. As a consequence of it all, Laurie spent the most part of her teenage years growing up with her father.

It was no secret that Laurie resented her mom for her five years of absence. When she finally reappeared, she tried to move in like nothing happened, and that only seemed to tick her off more. Eventually, everything did seem to fit in place for her; her relationship with her sister, Ally, and even her ex-husband, but Laurie could not get past being abandoned for selfish reasons for a long time.

That was all years ago. Since then, both had found a way to mend that bridge, so it was not the reason Laurie found her mother infuriating.

The truth was, the family had first thought that Wendy was somewhere getting drunk and drowning in self-pity. So it had turned out to be quite a shock when she came back looking better than ever—both in appearance and attitude. Perhaps, it was what drew Laurie's father back and renewed whatever spark was still left. Truth be told, Aunt Wendy never stopped loving her husband and neither did he which was still evident as they were still together.

To Laurie, all that was more appealing compared to the new attitude and lifestyle her mother brought with her. Her new wardrobe included maxi skirts, head wraps, sandals, and jewelleries with beaded styles. Her mother started acting like a seer, and it only got worse when she was mostly right with the things she said, getting into people's private and personal business. So they were always at loggerheads about Laurie's lifestyle. There was always a new 'prediction' about Laurie's life whenever her aunt came around.

"And why is your mom scary again?" Mike asked.

Laurie stared at him for a second before she frowned, leaving Mike to ask what he did wrong.

"You have to leave."

"What?"

She looked at her cousin in surprise. Was Laurie taking it out on Mike now? She was being unreasonable.

"You want me to leave?" He looked shocked.

Laurie finally realised what she was saying. "No. Not now. I mean… you shouldn't be around when my mom's here."

Mike let out a breath of relief but masking it enough for Laurie not to notice. "It's not like I'm going to ask her for your hand in marriage."

Laurie stared at him wide-eyed.

He was not thinking of that, was he? Ally wondered.

"Calm down." He chuckled. "Does it matter that we are together?"

Her laughter drew both of their attention. She mouthed 'sorry.' She just really felt sorry for Mike's situation at the moment. Maybe Laurie had a point. Aunt Wendy was not all that bad, but she could be a little... intense.

Laurie raised her hand towards her direction with her palm upturned. "Thank you, Al, for the obvious contribution to something this serious."

Mike was starting to get amused; he probably had never seen Laurie being so dramatic. He tried to keep from laughing when Laurie faced him again.

"Whenever she's around, in no way must you touch, speak, or look my way."

"Isn't that a bit far fetched?" A smile escaped his lips.

"Why are you smiling? I'm not joking," she said with a deadpan expression. She sighed and flopped back on the couch. "You haven't met her. She's got a sixth sense. Or she thinks she does. She knows about everything and wants to know even the things you don't know yourself. She'll know we're dating and try to get her claws in you. When that happens…"

The rest of Laurie's words were lost to them. The fact that Laurie kept ranting was proof that she probably did not realise what she had just said.

"What?" Laurie asked when she saw the looks she exchanged with Mike. She got into a sitting position and looked between the two of them.

"You just said the word," Mike answered.

She did not feel it was her place to interrupt, and she quietly stood up to leave the two alone.

She thought the pair was a little unusual. Whenever she was around them, they argued a lot, most of it teasingly. They flirted a whole lot; you would think they were just trying to get together. She has never caught them hold hands, kiss, or get frisky, but who knew? She has only been around them a few times—for three weeks, exactly. Only they would understand what they had going on.

Ally understood, really. People thought she and Xander were opposites in every way—and they truly had been that. Back then, no one could understand how happy he made her when she was with him. She was in love then, and the differences did not matter. She understood those two must have something they found in each other that people just could not get.

"What word?" Was the last she heard before their voices disappeared behind the closed door of her bedroom.

***

"Babe, are we *dating?* Do you like me? So, boyfriend?" He winked at her.

Laurie looked away and stood up. She could not let him see she was flustered by his question. "Idiot. I sleep with you. Of course, I like you."

She has never been intimate with someone just for the heck of it. There had to be a driving force; a definite attraction. Laurie admitted to herself she felt a strong and passionate attraction with Mike—the second man she felt that way about. The first man she had that kind of feelings for turned out to be married, making a waste of some of her years. Another thing she could not yet admit was that there might be more emotions laced with that attraction when it came to how she felt about Mike.

"Let me rephrase that," He said.

"No need." She started to walk away from his reach.

"Yes, we need to."

Mike stood up, following after her. He knew she was trying to avoid the topic. He liked Laurie. He more than liked her, so hell if he would miss this opportunity to know how she really felt about him and not just his body and the benefits it brought along.

"We are not having this convo right now."

"Yes, we are bunny. I don't see why not."

"Don't call me that in front of Ally."

He smirked. "Ally isn't here right now." He moved closer, trapping her body within his, and leaned his face close to hers, not giving her room to turn her face away. "Laurie Callahan, tell me what is going on in that pretty head of yours."

"You're not being fair," she whispered.

He knew that. He purposely put her in a position that always got him what he wanted. He wanted to hear her admit they were more than just a romp in the sheets. If she did not, he knew what their proximity will lead to: getting in the sheets, which he knew Laurie will not let happen knowing Ally was in the other room. He would be fine, whichever the outcome. Only, one seemed more important than the other to him at the moment.

"I'm not going to say what you want to hear," she said, putting up a brave front, but it vanished as soon as she saw the consequence of her answer on his face.

Mike smiled. To him, she just gave an admission even if she did not know it. "Then how quiet can you be?" he said with a wicked glint in his eyes.

***

Ally laid out her one week plan before her.

How had she overlooked all these? There were so many things to be done, to learn, and to catch up on. She had planned out a rough draft for her upcoming birthday, her plans for school after the baby, and how she could make what she enjoyed doing most fit into all that. But most especially, she was slowly getting ready for when the baby arrives. By next week, she planned to be back at her mom's and was expecting that a lot of things would be different. She had great expectations for the months ahead, and she could not wait to see how it all turns out.

It had been a week since she talked to Xander about focusing her attention on the baby. What she left out was, she wanted to focus on herself too, her school and a career. It would be stupid to deny Xander's presence and effect around her, and she just thought it was best to make it clear to him that she needed some time.

She was certain of it. She, Alicia Storm, still had strong feelings for Alexander Cross. So it was hard having him around. It brought out all too familiar emotions—the exact same feeling she felt the first time he introduced himself at that charity event. And whenever he was not around, her thoughts tend to stray towards what he did and how he looked like.

His calls have dwindled, and the unnecessary touches had disappeared. She missed all that. She would often reprimand herself for the secret glances she stole when she was the one who had suggested the new arrangement. It was not a pain to smile back at him when he did, and she liked that she had caught him looking at her. But that had only happened once.

She knew she only had to be brave enough to suck it up for a few months. "He is making it impossible to not think about him, right? All I can think about is him this and that." She felt a slight movement. "I know. I can't keep playing with your daddy's feelings."

She heard a scream from outside her room before it all went silent again.

It had to be Laurie, and she wondered what Mike was doing. She was going to give those two some space to themselves. They were major stepping stones for her recovery, and she could not have been more thankful she had them. Fate was funny like that.

She moved the laptop in front of her aside and lay on her side. "I'm going to work at making things right, starting with you," she said, rubbing her belly.

She looked forward to the next day; a day out with her mom, Laurie, and Liliana.

CHAPTER 28

Ally was close to regretting her decision of letting her cousin go behind the wheels instead of Liliana's nice chauffeur, Raul. Then again, it would not have made a difference anyway because Laurie would still be in the car, grumbling a thing or two about Aunt Wendy like she was doing now.

Thankfully, she was seated in the back seat with Liliana, and her mom was the one having the full pleasure of hearing Laurie's whining. She stared out the window, managing to block out the rambling noise as she focused on the view. Feeling a soft touch on her hand, she looked down at it before looking into Liliana's warm light blue eyes. She read the question on them and gave a slight nod in return to let the woman know she was fine before tilting her head a bit towards Laurie's direction to indicate her cousin was just being herself.

Liliana smiled back.

"Ally, please do not forget you are staying at my place so Aunt Carla can catch up with mom," Laurie said.

She had not decided on that yet. She heard her mom's chuckle fill the car.

"Now you're just badmouthing my sister."

"Liliana's part of the family. It would be no secret since she'll see for herself what I mean."

Part of the family? She was surprised that it actually came out of Laurie's mouth. Maybe she was not wrong, though; Liliana is her baby's grandma and her mom's closest friend as of present. Really, it was a wonder how all that happened.

"I can't wait to meet her. I've heard a lot about her," Liliana said as Laurie shuddered exaggeratedly. "But I am a little anxious for my son. Carla told me she wants to meet him."

Ally's eyes widened. "Why?"

Her mom replied from the front. "You know how my sister can be. She wants to have a read on him."

A frown began to form on her face. Suddenly, she understood Laurie's reason for wanting Mike to stay away.

"You should have said that when you told me about her plan to visit," Laurie said to her aunt in an excited tone. "It's a great thing if mom has a focus. Not that I pity the guy. He deserves every scrutiny my mom shoves up his a—"

"Laurie!" she exclaimed lightly.

Her cousin only snickered and looked in the rear-view mirror. "No offence, Liliana. Just stating facts.

Liliana started to laugh. Unbelievably, her mom joined in.

"You don't speak what you don't mean. I've come to know you well enough to know that," Liliana said in between laughs.

Laurie nodded in appreciation of Liliana's words. "That's the second time you've defended Xander this week, Ally. You couldn't make it more obvious that you're in love with the guy."

"I—"

"Here we are." Laurie interrupted her as they reached their destination and found a parking space.

She felt embarrassed. Liliana was sitting beside her, and whatever they talked about could easily reach Xander's ears. But when she saw Liliana's face, the beautiful woman just gave a smile of assurance.

What it was about, Ally was not sure.

***

When the door of the store was opened to them, Ally was amazed at the sheer size of it. She could not possibly imagine there was an accessory missing in here for a baby. This was her first time being in a place like this.

"Wow! Are babies lucky or what?" Laurie voiced out, and a smiling girl none of them had noticed approached them from behind.

"Welcome to Happy Babies and Forever Moms."

"What baby wouldn't be happy with this perfection, and all these colours! I think for the first time I'm going to slump from shopping," Laurie said.

The assistant smiled. "That's why I'm here. I can assist with whatever you need and help with your choices." She looked down at her visibly pregnant customer.

Her. She smiled back.

The attendant looked quite young to her; she was either around her age or just a bit older. She still had the smile on her face which seemed to be permanently plastered there, but at least it looked genuine. She acknowledged her, and the women began to move around.

She walked beside Laurie who was pushing a large cart as the assistant flanked her other side and the two older women walked in front. At least those two seemed to know what they were doing. When any of them saw something that they thought cute or beautiful, they put it on the cart… but not before taking a vote on which colour to pick.

The attendant who introduced herself as Mandy, looked at her, asking about the sex of the baby, and she mentioned her decision with Xander to find out until it arrived. Eventually, they picked items in pink and blue, going for more neutral colours that would fit well for either sex whenever possible.

"Everything is so tiny," Laurie said in amazement as she held up a pair of socks.

She smiled. "It's supposed to be tiny."

"But I don't think any of these will fit one of my fingers. I have never held a newborn. Are they seriously *this* tiny?"

"It's only a matter of time." Carla piped in.

"That's a *very* long time," Laurie replied, knowing what her aunt meant.

"There's nothing weird about shopping for your baby. When you have yours, you'll find as much joy in it as you find in your love for shoes and whatever else it is you get."

After getting quite more than what the baby would be using—from clothing and toys to preparation for a nursery—they asked for it all to be delivered to Liliana's home, and Liliana gave her address. It was only logical because they were all spending the night at her place, and no one would be home to receive the delivery at her mom's place. The help at Liliana's who could receive it.

They went on to a salon after, deciding to get a manicure and pedicure treat. Laurie pitched in a mini makeover as well. Her mom disagreed at first, but Liliana assured her it would not be anything drastic.

"Hi," the stylist greeted her, taking her position behind her chair.

Ally smiled at her. The curvy dark-skinned lady reminded her of Helen back in Valley Top, and she smiled, thinking of what another day at the salon would be like. What could be the latest gossip in the small town this time?

"Hi," She replied.

When the lady asked what she wanted to do with her hair, she explained her dilemma, telling her it was no use because it would only take less than twenty-four hours to get back to its original state. The lady convinced her to try it anyway since her friends said something about change, and she thought, why not?

She was always lazy when it comes to touching up her hair, so why not have someone do it this time and relax for a change? She smiled and gave her the go ahead. The stylist, Monique, realised she was no novice in the hair department, and they ended up chatting about their common passion. They talked about current hair trends, products, and women who had hair similar to hers and the problems that came with it.

The conversation gave her an idea.

She had been sceptical about what she really wanted to do with her passion, and it seemed like she finally knew the answer. Talking with Monique was a gift she could not overlook. But first, she had to broaden her research. It could work in the long run.

Laughing over a comment Monique made, she stated. "We should partner up and create a business of our own."

"That would leave us short of one of our best hairstylers." A pale-skinned woman probably in her thirties approached them. "Hi."

She turned to return the greeting. She had a short bright red hair, visible tattoos on her body, and several piercings on her face. Despite her appearance, she had a bright smile on, and she found herself returning it.

"I'm here to do your make up."

"Makeup?" She already had on a double coat of mascara and pink lipstick. She did not think any addition was necessary.

"Your cousin asked me to tell you that no matter what you said, you should suck it up. It's just for the day."

She faced the far end where Laurie was seated, having her nails done. Laurie must have expected that she would turn to her because she was waiting with a massive grin on her face. She burst out laughing.

"Don't worry. Nothing too drastic. When I'm done, you'll hardly believe I added anything to your face, only you'll look more gorgeous than you already do."

It was easy for her to give in. Really, what was there to worry about?

Who knew getting all pampered and dolled up could be tiring? She felt her back aching a bit, and she was really hungry. If she could get some food in her and stretch her legs, she would be really grateful.

When they were all done, she admired her mom's new look. It made her look younger. Her mom and Liliana could easily have men of different age drooling for them.

She could not help but appreciate her brand new mane as she stared at her reflection. Her hair now fell in a smooth, silky curtain behind her back. She loved the bounce it had to it, and its natural golden brown colour was a winner. Monique had given her a side part.

She had to admit she loved the way she looked. This was a feat she had not achieved in her teenage years. Even if Monique said that it would only last at most two days, the thought of what Xander would think about it ran through her mind. Would he like the temporary look?

She loved it, anyway. It gave her a totally new look.

While her mom and Laurie checked out the menu at the restaurant they were to have lunch at, she thought about eating anything that would not make her puke. She saw Liliana bring out a camera, pointing it towards her. They had all taken pictures outside the salon earlier.

"Alexander looked like he was sulking a bit yesterday when I told him about our plans. Just something to keep him curious." Liliana smiled.

She unconsciously put a hand to her hair, posing as the flash went off.

"I'm sure he'll find you as beautiful still."

She got hot with embarrassment especially since the comment came from Xander's mom. Liliana could not have known her thoughts, right?

The waiter came along to take their orders, and she noticed her mom and Laurie keeping quiet, listening in on their interaction. They all knew her and Xander were not particularly together. No one was willing to ask why her head and heart did not seem to be in sync.

They had their guesses, but she had never discussed her conversation with Xander with anyone, and it seemed neither had he. For now, where they stood was only known by the two them.

Lunch was well enjoyed by them all, and she felt satisfied. The kick she got was a good enough confirmation. So far, she had no negative thoughts. News about her and Xander has died down. Meeting other pregnant women and new mothers had been enlightening. Like Dr Stack had said, she was quite surprised at the stories some of the women had shared. She thought she had it bad, but there were worse situations out there that could completely break a person. She was thankful for the experience and the freedom she was getting.

They were taking a walk around the mall, window shopping, when Laurie stopped in front of a lingerie store. Liliana and Carla refused to go in and asked for them to meet at the car park in thirty minutes to catch up on a spa appointment. They parted directions, and she entered with Laurie.

Unknown to them, someone took their pictures repeatedly before they entered the store. Ally was the focus.

Laurie was filling her in on how she was planning to get it on with Mike when she gave them their privacy, of course. Laurie continued talking and considered if she should get something to get into role play mode. She laughed at the expression on her cousin's face. She really liked Mike—or maybe what they offered each other. Whatever it was, she did not want to hear about what they did in the bedroom. Laurie followed her, and she had to make it known to her cousin that she was not interested in what Mike was into. She should keep that information between them. She did not want to see Mike's face the next day and have this particular conversation crop up in her thoughts.

Laurie tried to convince her to pick a set to wear for Xander after the baby arrived, but she only grew hot and stammered a denial.

"I'm getting confused with you. You want the guy or not?"

"I talked about it with Xander. He knows—"

"I'm asking what you want. You can't deny you have feelings for him. Am I seeing things wrong?"

"No, but I want to put my life together first. If I'm going to build my future around him, I don't want the past clouding us. He understands that."

"Ally, as much as I want to tell you take your time—hell, take twenty years if you want to make him pay because of all the shit he did—that's fantasy. He's a man. How long do you think he can wait around for? He loves you. Now, I'm not saying jump into his arms and suck up your issues in one go, but have you considered putting him in the equation instead of doing it alone? At least that way, he knows he has something else he's holding on to with you besides the baby."

She stared at her cousin at what she just heard. She never really considered Xander getting tired of being patient. She never really thought there might come along another woman who could get his attention. At this point, she had literally told him they weren't together, and it was not happening anytime now. What if in between that someone comes along? It would not be his fault. Had she been overconfident because Xander had said he loved her?

"I'm just saying think about it. In the end, only you can make the decision about what you want."

Laurie was right. She knew she should know perfectly well what distance did to the heart especially when it seemed getting back was unlikely. Then again, she did not give him the impression that there was no hope between them. But maybe she needed to let him know that clearly.

They went over to the counter to pay for Laurie's purchase.

"No way," Laurie said in disbelief.

Laurie's words grabbed her attention. "What is it?" She looked at where Laurie was staring and saw what she was looking at. She tensed up, and when she realised Laurie was about to approach who they were both staring at, she held her back, grasping her arm.

"Let it go. She isn't bothering us."

"Like hell, I would. I just saw her come out of the room beside the one we were in."

Okay, maybe that was just a coincidence. "It could just have happened. She wasn't there when we came in."

"How do you know that? This place is big enough for her to have been anywhere without us noticing." Laurie ignored her requests of ignoring Xander's ex-assistant and went on ahead, confronting Julia head-on.

She was left with no choice but to go to them. She grabbed the bag that housed Laurie's purchase.

Julia looked at her direction, particularly at her stomach, a second after she approached them.

"I told you she was listening in on us," Laurie said without taking her eyes off Julia.

"It was difficult not to since you were particularly being loud about the men in your lives," Julia said to Laurie before turning to her. Julia looked her up and down, finally resting her eyes on her visibly large bulge. "Congratulations. You got him. I never thought in a million years a girl like you would be the one for him."

She was about to say something, but Laurie cut her off.

"A girl like her?"

Julia raised her bra filled hands, amusement clear on her face. "No harm. Just saying if I had known this was all it took to pin Xander, I would have taken the initiative. But I knew better."

She continued before she could be interrupted. "He would not have cared. I tried. I overlooked a lot of things, but he obviously feels differently about you. I envy you, Alicia. What does it feel like to be cared for by the man you feel the same about?"

She could not answer that. Meanwhile, Laurie's anger only simmered at Julia's blatant dismissal of her question.

"We'll probably never see each other around again."

"The wisest thing you said all day. Come on, Al," Laurie said, letting the rest of Julia's words hang in the air.

Neither of them turned to look back at Julia. She went silent, already deep in her own thoughts. Something that Julia said resonated with her. She had someone who cared for her as much as she did. Why couldn't she let herself have that? Everyone was convinced she meant everything to Xander. Why was she delaying things for?

Right there and, more of Ally's pictures were taken, unbeknownst to her.

***

All four women were ready for the ladies in uniforms to unknot the stress stuck on their muscles.

They had random chats as the masseuse got to work. She released a light groan when the masseuse got in touch with her back. Her mom asked how she was doing and the three turned their heads to her direction.

She was currently lying on her side and murmured an approval before speaking out. "She's really good."

The lady gave her a smile of appreciation.

It felt like days had gone by when she woke up to what sounded like whispers around her. When she was finally fully aware of her surrounding, she knew it could not have been days unless she came back here without remembering any of it. She looked to where Laurie, Liliana, and her mom were seated, talking quietly. They were all dressed and looked relaxed. She felt the same way, but only she was still without clothes.

Had she slept off? When she realised that was what happened, she could not believe it.

"How long was I out for?" All eyes were on her, she carefully got up. It was then that she realised there were two more benches added to the massage table; one on either side of her, giving her enough room to avoid falling off.

Her mom raised her hand to look at her wristwatch. "About an hour."

"You did not wake me."

"You looked like you needed the sleep. How do you feel?"

She stretched. "Great, actually... and hungry."

They smiled at her, relieved. After she got dressed, they grabbed a quick snack, took more pictures, and planned to head on over to Liliana's place and call it a day.

***

While leaving with Carla and Liliana walking behind them, Laurie was telling her about her encounter with Tony and how he got angry that she was seeing someone else. Laurie was laughing about what she had said to him when she bumped into a girl—a pretty face that appeared to be younger than them with a man who looked like her father… or not.

The girl smiled at Laurie. "I'm so sorry. It was my fault... or rather, Dad's." She looked at the man, giving a mock frown, and he smiled back.

"Sorry, young lady. My fault," The man said in a deep voice with a hint of a foreign accent.

"Sorry again," the girl said.

Laurie assured them it was no big deal. She had not been concentrating either.

***

"Why the hold up?"

Laurie and Ally turned to face Carla and Liliana who were walking towards them.

"Laurie must have done something," Carla commented.

Laurie frowned at her aunt although she knew it was meant to be a joke.

"Carla."

There was surprise on everyone's faces as they turned to look at who called her. It was the same man. How did he know Carla Storm?

Carla marched forward until she was standing directly in front of him. She was in no way matching his height, but she still looked defiantly into his eyes, ascertaining her control over them.

"Are you following me now?" she asked silently, hoping that no one but him would hear. But that was impossible since every one of them was standing close enough, especially the girl beside him.

“Of course not. I'm here with my daughter."

Carla calmed her facial expression, but her stance still remained the same. She gave the girl a smile she hoped did not look too forced and got shocked at the sincere and bright smile the girl returned.

"So this is Carla," the girl stated.

She looked happy. Carla was not sure what her presence meant to the girl except...

She turned to Pedro and gave him a look that said, *you did not.* But his look gave her the answer. After murmuring a brisk excuse me, she walked away.

She was angry, and she had every right to be. What was Pedro thinking—or better yet, what did he think he was doing? He was still married, wasn't he?

Oh, she forgot. He mentioned something about being separated from his wife, but that was hard to remember when he still had a ring on his finger. And what was that smile about? His daughter knew about their history and she was smiling at her? That was what it was: history. She just wished he would let it stay that way and not try to find ways to get her back to him.

Carla did not want to look back.

Meanwhile, Liliana followed behind her, giving a short nod of acknowledgement to the man. Laurie did the same and greeted his daughter, and Ally followed behind her cousin. She stood in front of the man, and they both stared at each other as if they fully knew who the other was.

She was not sure though why his presence bothered her mom as much as it did, but she could take a wild guess.

***

The evening in Liliana's home got all the women to relax. They were all currently changed into comfy clothes, definitely down to playing a game or two before watching the movie—a flick they had previously debated about. Their votes were based on which actor was hotter: Ryan Reynolds or Chris Hemsworth. The argument only made Ally smile, remembering the last time she watched a movie with a certain someone. Back then, she slipped up and told Xander that the main guy was hot. It was no problem whatsoever here among girls.

None of the women had spoken up about that strange encounter at the mall, but she was unable to forget about it. So she had asked her mom about it in private, cornering her like a seasoned paparazzi. It was then that she found out he was the man that broke her mother's heart—her first love. She could now put a face to the story. She had tried to search her mother's face to see if something else was lingering because earlier, it did not look like it was their first meeting after years apart. Her mom should have been shocked or surprised to see him, but not angry… except if his betrayal still hurt.

She got nothing.

A blinding flash of light distracted Ally from her thoughts, she saw Liliana taking more pictures. Before she could even ask, Liliana gave her an answer. "I'm sending pictures of our day to Alexander. He's relentless after I baited him."

She did not know what that meant, and she did not ask. All that she could think of was that Alex would see her hair in a top knot. Would he like it?

***

Xander looked down at the new message he received on his phone, and his face morphed into a groan. "This is unfair." Though he only mumbled the words, he was heard.

"What's that?" Dom asked.

They were all currently in one of the most expensive and popular bars in the city, having what he referred to as a guy's night in a text he sent his mom.

The other two stared at him, and when he did not say anything, Jay took a swig from his beer bottle. "I'm sure it has something to do with Ally and him not being there."

Dom shook his head. "I seriously would not believe it if I'm not seeing it myself. You're *whining*? The great Alexander is bitching!"

They all laughed at him.

"Fuck off, Dom." He ignored his friends and took another look at the pictures. The problem was not what they thought it was. The problem was the pictures his mom sent him. Ally in her wild waves was hot, especially when he had his hands in them as their naked, sweaty bodies tangled together, but what he was staring at was equally making him horny as fuck. He seriously needed to get off. It was frustrating because he knew he was not getting any soon. Still, he had to do something about it, and these pictures were not helping.

She looked really beautiful. It suited her, and he could not stop staring at the pictures—especially the last one where she had her hair on a topknot, wearing just a large tee shirt. She obviously had no underwear underneath as he could faintly trace the large mounds he recently had the pleasure of getting up close and personal with. He was not sure if it was the same down there, but he could obviously see her exposed thighs.

Oh, shit, his thoughts are not helping at all. He shifted uncomfortably in his seat.

Dom laughed out loud again. "Oh, boy. I know a horny look when I see one."

"What?" Mike and Jay said at the same time.

"It looks like Xander here is frustrated. Not getting any, huh?"

He was tempted to roll his eyes at his best friend.

"I thought this was about being left out? Ally's coming around, you know? You shouldn't give up," Mike said, looking straight at him.

That made him frown. "I'm not giving up on anything. You think because this douche here says I'm frustrated I'll get the next girl I see under me?"

Dom laughed again, obviously enjoying his frustration.

"Honestly, man, cut it out."

"It's just really funny. You should see your face. I'm sure one of the lovely ladies around here will lend you a mirror if you need to," Jay said, grinning at Dom's constant bugging.

"So what's really eating you?" Mike asked again.

He kept quiet for a moment. He could feel their eyes on him, so he looked up. Even Dom's playful look had somehow vanished, replaced by genuine concern.

He let out a sigh. "I have these thoughts at the back of my mind that Ally will get the future she deserves without me in the picture. It's crazy. I keep telling myself she was once in love with me and she's having my baby so that can't happen. But whatever I do, I always go crazy, thinking myself out of that picture. I want to be selfish; I don't fucking care, but I know I can't do that to her a second time."

"Shit, man," Dom said.

"Xander—" Mike was starting to say something, but he interrupted him.

"I got Collins to get me in touch with William Fraleigh and made tons of baby shopping yet to be delivered at my home. Sometimes, it just feels like I'm only hanging on by a thread, holding on to the only connection I have with her. She said she was not saying no forever, but it did not seem convincing. It's unspecified."

The guys kept mute until Dom spoke up. "William Fraleigh? The real estate dude? You're on the hunt for a home?"

William Fraleigh was not just any guy in the real estate; he was the best in the business. He wanted him to attend to him personally and not just any people working him. He was still young, yet the man was already a legend, always delivering just what his clients wanted. He had the skills to make a dream house into a home; tons of media reviews attest to that. Even though the majority of his clients were wealthy, his service was well worth the price. The guy has always been referred to as perfection, and not just because of his looks, wealth, and status. It was also because of his flawless wife, a well-acclaimed Hollywood sweetheart. He has an adorable son and a solid five-year marriage under his belt, but recently, rumours of an affair almost broke up his family.

All that crap was really not his business. He would be happy as long as he got what he was paying for. As far as he knew, the guy was already getting it together again. William himself told him this was the first job he was taking after the whole scandal.

"A family home, to be precise." He chuckled bitterly.

He sounded pathetic even to his own ears. Maybe it was just the drinks though he was still on his first glass. Perhaps he was indeed sexually frustrated. He had been without it for months, and he had done fine. Not really since his balls would disagreed to that, but he stuck through it. And then he got it on with Ally. The fact was, he was burning with want twice as then.

"I don't see how that's a bad thing," Jay said.

"Yeah, man. You've seen it yourself. When your name is mentioned, she flushes and defends you. Laurie tells me so. I never saw how you two were before, but you'd be blind to not see she's into you—again, I guess."

"And you can just get off with your hand."

Everyone looked at Dom.

"What? Don't tell me you don't give it personal attention."

"I don't know what you're talking about. I have a girlfriend," Mike said, placing the bottle to his lips.

"And I'm too busy with work to think about that," Jay said.

"Now, that's the definition of a lie," Dom said.

"How did the conversation turn to this again?" Mike asked.

"Helping old boy Xander here with some options," Dom replied, giving Xander a pat on the back.

Xander, just shook his head at his friend.

Jay turned his head around the room and saw three sets of eyes drifting over their table. "I think we have company," he said dismissively. Realising what he was talking about, he and Mike said nothing.

"When was the last time you got laid?" Dom asked.

Jay frowned. "What does that have to do with anything? I'm not picking up a girl."

"You should reconsider that decision. They've been giving us curious glances from the start."

"If you're so in touch with your crotch, why don't you pick them up?" Jay fired back at him.

"And leave you three alone? What would you talk about? I don't want to wake up tomorrow after a night of passion and hear you all died of boredom. So I'll just stick around and be the great friend I am," he said, grinning.

He and Jay scoffed. They knew him longer so they were not surprised at all.

"Besides, I bet you're the only one who hasn't gotten any in a long time," Dom added.

Xander felt their eyes on him and saw Jay staring. He knew what his friend was doing; trying to make him the focus of the conversation. "I'm not discussing my sex life with you guys, but I'm sure Dom's right about that."

Dom smirked, laughing out loud once more. "Hear that, Jay?" He looked to the table where the three attractive ladies sat. "You're the only one who can cross over to that table. Xander is an expecting dad, and Mike has a girlfriend."

"She's not really my girlfriend." Mike explained what his relationship with Laurie was, and the guys made it clear that it seemed like he was the one who wanted more out of the relationship. He did not deny it. "I'm thinking of moving here because of her."

"That's not right, man. You can't turn your life around for a relationship you're not sure about."

"And you wouldn't if it were for Julia?" Jay said.

Xander saw how tense Dom went after that statement. Julia was a sensitive topic for Dom, and he sure as hell did not know why Jay brought it up.

Mike, on the other hand, was left wondering why the name left a sour mood.

Jay realised what he had said and apologized. Backing off for a bit, he stood up to get more drinks, and Mike followed him.

Mike and Jay left the table in silence, but that lasted only for a while.

"Has she tried to contact you?" Dom asked him.

"No. And I don't think she would again."

Honestly, he did not want to talk about Julia in front of Dom. It always left him feeling sorry for his friend. He could not imagine what it was like when the person you are in love with is attracted to your best friend, never sparing a glance your way. Dom has been in love with Julia since college, and it always left him wondering what his friend was holding on to for.

Wasn't that hypocritical, though? His situation with Ally was not that different. Would he wait years if it took that long for Ally to want him to be in her life?

"Hey, Xander." The guys came back with two beer bottles each. "Your brother just came in. You expecting him or something?"

He almost told them he had no brother. He was still getting used to having one. To others, it was no problem all, but it needs some getting used to for him. A tall, dark figure overshadowed their table along with a leggy blonde trailing one step behind. He slowly met Theo's eyes.

"Mom said you were sulking. I didn't expect the pleasure of seeing it on your face tonight."

Mom? Yeah, he was still getting used to that too. His mom had talked about it with Theo? Xander ignored it and concerned himself with the woman he had with him.

Theo bent his head towards the girl, saying something to her ear. She gave a slight nod and excused herself before she turned to walk away.

"Room for one more?" Theo said, cocking his head.

He ditched his date? He was not friends with anyone here.

Mike and Jay were already moving in their seats to create some space for him to sit. Dom could not have done so if he wanted to because Xander did not move from where he sat—just watching.

He was curious. Did the girl in his arms mean Ally was out of the picture for him?

The vibration in his pocket forced him to excuse himself. He saw the caller id on the screen. It had to be important. When he was in the clear outside, he picked up.

"Boss, we had her followed like you asked, but there was nothing suspicious. She had nothing on her."

Paul had called him earlier that the men he had on Ally spotted Sophie Lane in the same places Ally was. He had instructed Paul to take care of it quietly. He found no use in alerting his mom about it; it would only ruin their day and have them worried. It got him furious thinking Sophie was following Ally, but now Paul was telling him it was nothing and it could have been a coincidence.

"And?"

"I suggest we keep track of her for at least until tomorrow. The fact that she was where Miss Storm was today does not feel right."

"Do what you have to do then. I just don't want Ally noticing the men you have around her. Be discreet. You know that."

He felt a presence behind him. He cut the call and put his phone back in his pocket before turning to face Theopolis Christakos.

"Is there something you want to talk to me about?" Theo asked, folding his hands across his chest as he leaned on the wall behind him.

"You came out here looking for me. If anyone has something to say here, it must be you."

"Okay. I'll get it out. For months, we've been working together, and it's not hard to notice that my presence bothers you. I'm trying to figure out why you don't seem to want me around; is it because of mom... or Ally?"

Both, actually. Xander gritted his teeth.

"I'll make it easier for both of us." Theo straightened his posture. "I get it if you're not comfortable with a brother being sprung on you. Afterall, I was prepared for that for years. I knew all about you, and I expected to meet you someday. And that you have to share a mother you just found? I completely understand. But Liliana has been my mom since I was a young boy. I love her, and her being my mother isn't going to change. You'll just have to get used to that."

Xander knew he had a point.

"And about Ally, she's a special woman, and I'll confess I had every intention of getting to know her because yes, as you must have guessed, I was attracted to her, but that girl cares about you and if I got in the middle of that, it would tear mom into two. I won't do that to her and have her think she has to choose between her sons. I know how much you mean to her."

He was saying he was backing off because of his mom and not because he was over his attraction?

"If I wasn't in the picture, would you still be interested in her?" he asked.

Theo smiled. "The thing is, you'll always be in the picture." He turned to leave but stopped and added. "I saw the way you looked at the woman beside me. She's just a friend."

And that information was helpful in their discussion and his peace of mind? How?

He went back to his friends, and they were quick to ask him questions, knowing Theo had left to find him. He answered a few of them, and when they asked if Theo was coming back to join them, he silently murmured that he went back to his 'friend.'

"At least someone's getting laid tonight." Dom finished with a chuckle leaving his friends to glare at him.

CHAPTER 29

"So, after your twelve o'clock meeting, you have an appointment with William Fraleigh by two, but before that, I think you should see Mr Cross. He asked to see you earlier this morning."

Xander looked at Collins who was sitting across him and reading out the rest of his schedule for the day.

He has been fairly busy again lately, but he was thinking of making time to see Ally today. The last two days have had him burying his head deep in work, leaving late at night; which meant he had not seen Ally in three days. The day after he went out with the guys, he had wanted to see her, but work interrupted. They had not made any plans, but he didn't want to come see her only when a reason or a plan came up. He didn't want things to get to that point

So it surprised him when Ally called the day before yesterday at around nine o'clock in the night just to check up on him. He was still in the office but didn't mind; he was happy she called since he also got the chance to take a break from work. They talked for thirty minutes, nothing awkward about the topics raised, and it almost seemed like how it was at the beginning of their relationship. He told her he would check on her the next day, and when he realised he was not going to make it, called to apologize, and they had another lengthy talk on the phone.

No matter what, he was going to try and squeeze time to see her today because he knew his late nights at the office would probably continue for at least two months. That was close to when she would go into labour, but he knew no matter the amount of work, he was going to be there. He specifically told Collins not to schedule any business trip outside the city or country around that date.

"I really don't like when your father stares at me. The man is scary when he's staring straight at a person. His eyes automatically glare fear. You're the only one I've never seen him glare at, but that's understandable; you're his son."

Well, you came to know him a bit late, Xander thought.

"So please see him."

He ignored his exaggerated worries; they were done. He looked up to ask why Collins was still in his office and saw the kid grinning.

"What?" He has been trying to put Collins at arm's length, but the kid was very hyper about a lot of things, and getting personal with his boss seemed to be on the top. He said it made him work better if he had a good relationship with his boss. He did not buy the crap, but he let it go because the kid had not overstepped his boundaries—not overbearingly so, and he was quite smart.

"Ally's birthday. What do you think I should get her?"

He frowned in exasperation. "You don't know her, you're not friends, and I'm sure she did not invite you."

Collins smiled. "Ahh... yes, I do know her because she's your girlfriend. We're friends because we chat on facebook, and actually, she did hint on an invitation."

He almost rolled his eyes at his answer. All were flimsy excuses for inviting himself.

"So what does she like?"

What does Ally like?

He thought of how he was still finding all that out himself. He was still getting to know who Ally was; what she liked, disliked and loved. He had an idea for a birthday gift himself, but he was not sure how appropriate it was for her and her condition at the moment.

"Get out of my office Collins and put your head in some real work."

***

Xander just finished one of his meetings for the day, and he knew he was going to be as busy as he had in the morning. He knew this was the only time he could take and spare a few hours to see Ally, and he was still yet to see his father.

He picked his office phone and called his father's secretary to ask if he was still in the office. When it was confirmed that he was, he made a move to go, and from there, go over to Ally's. On his way, he informed Collins of his plans, asking him to cancel anything in between now and his meeting with Fraleigh.

He knocked on his father's door who was already expecting him. "You wanted to see me?" He walked closer and took a seat opposite his father.

His father was not giving him much of his attention when he started to speak. "I've been informed of the nights you spend in the office working."

"And?"

His father stopped what he was doing and gave his son his full attention. "Don't you have a woman and a child to go to after the day?"

He stared at his father and tried to take a guess on what was going on. "I'm sure you know the current situation with Ally and I. So technically, I don't have them waiting for me at home or something." A small frown was still present on his face even when he finished talking.

He watched his father drop the silver fountain pen in his hand and swivell in his chair. He was looking straight at the busy view outside of his office before standing up and walking towards the large glass separating him from it. His hands went into his pockets before he turned to face him again.

"You want to know how important family is?"

And his father was going to teach him that? After all the years all these years of his father not giving a care in the word? He was a big part of the distorted view he had of a family.

"Dad—"

"You are going to lose them if you keep up with such attitude."

He heard enough. His father knew nothing of his relationship with Ally, so he had no right to cut deeper into what he was already aware of. And who was this man in place of the cold-hearted guy he knew as his father?

"Why do you care?"

They stared at each other before Cameron took his eyes away and sat back in his chair.

"I've seen the look in your eyes, and I've certainly heard a lot about what you are doing about the whole situation. You love the girl. At least even I know that this time it's for real—the girl and the baby."

He knew his father was talking about Barbara. Was his father never going to let him forget his mistake just because he had been the first in line to warn him about it all?

"Did you invite me into your office to lecture me on my mistakes?"

"It's the only way we've ever had a talk that rarely ended leaving you cursing me inside."

That was true, he thought, and the changes had only been recent.

"And knowing we would not be having a drink together any time soon to discuss our lives or mending a father-son bond, I'm taking the only way. I know you blame me for some things that went wrong, and maybe that's true..."

Maybe?

"When I saw you, it was impossible to be around you. You look so much like her. I'm not talking physical appearance. You acted a lot like your mother when she was younger... when I first met her."

There was no smile and no sign of regret on his father's face as he talked; just a straight face telling it as it was. "You were angry, always so angry that it mirrored how I felt when she betrayed me."

"I've heard you say that before but what does that mean? What did she do?"

"I did not ask for you to come listen to the past."

Xander said nothing. He still found his presence here a waste of time, precious time he actually planned on spending with Ally.

"I met the girl."

"What girl?"

His father just stared straight at him in all seriousness, telling him he should already know the answer.

And he did.

"Ally? Why? When?" Ally never said a word of it to him. Whatever could his father have had to say to her? Maybe he should not have had his men off her since Sophie Lane and the paparazzi backed off. Now he did not know about any of this.

He listened to his old man talk some more, but all he heard was his father getting into his personal business.

He was getting more confused each day; his father was getting *soft*—towards him alone really. But he did not say a word about that. Before he left the building to go see Ally, Xander wondered if maybe someday, he and his father would be in a position to have that drink together as father and son.

***

When Ally opened the door to see Xander in all of his dashing glory in the suit he had on, they both looked shocked, albeit for different reasons.

Ally was not expecting to see him because she had heard how busy he was recently. She did not think he would have the free time to be standing on her doorstep this afternoon to see her. Xander was just as speechless, expecting to see a new look, the different look on her. But her hair was back to its original state, in uncontrolled waves, and it was not just her hair that looked unsettled.

She invited him in, and when she was sure he had his back to her, she ran her fingers on her face, clothes, and hair. When he turned to face her, he was staring at her. Had he caught her panicked attempts to look good? If he had, he did not say a word about it. It was not fair that he was looking handsome, calm, and collected while she was trying to get over her urge to eat everything as she worked, and it had an effect on her overall appearance. Yeah, she was not a pretty sight right now really.

"Are you busy?"

She walked towards the laptop she had on and the papers and pen all over the kitchen counter, not to talk of the snacks and crumbs scrawled alongside it. She walked towards it as quick as her round stomach would let her, not bothering to clear it up since he's seen it.

He took a seat beside her. "What are you doing?"

"Just working on an idea and doing some research." It was nothing much as of the moment, but she was still working on it and it looked promising. She was excited after all, to see what she would eventually come up with in the end.

***

"It's good to see you happy about it," Xander said. Though he had heard once from Ally when they were dating about her passion and talent, he had not given it much thought. She had mentioned it then, and he had listened and forgotten about it in the next moment. But now, he wanted her to know he cared and that he was ready to grow with her—and that included her future plans.

"If there's anything I can help with... I know nothing about women's hair or products, but I can be helpful when it comes to the business aspect."

She gave him a smile and looked at him with one of those looks she always had for him in their early months together. He was not hallucinating right? He cleared his throat.

"Thanks. I'll remember that."

"Um… Are you getting cravings to eat? Is there something you want in particular that isn't here right now?"

She shook her head and smiled again, almost letting out a chuckle. "No, Xander. I'm fine really. I just can't seem to get my hands and mouth off food while working. And talking about working, I'm surprised to see you here. Shouldn't you be working? Owen mentioned how busy you've been working, and I know too from the conversations we've had."

"That damned magpie of a guy," he murmured to himself but loud enough for Ally to have heard every word clearly.

"No cussing in here please." She reprimanded lightly. "You don't want your child learning that from you, do you?"

He was not sure how to digest the words Ally uttered just now. It was nothing special, but the weight and meaning behind it squeezed a part of him that had always wanted that connection with her. At that moment, it felt like it was just the three of them in the world. Still in that euphoric bubble, his hand found its way into her hair, and she stood still.

Since the night they made love, there had not been any voluntary or conscious act of closeness between them.

"What happened to your hair?" She looked a bit confused by the question until he clarified what he was talking about.

"I told you, my hair always has a mind of its own."

He let go. She must have mentioned something like that, but he honestly could not remember if she did. He had not been listening. He realised he never listened to a lot of things, but he was changing that; he was learning to give and not just receive.

"I saw the pictures. I've always loved your hair, but the change was nice. You looked beautiful." He stopped at that so he would not make the mistake of telling her what else her look had done to him.

"Um... about... I met Julia."

His features went tense. They had never really talked about that woman he cheated on her with, but then again, Julia was not the real problem they had drifted apart.

"Did she say something to you?" Did she say something hurtful?

"No. I guess in her own way she was saying goodbye and wanted to know what it was like to have you…"

"I'm sorry." He stopped whatever she was about to say. "We've never really talked about what happened with her, and I know it's still hanging there. You once told me you could not get over what you saw that day, and I can't imagine what that says every time you remember, but there has to be a way. It might be impossible to forget, but there has to be a way I can earn your forgiveness—a way for that not to come in between us."

When he finally stopped talking, she breathed out. "You're right, but if you had let me say something, maybe you would have understood where I was going when I brought it up."

He gave her his attention.

"The memory might still be there because I can't undo it, but I honestly don't resent you for it anymore. When I said her name, I felt no anger build up, and that... that means a lot for me. I meant it when I said I forgive you Xander, and I meant when I said we…. *Us* isn't hopeless. I need you to know that."

Had Mike been blabbing to her?

"When Laurie mentioned to me how I could be taking the situation lightly... I realized she was right. I needed to talk to you about it and let you know I did mean all I said. I'm not saying no to us because... I care about you."

He was absolutely fine with that. It meant a lot to him that Ally was admitting this, and he knew it must mean something to her to have said those words. He loved her, and he has passed on the message. She might not be in love with him, but he was taking this for now.

He thought of telling her the whole story with Julia, but then again, why bring that topic up when they were trying to get past it?

"You remember what I once said to you when we were dating? We don't have to listen to what people say. Media, friends... let's just focus on us. Let's focus on what we have to say to ourselves and what we mean to each other."

She smiled in return. "I can do that."

He could honestly say the past two days had made a major difference in mending some cracks in their relationship. They communicated better face to face, and he was glad it was not just on the phone. She was not unconsciously recoiling from his touch anymore, and she was a bit more open to him about her feelings.

"So, this would be like courting you all over?"

"What do you mean?"

"I have to woo you obviously. I feel like I have my work cut out for me now compared to when we first met," he said, running his hand through his hair.

Ally laughed, standing up to get herself some water, having eyed the empty jug on the table. "What era are you from?"

He stood and followed her path but created enough space to not crowd her. "It just sucks that I have lots of work to cover right now."

"You want to spend a day together?"

He stared at her and knew it would be stupid to turn this down. He was swamped with work at the moment, but honestly, a day off would not kill him or the business tough it would definitely leave some huge catching up to do. A Saturday or Sunday should do.

"I know you're busy with work... so any time is fine. Probably after the party Mom has taken out of my hands."

That was fine with him too. That was about ten days from now. It would make things much easier to adjust, and he was not oblivious to the fact that Ally might have considered his work schedule for his convenience. He agreed to it, and they set a date after her birthday.

"Ally?"

"Yes?"

"I have to ask. You met up with dad. He didn't threaten you in any way, did he? I want you to tell me if he said anything demeaning to you." His face changed in that instant.

"How did you find out?"

"Actually, he told me. Why didn't you tell me about it? We talked after that."

"I did not tell you because I knew what your reaction would be." She raised the glass to her mouth and finished the glass of water.

"Don't you think that would be justified?"

She shook her head. "I wanted to hear him out."

"What?" he asked, surprised.

"When he called me, the first thing that came to mind was how he got my number, but then, I thought, his son's the same way. He has people watching my every movement

He saw that Ally did not mean her words in a bad light of him. In fact, it felt like she was making fun of him. She walked back to where she sat earlier, and he walked behind her.

"I do that because I worry about you. Besides, I took them off you. Maybe I shouldn't have. I would have known about it if I didn't."

"That's your excuse; I'm sure he has his. When your dad called, he told me he was not calling to offer more money or tell me how bad I was for you. He just wanted to talk."

"And?"

"He apologised."

His jaw dropped. He saw Ally smiling at him, and he frowned. "And you believed him?"

"He had nothing to lose or gain from it. He didn't request anything from me. I thought he would, but he did not. Instead, he had a lot to say about how stupid you can be sometimes."

"What?"

Ally full out laughed.

"That's funny? What the hell does that mean?"

She gave him a serious look at his choice of words, and he sighed, knowing he had to control his words in front of Ally and her rules. It did not take long for her to go back at making fun of him, or at least that was what he thought it was.

"Your dad had a lot to say about you."

"Oh, I'm sure."

"He had your back the whole time. He was pitching for you. He specifically told me not to give up on you. All he talked about was you."

"Maybe dad's dying," he said without thinking.

"What?" A stricken look covered her face.

"I mean, that's the only explanation."

"You assumed?" She hit him hard on the arm which had him pulling back, the impact unexpectedly stung. "You ass!"

He smirked. She just broke her own rule. "You just cussed."

"That was needed, and coming from me, the baby would understand why his daddy deserved it."

Daddy. He was not sure if that had come out intentionally, but he smiled and he could not help that it grew wider along with the look of annoyance on her face.

"His attitude has been very confusing lately: talking to me, talking to you about me, and acting like he cares."

"It does not mean you could use that word lightly." She obviously was still annoyed, and then it clicked on him about her own father and what she must have gone through. He had inconsiderately said that.

"I'm sorry." He apologised. He was aware of how easy her emotions could spike, and he hoped she would not start crying. He would honestly take more slaps to the arm from her for it,

"And what if he's just trying to be a father to you? What if he's trying to change?" she said empathetically.

"Not my father."

"You did not know how to be a father too and you eventually got around to it; why should your father be any different?"

Maybe she was right, but his father is hiding a lot of secrets, and his involvement in his past was still unclear. He needed to know.

The doorbell rang. Ally's eyes told him she was not expecting anyone. He offered to get it when she told him she needed to pee.

He opened the door to see a woman standing there. She had a bag in hand, and he assumed she probably had the wrong house. Before he could open his mouth to speak, she closed her eyes and took a deep breath, murmuring something before she opened them and stared straight at him with an unfaltering gaze

"You are the man my niece fell in love with."

He could not help but assess the woman standing in front of him. *Could she be—*

"And most certainly she means a lot to you. Alexander, is it?"

"Yes. Xander." He took a pause. "You're Ally's aunt?"

"The one and only." She handed him her bag and walked in, leaving him a bit speechless. He got himself together and closed the door behind him. He stared at her where she was stood with her back turned to him. She was dressed quite.. differently, and every move she made announced her presence, a result of all the layers of jewelries she had on her wrist.

"Your assessment of me is quite... enlightening," she said before turning and walking towards him. She took his left hand in hers, staring at his palm before looking up at a confused Xander.

"Hmm. Danger." She mouthed lowly, but he heard.

He was trying hard not to be disrespectful, but her attitude was honestly irking him.

"Aunt Wendy?" Ally's voice was heard as she walked into the room.

Wendy was smiling at him. "Don't be afraid, boy. You and I need to have a long talk. You've got quite a journey ahead of you."

He frowned at her words as she turned away from him and went to give Ally a hug, staring and touching at her protruding bump. "I can't believe my baby is having a baby. Such at a young age."

Ally had her eyes on him as her aunt smothered her with attention. His phone vibrated in his pocket, and for once, he could not get angry at Collins' interference in his life. If Ally's aunt was this intense, he was not sure he wanted to be around her alone for another second. The woman sort of creeped him out.

He raised his phone, signalling to Ally that he was going to take the call in private.

"You are supposed to meet with someone at two o'clock. It's one forty five. Are you with Ally?"

Idiot. Where else would he be outside of work? "I'll be there." He cut the call, and before he could walk further, Ally approached him, her aunt nowhere in sight.

"Did she weird you out? She must have sounded strange to you."

"You could say that." *And more.*

"Most people aren't a fan of hers, but she hardly cares. She's here for my birthday."

He knew about that. So she was going to be around for longer. He would have to face her when he came to see Ally.

"I have a meeting by two. Sorry I have to leave."

"It's fine," she said.

He hesitated a bit but threw caution out. He could not walk on eggshells forever. So he drew her closer to him and placed a kiss on her forehead before slowly bringing his mouth close to her ear. It almost seemed like he was seducing her, but it honestly was not his intention.

"I'll call you later. Is that fine?"

When he received a positive reply, he walked out the door to meet with Fraleigh.

***

Ally's body seemed to freeze at Xander's breath grazing her ear and his closeness. She had only been able to nod as a reply, and she still stood in the same spot she was when she watched him leave. Her aunt's voice was the one that cut through that short reverie.

"Come tell me about that boy."

CHAPTER 30

It all seemed like yesterday when Xander had visited and her aunt arrived, but all that had actually happened nine days ago and her ideas are slowly turning into a possible project she could actually worked on. Her relationship, on the other hand, with Xander got better and better every day. He was still cooped up with work, and he never failed to apologise for it. They talked on the phone a lot, and that got her suspicious that he was avoiding her mom's place because of her aunt.

The next day was her birthday, and though it was not something loud or extravagant, she was excited to have people she loved around her, celebrating another year to her age with her, except it was going to be in Liliana's home and in her massive garden. Ally realised she knew more people this year than the last and her mom's place would have been too small. She was finally going to be twenty-two.

Everything seemed in place, but she felt like something was missing—someone.

Her father.

She pushed away the sadness because, just as he had once told her while he was sick, she would not always be as sad. He was right. Ally had totally been a daddy's girl, and nothing could replace the love of her father who had always put her first, but now she knew she also had the love of people she could count on. She wished her father had met Xander, though. But, on the other hand, she wondered how that would have gone. If she had met Xander while her father was still alive, her father might have accused Xander of being a pervert because she would still be in her teens then.

That thought got a loud laugh out of her, and she was suddenly grateful she was alone.

Tthe only thing she thought she needed to worry about was a dress to wear on her day, but that ones been sold

Even if it was not to be a black tie event, she still felt the need to look good. With the large bump she was sporting, she knew it was going to be challenging to shop for the perfect fit. Heck, it was getting harder to stay up on her feet for long! She had been considering asking Laurie's help when her mom came home three days ago and surprised her with a simple red chiffon sleeveless long gown which turned out to be just the right size. Her mom had told her the dress was from Liliana and herself. They had it made for her. Ally knew her mom had to be the mastermind behind that.

Her insides bubbled when she had it on as she wondered what Xander would think of her in it. He used to love the colour on her, but things were a bit different now. Would it make a difference to him?

***

Eight forty-five p.m.

Everyone she invited were already gathered in Liliana's home.

It was well into an hour since the night started, and she rarely saw Xander because her aunt had hijacked him. But she did meet him, and just like she hoped, he admitted the dress looked beautiful on her and even had the guts to flirt openly with her, always finding a spot on her body on which to land his hands and eyes on.

She had tried not to laugh when she saw his horror-stricken face when her aunt finally caught him. He was obviously avoiding her. Maybe Laurie was right; it seemed like she was one of the very few people who did not think her aunt was a piece of work. But right now, she really wanted Xander beside her.

***

"So, maybe you were right."

Laurie watched Mike closely, wondering what he was referring to.

"Your mom."

"You met her?"

"No, but I've been in the same room as she is. She's quite..."

"Yeah, you can say it. I did tell you so. So you see for yourself I was not blowing it out of proportion. If she didn't have her eyes set on Xander, I wouldn't be around you right now."

"Then I guess I should enjoy my freedom until I meet the parents."

She stared at him in surprise. "You want to meet the parents?" She almost choked on the words herself, saying it out loud.

"Ah..." Mike's hand rested on the back of his neck, rubbing as if the action would not make him spit out the wrong words. "I mean, I hope I get there... we get there."

She said nothing to that but smiled secretly as she raised the flute to her lips. *How cute.*

She spotted her cousin a moment later looking rather somber for someone who was meant to be enjoying the night the most. "I'll be right back." And she explained to Mike why.

***

"A penny for your thoughts?"

Ally looked up at her cousin, looking beautiful as always with a drink in hand. "Just wondering how long Aunt Wendy will hold Xander hostage."

Laurie laughed out loud, not holding back. "Okay, tigress. You obviously miss your man beside you, and girl, did I ever imagine you would say that? You thought my mom was a saint."

She rolled her eyes. "Not a saint, but today's my day, and I want him here."

Laurie smiled connivingly. "I feel your pain sister, but have you heard the words, 'one woman's loss is another woman's gain?'"

"I'm sure that's not how the saying goes."

She knew what Laurie meant: Xander not being her meant Laurie got to be with Mike. Her cousin was not being fair right now.

"I'm just glad she's not in my case. Don't be selfish, baby mama." Laurie teased, nudging her lightly, but Ally knew who the selfish woman was between them as she watched her cousin strode towards Mike's direction.

It was not fair. She could not drink, stay mad, or stand on her feet for too long, and now she could not even have the only eyes she wanted on her for the night? Everyone seemed to be engaged in one thing or the other, and for the second time in the night, she was alone. She was tired of sitting and decided to stretch her legs as she spotted a secluded spot in the garden.

"Hey."

She thought she was alone. "Hey."

She turned in her seat to see Theo smiling down at her. It didn't seem like he was even trying, his actions looked so effortless. He was a very attractive man, and she was sure some woman would be lucky to have him.

He took a seat beside her, the bench was a bit small for both their frames, but they weren't squeezing each other for space.

"How are you feeling?"

"Good, just tired feet. Thanks for the present," Ally said although she was not sure what was in the wrapped gift he gave her amongst the many she had received tonight.

"You should open it before you thank me."

"What? Is it something I probably might not like?" She joked.

"I don't know until you see for yourself."

Ally shrugged. "Well, it's still good manners to thank you for the thought."

He reached into his pocket. "I have something else for you," he said quietly in his smooth, rich voice.

She stayed quiet as he reached into his side pocket and brought out a neck chain with an emerald green pendant and another small pendant beside it with the letter a. It was beautiful, but she had it in her mind to refuse. She possibly could not accept it for many reasons.

"Before you refuse it, I had this with me the week you got back from that small town." He unclasped it and leaned forward as he placed it around her neck, not giving her the chance to think as he continued speaking. "The man I was having a business deal with practically dragged me along to his wife's favourite store. I saw it in your favourite colour, and I pictured it on you."

She remembered he had found that out by accident.

"I'm still not sure why I kept it with me but..." He looked at it on her as she placed her fingers on the pendant, caressing it. She looked up at Theo to see him already looking at her. "It's yours. I have to let you go. Really, this time."

They both understood what that meant without saying anything further.

Theopolis Christakos was really a perfect man, and she was starting to see why it was not hard to get attracted to him. He still had that pull on her, but whatever it was, it just was not strong enough to drag her in way over her head like before. She had spent some time with Theo months ago when she still could not stand Xander's presence. Things happened, but then it changed. She was running from everything that went wrong in her life then, and Theo seemed to be the perfect getaway, but she was not going to deny she had felt something in return for him.

"Thank you," she whispered.

He gave a faint smile before tucking a stray hair behind her ear.

***

Theo has never placed himself in a position where he would be forced to give up, stay away, or eventually lose, but earlier today, he had decided that the situation with Alicia Storm and his brother was one he needed to concede to. If he held on, he would eventually lose.

That was just stroking his ego—he knew he had lost already. Ally was in love with Xander, and Theo knew there wouldn't be as much room as he would like in her heart for him.

***

Xander watched the scene play out in front of him. Of course, he was pissed to see them in a somewhat intimate position. Maybe he needed to confront Ally about what kept bugging him since the first time he saw them together.

A loud laugh and what sounded like a glass shattering from a small distance exposed his presence. He looked back at the eyes staring at him now. Theo's eyes followed Ally's, but Xander was more concerned about why Ally looked guilty.

"Alex," she said, shocked.

Theo said something to her, but her eyes were still focused on him. Xander looked at him in the eyes, and Theo left them without another word.

Xander casually walked towards her, and she watched in silence as he just stood above her with his hands in his pockets.

"Hey," Ally said.

He did not say anything and kept silent for a few seconds. His thoughts seemed far away.

"The most important thing in my life right now is you and the baby."

He was not sure what he was more irritated about: the fact that he caught them so close together or the fact that Ally's was holding on to that necklace she got from Theo when her neck was bare when he left her side. Seeing them so close tonight made him realise he needed Ally to understand what she needed and be sure of what she wanted. It could not just be him fighting to hold on... or was he just trying to bring back a past where it was all about him for her?

He has also considered the possibility that Ally was attracted to both of them and was just confused. As much as it brought a bitter taste to his mouth, it was something he needed to address. They had never talked about Theo.

"Xander—"

"I love you, and as much as I want to bring back what we had, I have to face the fact that you might not want the same."

"It's not—"

"If you like him, Ally, tell me. I can't keep playing a fool. It's alright if—"

"No. It's not alright! Yes, I liked Theo, and it scared me that another man could make me feel what you got out of me, but it honestly was not the same. It's not like that. Truth is, I got over it faster than I should have if it had been anything close to what I felt when I met you. He was not you."

He wanted to hold her badly but he needed, *they* needed to get things clear. So he resisted by clenching his fists in his pockets. "If I ask you if you still feel something for him till now, would you still say no?" Before she could utter a word, Xander added. "Nothing at all?"

She opened her mouth and closed it. "Why are you doing this? Whatever I felt for Theo, it's not even a fraction compared to what I feel for you now. Is there a reason why you're trying to"—she swallowed—"let go?"

"I'm not."

"It doesn't feel like it."

He sighed. "I want to stop being the selfish one that's always pushing."

"Where is this coming from?" She frowned. "What did my aunt say to you?" she asked, a deeper frown forming on her face.

"Nothing."

"You're lying. Did she get in your head and fill it with crap about the future and whatnot?"

"My decision has nothing to do with your aunt."

"Your decision?"

"I want the doubt to stop. I don't want to give up on us, believe me. It would be stupid to give up, but I've always seen it."

"Seen what?"

"The way he looks at you. It's always there at the back of my mind even when I'm trying to ignore how much it affects me. And it would have not mattered if you did not feel the same way." He walked closer to her. "Ally, I'm not saying this to get you out of the way or get me out of the way. Heck, I'm not saying any of this to get him *in* the way, but I honestly want you to know what it is you want."

"Are you stupid? This is what I want," she answered, sounding a bit frustrated. "Whatever tiny fraction left for Theo will fade. I know that."

That was exact what's eating at him. He knew she was not in love with him, and maybe she was right: whatever she felt for him could be much stronger than what she felt for Theo. But the reversal of their roles is such a pain in the ass. Now, he could say he knew what it felt like being in love with someone who did not return it just as much.

He only nodded. He was not sure how else he'll get Ally to understand where he was coming from. He put them in this situation, and seeing her try to convince him that she wanted them together was lifting his mood. He saw in her eyes that she meant it, but he also needed her to see that whatever decision she makes shouldn't be done while another person's name is hanging at the back of their minds.

If the situation were reversed and he had another woman he still had lingering feelings for, he was sure Ally would want to know. She would want to be sure why she was the one for him and not the other, that they both needed to know it was just the two of them and not with a shadow of a third person hanging around them.

The fist in his pocket balled the necklace he had with him, the gift he wanted to give her tonight.

***

The tiny bark woke Ally up, and she felt a soft ball of fur close to her face. It brought a smile to her face, and she accepted the wet greeting. The pup barked again, and Ally laughed because it seemed to be telling her it was time to wake up and get her breakfast. And she did just that.

It had been a week since her birthday, and she had not seen Xander for days. It was almost like he was avoiding her, and all she wanted was to tell him to stop his insanity, that she missed having him around her. She had been tempted to go to his office to give him a piece of her mind, but two things stopped her: one, he was always busy with work and two, thier names somehow found its ways in one gossip or another since she had that party.

Her mom had complained about the attention she was getting and how it bothered her and her employees at the shop. Her mom did not like the fact that her friendship with Liliana was being questioned. Some reports have even suggested that it was all a ploy from her side to get their kids married.

A lot of things got exaggerated, and that got Ally wondering how details got to the media. The one which really had her attention was the headline that read: *Alexander Cross throws lavish birthday party for his mistress.*

She hated being referred to as that. The word did not describe what they were or ever were to each other, but it was not like there was a word that would have been approprite at the moment. She was not his girlfriend, they were not friends, but she certainly was not his mistress. She really did not have an idea what they were, except she knew for the past week that Alexander Cross was the man she wanted, and it was a lot of work trying to get his attention.

"For such a tiny thing, she sure barks the entire neighbourhood down."

She smiled at her mother's words as she looked down at her snow-white Japanese Spitz currently fixated on her breakfast. "She's so adorable."

"You need to give her a name and teach her some manners. She looks like one expecting to be spoiled rotten."

Ally laughed. "You don't know that. We'll take our time to learn some skills. At least she doesn't jump all over me." At that, the dog barked staring at both women, and Ally laughed out loud while her mom walked out of the room, snickering.

Xander got her the dog two days after her birthday, and she was overwhelmed at his gift, never imagining owning another dog after Paddy. In just five days, it was amazing how much she and her unnamed dog had bonded. She had thanked him for the surprise, and that was the only time Xander received her call. Even then, he still did not say much and blamed his absence on his busy schedule, but they both knew better.

"What has got you thinking so hard?"

"Xander." She did not hesitate replying to her mom's question.

"He's still not picking up your calls?"

She shook her head. "Says he's busy."

"Honey, I somehow understand where he's coming from. You would question if Alexander had another woman you knew he was in love with and chose you. Would you not want to know why it was you and not the other woman? Wouldn't you think that maybe that other woman might still be in his heart?"

"Thare's a lot of sense in your sentence, Mom, but I'm not in love with Theo."

"Then are you in love with Alexander?"

"I don't know, but I miss him. It's all just getting to me. I can't stop thinking about him."

Her mom smirked.

"What?"

She shrugged. "I don't know. Maybe the fact that you might have your answer already?"

"I think I would know if I was in love with Xander. I once was."

"Then maybe you need to stop trying to recreate what you two had or what you felt for him and build on what you have and feel now." Her mom moved closer to her, a smile resting on her face. "I'll let you in on a secret I asked your father we never talk about."

Ally raised an eyebrow.

"I proposed to your father."

"What?"

"Well, after he asked me two times and I said no, I expected the third to be the charm, and when it seemed like it was not coming, I took the bull by the horn myself."

"What?" she said in between laughs that erupted from her.

"Laugh all you want, honey. You just might be in the same boat as I was. When I realised I was in love with your father and it seemed like he was giving me my space after two tries and it had seemed to him that a certain other man was still in the picture, I had to rethink and realized I could not lose him."

Ally understood clearly.

***

It's been two weeks and it seemed like her mother's words were really happening to her. Xander still refused to see that she wanted to be with him, and it only got her more angry and frustrated. Maybe the man was really stupid like his father had said. Cameron Cross had told her not to give up on him and she was ready to give the stubborn man a piece of her mind.

If he wanted to listen or not, if he was busy with work or the world, he was going to hear it.

How did it turn out to be her trying to convince him they were good together? Wasn't it him who said he's not giving up on her and the baby?

Maybe because he was tired of playing that role, a voice replied in her head.

She looked around to make sure she was not forgetting anything. It was almost nine o'clock in the morning, and Ally knew what she had to do today. After her appointment with Dr Stack, she was going to head straight to Xander's office.

She had hesitated a bit, remembering her last memory of Xander's office and realising she was going to get a lot of stares from the employees considering how she looked now. It had been what? Six, seven months? But Ally knew all that were excuses. She had to take the step for not just the both of them but for herself. Going back to the *crime scene* would tell her if she had truly let go.

She went out the door, confident about the day.

***

He was furious. He was sure she could see that, but she was just smiling like none of it mattered. This was not part of the plan. He knew she was crazy but... not this crazy.

"I did not agree that we kidnap her or bring her here." He gritted the words at her, trying to keep his voice low not to wake her up. "It's dangerous for you and me."

"Relax. No one will know she's gone," Sophie replied.

"How do you know that? He'll go crazy if he finds out, if he finds her missing. You're crazy. This was not the plan."

"Plans change. I don't need you to get involved in what comes next. Just watch her. You can do that much, can't you? I'll take care of him."

"Why do I get the feeling that you're still going to deviate from the plan?"

Sophie smiled, looking at the man willing to help as long as he got his pretty fat cut. "I'll take care of it." She spelled out each word for him.

"You better. If this goes south, you're on your own."

Sophie smirked. "I got this. He'll never know what's coming."

CHAPTER 31

"Not much has been revealed yet, but currently, we do know that the second floor is the only room in the building taken hostage. No names have been released yet on the attackers and people inside, but according to some employees in the bank, that's where the bank manager's office is, and it's been said that William Fraleigh and Alexander Cross were with him minutes before the shot was heard. There's no confirmation of that yet, but we'll wait and see as the cops just got to the scene five minutes ago."

***

"What the hell do you think you're doing?" Xander asked in anger.

"What I'm supposed to be doing. It's the only way we can be together. You want that, but as long as she's there, we can't have that. The world has to know we're in love. We're going to be famous. Better than Romeo and Juliet." Sophie gave him a sickly sweet smile, cupping her cheeks in her palms as the gun in her hand kept everyone in place.

Both men stared incredulously at her. She was talking crazy, and they knew they had to overpower her.

The same phone kept ringing; it was Xander's.

"Make that stop!" Sophie screeched, not talking to anyone in particular as she saw Ally's name flashing on it again. She dropped the phone on the floor and smashed it with her heels. There was nothing but fear in the eyes of everyone in there as they watched the action, but Xander's anger simmered as she continued smashing his phone. Meanwhile, William's face switched from anger to disbelief.

"She would have never stopped. She never stops, does she? I should have taken her away from you. At least then, she would be free from your deception. Ally was it?"

"Take her name away from your lips."

"And what beautiful lips I do have, I'll admit. Right, William?" Sophie asked.

"What do you think you're doing? You'll never get away with this."

"You think?" She smirked. "Not even when I have a card to play? A particular woman in my good care?" She mocked.

Both men narrowed their eyes at her as they made a move from their position.

"You..." Xander attempted to stand.

A shot was fired and she shouted at them. "Hey! Stay right where you are or I'll put you down. I have her. So you better give me what I want, or you get her lifeless body. Deal?"

"Mommy, I'm scared." A little girl moved closer into her mother's arms, hiding her face away. Xander watched as the scared mother tried to soothe her child. He looked back at Sophie, more furious than he was before.

He was worried about Ally. He was not sure if he should be relieved that she had been calling his phone, but he could not guarantee anything from where he was at the moment. Or maybe it was just what the crazy girl in the room wanted him to believe. She was pregnant, for goodness sake, and he did not want to imagine the worst, but at the moment, Xander was trusting Paul and his father to work things out and not let things get out of hand. They would know the first thing he would want them to take care of: Ally.

How the hell did he encounter this tiny evil girl?

***

Three hours earlier

Ally walked out her door, getting into the car Xander supplied her as Garry, her chauffeur for the next month to two, held the door open for her. Xander insisted she needed this considering the situation.

"Morning, Miss Storm."

"Garry, come on. After two weeks? You're old enough to be my father."

He smiled as he got in position. "I don't know about that. Maybe old enough to be an uncle, though."

She smiled.

"Besides, I don't think Mr Cross would like that. He left specific instructions."

Ally turned up her mouth in silent disapproval. He was not talking to her but leaving instructions for people concerning her? Typical Xander; almost like the old him she knew—getting things his way. She had less complain concerning that, but after her day with Dr Stack, she was going to have him listen to her.

She was doing a lot better; Dr Stack had confirmed that. Ally knew without being told that some things had definitely fallen into new perspectives for her. The nightmares had stopped, she was not anymore overly intimidated by what people thought or said of her, and most importantly, she was accepting the fact that she was a mother and her baby deserved to have her. She was learning to forgive her mistakes and give her baby protection as much as she could.

She had also met Andriana for the second time today by chance—she was her gynaecologist's student. The girl had witnessed her initial breakdown at the peak of her depression. They never spoke at length but always acknowledged each other, but today, they had a long chat, and Ally found out she also has a kid and her pregnancy did not come without its own challenges.

Andriana revealed it was the worst moments for her family.

"My son does not have a father. He does not even know about my pregnancy, and my mom had to take care of us after my dad's disappearance. He is her life and everything just went wrong. But we got through that. So you see, Ally, you're going to be fine."

To Ally, Andriana did not look anything like the story she just revealed, and she knew she made a new friend in the young aspiring doctor.

After another fulfilling session, she asked for Garry to take her to Xander's office. He looked surprised for a moment, but he did not refuse her instruction. When Garry announced their arrival at the front of Xander's office building, she looked out from where she sat, trying to gain composure before her next move.

"Miss Storm?" Garry questioned her hesitation.

"It's fine Garry. Just taking a breath." She whispered the last part to herself. She eventually got down and off the car.

***

"We have an appointment with the bank manager, so he's expecting us. We just need to sign some documents, and you can see for yourself the progress we've made on your home. This inconvenience should not be, but there's something else I need you to be present for."

William Fraleigh, who Xander had gotten used to calling William, told him as they both entered the back seat of William's car, taking them to the bank.

Xander simply regarded the man as a business associate before, but in the past few weeks they saw and discussed more, and they got along well despite having very few interests in common. He was a cool guy to be around and definitely intelligent. He wanted to say he's smart, but the rumour about his infidelity that spread like wildfire in the media would contradict that. But who was he to judge? He also made the same mistake, only he was not a married man when he did. He did not know the whole story, and he was not making it his business.

Xander was unable to shake off one thing, though. He had the same name as his older brother who he never got to meet, and that might have weakened his resolve when it came to the guy.

His phone started to ring and he excused himself, picking up. It was his mom. "Mom?"

"Alexander, are you okay?"

"I'm fine. Is something wrong?" He tried to sound calm despite hearing his mother's nervous tone.

"You're sure?"

He asked again what was going on with his mother.

"I just had this tight feeling in my chest, and I've felt uneasy all morning. I called your office, but Owen said you were out. Your brother,Theo, called me earlier and told me the same."

That was the first time his mother referred to Theo as his brother while talking to him. He had made it clear he was still not on board with that idea. She would slip now and then, but she would always correct herself before completing her sentence.

"If you're feeling unwell, you should call for a doctor," she said. There was a short silence, and then he heard a small sigh from his mother's end.

"I'm fine. I have a meeting soon at a bank. I'll call you when I'm done."

"Please do. I'll probably call every hour. It might inconvenience you, but I just need to be at rest. I don't feel right today."

"I have to go. I promise I'll call you in an hour." He hung up as they reached their destination.

The manager was awaiting their arrival and escorted them upstairs into his office. The employees stared at them as they passed by. The stare was more about recognising William and Xander and the fact that their boss never came down for customers unless they were very important to the bank.

***

Somewhere in the building

"Are you sure about this?"

"I'm not backing out now. I need you to just do what you're good at. Leave the rest to me."

"I owe you no more favours after this. We good?"

"Yeah, we're good. We agreed on that. Now, make sure you don't blindside me in there. I'll be going in after this call."

"And I'll be watching your every move. I got your back."

Sophie cut the call and placed the phone in her bag. She took another quick look at her appearance, or better yet, her disguise and walked towards her mission. She had set her plan in motion a week before by making her first agenda, setting up an account with the bank and setting herself up as an important personality through her fake identification. She had been here last week so she had no need to scope the floor.

It was a relatively isolated floor, and that was just perfect for her. She took a seat on one of the chairs, and even though the floor was a bit crowded than what she would have wanted and preferred, she had no choice because it was the day he was supposed to be here. This was the only way she could get this done. It might just be the only perfect opportunity she would ever get to reach center stage.

This was her comeback.

Sophie mentally counted the number of people on the floor and came up with total of nine, including the two employees in their space. She looked straight ahead at the large office that read bank manager on the door, and though she could barely see the three figures in there, she knew who they were. She looked up at the camera on her right and winked, knowing who currently had control over it.

Just as soon, she stood up to set the plan in motion.

***

The men had just concluded on the first part of their business, and when the manager rang for his employee, there was no answer. He seemed a bit embarrassed at the situation and excused himself. The manager closed the door behind him, and Xander's phone started to ring. He stared at the screen and saw Ally's name flash on it.

William seeing the back and forth hesitation on his face, spoke up.

"If that's the same woman you're doing all this for, I say you pick up," William said. "Not my business, but if there's anyone who can tell you to hold on to what you have now instead of trying to patch things later, the best candidate would be me. I don't know the story, but I'm sure you love her. Regret is one of the worst feelings in the world. All those what ifs will haunt you every single day of your life."

The phone had stopped ringing, and when Xander made up his mind to call Ally back, they heard a scream. Both men looked at each other before getting up in their seat to check what was going on.

What they saw was beyond what they could have imagined.

All they saw was one woman.

One woman who looked awfully familiar to one of them. She grinned as she expected their presence, pointing the gun towards them. William looked on shock while Xander gazed at the manager on the floor who had blood trickling down his forehead, but alive.

"Sophie?" William said in disbelief.

A look of pure happiness on her face, splitting in a wide smile. "I knew it. You do love me. You recognised me in an instant. Our hearts do beat as one. I knew the decision to cut me off could not have been yours. It had to be that ugly bitch." She sighed blissfully. "William."

Xander stared in horror at the crazy woman not far from him.

***

Present

Walking inside the building, eyes followed Ally's every move as she walked to the elevator that would take her to Xander's floor. It was disconcerting, but she edged it out. Approaching Xander's office, she saw Owen talking to a man. When he spotted her, he dismissed the other guy and pleasantly grinned at her with the warmest greeting she has received so far since entering the building.

"What are you doing here?"

She smiled back at the young man who was always smiling at her. "To see Xander. Is he busy?"

"He's not in at the moment. He left the office about an hour and a half ago with a business associate. Why don't you give him a call to let him know you're here? Perhaps he'll wrap up the—*Ahh*... what he... whatever he is doing."

She wondered why Owen was choosing his words carefull, but she did bring out her phone and dialled Xander's number. It kept ringing, but there was no answer. Was he ignoring her again?

Really, Xander? This was getting unreasonable.

Owen tried to change the sullen look on her face, but all his attempts turned futile. Her phone started to ring in her hand, and it turned out to be one she was not expecting. She took a seat to rest her aching back, a common occurance lately.

"Liliana."

"Ally? Is everything okay? You don't sound yourself."

Was it just her imagination or did Liliana sound anxious? "I'm fine. I just made a wasted trip to Xander's office is all."

"Oh." Liliana sounded relieved. "He has a meeting this morning at a bank, I suppose."

"Oh, how do you know that?"

"I called him earlier, and he told me."

Ally rubbed her forehead and she heard Liliana ask if everything was okay between them. "I have to go Liliana. There is something I have to do."

She hung up and saw Owen watching her. She lied to the woman; she had nothing planned. If she left here, she would probably go back to her mom's place and stare at her laptop all day, pretending to be working. It made her realise how everyone around her was so busy.

He picked his mom's call? That meant one thing to her—he was ignoring her call on purpose, and he did not want to speak to her. Was he really serious about giving her this much space? She did not think he would take it this far. She knew there was hardly much she could do in his absence, and so she moved on. Owen was beside her all the while as he followed her downstairs. She forgot about giving Garry a call before getting down and had to do it then. Owen kept her company for that short while. She smiled at something he said, and he looked happy that he finally got a smile out of her despite her mood.

"Do you have a name yet?" Owen asked. During her birthday, he had asked if she would consider his name for her baby in case it's a boy.

She had laughed it off, knowing she was choosing the boy names, but in the end, it had to be a name she and Xander would love.

"I have." She had decided on the names she wanted, but she was not sure if Xander had.

Garry arrived. And before she got into the car, Owen promised to reprimand Xander for his behaviour, but she knew better. That was just for her to feel better.

"Could you just tell him I was here?"

"Of course."

***

Owen watched the car drive off and received a short text from Paul asking him to keep Ally with him and make sure she did not leave. Owen smiled to himself. Was his boss back to his senses? How did Paul know Ally had been with her? That man had eyes everywhere.

He was still outside the building when his phone started ringing. He picked up and heard Paul's loud voice, asking if he did what he asked.

"She left already."

"What!"

***

Paul disconnected the call and placed one to Garry. He left a strict instruction to take her to Liliana's place where his men were waiting. Garry, without questions asked, changed their route.

Ally, noticing the change in route, asked Garry what was going on and where she was being taken, but he gave her no answer except assuring her that everything's fine.

She frowned. Everything did not seem fine. What's up with his sudden change of plans? She was not sure why, but for the second time since she left Xander's office, she dialled his number again.

She got the same response: nothing.

***

The room was sealed, and everyone was seated on the floor in fear. Sophie made sure to warn them against trying anything funny because she was not alone. The cameras were in her favour and the doors had been remotely manipulated to shut off outside interference.

They were all clear on that, and it was the only reason she still had the advantage.

Sophie had just smashed Xander's phone when Ally tried calling again. Even though they knew the cops were right outside, he was not sure if Ally knew what was going on right now. It was only a matter of time, but he hoped she did not because of the state she was in. He had tried giving her some space in the past two weeks, and they barely even talked when she called to thank him for the puppy. She must have thought he was ignoring her like always, and now that the psycho girl had smashed his phone, Ally might be thinking he switched off his phone.

William was right. Regret had a bitter taste.

He looked at William beside him who had just been shown a picture of his wife being held in some place by probably the same man helping Sophie. William had tried to talk Sophie out of this situation, but one moment, the girl was gooey eyed and listening to every word from his mouth and the next, she was acting crazy and pointing the gun at the two of them, blaming them for where she was.

Xander, on the one hand, was glad that Ally was safe, but he still was uncomfortable with the way Sophie had taunted him, watching her every move for a few weeks. Apparently, William's wife was more important to her, and Xander almost choked at the statement Sophie had made earlier.

"I considered letting her free from you. She doesn't have to go through what I did. She doesn't need to be alive to see you destroy her."

He still tried to understand why he was being involved in this mess. He did ask, and Sophie only shrugged like it was none of her problem.

Having confirmed that all the phones in the office had been disconnected, she dragged a chair and sat down. After that, she stood up smashed everyone's mobiles, telling William she really did not want to talk to the police because they would never understand. She had no business with anyone but him, insisting only William would understand her because, after all, he had been in contact with her, telling her to fight for them and take their stand against the world.

Xander stared in shock at William but only saw an angry look on the man's face.

"I did *what?* I never called you."

Sophie smiled. "Of course you did, silly. You don't have to hide it anymore. I heard every word you whispered to me at night."

Xander stared back at the girl, now knowing she was either crazy or being manipulated by someone.

Sitting back and facing everyone, Sophie crossed her legs and kept talking as the gun swung in her hand.

"I'm going to be so famous. Better than how Tony treated me. They'll all come begging for me. Oh, Will, don't you see? We'll have our own love story. They would talked about for years what I had to do to get us together. It's better than Romeo and Juliet!" She grinned widely. "What do you think? They'll make a movie out of today. I've always wanted to act too, but don't worry, I won't let another man touch me if it isn't you, so I'll probably never agree to the part." She laughed. "Unless you take the part."

Xander could not imagine how William got it on with this crazy woman. She had to be high on something.

"Say something. You've been awfully quiet."

"I'll never be with you. You know what really happened. I was stupid to fall for your lies. I love my wife, and you better get us the hell out of here because when I do, I'll make sure you get your name famous behind bars."

Sophie smirked. "I knew you might say that, so I came prepared." She gave a signal to the camera in the room.

Xander could see the determination on Sophie's face to end things her own way without a care of who got caught in between. From the way things were going, he was guessing she would prefer a twisted end to her tragic love story.

He had a child to welcome into this world, and there was no way he was losing that by letting his life end here today.

CHAPTER 32

Xander stared.

No.

He plotted.

He plotted in his head, but none of his plans came out with a good outcome. He had taken every angle into consideration, but came up with nothing. Sophie's accomplice manning the camera was watching their every move, he couldn't be reckless and take the gun from Sophie's hand and knock her out. Whatever he tried to do here might risk the life of William's wife, and he was not going to shoulder that responsibility. So far, there has been no human casualty yet, but things were getting more insane by the minute.

No one knew what she was thinking. What could be going through her head at the moment? He watched her every move, and noticed that moment she sat in a corner and murmured to herself. For a while, she had her hands to her rocking head, and it made those who caught her concerned—not for her but of what her strange actions might turn out to mean for them.

"I need to be famous again. I was getting there when you snatched it away from me." Sophie told William when she joined them minutes later, acting like nothing had happened. "It was the only thing I had. The only thing where I was better than them, the only thing which proved to them I made it, that they could not get to me again."

What she was saying made no sense to them at all, and Xander saw no reason to listen to her, but maybe William should because, at this point, it seemed like he was the only one she would listen to.

"That's why I never changed my name; for mom, Bernard and his brats to see… to see who I was! But I bet all they do now behind the TV is laugh at me." Sophie kept quiet for a second before she continued. "I ran away from them—for my independence and to prove that I was much more than a slave and a foot mat for my creepy stepfather, my so-called step-siblings, and for my mother who always chose them above her own flesh and blood."

She turned to William.

"She took that away from me, your wife did! The whole media pitied her and only saw her as a victim. What about me? Was I wrong to fall in love and have my career, my life, taken from me? Why is she special and I'm not? You're the only man who has ever treated me well."

"You should have thought twice before getting involved with a married man."

Sophie turned her sinister eyes towards Xander who had just spoken. "And who are you to talk, Alexander Cross? Excuse me for the mistake." She laughed a little before settling her eyes on both men. "From the start, I thought you two were friends. I thought you knew each other. Afterall, you both treated women the same. I've heard a lot about your story with that girl that's pregnant with your seed."

She was giving Xander her full attention now.

"I hate it when men use helpless women for their sick satisfaction. I really wanted to help by taking you out of her life forever, but it's so hard getting to you for anything really. That's why I resorted to using the media. Your father is a really scary man, do you know that? He warned me against getting near you, but today could not be avoided. I had no idea you two would be here together, but it was too late to back out. It was the only way I could get William's attention."

Sophie pointed the gun to her chest a couple of times. "She'll learn from me. I'm sure when she sees my interviews and the movie made out of today, she'll learn what love is and see who you really are: a player. I think it would be nice to make you a part of it." She let out a sigh. "Men like you really should be extinguished. Women like his wife should be condemned."

"Where's my wife?" William asked, trying to appease Sophie with his to get an answer.

"She doesn't love you. If she did, she would want you to be happy, right? And I know I make you happy. You always tell me that."

"Why do you keep saying that? I never talked to you except for that night, you know that. I only helped you. Why are you blowing this out of proportion? If this is about your fame, why don't we do something about it? I can talk to the police and the media for you. It's going to be fine. You just have to trust me."

"If you do that, you also have to tell them about our love story. You have to tell them about us—how we met and what we mean to each other."

Xander groaned. It was no use trying to get through this girl; she was clearly delusional. If they continued like this, something uglier might rear its head. By now, he would not be surprised if Ally had heard about what was going on. He just did not want to have her worried about him because he was making sure he gets out of this alive.

He owed her a lot. He had disappointed her and broke her heart in many ways. He was not going to let today be an addition.

The doors were locked, they were being watched, and there was a life being held hostage out there, but he had to get the gun from her somehow. But how? He moved closer to William and whispered his idea into his ears when Sophie picked up a call that came through her phone. Their hushed words suddenly died when Sophie screamed into the phone and cursed at whoever was at the other end.

Is it the same guy watching us? Xander wondered.

Seeing her disoriented look, Xander suddenly saw an opening. He looked around, and his eyes caught the woman who held her child to her bosom trying to comfort her.

This was not a place for a child to be in. This was messed up, and it bothered him. What would he have done if it happened to be Ally and their child in this same situation?

"Is she okay?" he asked loud enough for the woman to hear. The mother only nodded, obviously still frightened out of her wits. He moved his eyes once more and saw the manager seated on the floor, pressing a hand to the blood-soaked handkerchief resting on his forehead.

"AAHHHHH! Impossible! Incompetent."

All eyes turned to Sophie's erratic yelling. She obviously got news that displeased her. She threw her phone to the wall, and before Xander could voice out his concern for the manager, she shot twice through the roof.

The action made the little girl scream.

"Shut her up!" Sophie shouted at the mother who frantically tried to console the frightened child. "It doesn't matter," she said to William. "This is not the end of it. By the time she sees you again, I'll make sure we're inseparable by then."

Both men looked at each other. Did that mean...?

"SHUT HER UP! She is distracting me." She pointed the gun at the mother and child.

"I'm sorry, please. She's just scared," the mother said in fear, covering the little girl from the gun with her body and rocking the child.

She was whispering into her ear, but not even her mother's efforts could settle the child.

"Shut her up or I swear—"

"You will do no such thing!" Xander stood up, and this time, Sophie pointed the gun at him. He stood his ground and saw a shadow stand up to his height. He turned to see William standing beside him.

"You don't have my wife anymore." He was not asking, and they got the reply they wanted from her body language.

The shouts of the police from below did not change what was going on in that room.

"So what? You tell me what I want to hear or I'll start taking action."

Xander moved forward. "If you wanted to, you would have by now. If you really meant to hurt anyone today, you would have done that with William's wife and you would not have constantly checked that man's bleeding head and frown."

"Stop moving! You know nothing about me. The likes of you think life is easy. You get everything handed to you on a sliver platter, but I had to work hard for all I have achieved only for all of it to be taken away from me because of one woman, because of a woman deemed perfect for a rich husband! None of you know what it's like. I said, STOP MOVING!"

He halted, raising his hands. "How long do you think it will take before all this ends? Let's stop this."

Sophie shook her head violently. "I'll have nothing. No one. And don't talk to me. You're part of the people against me. You're part of those plotting against me." She made quick steps towards the woman and snatched her daughter from her, still pointing the gun at Xander.

"William, tell them you love me. Tell them I'm a good person and how good I am to you. Tell them how you trusted me and spoke to me about your troubles."

"Sophie, it's over. Let the girl go."

This was it. Her thoughts were getting more and more irrational. It was a gamble assuming they were being watched. But then, his fear of reacting was all because of William's wife and Sophie has lost that power over them.

He gave a slow nod to the man creeping behind Sophie as William engaged her in small talk. The ringing of a phone diverted her attention and made Sophie spot the man behind her. She faced the man, who stopped in his tracks and concentrated back on the little girl.

Xander ran towards her, and in panic, Sophie wondered who to concentrate on; the man behind her, the girl she had, or the man running towards her? She flung the girl away from her and fired a shot.

Screams were heard, but Sophie's screams rsng louder, piercing the room as she started sobbing and murmuring incoherent words on how it was not her fault. The events that followed felt like minutes but it all just happened in a flash. She threw the gun away from her and stared at William. Someone grabbed the gun from the floor while someone broke the window and shouted for help. A woman pulled at the door, but it was still locked.

Xander was a bit relieved that the crisis seemed to be over, but was he leaving here in one piece? He found that one hard to answer as he stared at William's face.

***

"Oh my god, will someone just tell me what is going on?" Ally asked no one in particular as she stared at the people in the room.

Garry had taken her to Liliana's house. About why, she still was in the dark about. Then she saw men waiting for them. Her first thought was that it had to be Xander's instructions. As if that was not weird enough, she found her mom barging into the house minutes after she arrived.

Now she was just plain confused. Why would they go to such lengths? Unless their lives was being threatened... or that sort of thing.

Liliana had a far off look on her face. She looked stressed and anxious. Even when she first met Liliana and she panicked about facing her son after a long time, this forlorn look on her beautiful face was not there.

Which begged the question again: what the hell was going on?

"Where's Xander? Is he here? Is he on his way?"

"Relax, baby."

"I can't, Mom, if no one will tell me what is going on."

"I will. Sit down."

She reluctantly obeyed. "What are you doing here, Mom?"

"Alicia—"

Ally was familiar with that look. It was like breaking her father's illness to her all over again. She could only think of one thing or two. "Xander and Laurie… are they okay?"

"Laurie's fine."

"X-Xander? Please tell me he's just as fine and he's just purposely ignoring my calls. I can handle that. Really. Tell me that's what's going on."

"I'm afraid it's more, baby."

"Is he okay? What's going on?"

"Xander is in a bit of a hostage situation."

"What? Hostage... Hostage as in the real sense?" She tried to stand up, but her mom gently put her back to sit on the sofa.

"Remember, you're pregnant and you need to consider the baby's health."

She slowly nodded. Her mother explained everything that she knew to her.

"He's fine. He has to be. He isn't a target, so everything is going to be fine," Liliana interjected.

She looked at Liliana and wondered who she was trying to convince. Liliana looked like she said the words for her own peace of mind. She looked scared.

"Then why are we sitting here?"

"Xander's father asked for you to be brought here for safety."

Why? If he was just in the wrong place at the wrong time, why should they be concerned about her safety?

"What else are you not telling me?"

"We honestly don't know anything more. This is all just for precaution."

She accepted her mom's explanation with no further questions. Instead, she played back today's events in her head. She had been calling him; what if she had put him in danger with her calls? What if something happens and she ended up alone? She had thought he was ignoring her, but he was... She wanted to cry out in frustration and helplessness. Her heart squeezed at the unknown, and she did something that she had stopped doing five years ago.

She prayed fervently.

***

"Hello?" Carla picked up the strange number. Liliana watching in apprehension, worrying that it had anything to do with the current situation.

"Move away from where your daughter and Liliana are."

"Who is this?" she asked curiously and saw Liliana and Ally's curious faces.

"Alexander's father. I have news, and they are the last people I want to know at this point."

Carla understood and moved away after shaking her head and waving to the two, as if telling them it had nothing to do with what was going on.

"I'm good. What is going on? Those two are worried sick."

"I need you to stay calm because those two would be far from it. Can I trust your judgement?"

"Speak."

"Xander's in the hospital. He's been shot, but I don't want you to reveal how bad it is."

Carla closed her eyes and took a short breath before speaking. "That bad?"

"He's in surgery."

"But you can't keep that information from them. They have a right to know and be there for him."

"Exactly what would they be doing for him except panic? I have no intention of keeping them away, though. I have instructed Paul to bring you to the hospital, but for now until they reach the hospital, I don't want them to know what the situation is. If one of them is going to need a doctor's attention, they might as well get it here. That's your job: to keep them together."

Carla had the urge to stare at her phone. Who did he think he was talking to? She let it go because of the current situation and went back into the room wher her daughter was. Carla was worried about her daughter. Ally was emotionally fragile, and she did not want to see her daughter losing someone she loves again.

When she got to the room, Paul was already waiting. Of course, Liliana and Ally questioned what was going on when they were moved into a car, and Carla explained as calmly as she could, leaving out some details.

***

Liliana's phone rang in the car and she picked up. "Theo."

"Mom, I heard. How are you holding up?"

"I don't know. I'm so scared for your brother."

"He'll be fine. I'll join you there soon."

The three women sat in the back seat of the car while Garry drove. Paul occupied the passenger's seat, looking as professional as ever as another car with two of Paul's subordinates followed them from behind.

***

Hastily leading the way to Xander's room, the first person Liliana saw waiting was Cameron. She did not hesitate to move closer to him. Her son was more important than the resentment she had for the man.

"How is he? How's Alexander?"

The first thing Cameron did was look at Carla who shrugged and shook her head. "Are you going to pass out?" he suddenly said, turning his attention to Liliana who was currently holding his arm.

Liliana frowned and dropped his arm. "What are you talking about? Is this a joke to you? Don't you care?"

His hands went into his pocket, and Ally watched nervously. This was the first time she was seeing Xander's parents together in a room, and not to mention talking. Cameron was smartly dressed in a clean cut suit and intimidating like always. Nothing looked out of place for him.

"This isn't about you, so I'm going to ignore everything you throw at me. He's in surgery. Panicking will do you no good. It's been two hours, but I'm sure the doctor will come out with news soon. So relax."

"Easy for you to say," Liliana muttered, but not before giving him a dirty look. She turned on her heels, walking away from him.

She took a seat beside Ally and Carla. She was not sure why she let Cameron's words get to her at a time like this. She was still as concerned and nervous, but her heart gained a ray of hope that her son would be okay.

Despite how much she despised Cameron, he was once that man that calmed her when she needed it no matter how absurd his words were. She could at least acknowledge that Cameron provided for their son in her absence—an absence he caused, but it was not right to bring it up right now.

***

It felt like hours, but in reality, it has been just minutes since they arrived. The doctor came out and gave them the news, saying the surgery was a success but they had to wait for him to wake up and monitor his vitals to know how well he was responding post surgery.

They had relieved faces at the doctor's news. Liliana asked for them to see him, but the doctor gave his apologies and said it was only possible for one of them to go in for now.

Ally gave way for Liliana, but the woman smiled at her.

"I'm glad he's okay and alive. That's enough for me for now. You want to see him, don't you? You should. Go."

A tear fell from Ally's left eye, and she barely managed a smile in thanks. When she walked into the white room, she saw the man she's always known to be in charge lying so still, and it threatened to break her wall of strength. She took a seat beside him and held Xander's hand closer as the uncontrollable sobs escaped.

***

Ally took the usual position she took from the very first day she entered the room. She took Xander's bedside, holding his hand and talking to him. Sometimes, she would even scold him.

Liliana had just stepped out with William and his wife who came to visit, and she was sure the guys would soon be here as well. Dom, Jay, and Mike visited from the very first day, and they usually had quiet little banters. The guys were sure he would be out of it soon. After all, it was not Xander's style to lie still in bed because the guy hated being stuck in one place, wanting to command his own freedom.

Xander recently went through a major abdominal surgery, but the scans revealed he had no life threatening damage to his head after the fall he took, and Ally could not understand why he looked the same as he did five days ago.

She rested a hand on her lower back and rubbed. The same pain kept coming every now and then, but it had been more frequent than usual, not to mention the frequent bathroom breaks she had to take. Her body has been switching between being tired and bursting with energy lately, but she decided to hide all of it from her mom and Liliana. They would only fret and ask her to rest; it was not like she was doing anything tedious anyway. She could manage this at least.

She got on her feet and walked back and forth within the walls of the hospital room. She took deep breaths in and out, and it got to a point where she had to hold on to something. She felt like screaming out at the sudden sharp pain she felt.

She couldn't be.... No, no way. She was not due yet. Besides, Xander had to be present.

She managed to walk closer to Xander's bed and held his hand that probably would be wrinkled from her frequent holds now.

"You have to get up. This can't happen without you."

Immediately, she felt a trickle down her legs. "You have got to be kidding me." She gritted the words, trying to hold on and overcome the tinge of pain she felt. "Alexander Cross, you cannot do this to me."

Her wet face was what Laurie saw when she came in.

"Al? What's wrong?" she asked, gently looking at her cousin's crying face.

"He has to wake up."

"He will, honey. Why are you doing this to yourself? You need to take a break, you've been with him-—"

"No."

Laurie took a step further to see why she could not stop crying and gritting her teeth and felt her shoe step on something wet. "Did you call for a nurse to get someone to clean this up? You could slip on it."

Ally forced a muffled scream out.

"What the hell?" Laurie said, a bit frightened at the sudden scream.

Laurie looked at the wet floor and back to Ally. "*Oh shit!* Are you... are you about to give birth? Did I step on... Gross! I'm already making history with this baby. Why didn't you shout for help?"

"What do you think I'm doing right now?"

"Come on, let's get you out of here and ready to pop."

"No."

"Excuse me?"

"I'm not going anywhere. Xander has to be there. He promised."

"Are you insane? Does he look like he can be there at the moment?"

She let the tears out again, obviously in pain. "I can't do this without him, Laurie."

"You'll have to. Are you trying to kill yourself? I'm getting a doctor." And just as Laurie walked out the door, Ally tried to hold on to something as she gritted back the pain.

She was doing the best she could, holding firmly to Xander's hand while she tried to breathe in and out. She just did not understand why the tears won't stop flowing.

"The only reason we agreed to not find out the sex of the baby was to find out together on this day. Please."

"Alicia." She looked up to see her mother, Liliana, and Laurie running towards her, entering the room along with a nurse. "Baby, what's going on? Why won't you go—?"

And she repeated the reasons she refused to go in alone.

"Oh, sweetheart," Liliana spoke. "You can't do that. I'm sure Alexander wouldn't want you to make that kind of decision. You have to think about your baby."

Ally shook her head. "I'm not ready. Something else has to be wrong. I have three more weeks to go."

"Alicia, stop this nonsense. You're being unreasonable."

Two people entered the room. It was Cameron and Xander's doctor.

"What's going on?" Cameron asked.

"She's in labour, and she refuses to leave unless Alexander's with her," Liliana answered.

Cameron looked at the scene in front of him. He walked closer to where Ally sat beside his son and stopped just before he stepped on the wet ground not far from her. He looked down at it before looking at the hand of his son she held and finally.

"What the hell do you think you're doing?"

"There's three more weeks—"

"If he doesn't wake up until the following week or the next month, you're saying you'll hold on till then? Did you carry that child just to put it's life in danger in the end?"

Ally stared up at the emotionless face frowning at her.

"Get up and do what you're supposed to do as a mother. He's not going to be there, deal with it. He does not look like he has much of a choice right now, does he?"

"But I've never done this before. I need him."

"And? You think your mother had gone through it before she had you? Or Alexander's mother? I was not there when she had him, and she did fine on her own. You have your family. Suck the bratty attitude up and get into labour. You'll only have more to tell my idiot of a son when he wakes up. Put your child's life first."

Every person in the room heard Cameron's words and was left with a mix of emotions. Liliana was not surprised. She knew this side of Cameron all too well. He was such a difficult man to understand.

Ally nodded slowly and let Cameron help her up. She dug his nails in into his hand, groaning as she summoned what little strength she had left. Laurie and the nurse helped her. The doctor brought in a wheelchair and gave the nurse instructions, asking her to call the obstetrician to attend to Ally.

***

It has been almost twelve hours since Ally started getting into labour, and all the while, her mom and Liliana kept her company. Laurie, who didn't want to witness her pain, waited outside waiting. Cameron was probably with her.

"How did you do it, Mom?" she asked again. She had asked the same question countless times in the span of two hours.

"Come on, baby, you can do it. It'll all be over soon."

"You said that two hours ago," she screamed out.

Liliana smiled and encouraged her to not give, but by now, Ally has turned her ears to the female doctor, who was around her mom's age, currently instructing her. About seven minutes later, Ally screamed, and the cries of a baby filled the room.

The mothers were happy.

"You did it, honey," Carla said, teary-eyed.

"I did?" Ally asked, tired. Her whole body felt heavy. Hours of pushing had taken a toll on her.

"It's a girl." The doctor announced, and when the baby was cleaned and declared healthy, she was introduced to her mother. The baby was laid on her chest, their very first skin to skin contact, and Ally savoured the special moment with her baby girl.

Ally's tears wouldn't drop; it felt like everything she had done in her life led to this singular moment. All of a sudden, she laughed. Xander was right. It was a baby girl. He was going to act all arrogant when he knew that.

"Daddy loves you," she whispered to her girl. *And I love you too, so much. Thank you for coming to our lives.* She brought the child closer to her.

"Do you have a name?" Liliana's voice cut in.

"It's a girl, so Xander gets to name her." They never got around to discussing the names with all that happened after the birthday party.

Ally nursed her baby, staring at the dark haired and grey eyed cutie as her heart swelled with love. By the next hour, the baby was asleep, and as with new mothers, Ally asked every minute if the baby was fine and breathing well.

***

Later in the day, Ally was laughing with her mom and Liliana who currently had the baby with her when a trio of noisy men came in. One of them, obviously Dom, shouted as they entered.

"We heard! Where's the princess?"

CHAPTER 33

"Alex, I know I've always liked the stubble look on your face, but this time, I really want you to shave... but you have to get up first to do that. I love you, Alexander Cross, and your daughter is still without a name. That responsibility is yours, remember? You have to give her a name, and will it be too early to discuss her next five siblings? Maybe." Ally chuckled lightly. "I know I'm still young, but we can manage it before you turn into an old man, right?"

She squeezed his unresponsive hand.

"You should have seen your father... I know I told you all this before, but I'll keep repeating everything until you tell me to shut up." And she told him again how she had wanted to wait for him during labour and how his father scolded her for the sake of the kid.

It was just two days since she gave birth to their daughter, and she had cleared all postnatal checks. She had been hoping for some kind of miracle, that the next time she saw him, he would be staring right back at her. It hadn't been the case, and she had taken every free time she was not spending with their daughter to be with him and talk, telling him about anything and everything she was feeling in the moment.

She admitted that she loved him for the the first time in a long time yesterday. The words fell out before she even realised. And she meant it. Saying it again today without hesitation burned away any second thoughts she might have had.

"She's a beautiful girl, and I know you can't wait to give me one of your know-it-all faces. Trust me. When you wake up, I'm going to whip you back into that coma for being so stubborn."

"I'd rather prefer a much different kind of whipping," a groggy voice replied.

"Xander?" She saw his eyes flutter open.

He coughed. "Has someone else taken over my body?"

She flung herself towards his neck. He tried to chuckle but came up with another cough. She released him and apologised for being reckless.

"I should get shot more often if this is what it takes to receive such a bosom hug."

"You think that's funny?" She lightly hit his arm. She probably had flung the whole of her chest towards his face. Yeah, she did. "You're in so much trouble, mister," she said, and her tears dropped involuntarily before she wiped them away.

Xander smiled and closed his eyes for a moment before opening them. "Carliana," he said softly.

Ally heard what he said, but she was confused about what he meant by it.

"Carliana." He repeated more clearly. "That's the name I came up with."

How did he know the baby was a girl? Had he been awake all this time she was talking? Then he might have heard all that she said to him from the moment she sat beside his bed.

"I like it," Ally said, repeating the name on her lips. “Carliana…”

"It's your mom and mine's."

Carla and Liliana. How cheesy could this man be? "It's perfect. I think Mom and Liliana will love it the most."

Xander just stared ahead for a while, a frown suddenly showing on his face. He tried to move, and the discomfort he felt drew a map of pain on his face. She tried to get him to lie down.

"I don't think you should be sitting. You just—"

"Got shot, I know. I've been on that bed for how long?"

"Eight days."

"I just want to stand up and do something."

She felt anger in Xander's voice, and even though he tried not to snap at her while he spoke, he still did a poor job of letting it show.

"I'll get the doctor." She walked out without saying another word.

***

Xander wanted to hit himself, if he could. The last person he wanted to take his anger out on was Ally. Was there anything he could do right by her? She deserved so much more. There was so much more he could have asked her; that was the most important thing, but he had not.

The door opened, and he intended to apologise to her. But instead of the beautiful face and wild waves of the woman he loved, a doctor and nurse appeared. Ally was nowhere in sight.

And as he was spoken to, Xander's mind drifted far off.

***

It had been barely three hours since he opened his eyes, and his room began to flood with people. He didn't need sympathy, but it was not like any of the people who came to see him gave him that. Well, save for Collins, but he snapped it out of him until the kid acted his normal upbeat self around him again.

His mother had been all over him as if he was a kid who got his first scrape and needed to be rushed to the ER. She also could not stop gushing about her little grand daughter who obviously, according to his mother's words, had significant resemblance to him. Carla had just smiled at him and wished him to get well. It was the first genuine smile he got from Ally's mom since he knew her. Carla eventually dragged his mom away to let him rest, and he was grateful for that. He needed to breathe a little.

His father came in minutes after his mom left. It had been a silent conversation between them. Both wanted to say something to the other, but nothing came out.

When his father walked to the window in the hospital room, Xander said softly, "Thank you."

For making sure Ally and my child were protected and for talking some sense into her in his absence…

He knew his father heard him.

His father turned to his direction. "Get back on your feet soon so you can take over your duties. That includes your new responsibility, of course."

He understood; he was a father now. He had someone to look after now, and he did not need a reminder for that.

Paul came in before all of them, briefing him on all that happened while he had been out of it. The only person who had not come back to see him was Ally.

"No one knows the whole story, but there has been no suspicious person lurking around," Paul had said.

Paul and his father would have made sure of that. The last time they were lax, things ended up badly.

Collins later joined them in the room, and Xander collected from him what he had asked him to get in his office.

Collins was talking too much. Xander was not listening anyway as he stared at the box he moved around in his hand, but the sound of his assistant's voice was making him more irritated, and so he sent him away to find some other person to bother. Collins, being who he was, had murmured before leaving that he only had free time because his boss was not in the office and his father took on most of his work.

He opened it and brought out the white gold necklace with a neatly cut diamond pendant hanging below it. He just kept on staring at it for a while. He had gotten it for Ally when they were dating, but the timing had been bad. He kept it with him for so long because he did not know what to do with it. It was a reminder of what his heart had realised, but his brain was too slow to pick up on that. Alicia Storm was not just a woman he liked hanging out with in and out of bed.

She was so much more.

And then all that stuff happened—his reaction to the news that she got pregnant. He sighed, squeezing the chain in his hand and closing his eyes. He had come far since then; he wanted to believe he was a much better man than that foolish one in the past, but what did he do? He planned everything just to be there for his daughter's birth and he had to go get himself shot by a delusional girl.

He broke yet another promise to her. He failed yet another female in his life—his little girl.

The knock on the door made him put back the chain, placing it beside him under the sheets.

"Look who's awake!"

Xander almost rolled his eyes at his best friend who was grinning at him.

"You don't look any different."

"Have you come to bother me?"

"What? No one told you about how I was bawling my eyes out for you?"

"It wasn't like I was dying," he said in a monotone voice.

The humour on Dom's face disappeared, being replaced with a serious one. "She was right."

He just stared at Dom as he stood at the foot of his bed, wondering what and who he meant.

"Ally called us that you were awake, and you know what? She was waiting right outside for us."

Xander frowned. *Why?*

"She told me how she was scared something was wrong. She was sure something was upsetting you because she expected you to be happy. I thought she was exaggerating until she told me you did not even ask about your child, and I just had to see for myself. And here you are acting like someone took a piss on your ego."

Xander's frown was still prominent.

"It wasn't like you were dying? Idiot, you got shot and had to go through surgery. You should have been awake a day after at most, but you decided to take a long nap. Do you know how many people you scared? Everyone. Everyone that cares about you. And you wake up with that attitude? I thought you were past being that ego-driven spoilt brat."

"Don't talk shit you know nothing about."

"That's your problem. You never talk. You just do things that are most convenient to you."

"How is this convenient?" He pointed to himself. "I'm angry, Dom. I'm angry about a lot of things. I can't get what I should have done out of my head. What if I did die? I would not have forgiven myself if I left her and never got to meet my child. I'm angry I let a little girl manipulate me. I'm angry I wasn't there for her when she gave birth. I'm angry because it doesn't seem like I'll ever do anything right with Ally. I love her, but it does not seem like it's enough, right?" He breathed out heavily.

While Dom tried to let his words sink, he gave a slow smile at him. "Well, I'm glad. You're angry at yourself, but you couldn't have changed the circumstances even if you wanted to. You wanted to play hero? What if it had gotten you killed? Be thankful for the life you still have and appreciate it with those around you. You have a family now; you can't let situations get to you and moan about them in solitude."

He did not want to play hero. He had wanted to get out of there alive for his family.

It was not just for Ally. He had been a real jerk to his mom, Carla, and Collins.

"Jay and Mike?"

"The perks of having a job that's flexible. The doctors are busy, but promised to check on you soon."

"I have no intention of staying here any longer."

"Good for you. The nurses around here, though *beautiful*, beautiful women, shouldn't be bothered. I can't let my presence distract them any more from their service."

Xander huffed, shaking his head, and Dom smiled. "You good?"

Xander gave him a nod.

Dom took a seat and crossed his legs, hiding his hand in his pockets but did not say a word. Xander watched his friend and knew something was eating at him. Silence and seriousness were two traits rarely seen on Dom.

"What?" Dom asked when he realised he was being watched.

"You've gone serious. What do you want to talk about?" he asked.

Dom didn't answer.

"Dom." Xander repeated. "Now I know." He sighed and looked away. "I won't ask you to let her go. That's almost impossible; it's like asking you to stop breathing."

"But I want to exhale every breath that reminds me of her. Even when I promised to stop acting pathetic in front of you guys, I don't realise when I'm wearing that pathetic face again. I tried to let it go—in every fling, every work, and every other thing I tried to do. Nothing worked. I've come to terms with knowing she won't come to me, but how do I purge her out?" Dom stood up. "I'm still waiting."

"Waiting for what?"

"For a girl who will help me with that. I'll eventually fall in love again, but knowing when is the problem because that could be a damn long time."

And as if they're done talking about the troubles of their hearts, Dom went back to his usual mood.

"I'll let the guys know you're back to being an ass. At least they'll know it means you're fine. I'll probably come with them if they get the time to show up." And before Dom walked out, he stopped by the door. "Don't try to lose what you haven't lost. I'll let her know that."

He pondered on Dom's words and picked up the phone to dial William's contact. The surprise was evident in William's voice, hearing him talk.

"How are things going with the house?" He cut the man off before he could ask about his health and went straight to business.

"It's ready. There are still some papers to be signed, but that can wait. If it can't, I can bring them over."

"No, it can wait." He did not need William's face reminding him of why he ended up in a hospital bed.

The house was ready, but was it ready to be moved in to? Would Ally agree to move in together? And what would she say if she found out he got them a house? He thought of the three of them as a family, but he never gave emphasis to the idea of marriage. He honestly was not sure if he was ready for that; nothing he had done so far proved he was a man fit for such level of commitment.

If he asked Ally to move in with him without the marriage card on the table, would he be another disappointment for her?

***

Xander had more than half an hour to think, and he could not wait anymore. No one came to his room, so he had to stand and find her himself. He was already up on his feet, trying to get past the discomfort and pain he felt in his midsection, when the door opened. He looked up and saw Ally walk in, and safely tucked in her arms was a bundle.

"Knock knock. Someone's here to say hello."

Ally walked closer to him, and he just stood where he was, staring at those adorable large eyes looking around the room. Her eyes settled on Ally, and she made some noise. Ally rocked her and spoke to her, introducing who he was. A few precious seconds later, she was trying to place their tiny little girl in his hands.

"Uh..." He hesitated.

"Come on." Ally was smiling at him, amused it seemed. "You can't be this nervous carrying a baby."

Heck, he was. She was small and looked really fragile. He's never held a newborn child. It shouldn't be hard; he had definitely read every page there is about expecting a kid, but nothing in the book prepared him for her size.

"I'm not nervous." He swallowed discreetly. "It's just that I'm not particularly stable on my feet and I don't want to drop her."

Ally laughed. "You won't drop her. You need to hold her, Xander; she wants to meet you. You've been waiting for this, right?" She carefully placed the baby in his hands. "You look stable enough to me."

He did not hear, too aware of the life he held in his hands. He was not sure how long he stared at those shining grey eyes looking back at him.

"You should sit, Xander," Ally said.

"Hmm?" he said, obviously not in the same dimension as her. Ally repeated her words, and he sat on the chair he could rest his back on, still getting familiar with his child. Finally past the silly idea that he might drop her, he had a feeling he would find it hard to put his baby girl down from now on.

"Are you sure you're fine?"

He nodded, glancing at Ally. He was very comfortable the way he was right now. He took another glance at the mother of his child and saw her watching him. He should explain his earlier behaviour and apologise.

"She honestly looks nothing like me," she said.

"You can't be so sure. She still has years to grow." He could not deny that when he hoped it was a girl, he also wanted one that looked like Ally, but she was right. Her hair and facial features had nothing similar to Ally's.

"Your dad started boasting about of the dominant traits of a true Cross the minute he saw her."

"Dad said that?"

"You look and sound surprised. Your dad has been very helpful. You never know, like father like son." She teased.

He was trying to be a better man, and it seemed like Ally's saying his father was trying to do the same. He would have to see the results to believe that. He looked down at his little girl. Lying right here in his arms was the one thing that would make sure he becomes that better man. He was going to right his mistakes.

"I'm going to work at being the best dad for you. I promise to always protect you and be there, always"

***

Ally was silent. She had no doubts that he was going to be a great dad. Carliana would most probably turn out to be a daddy's girl, just like what she was to her own father.

Dom had explained things to her and why he was angry. Xander was going to realise he was not going to be there for everything forever, but she understood where he was coming from, and she was not going to burst his bubble. He was going to have to learn some things for himself in the future.

"I'm sorry..." He looked down at Carliana who was trying to close her eyes, battling to keep them open. She looked sleepy. "I'm sorry about earlier and for not keeping my promise. I should have been more careful," he spoke quietly.

"Xander, stop. Dom told me. I don't blame you or hold you responsible. You're here, she's here. It's all that matters to me now."

He kept silent, and after a while, she spoke up. She wanted to know if he heard her confession. "How did you know it was a girl when you woke up?"

He took a moment to reply. "I didn't. I just wanted you to know the name I came up with."

"Oh, so you did not hear a word of the things I said to you before that?"

"What?"

That I love you, among other things, she thought.

She shook her head and changed the topic. "Nothing, where are you going to stay when you get discharged? I know you'll want to see Carliana, and you should have someone taking care of you for now. I can—"

Xander looked down at his now sleeping daughter. "You should stay with your mom."

She was disappointed with that answer.

"You just gave birth, and I can take care of myself. Seeing Carliana every day will not be a problem."

"Xander, are we okay?"

"What do you mean?"

"We left things... confused before all this. I haven't even thanked you for Snow."

"Snow?"

"My puppy. But... you should know before all this happened, I meant what I said to you. I want to be with you. I was attracted to Theo, and maybe there could have been room for more, but that's not the case anymore. I couldn't even compare what I felt for him to what I felt for you... how I still feel about you.

He still refused to acknowledge her words.

"Xander—"

The voices approaching stopped whatever she was about to say. Liliana and her mom walked in, and she turned to look at Xander upon hearing a groan from him. She thought it was because he felt some pain, but she only had to look to understand that pointy look was because their moms were here.

They could talk later, she decided.

Just as she had thought, their moms could not get over the fact that their daughter's name came from theirs. Liliana was tearing up, grateful for this second chance with her son and for another blessing. She thanked Xander for giving her that, and Xander apologised to her and Carla for being unbearable all this time.

Ally took the baby from Xander who was visibly reluctant to release her, leaving him and Liliana to talk. It also gave her and her mom room to talk which they barely did since the incident.

Her mom asked if things were right between her and Xander now. They were not there yet, but she was going to make certain his stubbornness and insecurity were kicked out of his rear. She was not sure how she's going to that, but she vowed to make it happen.

***

Liliana and Carla met outside the hospital building, waiting to get home together. Awaiting Theo's arrival, they engaged in small talks as Raul,

Liliana's chauffeur, waited in the car. They did not have to wait for long. Theo appeared, striding forward in his black fitted suit.

They talked a little about Xander, Ally, and the baby, and Liliana could not help spilling the baby's name to Theo. The carefree look and smile on her face only made Carla and Theo laugh at her obviously happy mood.

"Carla," someone called her name.

Carla turned to see Pedro standing two feet away from them. She was surprised. What was he doing here? She did not think he would come after her. Here, of all places. She had made where they stood clear enough for him. He had to be here for another reason, and Carla knew meeting someone at a hospital is never a good sign.

Theo excused himself to go see Xander and gave his mom a peck on the cheek before leaving the women. He walked to Xander's room without stopping to ask for directions. He had been here twice after all: on the day he was brought in unconscious and the day after Ally gave birth.

When he walked in, Xander was alone and busy with a tab in his hand. Was he working?

"You shouldn't be doing that."

Xander put the gadget aside. "What should I be doing then? Why don't we exchange positions to see what you'll be doing?"

"I'll have to decline, but you're probably right. How are you feeling?"

"Like I've recently been shot, and there's the uncomfortable evidence in my midsection."

"I was expecting you'd say you're thankful for being alive."

"Anyone would be thankful for that. What are you doing here besides coming to throw words around like your ego?"

"Then we certainly do have something in common."

Xander looked uninterested.

"Grow up. You had a pregnant woman anxiously waiting for you to come to your senses."

Xander raised an eyebrow. "Grow up? Are you playing the big brother card with me right now?"

"Hmm... maybe." He shrugged one of the arms he currently has folded together as he spoke.

Silence hung heavy between them. Neither wanted to add a word. But this time, the word 'brother' did not leave a sour aftertaste—a first for both of them.

"Since you'll be off work for a while, our work together should be done in a month give or take. Your father's taking over the reins. He's a good businessman, but I personally still don't like his guts." He unfolded his hands and put one inside his pant pocket. "I'll be leaving after that."

Xander looked at him to see if there was another meaning to his words. When he realised it meant exactly how he had heard it, he frowned.

Theo smirked. "Are you sad?"

"That you'll be gone?" Xander huffed. "Just because all I'll probably hear from Mom will be your name and what you're up to in god knows where."

He laughed a bit. "You want to know where I'm going, don't you? You can ask. You look pleasant when you're jealous."

Xander was aware he was making fun of him in a light way.

"I'm going back to Greece. I have business to take care of, so I can't be certain for how long I'll be gone."

Xander did not say anything to that.

"Maybe someday you can openly refer to me as a brother without those frown lines showing up on your face."

"Maybe someday." Was Xander's only reply.

"She loves you. If she hasn't said the words, you'll be a fool not to know that when she's right in front of you. If you mess up—"

"I'm not leaving room for you to swoop in."

He smiled. "I'll remember that, but I was going to say I would kick your ass into shape. I promised her that."

When he had checked on Ally after she gave birth, they talked, and she made it clear where her heart belonged to and where it would always be. He respected that and promised to protect it in times his clueless brother might need some sense drilled into his brain. Though now, looking at the man in front of him, he doubted Xander needed any of that.

He prepared to leave but stopped in his tracks. "I mean it, Alexander, you can ask me anything, anytime... little brother."

Xander frowned again before shaking his head. He released a resigned sigh and a bit of fall to his shoulders. His reaction was comical to Theo, and it got a smile out of him.

He was already at the door when he stopped again to say something. "By the way, if I'm still away when the invitations are out, I'll expect one."

"Invitations?"

He gave Xander a knowing look.

Xander was starting to feel exasperated by his behaviour. "No one's getting married."

"I didn't say anything about a wedding. You did." He was out the door and has closed it behind him before Xander could even react to his words.

***

Theo's words made him think about what Ally asked earlier.

"Oh, so you did not hear a word of the things I said to you before that?" she had asked.

Xander had been conscious then but kept silent, unable to keep his eyes open at the time. So yes, he heard every word she said.

He had lied.

CHAPTER 33.5
Carla & Pedro

Carla wanted this meeting to be their last encounter and planned to get it over within an hour. She would give him that much time to know there was nothing else for them to say to each other.

Pedro stood from his seat he had been waiting at for the past twenty minutes, but she ignored his attempt at being a gentleman and got her own chair. When she was seated, he sat back in his chair; she did not look the least bit happy about asking her to meet with him.

He was not expecting much—they did part in the worst of ways after all—but he hoped she would at least want to hear what he had to say. He wanted to hear what she had to say, even if that meant that she would curse him because he never even got to hear a word from her after she found out about Lorena.

"Thank you for coming."

She was dressed in a silk ocean blue blouse which matched the colour of her eyes and dark jeans. A cotton printed scarf was wrapped around her neck and mingled her hair. She had makeup on, but it did not take away the woman he knew. She was older but still as beautiful in his eyes.

A young waiter attended to them, and Carla made it clear she was not here for food, something she tried to put out politely in front of the young man. She gave in to being served coffee, and Pedro ordered it for her. It was one of the few things he had learned she loved before things went awry between them.

"You still like it with lots of cream and sugar, right?"

Carla nodded. "I'm not here for the coffee either. Let's talk."

"You sound a lot scarier than you used to be."

"You don't know me anymore, Pedro. I don't think you ever did, really."

She was right. "How are you?"

Carla sighed. "What are you doing? What is this? I made it clear that I wanted nothing to do with you. We don't have a reason to see each other. I came here so you can finally accept that because frankly, I don't like the way I see you everywhere I go."

"Our recent run-ins have not been on purpose."

That was the truth. His daughter felt like the pattern was a sign that he should go for what he wanted and pushed him to call Carla to meet up and talk.

"About that... what was that about your daughter smiling at me like she knows about us?"

"Because she does. So you've never mentioned to your daughter anything about us?"

"I wouldn't have if she did not need to hear it."

Carla remembered when she had no choice but to explain to Ally her reason for disliking Xander so much in the beginning. She leaned back in her chair as the young waiter came back with their coffee and excused himself promptly. "Why would your daughter smile at some other woman her father's after?"

Pedro took a sip of his coffee, placing it back on the table. His mouth twitched which almost seemed like a smile to Carla, but she knew it was not.

"Bailey does not have much of a relationship with Lorena. When I adopted her, Lorena was not particularly looking to take care of a child."

"Adoption? What about your baby?"

She meant the pregnancy Lorena carried years ago, and Pedro understood. "It was a boy. Gabriel is fine, doing well. He currently lives in Spain." Pedro smiled, looking like a proud father. She was a parent, and she understood that well. He had to understand then that they had lives far different from the one their much younger selves had years ago.

"Bailey's a mushy romantic at heart. When she found out about you by accident, she wanted to know everything, and I can barely get away with denying her what she wants."

Carla smiled. It seemed like he had a really great relationship with his daughter.

"What about your daughter?" he asked.

Telling Ally about Pedro was definitely not an accident, but she was not going to get into the details about her daughter with him. "Alicia, that's her name. She's doing fine, and she recently gave birth to a beautiful baby."

He grinned.

Carla was happy, and he was happy to see her doing so well though the thing about her daughter was not exactly news to him. Bailey had previously come to him with the news about this man dating Carla's daughter and what happened to him recently.

"I heard about the young man she's dating. How is he doing?"

"Xander's fine." This was taking to long for Carla. They needed to talk about why they were here. "And how is your wife?"

"She's the reason I was in the hospital the other day. I was there to see her doctor."

"Is everything okay?"

"Lorena has been battling with cancer. She's tired of hospitals and the drugs. She's weak, but she refuses anyone's help."

Carla understood well. His wife's condition might not be the same as what her husband had to go through, but she at least knew what having a loved one suffering from cancer was like.

He saw the look on Carla's face. He really did not want to talk about that, knowing she had gone through something similar. He did not mean to remind her of such a sad time in her life. "I didn't mean to bring that up. I know about your husband passing—"

"Let's not talk about it."

They quietly sipped in their coffee to allow that moment to slip away.

"I'm sorry, Carla. About everything, about what happened. It was foolish of me not to tell you about the situation between Lorena and I. I was greedy, thinking I could have it all with you at that time. I thought I had it figured out; I would be responsible for the child, and I would also be with the woman I love."

Carla looked away from him.

"I tried to see you once when you went back home, but your mom and sister wouldn't let me through. They were impenetrable."

He had come to look for her? She did not know that. Well, she was not sure if it would have changed anything, but it could not change anything now.

"Then I watched you getting your life together—culinary school, getting married, and building a family. There's a point where even a desperate man would know how to stop. I knew then that I had to give up. Lorena never fought with me over where my heart lay all through these years. She encouraged me to talk to you and explain that we both had an agreement. I think she even wanted that more than me because then she would also get her freedom. Since she got sick, the only thing she talks about is her regret for walking in her mother's shadow and living the life that woman wanted for her. Lorena is a good woman, and I could not leave her after knowing she was sick." He smiled at Carla who was listening to him intently. "I'm glad she found love, though."

Carla raised a brow.

"She met the man the first year she found out she was sick. They had two great years together before he left."

Carla was confused, and he elaborated. The man was one of the patients in the hospital where Lorena has been getting her treatment.

"I'm sorry," was the only thing Carla could say. She was gobsmacked by what she just heard.

"If I said something crazy like I never stopped thinking about you, that what we had even in that short period of time, every word, still holds meaning to me, you would think me insane, right?"

Carla knew this would come. He could not be showing up everywhere just to apologise for the past. "It's been twenty-one years."

"Twenty-two."

She leaned closer to him across the table. She still remembered clearly the look in his eyes when she had first set eyes on them. He's her first love, but a lot has changed since then. Since Mac, she stopped harbouring any remnant feelings for Pedro.

"Pedro—"

"With that look on your face, you're going to tell me exactly what I don't want to hear."

"But you have to hear it… from me. I truly was in love with you, and I'm glad I had that experience, that feeling, and if you were ever unsure of it, at least I knew you honestly cared for me. I never doubted that you must have felt something sincere towards me. But I was young and did not understand why you would betray me. All that happened, and then I met Mac. He made me love again, and he loved me back—so much so that I did not have to linger or hold on to what we had or what we could have had."

"Every time you saw me, you always looked angry. Bailey was sure there was still some unresolved feelings."

Carla smiled. "Your daughter is truly a romantic at heart, but maybe she's a tad right. The first time I ran into you, I was angry, and that's because you approached me like we were best friends. But other times, I'd say I just did not like seeing your face," Carla said with a smile to let him know she was not serious about her last statement.

"That was no joke. What if you honestly don't like seeing my face because of what it might remind you of?"

"Trust me, your face alone won't make me fall for you again." If she met someone that looked like her late husband on the street in her shop, would that make her fall for the person? Carla was sure it did not work like that.

"I have a daughter, a granddaughter, and a business I want to give my attention to now. So no, Pedro, I'm not ready to be in a relationship. And if I'm being totally honest, there's still one man filling up every space in my heart."

She did not have to spell it out. Pedro knew who that was.

She thanked him for the coffee, wishing him well with his family and life. As Carla stood from her chair, Pedro called her name.

"Carla? Thank you for letting me know what it means to be in love, but I don't think I'll ever give up on my feelings for you."

She wanted to tell him to forget about her, but she had first-hand experience on what the matters of the heartfelt like. It would just be empty words to him. Only time could say when it will fade.

"Take care, Pedro," she said before walking out of the restaurant and out of sight.

CHAPTER 34

There was a routine. There shouldn't be one, but there was, and it was going on for three weeks now.

Xander has been stubbornly staying in his apartment, enduring his mom's 'beck and call' service which he never asked for and he honestly could do without. He was better—much better in fact—but he never complained out loud at his mother's fussing. He almost wished Theo would stay; he never knew Theo leaving would have this effect on their mother. Now she had her sole attention on him.

Was this the way mothers were? He was a grown man!

After all his insistence, she still wouldn't let him go back to office to work. So because the office was out of the question, he usually had Paul and Collins over to his apartment when he needed something to be done.

One person who had shown up all of a sudden even when he asked him not to, was his grandfather. His old man was there the day he had been discharged and had stayed around for a week before leaving, but he never for a day forgot to bombard him with calls, asking how he was and how Ally and Carliana were doing.

It was a bit embarrassing when his grandfather met Ally and started talking about the right girl, settling down, and having more kids. Ally did not seem upset about it—she did after all talk about more kids while she thought he was still unconscious. And five? She must have been honestly kidding.

His grandmother was away with her husband's family, but Xander had talked to her a few times, and she promised to check on him when she got back. It was no secret that he was never close to his grandmother.

Another person who started to come over in the past week was Ally and their daughter, and not to forget Snow. For two weeks after he had been discharged from the hospital, he regularly made visits to Carla's place to spend some time with his little girl.

The feeling he got whenever he held his daughter in his arms never faded. It was always the same, and it was only growing bigger. It felt like a swelling in his chest that needed room to burst open. He was proud, proud of the gift he was given. Looking at Carliana always made him feel like he did do something right in his life for the first time. It had not been without mistakes, but the product of it all in his hands was the best feeling.

"I can't wait for you to get back to the office. Working here isn't exactly motivating. You won't let me touch your fridge, and I need to eat."

He stared at Collins who's whining again. He has stocked his fridge for Ally's sake, for when she came over, and not for him. The groceries were specific instructions from her, and he was not going to let his annoying assistant mess with that. Ally scolded him about, and it was amusing the first time it happened, but then he let his imaginations take the better of him. He played himself.

So no, he was not going to let that happen. Allowing her to scold him some more wound only leave him hard again. He was not going through that. His torture was more dire than Collins'.

"Now that you're stocked up, you won't even let a starving, dedicated assistant help himself to some."

"If you go near my fridge, I'll cut off your balls."

Collins recoiled and looked at him to see if he was joking. "What does the need to feed have to do with my junk?" He murmured before speaking out loud for him to hear. "I don't use them for much these days so—"

Xander stared hard. He wasn't kidding.

That shut Collins mouth.

The door opened, and Collins felt like he had just been saved. They looked towards the door to see Paul come in.

Not really. A robot man wouldn't save him. Paul would not care if he lost his balls right there and then.

Paul started to relay the information he had, and Collins gave them some privacy, insisting he needed to get something to eat. Xander had never really asked Collins to excuse himself whenever Paul needed to talk to him, but the kid did it anyways.

As soon as Collins closed the door behind him, Paul gave him his briefings and handed him the file in his hand.

He went through it as Paul spoke. "She's receiving treatment, and from her file, her diagnosis does not seem falsified. I dug into her background like you asked, and you were right, she did come from an abusive home. Her mother's sick but still living together with the husband and his children. They live poorly and have lived more or less in the same condition for years. Sophie ran away from home and worked her way around to live until she got scouted."

So why did she end up like that?

"It's true she encountered William Fraleigh. She was also present at the party he attended; that was the first night they met. A witness said they talked and they seemed to get along well."

"Did that mean they had something going on?"

"That was the only time they ever met. She must have taken a liking to him because the people she worked with said she could not stop talking about him."

So she had been infatuated.

"She spiralled from there. She was the one who leaked the supposed affair between them to the media. She eventually broke down from the backfire and ran away when the heat got to much for her. That was around the time we met her. She must have found out who you were and decided getting with you would save her career. Her manager confirmed she was cut off by the label when her actions started giving them problems."

Xander did not think the first incident could have ruined her career totally. If she wasn't so unstable in the first place, there were better ways to have made amends. He personally thought the people around her just did not care about her as a person.

"She snapped when she lost all she worked for. She misjudged your business relationship with William Fraleigh for a personal one, especially after you rejected her. She saw Miss Storm as a vulnerable target to get to you, but that plan was foiled when your father went after her, but you asked that she be left alone."

That was a big mistake. But then again, his father would have been ruthless. He thought he was giving the girl a second chance at that time.

"And the men who were working with her?" Paul had informed him that there were two of them—one who had kidnapped William's wife and the other who manipulated the door and cameras in the room.

"Still awaiting trial."

Xander folded his hands... He had a feeling there had to be some truth to Sophie's words. Despite her craziness, he pitied her. Even though he could not forgive her for the situation she had put him in, he needed to stop losing sleep because of it.

He let it go and nodded, telling Paul it was enough. This was the last he would hear about Sophie Lane and that incident. Besides, he was aware his father had his eyes on the case, and his father was not a very forgiving man.

Paul excused himself to go pick up Ally and Carliana. Even though they already had two men watching over them, Xander still made certain that Paul was in charge and was around them whenever they were on the move. Paul was his most trusted man, and as long as he still felt on edge about the incident and the paparazzi wanting a scoop of the new addition to his life, he would rather prefer having Paul around them.

He could not wait to see his daughter today and of course, get rid of Collins for the day.

***

Three weeks after Ally went home with Carliana, Dr Stack asked her to drop by for a few post-pregnancy check-ups when she could.

The past weeks had not been without challenges. Caring for a newborn was tough, but she was getting by with the huge amount of help she had around her. Though Carliana was not too fussy, she had a lot of things to adjust to. Thank goodness she had her mom and Liliana helping out with the baby when needed. Laurie's contribution was mostly cooing at Carliana and trying to make her smile and laugh for her even when she was told it was not going to happen anytime soon. The godmother was bent on changing that. Those sort of moments brought smiles to her face.

Ally couldn't stop thinking of how Xander's been trying to help with his daughter. There was no stopping him from moving around and coming over. He showed up every day for hours at a time, and she was quickly getting used to it. Just last week, Xander baby-proofed his apartment, preparing everything for Carliana's stay. She smiled when they got to his place, seeing how overboard he had gone with the baby shopping. It was a surprise for her when he told her he bought all of it when she was still pregnant.

Xander's presence always bothered her—in a good way, if she could state it as such. And as if putting her into more misery, she once caught him shirtless with Carliana cuddled to his chest. A book he read recommended skin-to-skin contact with his child, and he was eagerly following it down to the last word. That was one memory that always played in her mind.

Oh, yeah? I would also want some skin to skin contact with him.

"What?" Xander had asked.

"Huh?" She had caught herself mumbling. She realised what she was thinking and fled the room as if any second more and she would actually act on her thoughts.

She came to reality and shook the toughts out of her head, sighing.

"What are you thinking about?" She turned to see her mom pacing back and forth the house frantically. Her mom was exactly like this when she had a big contract coming.

She remembered one particulary big deal her mom got, the night Alexander Cross came into her life, and a smile crept up her face when

"You're doing it again. Honestly, Alicia, are you okay? You seem out of your head." Her mom was still running around the room to gather her things.

Meanwhile, Ally stayed sitting comfortably on the couch with Snow cuddled beside her. Carliana was not far from her on her crib as she tried to work on her newest idea in her laptop, but she was aware of her mother's frantic movements. She wished she could be there for her mom like she used to, but she had a responsibility she could not re-schedule now.

Her mom suddenly stopped and faced her, asking the question Ally had heard three times already in that afternoon. "You're thinking about something. Are you sure you have this?"

"Yes, Mom, I have this." Snow barked beside her. "See? We have this. Besides, Paul will be here soon, and I'm sure Liliana would show up. I don't think she gets the hints Xander gives when she smothers him. He's been complaining about it lately."

"She thought she was going to lose him after just getting to know him. Of course she knows how he feels about it, but he should give her a break and bear with it for a few weeks more. He's a parent now, so he'll know what it's like to worry about your kid."

She thought about what her mom just said.

"And Liliana won't be showing up today. She helped out with the preparation and insists on being there with me. I'm nervous. I've never had this big a client before."

She smiled at her mom. "I can tell, but you'll be fine like you've always been. Dad would be so proud of your achievements."

Her mom smiled in return. "Thanks, baby." She turned, about to walk away, when she stopped and looked at her again. "Alicia?"

"Hmm?"

"Are you wearing that?"

She nodded. "Hmm. Why?"

"Trust me, baby, even if you love the guy, you don't want another baby along the way right now."

"Mom! It isn't even like that."

"Hmm hmm. Tell that to the dress you have on," her mom replied as she walked out of the room.

Her mom had to be teasing her. It honestly was not like that. It might be true that the floral printed dress she had on reached mid thigh, generously emphasized her larger bosom, and showed off her clean shaven legs, but she did not have it in mind to seduce him. Okay, maybe leaving her hair the way he loved it and putting on light make up on her eyes and a red tint on her lips made it seem like she had other intentions, but she honestly was not going for attraction. Instead, she just wanted a little attention for herself so Xander and her can acknowledge what he has been avoiding . She was just determined to do that today.

So yeah, she was a woman on a mission.

At the knock on the door, she got up to get it. She opened it to see Katie on the other side.

"Wow! You look great. Are you coming along like that?"

"Hello, Katie." She greeted as she let her in. "And no, I have other plans." Was she really that dressed up? The dress was not even new.

"Congrats on the baby. This is the first time I'm seeing you without the large bump."

"Thanks."

Katie traced her outfit again. "Must mean you have something planned with that hottie of yours. Remember that night? You looked uninterested, but then you snatched the exact guy we were gossiping about."

She clearly remembered Katie doing all the gossiping that night.

"I didn't even know that you two had met that night, but I called it first." Katie was smiling like a fan girl now. "I should totally start pairing people together. I'm a lucky charm."

Right.

"What does it feel like?" Katie asked.

Julia had asked her a similar question, a question she had no answer to at that time. This time though, she was sure she had a mouthful to say. Katie continued talking, and Ally heard her words mid-sentence.

"…so hot and handsome, and please don't let us forget, super rich." She had a dreamy look on her face now.

Carliana made baby sounds, and it was as if the little girl was protesting about the stranger going on and on about her father. Katie moved closer to the cot, looking like she was just aware of another presence in the room.

Katie turned to her. "You even have a baby that looks like him. I'm jealous, Ally. You've got it good while I still have to bake and cave at your mom's orders." She almost laughed at Katie's funny, sad look. Katie had always been the dramatic one, but Ally knew she meant well.

"Yes, you do," her mom's voice said as she entered the room. "Let's go." Her mom bid goodbye to her and Carliana, going out the door as Katie trailed after her.

See what I mean? Katie mouthed to her. "Bye, Ally. Bye, baby Carly."

"Bye."

What's with people and coming up with nicknames? Carliana's just fine.

She thought of Katie's words; yeah, she was happy, but she did not think her life was set. She still had a lot of years to grow into the woman she had always wanted to be. She had a lot of things to achieve.

Paul arrived less than ten minutes later, and Snow was the first one at the door. Even she knew the routine now, but just as expected, Paul just passed by, ignoring the puppy. He's always strictly professional when it came to work, and he never once budged.

"Hi Paul." She smiled at him.

"Good afternoon, Miss Storm. Are you ready?"

Despite the fact that Ally asked to be referred to by her first name, Paul still continued to call her by that. "Yes, please."

He helped her with the bag she had packed for Carliana and her laptop. Ally rarely used the gadget when at Xander's, but she usually packed it along anyway. Snow waited eagerly for her as she carried Carliana to the car and Paul locked the door behind her.

Adjusting Carliana in her seat, she gave Garry a warm greeting which he returned just as well. Snow looked just as excited to be in the car as she would not stop barking. Ally knew that when the car starts to move, she would stop. They had all gotten used to it.

***

Upon their arrival, Snow hastily scrambled into Xander's apartment and ran to meet the man himself. Ally went in and saw Snow all cuddled up beside Xander.

That was faster than usual.

She also saw Collins in the room who was now grinning at her. "Ally."

"Hi, Owen."

Paul dropped the bag and laptop in his hands before leaving the room with Xander to talk in private. Meanwhile, she chatted with Owen.

***

When Xander came out, he saw Collins smiling and cooing at Carliana. Paul excused himself.

"Collins, get out. I'm done with you."

"But I stayed to say hi to Ally and Carliana."

"Now you have. Get out."

"My boss has been that way all day," Owen said, and she looked at Xander, wondering why he was pissed.

She had noticed the way his face tightened as soon as she walked in with Paul. Maybe it was business related. Xander walked forward and took Carliana from her hands. The two exchanged their usual form of greeting which was Xander giving her a kiss on the cheek. After that, he would direct most of his attention to Carliana.

Much to Xander's annoyance, Owen started to chat with her about how beautiful the baby was, and when he brought his face closer to look again and started to coo at her, Xander gave Carliana to Ally and dragged Owen out.

"Keep reminding me of why I need to fire you," he said.

Owen said bye to her all the way out, and before Xander could shut the door on his face, he told her not to forget making him Carliana's godfather.

"Is he serious?" Xander asked frustratingly. "Godfather? I'm not letting that punk near my daughter."

She laughed softly. "You're being too hard on him. Owen's nice."

"Nice." He puffed out.

"I like him."

"Well, I don't. He flirts with you."

What? That was not true, Ally thought.

"No, he doesn't." She went ahead to place Carliana in her cot. He followed her into the room and waited a while to speak, waiting for their daughter to get comfortable.

"You don't see when a man is turning it on for you."

She faced him. Xander crossed his arms, and she was not sure if he was aware he was invading her space because she was entirely conscious of him. "I-I do."

He smiled at her. "You didn't see that with me when we met."

"I had an idea."

Xander smirked. She was trying to hold his stare, but she was failing miserably. She knew he was aware of that. She was supposed to be confident today and make him notice her. In a way, he was, but she wanted more. She wanted him to act on it, and that thought gave her a backbone even if it was temporary.

"But it doesn't matter." She shrugged. "I don't mind if a man flirts with me"—Xander's gaze turned hard before she could complete her sentence—"as long as he's the man I would like to flirt with in return."

She could feel his gaze burning hotter. *Yes Xander, you idiot, do something about it before I lose it here!* She was not taking her eyes away just like he was not doing the same, but she did not expect his next course of action. His eyes trailed down to what she was wearing and stoped at her chest area and exposed legs before finally resting on her lips. When he was done, she was sure he would kiss her.

He coughed out. "I stocked the fridge like you wanted."

You have got to be kidding me!

That moment of awkwardness and tension passed, and neither said a word about it like it never happened, but it gave Ally some comfort knowing she was doing something right even though she may be taking the wrong approach to reach that goal.

The mood had turned lighter, and they joked around in the kitchen. Just because of one perfect meal Xander learned to prepare when she was pregnant, he thought that gave him control in the kitchen, never failing to remind her how she ate it all and left no scrap behind. She reminded him that it was because she was pregnant and had been eating for two.

Their discussions and teasing of each other went further until they both stepped on what had happened later that night he turned chef. Just as soon, both of them decided to stay off that topic—for obvious reasons.

They talked about Carliana instead. It was a much safer and calming topic. "She sleeps and eats a lot," Ally said. She did not expect him to look at the source of their daughter's nourishment, but he did.

"Stop perving on me."

"I'm not doing anything of such."

"Yeah right." They both knew that was not true.

"It's just... they're bigger."

She looked away, a bit embarrassed. "Um... yeah, it's only normal for nursing moms. Come on, let's eat."

They dug into the light, healthy meal Ally had whipped up and talked about everything they could: his friends, Laurie and Mike's relationship, his grandparents, their parents, his health, and her plans. She told him about Laurie's failed attempts at making Carliana smile and the nickname her cousin came up with for their daughter.

"CC."

"Cece?"

"Carliana Cross. CC." She elaborated.

"No one's calling her that. We gave her a name. Carliana Marie Cross is much better." They had agreed on a middle name weeks ago.

"I'm thinking of making Theo the godfather," Xander said out of the blue.

"Oh." She was genuinely surprised. "Well, that's... I didn't know you two were—"

"We're not there yet."

"Okay. The choice is up to you anyway, and I'm sure you must have given it some thought."

Xander scoffed. "Dom is going to be disappointed, but doing that will at least stop Theo from harbouring any hope about you."

So maybe he made his decision partly out of selfishness, but she did not think it was a bad decision.

Ally just smiled at his petty act of jealousy, and then she remembered.

"You're not going to gloat?" she asked.

"About what?"

"That you were right about our baby being a girl?"

Xander looked away from her and shrugged when he answered. "I was sure of it." She snickered, and he turned to look at her with a smile on his face. "I know every sperm I let out, so it was inevitable." He finished with a wink.

She stared speechless, open-mouthed at his words.

He laughed at her expression. "What?"

"Alex, come on! Seriously? Carliana is like a foot away from your dirty words... Oh well, I'll watch you trying to get boys off her when she's fifteen."

As soon as she said the words which insinuated they might still be together by then, she expected some sort of reaction from Xander, but he spoke on like she had not said anything to ponder on.

"She's like a hundred feet away, asleep, and does not understand a word of it. And by fifteen you mean in a platonic way, right? Because I seriously doubt I'll allow her male friends. She'll be introducing a boy to me *if* I allow it, at twenty-one."

Ally smirked. "Says the man who seduced a twenty-year-old."

"You were twenty-one."

She was happy. This was the first time in a long while she's seen Xander truly laugh like he had found a reason to. She was happy the moment was with her.

"As much as being a protective dad is cute, no girl really likes an overprotective one. It gets tiring."

"What did I say wrong?"

She shrugged, trying not to laugh at him. "You're just starting to get a little too obvious."

Snow, who was snuggled beside Xander ran towards the direction where her litter box was placed, stepping on the papers that were neatly piled on one corner of the floor. She spotted the disarrangement first since it was behind Xander and stood to pack it up.

***

Xander followed her movements, and instead of seeing what Ally was doing, he was seeing a different sight entirely. She was bent not far from him, and he just stared at her exposed thigh and curves.

She turned to ask him something and caught him in the act. He was starting to feel like a pervy creep. And just like that, it was back. Well, it did take some naughty thoughts to have his erection answering without being called. When she stood up straight, he knew he was supposed to be looking away, but his eyes rebelled and tailored her front view of every inch.

The dress was messing with him; had been since she came into his view. It had to be new; he's never seen it on her before. That was why he had to distract himself by talking to Paul privately and had wanted Collins gone so bad. That way he would not bear witness to his manhood acting up. Xander did not even want to imagine what Collins would have had to say about it.

Right now, he was painfully hard, but he knew he was not going to go there with her just yet. She gave birth barely a month ago.

"I'll get that," he said.

***

Ally wondered what was really stopping Xander. She was sure he still cared about her, but she did not know why he was distancing himself from her emotionally. She was not asking to be ravished by him—she was not sure her body was ready for it. Tonight, all she was asking for was a kiss and for him to admit what he was avoiding.

He had taken the papers from her hand, and when he turned to leave, she clenched her hands, taking a deep breath. She was not going to wait for him to come around any longer. She had enough. She doubled her pace and caught up to him.

He stopped and faced her when she held on to his shirt. "Why?"

He was probably looking at her, but she had her face down.

"I've tried. I have no idea in the least what you're thinking. For the past few days, I've put myself out there for you to see me. I don't know how else to express it."

***

Xander barely heard the whimper. Was she crying?

"I love you, idiot." She looked up at him. "Don't say this is about Theo anymore." Ally wiped her tears. "I don't know why I'm stupidly crying in front of you like this. If it's that you don't feel the same way or something else ... whatever it is, I would rather you tell me to my face—"

He bent and caught her mouth in his. His left hand that was free caught her body and drew her closer to him. She was doubting his feelings for her, but at least she wouldn't have to doubt his physical attraction to her.

His kiss was sweet but almost frantic, a*lmost*. He wanted more. He needed to taste more of her, but he was not going to get that at this rate.

***

Ally was taking a good few seconds to get out of her daze. She did not respond to the kiss, and only when he nipped at her lips, did she catch herself.

Idiot... You're finally getting what you want, and you're freezing out? she reprimanded herself. She instantly hooked her hands behind his neck, going tiptoe to try to match his height. She fully gave in to him, sweeping her fingers in his hair.

The hand on her waist travelled to her butt, giving it a generous squeeze, and when she responded with a moan of approval, Xander freed his right hand of the papers and lifted her, welcoming her legs as it wrapped around him.

She felt him wince, but it did not stop his onslaught on her mouth and body. His tongue had found its way to explore more of hers, and she could not help the moans and the hunger building up in her.

Ally released her mouth from his. She needed to breathe, or he would just consume her last breath along with his kisses.

But Xander was not done. He was like a man that had just been handed the freedom to breath, and he was exploring the basics of it. His lips found and gave pleasure to her neck, curved at an optimum angle for him, while one of his hands explored her full and eager breasts.

The wince was still at the back of her mind, though. It was probably from the surgery or the papers that had to be important and were now scattered on the floor. She managed to ask him, and he momentarily freed his mouth from her skin to answer.

"I can probably take you right here. I can have Collins get me another copy of those any day."

She found her back against the wall and Xander's lower region pressing into her. He supported their weight with his left hand that was resting on the wall as his other hand devoured every part of her it could capture.

She wanted to touch him like he was touching her, but she avoided his chest, afraid to hurt him. Her hands found their way to the back of his shirt where she explored. Her response must have triggered something in him because Xander started to grind himself on her, and she moaned out loud. It was not enough, and she was starting to feel greedy. The kiss she hoped for had left the shore and was sailing into a full make-out session.

"Ally, you're killing me. I'm sure you're aware of that."

She gave a wicked grin, feeling more daring. Her job could not have been easier as she dug her hand into the drawstring pants he had on and cupped his package. Xander gasped, drawing in air. He let her engage in the act. Or rather, the feeling was too good for him to stop her. But that was until she tried to take him out. He stopped her hand.

"We can't."

"Why?"

"I can't get enough of kissing or touching you, but any more and I'll blow my nuts right here."

"So, why?" she asked again.

"You just had a baby. I don't think your body is ready for that yet."

That was true. She'd have to get the go-ahead from her doctor the next time she drops in for a postnatal check up. "Is that the reason you've been holding back?"

He kissed her briefly again. "Partly."

She cupped his face and started to kiss him again which he did not stop. When they eventually parted, their chest rose heavily from the assault as their green and hazel eyes stared into each other.

She rested her forehead on his, still aware of his rigid friend digging into her. It took Xander a while to speak.

"Please don't ever doubt how I feel about you. I love you, Alicia Storm. I didn't know how it happened, but now I know why." He continued without taking his eyes off her. "You and Carliana are the only people that makes my life worth living. I had a life before, but having you and Carliana in it now makes it precious to want and protect," he whispered softly enough for every word to resonate deeply into her heart.

She smiled, trying not to cry again. Xander could not see her face, though.

He created some space between them to see every inch of her face and saw that she believed him. "I did not mean to act like an idiot these past weeks." She believed him, and he was relieved. "Thank you. I've never said it to you."

"For what?" She looked at him confused, resting her hands on his smooth jaw.

"For giving me our little girl. For giving me a second chance."

CHAPTER 34.5
Liliana & Cameron

The week her father came to the city to see Alexander, Liliana had that long overdue talk with him. She has had enough of the ghosts of the past hanging around her. Her regrets has always held back her happiness, but still, she was thankful.

She was thankful to have met Aegeus at the lowest point of her life. The much older man was not supposed to be in the country on that day, but fate played its cards well and they met.

Aegeus believed in the fate of men the journeys that map out to their destiny. He was a philosophical man. He took her back to Greece with him. Getting used to life there was hard considering she left her child back home, but she couldn't be more depressed at that point. Aegeus did not want anything from her. He did not propose anything, and she never mentioned anything about the life she left behind.

That was when she met Theopolis Christakos, Aegeus and his late wife's only son, a young boy of sixteen at the time. They started out as friends. She bonded and found a bit of solace in the boy who still had a for his mother in his heart.

She had, in a way, lost a son, and he missed his mother. They needed each other.

Over the years, the two of them forged a strong relationship. Aegeus had articulated it so insightfully; fate led him to her not because of him but because of his son. Theo stopped socializing after the death of his mother, but Liliana changed that. Theo found strength in her as much as Liliana found strength in him.

It was only five years after that Aegeus propose marriage to her. And she accepted.

He became the second man she ever got intimate with and cared for. Though she never fell in love with him, she respected him. They had a good marriage born out of respect and admiration. Marriages without love never last, but she felt like theirs was an exception. So it shocked her to know that Aegeus did fall in love with her before he died despite realising that she still carried around the hurt her son's father caused to her heart. She found that out from Theo.

All along, he knew about her life—the life she left behind and hid from him.

She cried then, wishing she knew about it all before he passed. It felt like she had betrayed him. He did not deserve any of it.

Love? No, she did not fall in love with Aegeus for she did not think she was capable of loving another man. Her heart was shattered at a young age, and she never tried loving again.

Liliana looked at the file in her hand Theo had sent her. He had called earlier to let her know what was in it, warning her that what she would read flew in the face of what she thought was true.

So much for letting the past go. But she needed to know.

She read the report line by line.

***

Early 1989

The first time Liliana saw Cameron was at Betty's store. They did not meet per se. She just took a look at the handsome green-eyed man that was new in town, the guy every lady and woman could not stop talking about. Of course, Cameron seemed like a big deal because he was from the city, educated, and definitely gorgeous beyond what the town considered handsome. Even Eli, the popular town bachelor, couldn't hold a candle to the mysterious man.

So all that happened on that day was a meeting of their eyes, as she was helping Betty out with a favour and Cameron came to the front to pay for his goods. She must have been staring at him. It was after all the first time she was seeing the man face to face, and he caught her doing exactly that. He looked back at her and smiled.

Liliana took her eyes away in embarrassment and said a quick goodbye to Betty before fleeing away from the store.

All throughout that week, at home, during classes, and running errands, she could not shake the image of the man. He was truly handsome, and it was in those moments that she realised she had unconsciously joined the group of women who had an instant crush on him. It was not something she was too concerned about though.

For one, she probably might not see him again since he was supposedly in town for just a month or so. And two, he was older than she was, and he probably wouldn't fancy being attracted to a high school girl like her.

It was just a crush, and crushes fade.

Liliana, at seventeen, was already independent. Due to the dysfunctional house she grew up in, she learned to mature beyond her age. She had no real relationship with her father except for a biological one. He was a respectable man, and he might come off as a good man to most people, but she hated him. She hated the fact that he did not care about her growing up. She learned that he had never wanted her; he never asked for her. At least that was what her mother said; something along that line.

So what if she was the consequence of a loveless union? How did that turn out as her fault? It was her parents' mistake, but she was the one suffering from it now.

As for her mom, Liliana did not have much of a relationship with her. She spent most of her days trying to be noticed as a wife than actually trying to be a mother to her daughter. To save up and earn extra money, Liliana has been helping people out in town as a form of side job.

On a particularly sunny day while doing groceries, she saw him again. She was avoiding him at a supermarket, but then she fell into step with elderly Mrs Baker and hit her shoulder. She apologised profusely for her clumsiness and attracted his attention, the very thing she was avoiding in the first place. When Mrs Baker left, she sighed.

She didn't know what was going on with her. She was never a shy person, yet she did not feel comfortable with this strange, handsome man who has been messing with her thoughts. Well, she had nothing to worry about if they never crossed path. But that was off the table now.

When she looked up, she saw him looking at her. He gave her a wide grin, and for the second time in just a span of a few minutes, she got clumsy again. She was not bumping into another person this time. Instead, unluckily for her, she ran her head straight into the nearest shelf.

"Ouch."

She was rubbing the sore spot on her head when she heard a deep, caressing voice beside her. The gentle rest of a hand on her shoulder made her moving away and face up to look at him. He was quite taller than she was.

"Hey, are you okay?"

She managed to nod her head.

"I did not mean to make you run. It seems like you're the only woman around here who doesn't like me much."

Was he mocking her? His smile looked sincere, though.

***

Cameron expected her to say something, but she was still keeping mute. Maybe she disliked him, but he had a tiny feeling it was not the case. He wanted to know why she was avoiding him. She did flee the first time they met. If she had been successful today, it would have been the second time she avoided him.

But it was not the second time he saw her. No, not at all.

The truth was he noticed her first. On his third day staying in this town, he ran into her, and he stared at her for a good few minutes. After Chloe deceived him into tying the knot, he immersed himself in work, caring only about the business and his son. However, seeing the girl a couple of times piqued his curiosity.

"Do you find my presence annoying?" he said with a light chuckle.

He caught her frowning, and a quick reply followed. "Ah... No... It's not like that. I don't dislike you."

"So you like me?"

"Uh, no... Not like that..."

"Oh, so you don't."

She waved her free hand in front of him. "I don't hold such feeling like other women do for you."

"Uh, well, that's a shame. I like you. You seem like a great friend to have while in this town."

She frowned again. She was doing a lot of that.

But he was also a smart man. He figured what she might be thinking and quickly dismissed her thought. "I mean no disrespect, but you honestly can't judge me from what has been said about me, whatever it is you must have heard."

No one in this town knew about his marriage, save for the workers in his company,

"Can I interest you with coffee? I still haven't been around the town much." His hand went to the back of his head. "I'm not much of a social person," he said.

She cocked her head to the side. He almost laughed because it seemed like she did not believe him.

"What?"

"You're lying. How can you not be popular?" she asked blatantly.

"You judge pretty quickly, don't you?"

She looked away, and her body language showed embarrassment.

"And I did say social, not popular. I don't think they come as a package deal in men."

"You're old."

"Ouch." He was not offended, and he gave her a smile to show that. "I'm Cameron. What's your name?"

She hesitated, looking at his outstretched hand, but took it. "Liliana," she answered softly.

"It's a beautiful name. It suits you."

"I did not mean to sound rude. It's just, I'm seventeen. I can't go on a date with you."

"A date?" he asked.

Liliana flushed, embarrassed.

What was he thinking? This was a small town. Of course, coffee between a good-looking young man and a young lady meant that, right?

"Well, you might be right, but I don't mean trouble. I had no idea you were seventeen, and I don't want to cross the line or make you see me as a creep." He smiled again. "It was nice meeting you, Liliana."

Maybe it was for the best not to get involved with her. That was what Cameron thought.

***

All through the week, Liliana couldn't forget about Cameron and their meeting at the store. She had no idea if he truly liked her or what she was doing thinking about him at all, but she had not seen him around anymore. It had her wondering and thinking if she should consider being his friend and get to know him by accepting that coffee. She was, after all, going to be eighteen in three months time.

She tried to convince herself that she was not thinking of anything further than friendship. He was a man from the city, somewhere she has always wanted to be; he could tell her things about life there and advice her. She was planning to live there after high school, putting off college for a year so she could make some money for herself.

The second week after that went by, and on the day she was to do an errand for a woman whose husband worked at the construction site where Cameron was usually seen at every afternoon, she had made up her mind. She was letting him know about her decision—if she comes across him.

She did, and the rest from there, they say, is history.

In a span of one month, Liliana found herself closer to Cameron than any person she's ever known growing up. But there was that issue of just being friends

If they were just friends, why was she always aware of his presence and everything about him when they were together? She felt stronger about him with each passing day, and in just two months, Liliana was ready to admit she saw Cameron Cross as not just a friend, but a man she was attracted to.

If Cameron felt the same way, he never once showed it. He listened to her, made her smile, and talked to her. Sometimes, he would talk strange things, but she never once felt like he has ulteriour motives.

Her birthdays were usually a disappointment because her dad and mom almost always forgot. If her parents never bothered remembering that day, why should other people care and celebrate? She never expected anything out of the day.

But the year she turned eighteen was different, and Cameron made all the difference. He couln't cook for the life of him, but because he wanted her day to be perfect, he ordered from outside of town and even got her a small cake. He knew she loved cakes. And as if that was not enough, he handed her a gift; a beautiful bracelet that looked more expensive than anything she has ever owned. It was not surprising that she turned into an emotional mess right in his home. He comforted her, and after taking a quick break on his bathroom to compose herself, she took a risk and smacked him on the lips.

That was her first kiss.

He disagreed with what she did, saying it was just her being emotional about her big day. At that same moment, she got the courage to tell him she liked him. And when he finally admitted he was attracted to her too and did not dislike the feel of her lips on his, she encouraged him to be the first man to own her heart and body.

For three months, they continued to see each other: after school when she had nothing important to do, when Cameron asked her out on dates, mostly outside of town, and on the few nights she insisted on staying over.

Then the gossip started, and all hell broke loose.

At first, it did not bother her what the rest of the village thought about their relationship. It was not their business if he was almost ten years older than she was. She was an adult anyway.

She loved him, and she was sure he felt the same way.

***

Liliana closed her eyes. She could still remember to this day the week her mom went out of town and her father approached Cameron, threatening to have him arrested if he did not leave her. She had no idea what her father said, but Cameron broke things off with her after that. He tried to hide her dad's visit, but she was not stupid. She went home and confronted her father, and they shouted the house down

It was the first time she said to her father's face that she hated him. She then packed her things away from the house and left.

That same week, while she was still trying to see Cameron, a woman approached her after school and introduced herself as Cameron's wife. She introduced herself as Chloe Hillway. Even though she was not exactly the most beautiful woman, she was sophisticated. She had to be around Cameron's age if not older.

It was the only time she saw her. Chloe, who should have threatened and cursed her for being the other woman, thanked her instead. She said she had helped her decide how to hurt her husband for what he had done: taking his son away from him forever.

She didn't want to believe what she heard. Her heart shattered to piesces at that moment.

Chloe adviced her to stay away from Cameron because he was a greedy and dangerous man. It was hard to accept everything until she confirmed it all from Cameron himself.

Finding out that the woman who planned on leaving him with his son died a few days later in an accident, in his car no less, sealed their present fate.

Liliana remembered all of that... but Theo's conclusive reports were telling her that Cameron went to jail for the wrong reasons, something she had a hand in.

Did she get it all wrong?

She needed to see him. He needed to explain things to her... things only he might know. She would compare his story to what she had in her hand. She might be the last person he would want to speak to, but she needed Cameron’s side of the story... the whole truth.

She picked up her phone anyway.

***

"Sir? Liliana's on the phone again. She insists to speak with you or she'll come over."

Cameron dismissed his secretary after agreeing to take the call.

"We agreed no contact unless it had to do with Xander. I'm busy," he said to the receiver.

"I need to talk to you. This is important, Cameron."

"I'm listening." He sounded uninterested, though.

There was a short pause from her end before she spoke. "You knew. You knew all along."

Cameron was an intelligent man, and he had an idea what she was referring to; but he wanted nothing more to say on it. Whatever she needed to hear, one thing remained unchanged; she betrayed him.

"I'm not going to talk about the past with you. If you have nothing else to say, I'm hanging up."

"Cameron, please. I want to know the truth. If you hang up now, I won't give up until you agree to talk."

He gave her a resigned sigh coupled with a frown she could not see. His secretary came in and placed a white note in front of him with a message in her handwriting and walked out.

Miss Chang called. 7:30 meeting tonight.

Veronica Chang was the woman he was currently seeing. She was flying in tonight after a month's absence due to work.

It could wait for at most thirty minutes.

"Cameron?" Liliana confirmed at the other end if he was still with her.

"Seventy thirty tonight. Decide on a place and give my secretary the details." He hung up before she could add anything.

***

That night, they met at a luxurious hotel that gave the privacy they needed, and Liliana found out in that same night that the pieces she had did not quite fit the puzzle that was her past—Cameron's truth and the years he dedicated to finding out what he had missed and prove his innocence were.

Cameron did fall in love with the seventeen-year-old Liliana. He kept from the fact that he was married and had a son that meant everything to him.

When his father-in-law proposed he take over the supervision of their new business in that small town, Cameron was happy to have a breathing space away from the Hillways. His marriage to their only daughter, heiress to the family's vast wealth, was known only to a handful. Being in a new town helped him immerse himself in his work and forget about the forced marriage he got trapped into and all the mess that waited for him back in the city.

True, his marriage to Chloe was a farce, but he stayed because that it was the only way to be with his son. Cameron had no family—none that he knew of since his father passed away when he was fourteen. He was just a man struggling to make a name for himself when he met Chloe, and a string of casual meetings landed him in bed with her multiple times. Then the news of her pregnancy got out, and an offer, too good to be true, was given to him.

In return for marriage, he got to see his son, half of Chloe's inheritance, and the guarantee of the other half being bestowed to their son when he was of age. In the contract he signed, it was stated that Cameron could not seek divorce or separation from Chloe within the first three years. Not unless he wanted to risk losing everything—including his son.

He knew then what it meant to have power. What it meant to dictate things. It meant being in control.

He always thought of Mr Hillway as a senile, old man. What father would agree to such ridiculous conditions just to marry off his daughter?

He was not in love with Chloe; they all knew that, but he did it anyway for his son and the financial stability that went with it.

Afer some time it was revealed to him that the clingy, annoying woman who wanted him as a husband was sick, a condition of the heart money couldn't cure. So, like the assuming idiot he was at the time, he thought that the three years stipulated in the contract was the years she had left to live. It made sense especially when the family wealth would be eventually divided between him and his son.

He never anticipated Liliana in his equation. It messed up his plans, but he was in too deep. Letting her go would have hurt him, almost as much as he would have felt if ever he was to leave his son.

Having her meant losing his son and being with his son would have probably resulted in losing her.

So he kept his secret until things blew out of proportion.

"I considered so many times to leave the money and find some other way to at least share custody with William and have you with me, but in the end, it meant fighting against the Hillways' with no money or status," Cameron said.

***

She wished Cameron had told her the truth from the start. Maybe nothing would have been different, but at least things might have turned out differently for the three of them—for both of them and Alexander.

Cameron also revealed that when Chloe's father revealed his daughter was sick, they were lying about the details. Chloe and his son's accident was entirely Chloe's plan to make his life difficult.

"She was not sick in the heart, she was sick in the head. Her parents knew, and the few staff who witnessed her episodes were sworn to secrecy by her parents. I eventually had their testimonies to help with my case. I had nothing to do with their deaths. Chloe wanted me to lose everything in the cruellest way, and what better way that to lose the son I cared about, the money I was offered to be with her, and to go to prison for a crime she planned out?"

"She told me," Liliana whispered to herself and looked up suddenly at Cameron in realization. "I thought she meant leaving with your son. I had no idea…" The rest of her words faded.

"I avoided her for the most of the years together so I had no idea what she was struggling with."

She bit the inside of her lips. She was part of his unjust conviction. She was pestered by a detective to testify against Cameron about their relationship. When she did, still freshly hurt by his betrayal and deception, it only made him look guiltier in front of the court. She remembered clearly how Cameron pleaded for her to hear him out.

"I lied, I betrayed your trust, but I never did all those things. I would never do that to William. I love you Lil." His words replayed in her head. It seemed like

Cameron desperately wanted her to believe him, never mind that she was testifying against him

She remembered how she cried harder for days when she later found out she was pregnant. She washed her hands of anything related to that case after that and focused on the only boy that mattered in her life. But when Cameron reappeared in front of her years later and found out about Alexander, she was thrown into the spotlight again.

He threatened to take Alexander away from her. He made sure she knew how much he hated her with his words, and at some point, she was actually afraied for her and her son's safety. All she saw then was a man who did not hesitate to take out his wife and son. What would make her story different? She believed he hated her that much.

She asked him about it.

"You never knew me at all. That was not me. It was the old man. Chloe's father was bitter about my freedom, and then he found out I had everything he had just lost. He was trying to get me in trouble by using you. You were not the only one he played a game with. I received letters supposedly from you threatening to expose who I was and expose my secrets. I was just not ready to believe you would be capable of what he wanted me to believe."

That was when she gave her parents full custody of Alexander and ran away to keep him safe. She ran away... because of a lie?

"It must have ben tough forging your awful handwriting."

All these years of fear, hatred, and separation for the wrong reasons?

***

Cameron first thought that Liliana ran out of the country for fear of him getting custody of their son. Her father got to be his son's legal guardian. To fight then would have been messy considering his ongoing legal issues at that time, so he stopped trying to claim his flesh and blood and concentrated on making his name instead so he would never depend on anyone again.

He made it. He made lots of money and approached his son in his first year of college. Alexander, his son resented his mother, but seeing Alexander always reminded him of Liliana, and he hated that. He made mistakes and one of them was was taking it out on his son and feeding on his emotions.

But their was one thing he had sworn to himslelf he'd do. He failed to protect William from a crazy woman, and he made sure he never made the same mistake with Xander.

That was why he was always in the background in everything that went on his son's life, trying to protect him from his own mother, Barabara, and that delusional assistant of his. He's glad that he was wrong about one of them, though—Ally. She and her baby was the only good that came out of that crazy life he gave to his son

He wanted to say he understood Liliana's actions. She was afterall a teenager who found in him the only person she could trust in all of her eighteen years, and he messed that up by hiding the truth about Chloe, William, and the life he had before her. But what she did still felt like the worst kind of betrayal to ever hit him.

It ripped out his heart because he was so in love with her.

He took an instant gulp of the glass of whisky and placed it on the small table in front of him. He stood up and buttoned up his neatly tailored dark suit. "I have said what you wanted to hear. Don't bring this up again. I have another meeting."

He was walking out the door.

"Cameron."

He did not turn to hear what she had to say.

"I'm sorry," Liliana said.

She was not just apologising for not believing him then, she was sorry for the things he lost.

"It's the bed I made for myself. It's gotten much more comfortable to sleep on," he said and stepped out the door without even a second glance.

She sat back, feeling like she needed to relive everything that has been revealed to her about the past. Staring at his back moment before he walked out, she had wanted to ask him a question she was too afraid to ask, a question she was not sure she wanted to know the answer to.

Do you still hate me?

Maybe it was better if she never found out.

CHAPTER 35

It felt good to be be in his office again. but it meant less hours to spend time with Ally and Carliana and more time than he would like, seeing Collins' face. Xander still couldn't believe Ally thought his reactions to Collins meant he really liked the kid and his happy mood. True, he liked the fact that the kid was good at what he did and trustworthy, but the boy was awfully annoying for his liking.

Two months had gone by since that night he and Ally admitted their feelings for each other without hesitation. Their relationship was better now, way better than what he thought when they first met. Now, he saw himself as a patient, understanding man who always puts his woman and daughter before his needs.

He was getting used to the man he was becoming, and it was not bad at all. The only thing he was still keeping from her was the house he brought for them. He did not want her to feel pressured if he told her about it.

Ally was young and had dreams. He had already messed up her plans in life, putting a kid in the equation for her. He did not want this to feel like another one of that. He did not want to risk the good place they were at.

They were yet to get intimate, but this was much better, *much* beter.

He could not stop touching her whenever they're alone. Heck, the make out sessions was almost as satisfying as the real deal especially when they had both found ways that brought them to fulfillment. Ally could say 'I love you' without hesitation now, and that in itself brought him great happiness.

Seeing Ally and Carliana's face each day was the most satisfying moment in his day.

He had tried to talk to Ally about the house two nights ago when she and Carliana spent the night at his place, but their need for each other got in the way. They would have gone all the way, but Carliana's cry stopped them. He had made a decision then, to show the house to her instead of the date he had planned for them.

"Are you sure you still want to go ahead with the interview?" Owen asked for the second time in the day.

He had to. He was aware he was going to be asked about his private life, but what better way to shield his family from the spotlight? Besides, he had made sure the questions were in his favour. If he fed them with the kind of information they itched to have, they were sure to back off from his family—at least for a while.

"It's just... your father specifically asked that you cancel—"

"Dad's just being himself. Let it go, Collins. You're getting annoying. I'm doing the interview."

Collins sighed. He had barely taken two steps to leave his office when the door opened and in came Xander's father. Collins retraced his steps back to his original position, standing stiffly. It was almost comical.

"I asked you to have the interview cancelled." His father was staring straight at Collins without a twitch in his features.

"I-I tried. He would not listen. He insisted that—"

"Dad, stop bullying my assistant."

A smile almost broke on Xander's face just watching Collins' face. It was good to see him tongue tied and stuttering with words for ones.

His father faced him.

"I'm not cancelling. I don't like anyone coming near them. It makes Ally uncomfortable," Xander said.

"You don't need to give a bloody interview to make your woman feel safe."

"I'm not going to threaten everyone like you do."

"It's the only way you could get the message across to those nuisances."

"I know whether I cancel or not you would still have eyes on them. This is my way of doing things. Let me do it." Xander was aware of just how fond and protective his father was of Ally and Carliana, but he never showed it as such.

His father kept silent after that. "See me before you leave. There's something I need you to see concerning the Lantern deal."

"Of course," Xander replied.

When his father went out the door, Collins let out a dramatic sigh. "I think I'll start reconsidering working for you if it's always like this. He does not have to say anything and he scares years out of my age."

Xander looked towards the closed door. At first glance, his relationship with his dad was hardly different from what it was three months ago, but something had changed. He heard and listened to every detail of his parents' past from his mother, and it was quite a lot to take in. He now understood why his father always looked bitter. He went through something life changing, and to think he once accused him of having something to do with his son's death—an accusation he must have heard a lot in the past. His mom wanted them to have a better relationship, but he doubted his father would change that cold behaviour he always put on.

But still, he needed to apologize to the man. But till now, he had not done that.

He had tried to approach the topic, but it never felt right to him. Was it worth digging up the past and his pain? They needed to try to move forward, but it wouldn't be an easy task when it came to his father. Maybe one of these days, he would invite his father to have a drink and they could leave all things aside and talk like a son would to a father. Baby steps.

"Tonight would be especially lonely."

Xander did not spare him a glance but asked, "Don't you have friends?"

"Not the kind I would like to hang with. Most people just want you for something they know you can give."

He looked at his assistant's back. He never really tried to picture a different kind of Collins outside of work.

"Come to think of it, since you have drinks with your friends tonight, I can go say hi to Ally and—"

"No."

"It's not like you're jealous of me, are you?"

"I can't afford to let you go at this time, but you keep reminding me why I need to fire you."

Collins gave him a big grin. "I'm your best employee. Besides, I was only kidding about that. Thanks, boss."

"For what?"

He shrugged and walked out of his office.

Weird kid, Xander commented on his head.

***

"How was the interview?" Dom asked.

"What interview?" Jay asked while Mike looked at Dom and Xander for an answer.

Dom chuckled. "Haven't you seen the glow on this dude's face lately? Been looking like someone who just got told his crush feels the same way."

Xander ignored Dom and just raised an eyebrow at his statement.

"What are you going on about?" Jay asked again.

"Don't you see the difference? Compare Xander's face to the last time we were all gathered here. This guy's been getting some." Dom laughed out loud as he gave Xander's back a big slap.

"What the hell, idiot? Quit hitting me," Xander muttered, shooting Dom a glare.

While Mike sat amused by Dom and Xander's banter, Jay was not particularly surprised.

Dom teased him for a while about his relationship with Ally before he diverted his attention to Mike and Jay. "So does this mean you two will be off the grid?"

"It's a two-week course. Stop exaggerating things."

Since Mike made the decision of staying in New York, he got a job at the hospital Jay was working at, and the two already had a plan cooking. They realised they did not just have a common ground in the field of medicine, they also shared similar dreams. Jay's dreams of having his own hospital was now easier to realise with Mike on board. They were still not sure how they intended to do that, though. But it was no surprise that the two had grown closer over the months.

"So, do you regret it, Mike?" Dom asked him.

"What?"

"Moving places for your girl."

"No," he said, not hesitating in the least.

"You must really love her then."

Xander and Jay just listened on.

Mike exhaled. "Laurie's a tough woman, and she's not the kind of person who shows her affection or wants them displayed to her. The fact that she did not freak out when I asked her to move in together is already a massive progress. To be honest, I expected her to say no. I never told her why I applied for my job. I told her I was offered the job here in New York. I'm not sure revealing the truth to her is the best thing. I'm afraid of what it would mean for us."

"So you still have doubts about your relationship?"

"No, nothing at all. I'm just a little guilty for deciding things all on my own. I know she cares about us, and I should have had more faith in her. I should have asked what she thought. We should have talked about it and decided together. I was too afraid of losing her. In the end, I was just stressing over something that could have saved me the headache."

Xander listened intently. Was that not what he was currently doing with Ally? He was making the decision for the both of them, deciding what she would want. How would he know what she wanted if he never asked?

A grin formed on his lips.

"What's funny?" Mike asked, and the other two stared at him.

"You just solved my problem," he said, raising his glass to his mouth while they all looked at him with confused looks. They had an idea of what it was about, though. His living arrangement with Ally was not particularly a secret.

A comfortable silence fell on the guys for a few minutes before Dom spoke up. "We'll all be busy for a while. This might be our last drink."

"You make it sound like the world is ending." Jay said.

"It might as well be," Dom replied. "I hate doctors. They're always busy. I had to travel out of the country because this one was always busy with his work." Dom pointed to Jay and then pointed to Xander. "And this one was either trying to prove himself with work or engrossed with his promiscuous life."

"You're one to talk." He fired back.

"You said you took on a contract," Jay asked Dom.

"I did, but I'm starting to think I made a mistake."

Xander shook his head. "What kind of CEO delegates his work to his employees and only focuses on one contract per year?" he asked.

"The very rich kind." Dom smiled arrogantly. "Not every CEO can achieve that. Besides, I have other things to focus on. It's going to keep me busy for about half of the year."

"What other things? Like women and travelling around the globe... for *more* women?" Xander shot him down.

Everyone laughed.

The men talked more, and Dom had more to tease about each of them. They enjoyed each other's company, knowing the months ahead would keep them apart for a while.

"By the way, you haven't told us what your interview was about," Dom told Xander.

"Buy one tomorrow to find out."

"Cheeky bastard. Being in love as made you more of an asshole," Dom muttered, smirking.

***

"She's just too cute to be angry at."

"She's two months old."

"Well yeah, but I've been training her. It would be unfair if she smiles at someone else first."

Ally said nothing about the little smile she had received from Carliana last week. It barely looked like a smile, but it was something, and she was not going to tell Laurie that.

"I guess if it's you, I wouldn't be too angry. You're the mom." She moved away from Carliana and sat on a sofa. "So?"

She looked at her cousin while she attended to the baby, wondering what she was reffering to. She did not know what she was talking about. "What's that?"

Laurie looked at her surprised. "Tell me you have at least heard about it."

"Heard what?"

Laurie stared at her open-mouthed. "You're unbelievable. You should at least have an idea what is going on out there in the media. That's the kind of life you have now."

And the life she was trying to avoid.

She shrugged. "I've recently learned that it's better to ignore those things. They interfere way too much, and I've got enough on my plate for now."

"I wouldn't have bought it, but Mike told me about it."

She took her eyes away from Carliana briefly, looking see Laurie getting something out of her bag. "He had an interview done and guess who got asked about his love life." Laurie waved the magazine in front of her with a grin on her face and a wiggle of her brows.

Ally smiled at the way she was grinning at her.

"Don't you want to know what it says? Never mind. I'll read the juicy part out loud for you," Laurie says, obviously excited.

She watched as Laurie flipped the pages, wanting to hear what Xander said about her. It made the things she was doing go in a slow motion.

"Blah blah blah... Oh, here's a good one!" she squeleed after some time. "**You have a baby girl, right?** Yes. He's the cutest girl you could imagine. She's adorable and everything is different when she looks at me with those gorgeous eyes."

She listened as Laurie read on in that silly singsong voice.

"And for the juicier part..." She coughed out, stealing a knowing glance at her. ***"Are you single?*** *No.* ***So there's a special someone who has Alexander Cross to herself?*** *Of course. She's the mother of my child."*

Her heart swelled at hearing that.

"This is the part you should not listen to. I'm sure it's a woman, and she's just jealous.

Ally didn't think so. No matter what the person's sex was, he or she must have just been doing what he or she was being paid for.

"**Alicia Storm right?** Right. **There were rumours that after she stopped being your mistress, you two went your separate ways.** I'll make a lot of things clear. She was never my mistress. She was my girlfriend, and for every article that writes trash that includes her name, the writer would have to deal with more than they can handle on their back."

She returned her focus on Carliana but was still listening to every word Laurie was reading.

"**So, you two are very much together?** She's the only woman who keeps me alive each day and makes me want to be better man. Does that answer the question?"

Xander said that for the world to hear?

"What do you think, *Mrs Cross?*"

She stared wide-eyed at her cousin. "D-did he say anything about marriage? Did he say that?"

Laurie laughed. "I can't tell if you are freaked out or shocked. What if he did?"

"Did he?"

Laurie stood up and walked closer to where she was, placing the magazine beside her. "No, but you can have this to read." She made a kissy face at Carliana before looking at her. "I'm not even going to ask what that look was about, but it's good to see you happy, Al."

"I'm happy. How's living together with a man like? Any wedding bells near?"

She was quick to change the topic because she did not want any more of her and Xander's relationship being discussed. Marriage would be delightful, but it was nowhere near her thoughts for now. Yes, she always imagined the three of them together, but she was not sure if Xander was thinking the same way.

Laurie placed a hand to her hip and raised the other one at her to stop what she intended to say. "Okay, let's take a breath. Mike and I have an understanding, but I don't want marriage or kids for like the next eight years or so."

"I thought... It almost felt like—"

"What?"

"Like you're in love with him."

Laurie shrugged and went to sit, facing her. "I don't know if it's what it is, but I do care about him. Really, really care about him. It's borderline insane. I never thought there would be another man after what happened with Niel."

Ally remembered. Laurie was in a dark place for a long time after finding out that the man she loved was married. She defied everything and went on with the affair for seven months until the guy broke it off, leaving her with a broken heart and futile words.

'I'll always remember our time together,' he said.

After that, his cousin closed off his heart to men. Good thing Mike was relentless.

"But here I am living with a man who calls me his girlfriend. He understands me, and I don't know what he does and how he does it, but I get crazier and crazier about him. And the sex! You can't imagine—"

"I think it's better if we leave it that. I don't have to imagine it."

"Pssh. Look at you acting like you haven't been getting that man of yours to do—"

"Laurie, Carliana's near."

Laurie chuckled. "It's funny how you go off about that. She does not understand a word. And seriously?"

"What?"

"I thought you two would have this unquenchable thirst for tearing each other's clothes off all the time."

The thirst was there, but they had not gotten around to doing what they both really wanted. And she was still not comfortable talking about her sex life with her crazy cousin.

The message tone went off on her phone, and Ally went for it, having an idea who it might be.

Hey, beautiful. I miss you, the text simply said.

Short but sweet, and it brought a smile to her face just like what it has been for the past two months.

***

Two days after, Ally was all dressed and ready for the lunch date she had with Xander, but before that, she had to drop by at her doctor for an appointment. She and her baby was already cleared of all post natal checkups, but she had questions she needed to ask Gaby. She was really comfortable around Gaby and her student, Andriana. Afterall, they were there when she had her breakdown.

The last time she went to see Gaby, she finally met her son, Rafael, a beautiful kid with very different trait from his mom. Perhaps the boy took on his father that was not in the picture. She knew there had to be a story there, but she was not asking. She was not that close to Andriana to ask about her painful past.

She left Carliana with her grandmother and those two had a lot to catch up on. It gave her a few hours to spare and she was sure Xander could only probably spare a short amount of time too due to his work.

It felt more like Cameron had the intention of leaving the business in his care soon. Cameron never told her directly but his words insinuated that. Even when he talked to her and never seemed to elaborate on things, she seemed to understand the man and he had somewhat gave what seemed like a compliment about it to her.

She smiled to herself. Xander always complained about never being able to understand her being 'friends' with his father. She was sure Xander and his father would eventually bridge the gap between them. They were more similar than both of them realised.

Garry reached the front of the hospital building, and she stepped out.

***

"Is she asleep?"

Carla nodded when she joined Liliana in the dining room.

Both women settled for a glass of wine each as they talked about Carla's growing business and Liliana's new business plans. Liliana already invested in Carla's business, but since she was going to be around for a long time and had no plans of travelling back to Greece for a while, she needed something worthwhile to keep her busy. Knowing full well that setting up a flourishing business was not going to be an easy feat, she focused on studying and learning the hang of it. She had her heart set on interior designing.

From that, their conversation shifted to Liliana's private life.

Liliana smiled. "You're just like Theo. He calls me every minute to ask how I'm doing. Honestly, I'm still trying to wrap my head around it. I can't get out of my head what Cameron must have had to deal with for years. Everything kept replaying in my head… all the what could have been and what I should have done different.

"You think you might still have feelings for him?"

"Do I?" Liliana paused, deep in thought, before she looked back at Carla. "All I let myself feel for him in all these years was hatred, and I'm pretty sure it's the same for him. I feel like Cameron has more reason to feel that way, though."

"That's not true. You were lied to. You felt betrayed."

"But he had it worse. Cameron's hated me for more than twenty years, and I'm not sure he feels differently now."

"You can't know that." Carla saw the two of them at the hospital when Xander was in surgery. To her, Cameron did not look like she hated Liliana, but it was obvious that he didn't care much about her either. But then again, Cameron Cross didn't look like he cared about a lot of people.

"Well, it's not like I'm hoping we get back together. Alexander, Ally, and Carliana mean a lot to him even when he's not actively displaying it. I just hope having them is enough to make him happy. Ally and Carliana is a blessing to the Cross men," Liliana said, smiling. "And in a way, your daughter gave me back my son, too."

There was nothing more Carla could say. It was something Liliana and Cameron should figure out on their own, and all she could do was support her friend in whatever decision she ends up making.

***

Was there a way to wipe off the constant smile she had on her face for hours? Ally wondered.

Xander did not mind it at all, though, and that only turned her smiles into embarrased ones whenever he caught her.

After she left the hospital, Garry drove her to the restaurant where Xander was waiting. Xander had told her he had something he wanted to ask and show her. Considering what he recently said about her in that interview, she was nervous and speculated all through the ride, thinking he might propose.

They had lunch and talked about things between them, and it made her loosen up, forgetting about her nervousness.

Ally never pegged Xander for a funny guy, but he actually made her laugh out loud twice. It was great but also embarrassing because it directed attention towards her. And while she tried to mutter an apology every now and then for the disruption, Xander looked just as cool and perfect where he sat, looking at her like he was seeing her for the first time.

***

Xander just sat comfortably at the opposite end, staring at her with a smile gracing his lips. They were currently in the car that brought him, once again enjoying each other company as the car drove off.

She had no idea where they were headed, but he was going to show her the home he bought for them. He was going to tell her what he wanted for them and ask what she wanted, and they could come to a decision together.

Nobody knows how Ally would react, and that made him so nervous inside. He was not proposing now. It troubled him all through the night, but he wasn't confident he was the right man for her yet. He got some sleep eventually after coming to a decision that Ally's heart wasn't so narrow minded.

What he could not put in words, he had to express in his actions today.

The car stopped.

"Where are we?" She took a curious look at the large house outside the car.

He squeezed her hand. "Come with me."

***

Ally's steps were careful as she followed Xander who still had her hand in his pockets. He led her inside, and she was astonished at the view before her. The outside was stunning, but the interior beat it twice as much. It looked fully furnished, and everything in it seemed new. It almost felt like it would be against the law if she knocked anything out of their places as Xander showed her around.

"What do you think?"

She turned at Xander who had kept quiet as he obeserved her reaction to the house.

"It's beautiful. Really. Is it yours?" Ally asked.

"Ours."

Her eyes bulged out, and she swallowed the knot that formed in her throat. "What?"

"I've wanted to ask you for a while now." He held both her hands.

Was he going to propose?

"A-Ask?" She stuttered in her words.

"I want to come home to you and Carliana each day. Would you like to move in with me?" Before she could answer, he was quick to add. "It's sudden asking you like this, but I don't want you to feel obligated to answer now. I just wanted you to know about this, and if it isn't what you want or if you think it's moving too fast for you, we can go at the pace you want."

"It's really beautiful, Xander, and it's impossible not to fall in love with the sight." She looked him right in the eyes. "You're right. Moving in together will be a big step. I love you, but if we do this, it's going to be a huge commitment. There are so many things we haven't talked about yet... so many things we should talk about..." Her voice trailed off as she pretended the furnishings in the middle of the room was more fascinating than they reall are.

"Ally." He called her name gently as he caught her chin in his fingers, turning her face to him. "Hey. Tell me."

She hesitated a bit before she finally let it out. "Are you sure about this? I don't want you to feel obligated either because of you and me... or Carliana."

"I love you, Ally, and no other woman can come close to the meaning you've given me. I'm sorry I don't feel confident I deserve to put a ring on your finger. I'm still learning to be better."

"Xander—"

He locked their fingers. "I can't go down on my knee and ask that question yet, but I can do it to ask you..." He bent down on one knee.

She was shocked, unable to form words.

"Alicia Storm, I can't promise I won't do something stupid or foolish to disappoint you in future, but I never want to be the reason you cry again or feel less about yourself. I don't have the confidence to propose to you now, but I don't see myself falling less in love with you either. For the rest of our lives, I'm going to need you, Ally. I'm need you to teach me how to be the perfect man for you, flaws and without. So I propose we start the journey now together—if you want to, that is."

She was trying hard to suppress the sobs, but it was inevitable as the tears trailed down her face. She wiped it away with her free right hand.

"I'm making you cry when I just said the opposite." He smiled.

She chuckled amidst her tears. She bent down, match the position he was in to keep their faces level. "It's because you're being dramatic and I'm happy. This—"she paused, wiping away her tears"—is because you make me happy." She grabbed the lapels of his suit and placed her lips on his before looking at him.

"I love you," she said and placed another short, sweet kiss on him. "Yes."

"Yes?" he asked.

"I want to move in together."

She kissed him again, this time a few seconds longer than the previous ones.

When she released his mouth, he pulled her to him and gave her everything in full.

She had no objections.

***

"You should know what that does to me. If we continue, I can't promise we'll leave here by sunset."

Their makeout session was going further than either wanted. They haven't been able to make love in a long while.

She giggled. "I have to get back to Carliana."

"And unfortunately, I have to get back to the office," he muttered.

"Hmmhmm." She gave him a quick kiss. "You have another set of these in your car, right?" she said, mischievously grinning as she loosened his tie and went on to unbutton his suit. "Or you can have Owen bring one over for you."

He understandood what she was getting at. "I don't have protection with me, Ally."

"I'm on the pill. Besides, I'm not asking we go all the way. We can do what we've been doing. We can check out what our room's like in. How many minutes can we spare?"

He looked at his wrist watch. "Fifteen to twenty."

She winked before wetting her lips and doing a kissy pout.

He groaned, giving in. "Well, it's gonna be uncomfortable working around this tightness and what you just did." He carried her and led them into the biggest bedroom in the house.

"Even if you if you are on the pill, I'll still use a condom, but I don't have one on me now." He looked at her and placed her arms around his neck, carrying her to the room. "We do this together."

"Who are you?" She searched his face, amused.

He laid her down on the bed gently and crawled up to her. "I'm the man who isn't good enough for you but will make every day with me good enough for you to forget."

"Xander, I love you, and that makes you good enough for me. You're perfect for me."

After learning how his parents' love ended, he counted himself lucky that his mistake did not take him and Ally down that road. Every day with her helped him forgive himself, but he could never forget. He was not allowing himself to. He would always remind himself of what he almost lost and why he couldn't let that happen again.

He made sure to make the most of the fifteen minutes they had left. But with the way she was looking right now, he could make that twenty.

***

Five months had gone by since Ally, Carliana, and Snow moved into their new home, and within that span of time Ally and Xander had come to an agreement.

Ally was not disappointed that he did not propose. Instead, she was focusing on her ambition, finding a way to finish her education while taking care of Carliana.

Cameron once paid them a visit, and Xander had commented on how she was the only one his father opened up to. Ally was not sure that was entirely correct, though. She saw first-hand just how far the father and son pair progressed. They only needed to learn to open up to each other a little more.

She has done some adjustments to their new home with Liliana's help, and Xander never failed to show how satisfying it was to come home to his girls after a long day at the office.

Carliana gave her very first proper smile to her dad. His chest swelling with pride, Xander's boasted about it for days.

***

"Let's make a bet."

Xander chuckled, still finding it funny that she was not letting it go. He had made love to her for the second time, hoping she'd forgot about it, but she kept going at it. It was just amusing.

"It's not being funny. I'm serious."

"I know you are, and that's what makes it funny."

"Alex, I'm serious."

"Fine. What do I get if I get it right again?" He kissed her exposed breast.

"Anything."

"Anything? That's a pretty confident answer."

"That's because I'm sure."

Ally did not like not get their baby's sex right and was determined to get it right on the next one even if they already agreed that it would still be years into the future. Xander found that funny

"Fine. I say it's going to be a boy," Xander said, smirking.

"Come on, that's what I was going to say." She grumbled.

He laughed. "Or you just thought to go with me."

"You should have let me go first."

"It didn't seem like you wanted to go first."

The argument went on for a few more minutes before she excused herself to go to the bathroom. He used that moment to stand up and walk into his closet where he kept the ring he got.

He got it on a whim a month before after sneaking one of her rings to one of the famous jewellery designers in the city for a quick fix. He had not returned that ring yet, because she had realised it went missing and thought she might have dropped it. He did not want to give her hints if it suddenly emerged in her box.

He hid the ring back and smiled to himself as he heard Ally call his name.

Only you Alicia, and very soon.

THE END

Can't get enough of Ally and Xander? Make sure you sign up for the author's blog to find out more about them!

Get these two bonus chapters and more freebies when you sign up at ProlifickInstinct's account at prolifick-instinct.awesomeauthors.org!

Here is a sample from another story you may enjoy:

melissa bender

FORGOTTEN SWEETHEARTS

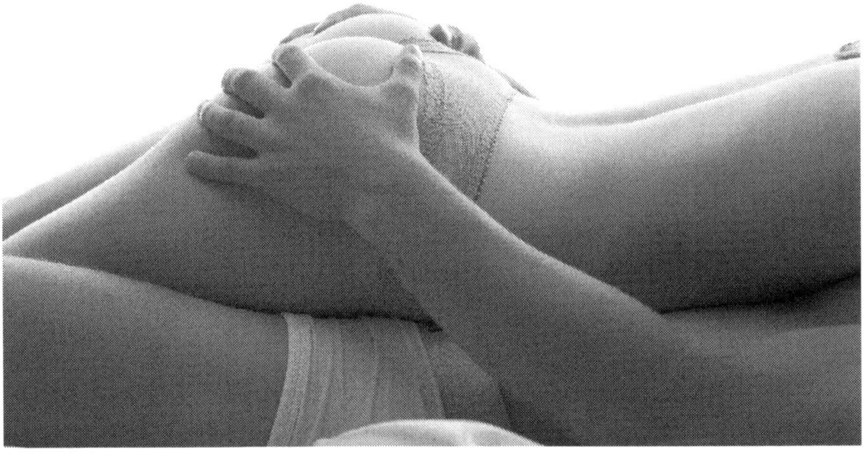

Prologue

Most would call us high school sweethearts. I fell fiercely and violently when we first met at fifteen. He was leaning against the lockers in the school corridor when I laid eyes on him for the very first time. My heart raced at the sight of him, pounding inside my chest so hard that I thought it would nearly explode. I walked past, blushing as my gaze dropped the second our eyes locked. Luckily for me, he felt the same way too.

I looked at him with love and complete devotion and always craving his deep blue eyes on me. Often, I'd look up to see him staring right back, gazing ever so lovingly towards me and sneaking hidden glances during classes. Even when we finished school and moved in together, he would always watch. At night, Brody would always hold me as if I were about to disappear, never wanting to let go.

Fast forward eleven years and two children later, the only thing exploding of late was my anger towards him. The fire of passion between us was no longer explosive. Lovemaking was a rare, occasional occurrence, and I no longer had a clue what foreplay was needed. Was it spitting on my own fingers or giving him a quick grab? I didn't know. I just knew it wasn't what it should have been.

Every touch, lingering kiss, and glance towards each other was just for show. Behind the large wooden door of our home, we were anything but happy. Living a lie was what we'd become accustomed to. This was our life.

To everyone else, we appeared the perfect couple. Deep down, I knew the divorce was near.

We spent most nights apart, sleeping in separate bedrooms. I hated it. I hated that we'd grown to loathe each other. The undeniable attraction was still here, just fizzled out. Neither of us was willing to try to keep the spark alive or to keep what we once had. Both of us had given up.

His personal life was suffering because work always came first. Brody worked hard all the time. I won't deny that. He had thrown himself into becoming the best he could, climbing the ladder to the top. I said nothing when I really should have spoken up the second I began feeling left out. My thoughts were kept hidden away and left unsaid.

His family never noticed, too busy engrossed with their own lives to notice just how bad things had become. Brody's mother loved her weekly family dinners and the yearly vacations. We would always manage to avoid those. Using work as the perfect excuse when in all honestly, we just couldn't stand to be in the same room with one another for two weeks, which was a sad and harsh reality.

I was unable to complain too much as Brody had given me a wonderful life, a beautiful six-bedroom home, much bigger than we needed, but it was ours. Brody earned enough to keep the bills paid and then some. After Noah was born, I stayed home full time, taking the new job title as a housewife.

It was hard at first as I had always loved my job, enjoying the daily interactions with other adults and feeling like I mattered. Now, I was used to being a stay-at-home mother, enjoying my children and living life through them.

Pathetic, I know. I just didn't know how miserable that would make me in the end.

Chapter 1

Quietly, my knuckles rapped against the wood before I reached down and turned the knob. Pushing the door open, I began to walk inside his office. My husband sat behind his large wooden desk, a soft glow against his face from the lamp close by. His office was filled with bookcases and family photographs. A couch was pushed against one side of the wall and a TV in the corner for the nights he spent in here.

This was his usual spot when home, working and away from everyone.

He looked so handsome with that dark brown hair and those blue eyes I wanted to lose myself in. For a moment, it was easy to forget that we were in a war against each other most days.

"The kids are asleep. I'm going to bed now," I said, interrupting him with a heavy sigh as I crossed my arms over my chest and leaned against the white wall.

Brody didn't bother looking up. "Goodnight."

I lingered, wishing things were different. How I wanted to go over there, walk across the timber flooring, pull his swivel chair around to sit on his lap with my arms draped over his shoulders, and kiss or just talk about our day—just to be close to him once again.

Paperwork scattered all around, his eyes were narrowed as he concentrated hard on whatever was on the screen. His fingers typing furiously on the Mac keyboard stopped. His head stayed bowed as his dark eyes glanced upwards. "Yes?" His voice was low yet still held authority over me.

I felt uncomfortable in here. Awkwardness filled the room as I stood by the door. "Did you need anything before I go?" I asked and swallowed the dry lump in my throat as he stared.

"No." Short and curt came his reply, and just like that, he was back typing away.

We rarely spoke about anything else other than the children or what our week entailed. As I went to close the door, I heard a disgruntled sigh. There was no need to say anything else. I left the room, making my way down the hallway to the children.

Lila was fast asleep, clutching her doll against her cheek as I pulled the light pink bed cover up over her shoulders to keep her warm during the winter's night. Her dark brown hair was curled and splayed out against her pillowcase as she mumbled something incoherent and rolled from her side to her back. I couldn't help but just smile, wanting to sit in here forever and watch her.

At seven, she was determined but stubborn at the best of times with a huge imagination. Her daddy was wrapped around her fingers, his little princess. Noah, who was a year older, was the opposite. He was very laid back and easy to keep happy. He'd gotten that from his father. The children were both often mistaken as twins with their age so close. Noah wasn't much of a talker, either reading a book or outside riding up and down the driveway on his bike. Lila loved to talk about anything and everything.

I kissed her goodnight and then made my way across the hallway to Noah's room. The second book of Harry Potter was on his face as he had fallen asleep reading again. I laughed softly to myself, placed the bookmark on the open page, and left the book on his bedside table.

I couldn't deny it. Brody and I made beautiful children. Biased or not, they were my life.

After kissing his forehead as my fingers combed through his dark, almost black hair, I stood up straighter, left his bedroom, and made my way back to ours. I paused momentarily and stared at his office door once more. I almost went in again. He was in there, shutting me out and blocking me away. Deciding against it, I left.

Slipping into the shower, I began to lather body wash into my olive skin and clean myself. I loathed the way my body looked after having children. Twenty-seven and I loathed my body. I could lie and say that I kept my figure or lost the weight, but I hadn't. I had leftovers from Lila, probably some from Noah too. It was too easy to eat and enjoy the sugary sweet cravings from being pregnant, convincing myself that I'd work hard to wear it off once they were born. It just never happened.

My hair hadn't been cut in years, just not bothering with it. It only went up in a ponytail, the way boring mums do. Even makeup went untouched, just a quick dab of blush and gloss. I really couldn't be bothered with it. The clothes that I used to wear, all those shorts and tight-fitting jeans were hiding in the back of my closet, hidden away for the day that I would finally be able to wear them again without the embarrassing belly fat bulging over the top.

Brody never once complained or said anything, but my subconscious told me that it bothered him. He'd only gotten better-looking with age, worked successfully, and grown into a strong man. It made sense for him to have a beautiful woman on his arm. However, I was never on his arm. I hadn't even been asked to join him at one of his work dinners since Noah was born. He would call up and inform me at the last minute that he wouldn't be making it home until late.

I was convinced he was fucking his receptionist, the woman who took his business calls. He denied it, of course. What man wouldn't want to be sucked off by a gorgeous blonde when his wife wasn't doing it to him?

The last time we were consistent with being intimate was when we were trying to fall pregnant with our youngest, Lila. I'd become increasingly aroused during my pregnancy with her, craving his touch, his kisses…to feel his hands on my skin. He never seemed to mind, always up for a quick romp between the sheets before work, before dinner, or when our eldest Noah was napping.

When Lila entered the world, sex and sleep were a distant memory of the past.

You could say our marriage began taking its toll when Noah entered our world. Brody had only just made it to the hospital. Another five minutes and he would have missed the first of his son, Noah. It was the same with Lila, another business meeting that he couldn't dash away from.

Sex was boring. Neither of us even really tried, and I had faked so many orgasms that I lost count.

As I stepped out of the shower, I quickly dried off in fear that Brody would already be in the room. I hated the thought of him seeing my body. Slipping into my flannel pyjamas, I sat down on the bed with my legs tucked up and put a braid in my half-dried hair. The bed felt cold and lonely as I slipped under the covers after brushing my teeth. It was too big, too empty.

We didn't have a TV in our room. When we first moved in, Brody said we didn't need one. The bedroom was for two things, sleeping and sexy time. Now, I wished there was a TV in here.

My eyes stared at the door, waiting, hoping he would come in and want to hold me. He didn't, and I fell asleep.

I could vaguely hear him undressing in our walk-in closet. Barely awake, I rolled over, picked my phone up and noticed the time, almost 2:00 AM, hours after I had said goodnight to him.

Putting the phone back down, I snuggled further beneath the covers as he joined me in the bedroom. "You awake?" his voice soft, half-heard.

"No," I replied.

I kept my eyes closed as I rolled to my back. This was his usual pickup line when he wanted some. I opened my eyes just as he walked around to his side of the bed, naked. Sitting down, I watched as he opened his side of the bedside table drawer and take out a condom. Tearing it open, he tossed the foil wrapper and began rolling down the condom down his thick length. I wasn't offended. Neither of us wanted any more children.

Raising my hips, I lowered my bottoms but still kept one leg in, easy to put back on afterward.

There was no kissing, barely any moans, and he was quiet after save for his shallow breathing. He'd always been silent, and it made me feel like shit. We weren't experienced with other people, only being with each other. I wasn't counting the bitch at his work until my proof was solid.

My hands gripped his strong arms, legs wrapping around his thighs as his body moved against mine. Closing my eyes, I laid here wishing…wishing for what wasn't. I couldn't have faked it anymore if I tried. This wasn't lovemaking. It was a job. As husband and wife, that's what we were meant to do—have sex.

Brody's hips began to move more forcefully, hurrying himself up. His breathing picked up slightly, and just when the actual pleasure began to sink into the pit of my stomach, he climaxed. I was too embarrassed to speak up, to tell him what I needed and wanted. It was okay, though. We'd have sex again in a month or so…whenever the urge came on.

His heart was racing, beating faster as his breathing slowed down. My arms draped around his neck, wanting to keep this closeness for just a moment longer before he pulls out and walks back to the bathroom. I knew that the second he moves, it would be gone. At least this way, we could pretend. Well, I could.

He didn't pull away, letting me relish in this small connection for a moment more than he possibly wanted. He was doing this for my sake. I felt his fingertips tracing against the nape of my neck. My eyes opened to darkness. I inhaled his scent, a strong musk of the aftershave I'd bought him for Christmas. I tasted the sweat on his skin as I pressed my lips to his shoulder, kissing him softly.

I began to feel a mere comfort. That feeling went as soon as it came when he began to move off my body.

I already rolled over and pretended to be asleep when he returned from the bathroom. He was spending the night in here, always in here after we'd slept together. Otherwise, he'd be in the spare, and I would end up with Noah or Lila, whoever wanted to snuggle with their mama that night.

I didn't stop them from coming in. I liked that they still needed the comfort of me.

My parents had been furious that we weren't raising them with Italian traditions. Hell, they were still furious that I hadn't married an Italian boy. What did they expect, though? They had come home from a holiday and announced we were moving to an island called Tasmania. I had not ever heard of the place before. My papa quit his job, found work over here, and the next thing I knew, we were moving, and I was enrolled at the school. It was rushed. I barely spoke any English and was the only Italian in my school. How could they not think I would fall in love with an Australian boy? I was fifteen for crying out loud. My hormones were raging all over the place for him once I laid eyes on his cute face.

I knew it broke my mama's heart when we had children even naming them Noah and Lila. She never mentioned it, but I knew she was disappointed with our choice of names for them. We didn't care. We loved them.

Waking early the next morning, I started my morning routine of getting ready: hair up, face washed, and the usual baggy clothes on which was a loose-fitting shirt paired with a pair of black mum jeans that sucked in my gut. Black was my choice of colour. It was more slimming.

Brody was still asleep when I entered back into the bedroom. His snores were the only sound filling the room of silence. I could have woken him up, but I didn't want to. He worked hard, providing for his family. I was just the housewife, not that it bothered me as I loved being able to take our children to school and clean our home, but still, he earned the right to sleep in more than I do.

Flipping the pancakes over, Noah was telling me about school when he brought up playing soccer. It caught me off guard, as he's never shown any interest in playing school sports. "Really?" I asked, genuinely surprised. "That's great."

"What's great?" His voice deep, masculine voice startled me as he entered the room.

Lila was already jumping up to run over to him. "Daddy!" She beamed, hugging one of his legs tightly. "Good morning."

Brody smiled back at her, bending down to her level and kissing her cheek. "Good morning, princess. Did you sleep well?"

"I did," she replied, going back to her plate of pancakes. She poked her brother in the arm on her way, trying to provoke him. He ignored her.

"Eat your breakfast and leave your brother alone, Lila," he lightly scolded, shook his head. "Morning, Noah." He went over to the breakfast bar where the children both sat, kissing them on the head while they both kept eating.

Noah had a mouthful of food, mumbling back, "Morning, Dad."

I set his coffee cup down on the white marble counter, poured milk into the boiling hot caffeinated water, and gave it a stir. Turning my back, I reached for the metal spatula and flipped another pancake. "Your breakfast won't be long," I said, getting ready to plate them.

Clearing his throat as he sat with the kids, I glanced up and watched the three of them chatting away and laughing. It made me smile on the inside that our children were happy with no idea about their parents. I felt like I was failing them. My eyes crossed back over to Brody, and I couldn't deny that he wasn't extremely attractive in a suit because he was. We were a mismatched couple. He was handsome, and I, just bland. Quickly, I looked away when I noticed him watching me.

"I might be late home tonight," he started, coming over with his empty coffee mug. "I have dinner with a client. I only just received the email." Pulling out his phone, he raised a brow. "Want to check for yourself?"

It was to mock me for not believing him the last time he had mentioned a work dinner. I had called bullshit, accusing him of heading out to screw the blonde at work and proved me wrong as he dialled his boss's number to confirm the meeting was an actual work one.

Biting my tongue, I wouldn't fall for it. "Fine, are you going to eat your breakfast? I didn't make it for you to watch it go cold."

His jaw twitched as his blue eyes glanced over at the plate of pancakes covered in maple syrup. "No."

Rolling my eyes, I snatched the plate up. "Asshole," I muttered, walking over to the cupboard and pulling out the bin.

"Bit dramatic for eight in the morning, don't you think?"

I spun around, glaring. "I should have known better than to think that you're going to eat breakfast with your family for once."

Pushing up his black jacket and white sleeves, he looked down at his watch. "Gabriella, I need to leave. I'm running late."

"More like running to your whore," I muttered under my breath.

Judging by the scowl on his face, I knew he had heard me. He ignored it and walked to each of our children again, giving them a kiss goodbye. I began to stack the dishwasher, just wanting him to go and get out of my face.

"Don't forget to kiss Mama, Daddy," Lila pointed out.

I froze. "Daddy needs to go," I reminded, looking ahead out into the garden.

She was stubborn, not letting this go. "Kiss Mama like in the movies, Daddy."

Sometimes I thought they knew just how bad their parents hated each other. Was it hate? I didn't know. It wasn't what it used to be, though.

Brody was already walking towards me when I had turned around. My heart pounded as his hand curled around my hips and he pushed my back against the sink with his strong top half and his leg between my thighs. I wanted to scream, "Get off of me," but the other part desperately wanted him to stay like this.

He was mad. I could tell by the way he stared into my eyes. His breath was minty across my face as he spoke softly, "The kids want a kiss, Gabriella. Are you going to say no?" He was pushing me, knowing I wouldn't refuse in front of the kids.

"Go to work," I said, keeping my voice low and quiet from the kids who were watching us. "I have beds to make since I guess you didn't do ours."

"Why should I? That's your job," he shot back, cocking a brow.

I could just slap that smirk off his face. I wanted him out of my face. "Asshole." I pushed my hand against his chest, trying to make him move, but he didn't budge.

"So I've already been called," he smirked again, fingers tightening against my hip to hold me in place as his other hand came up, cupping my cheek with a gentle caress. My eyes softly closed a moment as I felt his lips skimming against mine before he pushed them against nothing—just an open mouth. It was simple and enough to make Lila squeal with delight and Noah the opposite.

Pulling back, his eyes appeared darker as he brushed his lips against my ear. I thought he was going to kiss me. He didn't. His breath hit my ear as he spoke. "Unlike you, my dear wife, I'm not fucking anyone on the side." Letting me go, my body went cold as he picked up his black case and car keys, made his way towards the door, and left for work.

Hard to believe all those years ago, we were madly in love and inseparable.

If you enjoyed this sample then look for **Forgotten Sweethearts on Amazon!**

Introducing the Characters Magazine App

Download the app to get the free issues of interviews from famous fiction characters and find your next favorite book!

iTunes: bit.ly/CharactersApple
Google Play: bit.ly/CharactersAndroid

Acknowledgements

When I picked up a pen and started my writing with "Once upon a time", I did not think this far ahead. Growing up as an awkwardly shy girl, I had writing to help escape, be confident, and take over. I loved it, I enjoyed it, but I also wanted to share it, and I could not have done it on my own.

The quote, "There's nothing like family" is one I have been truly fortunate and blessed with, to experience. You bunch are my titanium pillar because I know I'm not going down easy with you always there to pick me up through every challenge of life I face. I never get the time to give up because I look around and you've all got your flag of support cheering me on. It's crazy how much you all believe in me, it gives me that recharge to believe in myself more.

Dad and mom, take you for loving me and caring about my aspirations in life. Without you two, there's a 99.9% probability that I might not be here.

Seun, Papa, and Seyi- my three adorable siblings. Thank you for always making me laugh. I laugh harder when you three fight over who will be my manager when I get published- and that was many years before I started writing *His Mistress' Baby*. Now it's happening, what do I do because it still cracks me now. I love you all.

Thank you Peejay. You asked me why I was just reading on Wattpad, and not writing. Remember? You gave me that final push, and here I am. Mr Hero, I think you published me before I even got published. Lol. You always telling people "she's a famous writer" is a great support and motivation. Thanks to you both for believing in me.

This moment would be incomplete if I did not mention the core support that has made this a reality and given this moment. A big thank you and massive hugs and kisses to all Wattpad readers that supported *His Mistress' Baby*. I did not do this…We did it! Though I haven't met you, I will always remember your contribution.

I want to thank AJ, my agent who believed in me and HMB, Aycee, for beautifully editing the drools and scribbles. Thank you for understanding and being patient with me through it all. Thank you BLVNP for making a dream come true.

And to God, who has brought you all in my life and never once let go of me. You gave me this gift, and for your guidance always, I am who I am today, only because of you.

Author's Note

Hey there!

Thank you so much for reading His Mistress' Baby! I can't express how grateful I am for reading something that was once just a thought inside my head.

I'd love to hear from you! Please feel free to email me at prolifick_instinct@awesomeauthors.org and sign up at prolifick-instinct.awesomeauthors.org for freebies!

One last thing: I'd love to hear your thoughts on the book. Please leave a review on Amazon or Goodreads because I just love reading your comments and getting to know YOU!

Whether that review is good or bad, I'd still love to hear it!

Can't wait to hear from you!

Prolifick Instinct

About the Author

Ola is a movie addict currently juggling getting a master's degree in Criminology and writing. She is a Christian, and believes in the significant change she will be making for children's well-being in a few years. Writing was a hidden passion until friend and family gave her the push, and now she writes to set her readers' imagination alive and full of emotion.

She absolutely adores children and can never say no to ice cream and cake. She is a full time Manchester United football fan who loves drawing and listening to Hindi music and would love to speak Spanish fluently someday.

15067115R00312

Printed in Great Britain
by Amazon